"The auth[...] [...]al and paranormal g[...] [...]can lifestyle with a touching romance... lots of hot fun."

—Romance Novel News

"Lydia Dare casts a spell on her readers! A scorching hot read, full of magick and desire."

—Love Romance Passion

"A deliciously delightful read... witty repartee, scorching sensuality, wonderfully complex characters, and an intriguing plot combine to make an unforgettable story."

—Romance Junkies

"Ms. Dare has proven herself with her writing, characters, storylines, and imagination. I'm a fan for life."

—The Good, the Bad and the Unread

"Sexy, witty, and wildly passionate... Just as riveting, sexy, and hot as the first two in the series."

—Star-Crossed Romance

"Delightful... funny and romantic and a joy to read... each book sucks you in from the first page to the last."

—Anna's Book Blog

ALSO BY LYDIA DARE

A Certain Wolfish Charm

Tall, Dark and Wolfish

The Wolf Next Door

T^{HE} TAMING OF THE WOLF

LYDIA DARE

sourcebooks
casablanca

Published by Sourcebooks Casablanca, an imprint of Sourcebooks,
Inc.
P.O. Box 4410, Naperville, Illinois 60567-4410
(630) 961-3900
FAX: (630) 961-2168
www.sourcebooks.com

Printed and bound in Canada
WC 10 9 8 7 6 5 4 3 2 1

One

Westfield Hall, Hampshire
January 1817

CAITRIN MACLEOD VOWED NEVER TO STEP FOOT IN England again—or at the very least, to keep her distance from Lycans in the future.

She stopped mid-pace to look out the bedroom window, her breath fogging the pane. She wiped it away with the flat of her hand and stared out into the darkness. She'd stayed in her bedchamber all day and now most of the night.

It was safer for everyone that way.

The visions had started days ago, wild visions where she saw wolves and their mates together under the light of the moon. There were several of them, all part of a family of Lycans. She was quite familiar with those particular Lycans, because her coven sister, Elspeth, had married into the family. Most days, they were simply the Westfield family. But one night each month, the male members walked on four feet instead of two under the light of the full moon.

Those visions weren't troublesome; she was quite used to them. But lingering around the edges of her visions was a wild wolf, an outsider. A danger. The Westfields were aware of the threat and had, indeed, prepared themselves to handle it.

She'd begun to see visions of a golden wolf, the wild one, earlier that very day. She knew what mischief he'd cause before the night was over. But she couldn't tell the others what she'd seen, or she'd risk affecting the future. And she didn't want to be the one to disrupt the natural order of events. The results could be disastrous.

To avoid breaking that unspoken rule, she'd locked herself in her guest room at Westfield Hall and refused to come out. She'd not set foot out the door and had only opened it briefly to take her meals. She'd wished several times for something to help her pass the time. At the rate she'd been pacing, she would wear a hole in the duke's Aubusson rug before long. That thought made her smile.

Caitrin closed her eyes tightly and tried to will the vision of the Westfield wolves into her mind. She sighed with contentment when she realized all was well. The danger to them had passed, and she was now free to leave the prison of her own making. None of them would return until the sun rose in the sky. The estate was empty except for her and any servant who happened to be still awake. No one would know if she donned her silk wrapper to sneak downstairs and retrieve her book while everyone was away. Maybe then she could try to get a few hours of sleep.

She crossed to the chamber door and opened it

quietly. On bare feet, she padded along the corridor and down the main staircase. The last place she remembered having her book was in the duke's study.

Cait turned the corner into the darkened study and stopped short. Standing behind the duke's desk was a tall man, one she'd yet to meet. Most of him was hidden in shadow, but his face was lit by the moonlight that filtered through the drapes. He was a blond Adonis, tall and lean. A vague memory of him, maybe from one of her visions, created unease within her.

A small gasp escaped her throat when he turned his amber gaze her way.

"I'm sorry. I dinna ken anyone was up at this hour." She turned to leave.

"Don't go," he said. Then he closed his eyes tightly and took a deep breath. "You needed something in Blackmoor's study?"

"Aye, I left a book in here yesterday when I came ta find Her Grace." She glanced quickly around the room, though she didn't immediately see her copy of Maria Edgeworth's *Patronage*. "Perhaps I left it in the library." *Perhaps I should run as quickly from this room as my legs will carry me.*

"Having trouble sleeping?" he asked, his tone amazingly familiar. As though he'd known her for a lifetime.

"Aye. At times, I canna get thoughts out of my head." Why had she told him that? He probably didn't care to hear how her visions played in her mind at all hours of the day and night, preventing her rest.

He walked around the desk and perched a hip on it. His hips were narrow, his shoulders broad. *Stop ogling the man's body, Cait.* His eyes narrowed at her, as though he knew she had a secret. She closed her eyes and tried to get a vision of him, something to tell her who he was. But her mind was blank, which was more than disconcerting. *Her mind was blank?* That had never happened before.

"I canna tell yer future," she muttered under her breath.

"Pardon?" He raised an eyebrow at her.

"Ah, there's my book," she said, smiling at him, hoping he'd believe she hadn't a care in the world. She picked up a small, black leather book that lay on the desk behind him. It wasn't hers, but it would have to do.

Before she could turn around, he reached out and grabbed her by the waist. She couldn't even utter a gasp as he drew her body flush against his. Her breath stilled.

"What are ye—" she began, but he covered her mouth with his, his lips hard and urgent.

She shouldn't let a man she'd never met before take such liberties. But he smelled so good. Felt so good. Tasted so good.

Her tongue rose to meet his as a whimper of pleasure left her throat. Her heart beat wildly as he tilted his head and deepened the kiss.

Cait had been kissed before, but never like this. Never so thoroughly that she couldn't think straight. Never so expertly that her legs threatened to buckle. Never with enough passion that she could drown in it.

A tug to her hair sunk into her consciousness. He pulled her head back and looked into her eyes. He gently tugged, guiding her head until it leaned to the side, exposing her neck. She nearly jumped when his lips brushed feather-light down the side of her jaw as he trailed a kiss down her throat. He pulled at the neck of her wrapper and nightrail until they opened, baring her shoulder to his gaze. She shivered.

When he reached the place where her neck met her shoulder, he sucked at the tender spot and then nipped her gently. It was the most sensual thing she'd ever experienced. Light-headed, she heard a moan escape her throat. *More. More, please.*

He nipped her again, then opened his mouth wide and bit through the tender skin of her shoulder, jerking her instantly from the passion-induced haze.

"Ow!" she cried and smacked his shoulder. "That hurt!"

The pain of the bite broke through the lust-soaked area of her brain, which she'd never known existed, and she smacked him again. One moment, he'd had her warmer than a fire in the grate on a cold winter night. The next, she was raising her hand to her neck to appraise the puncture wound he'd created on her shoulder.

She punched his chest. "Why did ye bite me, ye big lout?" she asked as she rubbed the wound, dabbing at the small amount of blood from the bite and scowling at him.

"I didn't mean—" he started.

But she didn't let him explain as she turned and fled from the study.

"Come back," he called quietly. She heard him, but she ran down the corridor and up the stairs as fast as her feet would take her.

Cait slammed the door to her room, threw the little leather book to the bed, and ran to the mirror. Baring her shoulder, she appraised the wound, which looked like a crescent-shaped bite mark, the same shape as his mouth. Blast him! He'd *bitten* her. And for the life of her, she couldn't understand why.

Well, she wasn't going to stay around Westfield Hall and let any other *guest* of the duke maul her. Not even if he looked like a Greek god and smelled positively delicious, like the outdoors and citric shaving lotion rolled together. They were ill-mannered English swine, the lot of them, and she'd had her fill.

Cait's cheeks were aflame as she remembered standing so close to the man in the study. She'd behaved like a common trollop. It was just another reason for her to leave for Edinburgh as quickly as possible. She was obviously losing her mind.

She'd always prided herself on her comportment, though her behavior in the study was seriously lacking. The man was just so mysterious. In her twenty years, she'd never met anyone whose future, either immediate or otherwise, hadn't popped into her head. The blond Adonis was like a blank page with nothing written on it. She couldn't blame herself for being curious, could she?

The bite on her shoulder burned slightly, and she frowned with a fresh wave of irritation. She'd already stayed in England longer than she'd planned. It was time to go home.

Cait stomped over to the bellpull and tugged hard. She probably woke every servant in residence, but at the moment, she couldn't be bothered to care. She needed to leave Hampshire, leave England for good and never look back.

❧

Dashiel Thorpe, the Earl of Brimsworth, sank into the Duke of Blackmoor's large leather chair and buried his face in his hands. What had he done? Of course, he knew the answer to that. Under the power of the full moon, he'd *bitten* the girl—a lady he didn't even know, for God's sake. He should have been shackled this evening, not roaming around free. How did the other Lycans manage to control themselves?

Dash groaned aloud. His circumstances had gone from bad to worse in the blink of a bad decision. The image of the angelic Scottish lass flooded his memory. She smelled so delightful, like fresh honeysuckle. Where did one even find honeysuckle in January?

The fact that she was stunning didn't help. He hadn't been in control of his thoughts or actions from the moment she stepped into Blackmoor's study. What was she doing padding through the ducal estate in the middle of the night during a moonful anyway? Didn't she know that Lycans inhabited the residence? Didn't she know it was dangerous to go around looking the way she did with men like him about?

Dash peered though his fingers and noticed that she'd taken his book, and he cringed. At first, he'd been amused when she had picked up his little journal, claiming it as her own. But he'd had no intention of letting her flee with it. The contents were not fit for a lady's eyes. The journal held details about every whore in and around Covent

Garden—physical descriptions, addresses, specialties of sorts, and ratings. The idea of her reading it made his stomach churn. Facing the pretty little Scottish angel in the morning would be more than difficult if she had read even one entry.

Face her in the morning?

Dear God, he hadn't meant to bite the chit, though he'd never forget the rush he had experienced when he'd marked her flesh. It was more intense than any release he'd ever enjoyed in his life.

It was best not to think about that, or he'd chase after her and finish what they'd started. Neither the Duke of Blackmoor nor Major Forster would forgive him that indiscretion. And he was already in enough trouble with the Westfield pack. If he had any hope of finding a Lycan mentor, he would have to be honest with them about his most recent actions. It was the only way to gain their trust after all he'd tried to do to them.

Dash wasn't accustomed to asking anyone for help, and the idea didn't set well with him. For twenty-six years, he'd suffered in silence, not understanding what or who he was. And now that he knew, he had to know more. He needed to find a way to earn the Westfields' forgiveness. That was the only way for him to obtain salvation.

He heard Major Forster before the old wolf opened the study door. The retired officer appeared much more at peace than he had a few hours ago. Dash wished he could say the same for himself.

The old man cleared his throat. "Well, I see you managed to stay put. That is something."

"I bit a girl." The words flew out of Dash's mouth before he could stop them.

Major Forster's brown eyes rounded in surprise. "I beg your pardon?"

Dash shook his head as he rushed to explain. "I didn't go looking for her. She came to me, and I was weak—"

"Where did you bite her?"

"Here, in His Grace's study," Dash moaned.

"Not *where*," the major snapped. "Where on her *body*?"

"What difference does that make?" Dash started. But then something dangerous flashed in the major's eyes. Dash pointed to the area where his neck met his shoulder. "Right here."

"Are you saying you *claimed* a woman?"

"I'm not certain," Dash admitted as he closed his eyes to block out the man's disapproving expression. "I thought you should know."

"Dear God!" the old man grumbled. "Now you'll bring Blackmoor's wrath down on both of us."

Dash opened his eyes. What did the major mean by that? "*Both* of us?"

The officer scrubbed a hand over his face. "I was supposed to keep an eye on you," he growled. Then he lowered his hands and leveled an intimidating glare at Dash. "Who was she?"

Dash shrugged. "I don't know. She was beautiful. Flowing blond hair and light blue eyes."

Major Forster gulped. "Did she speak to you?" he asked softly.

Dash nodded.

"And was she Scottish?" It seemed as though the words were wrenched from him.

"Yes," Dash admitted. "You know who she is." That much was obvious.

The major winced and rubbed his temples as if the action would relieve his pain. "Aye, I know the lass. Knew her mother, too. This isn't good, Lord Brimsworth. Not good at all."

"Well, certainly, there's something that can be done. I didn't mean to bite her, and she—"

"It doesn't work that way, my lord. When you bit her, the moon was full. You claimed her as your Lycan mate under a bloody full moon, you lummox. You're connected to the lass now. God help both of you."

"Well, what does that mean?"

"It means," the officer began as he dropped into one of the duke's leather chairs, "that she's your mate from now until one of you dies."

"My *mate*?" Dash gaped at him. "But I don't even know the girl. Surely something like this has happened before. There has to be a way to remedy—"

"Aye, Brimsworth. This is not the first time a Lycan, drunk on the spell of the moon, has claimed an unintended mate." The major shuddered. "I don't know of one instance where there was a happy ending, however."

"Why?" Dash asked as he sank into a seat across from the old officer, his heart hammering in his chest, still not ready to believe there wasn't a way out of the situation.

"Because the lass doesn't love you, my lord. You said yourself you didn't even know her. Marrying one of us, mating with one of us, is hard enough for women who love us every other day of the month.

"But you've attached yourself to a woman who cares nothing for you, and she's not bound by the same rules that apply to you and me. Whereas it will be impossible for you to take another woman to bed, Miss Macleod can marry whomever she wants. And you'll be left all alone until the connection is broken."

The prediction was troubling on more than one front. Dash wasn't a stranger to entertaining women in their chambers. He couldn't imagine not being able to do so anymore. He wasn't certain he even believed the man. It wasn't possible for him to lose that desire.

But what was even more bothersome was that his Scottish angel could choose another man over him. That hardly seemed fair. The thought of the delightful creature he'd held in his arms that very night marrying someone else was like a blade to his heart. Which didn't make much sense. He didn't even know the lass.

"Miss Macleod?" he asked. At least he had a name.

Major Forster nodded. "Caitrin. She's a friend of my daughter Elspeth."

Dash leapt out of his seat. "I'll have to talk to her."

"You'll do no such thing," the old officer growled. "And you won't say a word about this to anyone until I can sort out what to do."

"But, I—"

"Sit down," Major Forster barked. "In case you've forgotten, Lord Brimsworth, you are not a welcome guest at Westfield Hall. Your sins are numerous and we both know them, the most important being you are an uncontrollable, feral Lycan. And if you think

I'll allow you to stalk the halls of this home, you are sadly mistaken."

The air whooshed out of Dash's lungs. "That's why I've come to you for help, sir. I need a mentor, and—"

"You are here because His Grace, Lord Benjamin, and I kept Lord William from tearing you to shreds when you tried to claim *his* wife this very evening. Now *sit down* while I think," the man ordered gruffly.

"Trying to claim Lord William's wife was a poor decision on my part—" Dash began. If he could just explain.

"I said, '*Sit!*'" the major snarled.

Dash tucked his tail into a chair and watched a series of emotions flash across the other man's face.

Finally, the major sat taller and rubbed his chin. "You do need a mentor, and I need to keep you far from the Westfields."

"I mean them no harm."

"As you have already escaped from me once, my lord, please understand that I don't intend to take your word for it."

Dash could see the man's point.

"My family hails from Glasgow. I've got a cousin, a shipbuilder, who still lives there. I'm certain I can persuade him to take you on."

Glasgow? Dash shook his head. He didn't know anyone in Glasgow, and going there didn't solve his situation with Miss Macleod. "But the girl—"

"Does not need a feral wolf in her midst, nor would she tolerate one. You can take my word for that. Once you have control of yourself, you can seek her out and see what's to be done with the mess you've made."

Two

"LORD BRIMSWORTH," THE DUKE OF BLACKMOOR'S persnickety butler called from the doorway of the study. "Your coach has arrived."

Dash had sent for his carriage to take him to Glasgow, along with a letter of introduction from the major to his shipbuilding cousin, Mr. Niall Forster. Dash rose from his seat and stepped toward the old butler. Still, there was something he had to do before he set off for Scotland. "I'd like a word with Miss Macleod first, if you don't mind, Billings."

The old servant frowned at him. "I'm afraid that's not possible, my lord."

Not possible? Dash resisted the urge to snort. He didn't want to spend any more time at Westfield Hall than was absolutely necessary, but seeing Caitrin Macleod before he left for Glasgow was of the utmost importance. If he truly was connected to the chit until the end of time, it would be best if they got a few things straight before he departed.

"I'm not leaving until I speak with Miss Macleod."

The butler sighed irritably. "Miss Macleod is no

longer in residence, my lord. So it won't matter how long you wait."

"No longer in residence?" Dash echoed. How was that even possible? Only a few hours earlier, he'd kissed the girl, held her against him, *and claimed her.*

"I believe she has started for home, sir."

She left without speaking to him, without giving him a chance to explain? Dash thrust his hand into his pocket and crumpled the major's letter in his fist. He stalked out of the manor and was immediately assaulted by her honeysuckle scent. He continued down the stone steps and hauled open the door to his traveling coach. Dash slumped against the squabs and glared at the empty spot across from him. The journey was going to be a very long one.

"Glasgow?" His coachman, Renshaw, asked from the open door.

Dash nodded once. Major Forster hadn't given him any choice in the matter. Glasgow, for God's sake. Surely the old officer could have found him a mentor in England, someone who wasn't so bloody far away. The trip would take forever on the North Road in the middle of winter. Perhaps Forster thought he'd tumble to his death in the Pennines. Maybe that was the old man's plan.

Dash sighed. "I'm in a bit of a hurry, Renshaw, but safety is of the utmost concern. Watch the roads, will you?"

∽

Caitrin absently rubbed her shoulder as she tugged the blue Macleod plaid closer about her legs. Even though her gift of sight had allowed her to see many things she shouldn't, including many intimate scenes, she only hovered at the edge of those images. She never saw what actually went on between men and women behind closed doors. Of that, she was very glad. Until now.

She wanted more than anything to ask if it was normal for a man in the throes of passion to gnaw on one's collarbone. But that would be terribly improper. Who in the world could she even ask? All her coven sisters in Scotland were maidens, just as she was. Aside from Elspeth, of course, whom she'd just left behind in Hampshire. Cait sighed deeply.

"Are ye all right, Miss?" her maid, Jeannie, asked from where she rested on the other side of the coach.

The question drew Cait from her reverie. But just barely. "What did ye say?" she mumbled as she pulled the collar of her traveling dress over to cover the mark.

"I asked if ye're all right," Jeannie repeated, her eyebrows scrunching together.

"I'm fine. I canna imagine why ye would think otherwise." Cait closed her eyes and laid her head back against the leather squabs.

"I'm worried about ye, is all. First we leave Westfield Hall in the dead of night like thieves. Ye dinna even say good-bye ta Lady Elspeth. And now ye're so fretful ye canna even sleep."

Cait raised her head and stared at her maid. Jeannie was years older than Cait, a decade or so. Perhaps she could ask her. Caitrin shook that thought away as quickly as it arose.

"Does it have something ta do with that love bite on yer neck?"

Cait reached to tug her collar over farther. "I doona ken what ye mean," she gasped.

"Aye, ye do." Jeannie smiled and nodded her head, making her dark curls bob up and down. "Ye canna lie ta me, Miss. I'm the one who does yer hair, and I've kent ye since ye were a wee bairn. And ye definitely have a little love bite under yer ear, there. It wasna there yesterday."

"Under my ear?" Caitrin echoed in surprise, trailing her fingers up her neck. Jeannie wasn't talking about the bite. Did the blasted man leave *another* mark?

"Aye," the maid confirmed. "Who was he? And what made ye want ta run back ta Edinburgh when ye obviously enjoyed him so much?"

"Enjoyed?" Caitrin gasped. Then she muttered under her breath, "I wouldna go that far." But she had enjoyed it, right until the moment he mistook her for a piece of meat.

"Ye canna lie ta me, Miss. I ken ye as well as yer own papa, maybe even better." She shook her finger at Caitrin playfully. "So, doona even attempt it."

This was much too embarrassing to discuss after all. She'd known it would be.

"Who was he?" Jeannie persisted.

"I doona ken who he was," Caitrin finally admitted.

"Oh, a handsome stranger?" Jeannie let her voice trail off as her eyebrows arched. "Where did ye meet him?"

"In the Duke of Blackmoor's study." Caitrin finally sighed. "I was lookin' for a book."

"And?" the maid prompted.

"And he just… kissed me." Cait shrugged her shoulders, unsure what else to say.

Jeannie sat back against the squabs and eyed her mistress warily. "Without even bein' properly introduced? Yer father wouldna approve."

"Ye canna tell Papa, Jeannie. Promise me."

The maid frowned.

"Please, Jeannie," Caitrin pleaded. Her father wouldn't be at all happy about the situation, and nothing could be done about it now, anyway.

"Did this man just grab ye, Miss?"

"Well," Cait hesitated, suddenly feeling protective of the man, although that was a ludicrous thought. "He grabbed me," she admitted. "But I dinna mind," she quickly added. Then she drew in a deep breath and steeled herself before finally asking, "So, the 'love bites' as ye call them. They're what usually goes on between a man and a woman?"

"Aye, that and more. But yer *husband* will teach ye all ye need ta ken with regard ta that. You doona need the likes of me doin' it."

A husband. "If I ever find one," Cait said, holding up both hands in surrender. "Never mind… it's no' important."

"But this man…" Jeannie started.

Cait shook her head. "He's in Hampshire, and we're on the way back ta Edinburgh. I'll no' see him again." She laid her head back and feigned sleep, her heart a bit heavier than it had been before the conversation.

～◦～

The faint smell of honeysuckle tortured Dash all day. He growled as he peered out the window into the darkness surrounding the coach. All he needed was to follow Miss Macleod's scent for a fortnight. That would make him go completely mad. He snorted to himself and leaned back against the squabs.

Who was he fooling? He'd already lost his mind. Traveling to godforsaken Glasgow to ask a shipbuilder to teach him to heel, sit, and stay. A mentor. He snorted. It sounded insane. On the upside, if his father got wind of this, the news would probably push the old cur right over the edge. Perhaps Dash should post a letter informing his father of his plans.

He shook his head at the thought. No reason to stir up that hornet's nest. With any luck, the Marquess of Eynsford would forget he even had a son. After twenty-six years, the odds weren't particularly in Dash's favor in that regard, but a man could always hope.

Perhaps Glasgow wouldn't be so bad after all. Since Miss Macleod was headed there as well, he could keep an eye on her. Make sure no one snatched her from him before he had a chance to court her properly. An image of his Scottish angel flashed in his mind. Flaxen hair, so soft and long he wanted to wrap a curl around his finger and simply stroke it with his thumb. Light blue eyes the color of a cloudless sky. Lips so perfectly kissable that he grew hard just thinking about them.

No, upon further thought, Glasgow could be exactly what he needed.

The coach slowed, and Dash glanced out the window. He noticed a spot of light in the distance that grew brighter as the carriage approached. A coaching inn. Thank God. He could sleep for a sennight after the past few days he'd endured.

The carriage rambled to a stop in the coaching yard, and Dash didn't even wait for Renshaw to let down his steps. He threw open the door and bounded outside, stopping the instant the scent of honeysuckle tickled his nose. Miss Macleod was definitely here. She had to be. Her flowery scent was stronger here than it had been all day along the road.

What a stroke of luck! They could have a conversation about what had transpired the previous evening and get a few things straightened out.

Finally, with a purpose to his step he hadn't had in quite a while, Dash strode straight into the taproom. Without a doubt, she was here. Miss Macleod's scent was so overwhelming that he had to clench his teeth to keep from growling aloud for her.

His eyes swept across the dark room, taking in a few locals who were well-foxed, a swarthy fellow with a child on his knee, a couple of buxom tavern wenches, and one portly barkeep who sported a bulbous nose and a bald pate. Ah, perfect. Dash smiled. Just the man he needed.

He hailed the owner toward him with a wave of his hand.

"Yes, sir?" The fellow scrambled forward.

"I need accommodations for the evening."

"Of course." The man nodded.

"But first," Dash began, "I'm looking for a woman."

The tavern-keeper's dark eyes twinkled. "I'm sure I can find someone to keep you company, sir." The man looked deeper into the taproom.

Dash shook his head, which was certainly the first time he'd refused an offer of companionship. He was only interested in one woman at the moment. "You misunderstand me. I'm looking for a woman who is traveling this road as well. My cousin from the north. Miss Macleod."

The tavern-keeper reared back on his heels. "Beg your pardon, sir. I didn't mean—"

"Is the lady here?" Dash barked. Honestly, there was only so much bumbling a man should have to deal with.

Before the barkeep could reply, Dash heard *her*. The delicate lilt of her voice came from a private dining room far in the back.

"Never mind." Dash brushed past the man and pushed his way through the throng toward the back of the room where a heavy oak door separated him from the lass he'd thought of most of the day.

Dash took a deep breath, then slowly pushed the door open.

She was just as mesmerizing as she had been the night before.

Unaware of his presence, Caitrin Macleod chatted with an older woman, a maid or chaperone of some sort. Dash frowned. If the woman had been keeping tabs on her charge the previous night, he wouldn't be in this current situation. Well, he'd still be on the road to Glasgow, but he wouldn't be tied to Miss Macleod for the rest of his days. Though, now that she was within his line of sight, he couldn't quite find it in his soul to be sorry about the turn of events.

Dash scoffed to himself. He must still be drunk on the moon to entertain such thoughts. Then a frightening idea popped into his head. What if, since he'd claimed the lass, he could never get her out of his mind? What if he'd lost what little power he had over his own thoughts? Exactly how *doomed* was he?

The strangled sound he heard must have come from him, because Miss Macleod's gaze shot to him in the doorway. Their eyes locked, and all the air in Dash's lungs escaped. Her blue eyes met his, and for a moment the world felt right, as though everything made sense.

But then she sputtered. And coughed. Whatever she'd been chewing so properly was now lodged in her throat. She turned red and then a bit purple. And that was when Dash snapped out of his trance and realized he'd better do something. He strode forward, yanked her from her chair, and began to pat her on the back. When a choked gasp was his only reward, he clapped her on the back a bit harder.

Suddenly, she coughed violently and drew in a great inhalation of breath. Tears poured from her eyes as she turned toward him. He felt the oddest compulsion to brush her tears away with the pads of his thumbs. So strange. It was a sensation he'd never felt before.

"Are you all right?" he asked after he swallowed past the lump in his throat.

He was completely surprised when her eyes narrowed and she cuffed him on the shoulder. Outrage oozed from her. She stomped her foot and balled up her fists and growled, "Oh, *ye*!"

"Happy to see me?" He flashed a smile at her, the one that never failed to charm maids or serving wenches. "You left before we had a chance to speak this morning."

"Miss?" her companion asked, rising to her feet and glaring at Dash.

But his Scottish angel didn't answer. She just turned on her heel and bolted from the private dining room.

Dash chased her through the taproom and out into the coaching yard. He reached her before she could round a small stone wall that disappeared into the darkness.

"Where the devil are you going?" Dash demanded as he grabbed her elbow.

"How dare ye touch me?" she hissed at him, yanking her arm free. Without waiting for a response, she took off down a cobblestone walk leading away from the inn.

Dash followed, feeling like a puppy chasing after his master. "Miss Macleod," he called to her.

She spun around and shot one quick glance at him. "What do ye want?" she snapped.

"I need to speak with you," he said, closing the distance between them.

"How did ye find me?" She furrowed her brow as she looked past him.

How could he avoid it? Her scent had teased him the entire day. God, that would sound ridiculous. "Bit of good luck on my part," he hedged instead.

"What do ye want?" she spit out. Fiery little thing she was, with her blue eyes flashing indignantly.

Ah, to be in control of himself. To manage as well as other Lycans. To hold her in his arms again. "You," he admitted before he could stop himself.

She must think him the most insane man. Biting her the night before, chasing after her in the dark tonight. It was a wonder she'd stopped at an inn at all. Any woman of sane mind would have fled as far and as fast as she could.

Miss Macleod shook her head at him as though he were some sort of worrisome gnat. "*Me?* For what?" she asked, her lilting voice rising with irritation.

"You asked what I wanted, Miss Macleod. I want you." Among other things he could never explain to her. At least not now.

Three

CAIT BLINKED AT HIM, NOT CERTAIN SHE HAD HEARD HIM correctly. She tried to ignore the flutters in her belly that his confession stirred within her and focused on his amber eyes instead, concentrating on his future. A flash of *something* would be more than helpful. Her cursed power had never failed her until now.

A cool breeze tousled his golden hair, and her eyes fell to his lips. Heat flooded her, and the bite on her shoulder burned. Gently she touched the injury he'd given her.

Still, no visions came to her. Absolutely nothing. He was a complete enigma, which was more than disconcerting. Cait had never tried so hard to look into someone's future. Of course, she'd never needed to before. She stomped her foot in frustration and held in a scream. Why couldn't she see anything about him? Why was her gift failing her when she needed it most?

"I want you," he repeated, his gravelly voice rumbling across her.

She snapped back to her senses and punched her hands to her hips. "Ye want me, do ye?" she asked haughtily.

A small grin tipped the corners of his mouth. "You have no idea."

She scowled at him. How dare he find this amusing? "Well, I doona appreciate bein' mauled by ye—or anyone else, for that matter. So just turn around and go back ta Hampshire where ye belong."

The smile faded from his lips. "I'm afraid that's not possible."

"It's very possible," she informed him. "Ye just get back in yer coach and go the other way. I have nothin' else ta say ta ye."

He shook his head as his captivating eyes darkened. "Running away from me again? You struck me as a girl with a bit more fire in her than that."

A bit more fire? She wished her coven sister, Blaire, was there with her. The warrior witch could singe the man until he'd had enough *fire* to last a lifetime.

"I'm no' runnin' from ye. I doona ken where ye would get such a ridiculous idea. I doona even ken who ye are."

"Allow me to remedy that," he said smoothly. "The Earl of Brimsworth, at your service."

Brimsworth? Cait recognized his name immediately and took a tentative step back. She might not know his future, but she knew enough of his past. He was a man she should stay far away from. He was dangerous, and, even worse than that, he was a Lycan, distasteful mutts that they were. She was barely able to tolerate the one who'd married Elspeth.

This conversation was over. She did not need a Lycan in her life, no matter how much he made her heart race. Cait tipped her nose in the air and leveled him with what she hoped was her iciest glare.

"Yer services are no' needed, Lord Brimsworth. Now turn around and go back ta Hampshire or wherever ye came from."

A muscle twitched in his jaw, and Cait swallowed nervously. Lord Brimsworth took a step closer to her and said, "There's nothing for me in Hampshire, lass. My future is in Glasgow."

Blast him! Why did he have to say *future*? Cait almost swallowed her tongue. Why was the Englishman headed to Scotland? And why Glasgow? Did he think she was headed there? Well, wouldn't he be surprised to find he was mistaken? She certainly wasn't going to correct his assumption.

But what if her father met Brimsworth in Glasgow on one of *his* many business trips? Cait shook her head at her own foolishness. Her father would never meet Lord Brimsworth. Then again, she hadn't thought she'd ever lay eyes on the man again either.

What if Jeannie told Papa what Brimsworth had done to her? And then what if they *did* meet in Glasgow? Papa was there often enough. Cait's belly plummeted. What she wouldn't give to tell the man's future.

"Ye canna go there," she squeaked.

The earl's disarming smile returned. "I was unaware that I needed your permission to travel north, Miss Macleod."

Cait gathered up her courage and poked a finger to his chest. "I doona ken what ye're after…"

He captured her hand in his, and tingles raced across her skin from his touch. Then he lifted her hand to his lips and kissed her knuckles while his gaze seared her.

"Since last night, I haven't been able to think of anything but you and your delightful scent."

Cait's traitorous heart flipped, though she chose to ignore it and extricated her hand from his grasp. "I somehow doubt that, between yer acts of vengeance, my lord, ye've been troubled by thoughts of me or my scent," she replied tartly.

He threw back his head and laughed. "Ah, so you do know who I am."

She didn't find the idea remotely humorous and she nodded curtly, folding her arms across her chest. "I ken ye abducted Lord William and planned ta harm him." Not that she'd ever cared one way or the other about Lord William. But voicing the earl's crimes could only help her at this point.

Brimsworth shrugged. "Then you must also know that Lord William entered into a competition with me of his own free will. Then he cheated. I didn't take too kindly to that."

No. He didn't seem like the sort of man... no, *Lycan*,... who would take kindly to being duped. Not that Cait had any intention of standing in the cold without her tartan to continue this ridiculous conversation.

"Honestly, my lord, I have no desire ta applaud or deride the decisions made by either Lord William or his bride. The matter is moot, anyway. Now, do excuse me. I'm certain my maid is beside herself with worry."

Then she turned back toward the inn. She half expected Brimsworth to chase after her. He'd apparently been doing so all day. But his footfalls didn't sound behind her. She shouldn't have been disappointed by that. It was for the best, after all. She didn't have room for any more Lycans in her life anyway.

Cait entered the taproom and tried to avoid the visions of the other patrons' futures that assaulted her. In her mind, one man sat crying over the bed of a loved one, his wife, Cait assumed. A tavern wench at the far side of the taproom was about to learn she was an expectant mother. The portly tavern-keeper would stumble in a hole and twist his ankle.

She focused on the door to the private dining room and was relieved when she stepped over the threshold and blocked out all the unwanted sights. She hadn't appreciated the fact that her mind was clear and unburdened when she was with the Earl of Brimsworth. That in itself was fairly disconcerting.

As soon as she closed the door to the dining room, Jeannie threw her arms around Cait and kissed her cheek. "Ah, Miss, I was so worried about ye."

"I'm fine, Jeannie," she said.

"I've never seen ye behave in such a way. Who was that fellow? And why did ye run off like that?"

"Lord Brimsworth," Cait said casually. "He's an acquaintance of the Westfields."

Her maid frowned. "And the rest of it. Why did ye run off?" she asked again.

Cait should have known better than to think Jeannie would let it go that easily. "*Havers*! It's been a long day, and I just want ta go ta bed. Can ye save the Spanish Inquisition until tomorrow?" Hopefully, by then she'd have decided what to confide in her maid and what to keep to herself.

Jeannie slinked away. "I doona think Mr. Macleod would approve, Miss."

"Nonsense," Cait replied breezily. "There's nothin' ta approve of or no'. We'll no' be seeing his lordship again anyway." They were headed to two different cities, after all. They'd lose Brimsworth in the morning, and that would be that.

❧

"Sir," the tavern-keeper called from across the coaching yard.

Dash ignored the man as he was in no mood to enjoy the keep's company. His mind was still reeling from his conversation with Miss Macleod. The few moments he'd spent in her presence had stirred his blood in a way he'd never experienced before. Well, save the previous evening. And the moment she'd walked away from him had been excruciatingly painful.

Was this a normal reaction to seeing his mate? It was torturous being so close to her since she radiated warmth straight to his soul, but he couldn't touch her. He couldn't taste her. He had no claim at all to her, except for the mark he'd left on her neck.

The whole ordeal was a cruel torment. The major's dire prediction echoed in his head. She wasn't bound by the same rules he was. Dash didn't think he could survive a lifetime of lusting after her if she rejected him and chose another. As it was, he needed every bit of self-control he possessed not to storm the stairs, find Caitrin's room, and claim her in a much more intimate way.

"Sir!" the tavern-keeper called again.

Dash wanted to break the man in two. He stepped out of the shadows. "Yes?"

A look of relief settled on the portly man's face. "Ah, there you are. I thought you might have left."

"What do you want?" Dash asked, not even bothering to keep his tone conversational.

The tavern-keeper swallowed nervously and hastened to explain. "Your room key, sir. It's the only one left, and another fellow was wanting it. But since I promised it to you first... Is there anything else I can do for you, sir?"

Dash scratched his chin. "Actually, there is something you can do for me. And it involves that young woman I asked about when I arrived, my *cousin*."

Four

CAITRIN SIGHED DEEPLY AS SHE PULLED THE PINS FROM her hair and let it tumble about her shoulders.

"Tired, Miss?" Jeannie asked as she folded Cait's traveling dress and helped her mistress into her nightrail.

Cait leaned back heavily. "Ye have no idea." Being in places with a lot of people was utterly exhausting. No matter how much she tried to block out the names, faces, and futures, she was unable to do so. Except for the moments she spent with the dashing and dangerous Lord Brimsworth. Those moments were quiet. They were calm. The only emotions that roiled were within her. She received nothing from the people around her. It was almost heaven.

The desire for quiet nearly made her want to seek out his lordship again, just so she could see if he was truly a man who could bring her peace. Even now, she saw Jeannie in her mind's eye as she snuck from the room after Caitrin slept to go and meet with her suitor, Cait's coachman, Lamont.

"Why doona ye go ahead and go, Jeannie?" Cait finally asked, trying to keep the irritation from her voice.

"Go where, Miss?" the maid replied, feigning confusion.

"Ye ken perfectly well *where*," Cait chided. "Ye canna lie ta me. And ye ken that ye canna."

"Truly, Miss," the maid started, but Cait held up a hand to silence her.

"Please, doona tell me an untruth. Lamont is waitin' for ye." She tried to gentle her smile at the woman. "Go," she said, shooing Jeannie toward the door with her hands. The only head she wanted to be in was her own. "Out."

"Ye're sure ye've no need of me?"

"Positive." Cait sighed.

The woman nearly skipped out the door. Within a few moments, the maid would be wrapped in the arms of the coachman, and she wouldn't be back until the morning. Oh, if life were truly that simple.

When Cait was alone, she still caught snippets of the future, but when they weren't coming at her in concert, they were more like a dream. Or like watching actors at the theater. When they all came at her at once, they were more of a nightmare.

She crossed to the window and pulled back the drapes. The moon still hung high in the sky. She caught a flash of movement a story below her, the top of a blond head moving across the inn yard. Lord Brimsworth? No, that must be wishful thinking.

Wishful? She scoffed at her own thoughts. The day she wished for that Adonis to come and chew on her collarbone some more would be the day she was due for Bedlam. It was *peace* she wished for. Just a few moments.

A small shower of pebbles hit her window. She looked down and saw the man motioning with his arms, as though he wanted her to raise the window. She shook her head vehemently and let the drapes fall back in place.

Another shower of tiny stones hit the window. Maybe he would go away if she conceded. She thrust back the drapes and opened the creaky pane. Cold air rushed into the room, sliding beneath her nightrail.

"Lord Brimsworth, what do ye want?" She scowled at him.

He called back, his voice somewhat quiet, "You." He smiled.

Her heart clenched. He did have the most amazing smile with straight, white teeth. But he was also dangerous. She moved to close the window, and pebbles hit *her* this time. She gasped.

"Are ye tryin' ta kill me?" she hissed.

"I have excellent aim, Miss Macleod," he said, his stance completely relaxed. "If I'd wanted to do you harm, I would have done it by now."

She supposed that much was true. He could have done her harm in Blackmoor's study or on the cobblestone path this evening if he was of a mind.

"I only want a moment of your time," he added.

"Can ye no' wait 'til the mornin'?"

"You won't be alone in the morning," he said, raising one eyebrow.

She couldn't see his future. So, she didn't know if that much was true. But it was interesting to know that, from this distance, his future was blank to her, while others' still swarmed around her.

Caitrin heard a shout from the room next to hers. Then a guttural curse. She plugged her ears with her fingers and squeezed her eyes shut tightly. She could already see the future of the occupants of the room. And there wasn't a bloody thing she could do about it. This time, even their future emotions struck her, causing her to double over in pain.

"Miss Macleod?" she heard from the open window.

"I canna do this right now," she murmured to herself.

"You can't do what?" he asked.

How had he heard her quiet complaint?

Caitrin lifted the pillow from the bed and wrapped it around her ears, trying to muffle some of the sound coming from the nearby room. It failed to work. She sank to the floor and drew her knees to her chest and rocked, trying to find a soothing rhythm that could take her out of time and space.

"If you don't answer me, Miss Macleod, I'm coming up there."

She couldn't respond. Feeling anything at all was much too painful.

She did hear a loud thump against the outside of the building and then saw two hands grasp the windowsill. She bent her head and rested her eyes against her knees. Let him come. Let anyone come. It couldn't be worse than what she was experiencing at that moment.

"Aughhh!" She groaned aloud as he crossed the room and walked toward her. Then he touched her. And her world went silent. The images in her mind vanished. All she heard was the chirp of crickets from outside the window and the whinny of a horse in the stables.

She jumped up and threw her arms around his neck, hugging him to her tightly. Lord Brimsworth caught her in the air and didn't let go when she clutched him frantically.

"Finally happy to see me?" He chuckled quietly in her ear as he stroked her back.

❧

Dash had never been as scared as he was when he'd heard her cry out in pain. It was truly odd, because he usually gave little thought to the feelings of others. But he couldn't seem to *not* care about hers.

She clutched his neck tightly, her curves molded against the length of his body. She was a tiny little thing. Her feet dangled above the floor where he simply held her against him, her cheek resting against his shoulder.

"Doona let me go," she whispered.

"I won't," he assured her as he pulled his head back to look down at her. The wavy mass of her hair hung over his hands, the ends tickling his fingers. He wanted to bury his face in it and drink in the scent that had taunted him all day.

"Do you want to tell me what happened?" he crooned at her.

She shook her head against his shoulder. And only then did he realized his shirt was damp. She'd been crying. His heart clenched for her.

Nearly breathless with emotion for the very first time, he didn't know how to react. What was it? Empathy? Sympathy? Affection? He wasn't sure what to call it, but he'd never felt it before.

"Tell me," he prodded. "I might be able to help."

She raised her head and loosened her arms. He immediately wanted to kick himself for doing or saying anything that would make her pull away from him.

Without meeting his eyes, she said in a childlike voice, "In the next room, there's a little girl and she shouldna be there. That's no' her father. If she stays in that room, somethin' terrible will happen ta her."

"How do you know this?"

"I canna tell ye," she said, finally meeting his gaze. Her hand never left where it touched his arm. It was almost as though he anchored her in some way. "I'm no' supposed ta tell ye as much as I have. But I canna let her be hurt. Can ye help her?"

"I'll try," he started, but her face scrunched up with worry. He leaned and kissed her brow. "I will. Will you be all right by yourself for a moment?" he asked. "I'll be right back."

She nodded and tensed her body, as though bracing for an attack. Then she took her hand from his arm. He *would* find out what that was about.

Quickly and quietly, he slipped out the door.

When he was gone, the visions returned, taking Caitrin's breath with their intensity. She crawled onto the bed and huddled in the corner, rocking her body slowly, finding a rhythm that soothed her.

In no time, she heard a commotion from the room beside her own. It was as though the sun began to shine, obliterating the shadows in her mind. Thank heavens. The child would be unharmed. The perpetrator put to justice. All would be well. She took a deep breath.

There was a soft scratch at the door just before it opened and Lord Brimsworth slipped back inside.

"That was interesting," he said slowly, shaking his head in disbelief. "I think you just saved that child's life."

"I dinna do it," she said quietly, all the fight gone from her body. "Ye did." She wanted nothing more than to close her eyes and sleep.

But Brimsworth was in her room. And she was wearing a nightrail. And only a moment ago, she'd been clutching him to her like she needed him more than anything in the world. She didn't need him, of course. But she needed the peace he offered her.

He sat down on the side of her bed and held out a hand. She placed her own inside his, and his strong fingers closed around hers. He smiled half a smile. "May I stay with you for a bit?" he asked, his voice a little more raspy than before. "I'd like to know you're safe."

"My maid will return," she began.

"I'll be gone before then."

Usually, Cait could confirm or deny it when someone made a prediction like that. But not with him. Dare she trust him?

She craved the quiet he could bring her more than she wanted anything in the world at that moment. A few hours of peace, that's all she wanted. Besides, no one knew he was there.

"How did ye get in the window?" she blurted out.

He chuckled and lay back on one side of the bed, one hand beneath his head, the other clutching hers. "That's a bit of a story," he hedged. Then he asked, "How did you know about the girl?"

"That's a bit of a story, too," she mimicked him.

He chuckled and rolled toward her. The dip in the center of the bed made her roll toward him as well. She froze as he pulled back the neckline of her nightrail and examined the wound on her shoulder.

He sighed deeply before he bent and touched his lips to the area, his lips no more than a tender whisper across her skin. "I'm sorry if this hurt you," he said in a voice she could barely hear. "But I'm not sorry I did it."

He rolled back away from her and put inches between them, but he still clasped her hand in his.

Within moments, the peace in her mind allowed sleep to overtake her. And Cait drifted off to a place where the only dreams she saw were her own.

Five

Morning light invaded Cait's small room, and she sat up with a start. Had she actually lain in this bed with Lord Brimsworth? She cringed and fell backward, blocking the sunlight with her arm. What had she been thinking? She'd behaved like a young witch who didn't understand her powers. Foolish. She'd behaved recklessly.

She rarely left home, and had only done so in this case because Elspeth's family had need of her in Hampshire. On the journey to Westfield Hall, they'd only stopped to change horses—never staying the night at an inn along the way. Of course, she'd been in a bit of hurry then, and sleeping in a bed at night was a luxury she hadn't had time for.

She should have known better than to stop for the night. She was accustomed to visions of Jeannie and Lamont. But being alone with so many unfamiliar people had been a strain and more than overwhelming.

Cait groaned. She hated to think of herself as weak, but there wasn't another word for her actions the night before. If Lord Brimsworth hadn't arrived when he did…

Cait groaned louder. The man had seen her at her worst. That was quite embarrassing. No one had seen her like that since her mother had taught her how to use her powers.

"That's two groans, Miss Macleod. Are you quite all right?" Lord Brimsworth's smooth voice from a nearby chair shattered what was left of her nerves. *The man was still here?*

Cait gasped and tugged the blanket up around her chin. "Get out of my room, sir!"

He chuckled lightly and let his booted feet drop from where he had them propped up on the corner of the bed. "A little late for modesty now, my dear."

Cait's heart pounded in her ears. "Wh—what are ye doin' here?" Her voice came out as a squeak.

"I wanted to make certain you were all right and you were able to sleep."

There was no reason for him to remind her of what a fool she'd made of herself the night before. Cait scowled up at the ceiling, not daring to look at him. "I doona need a nursemaid, Lord Brimsworth."

"I've spent the night with you, angel. I think we can dispense with the formalities, don't you?"

That was his plan? Cait sat up and pulled the blankets around herself, glaring at him. "Are ye tryin' ta compromise me?"

Looking at him was probably a mistake. Until now, all of their encounters had been at night and she had had no idea how handsome he was in the light of day. His golden hair was tousled, radiating warmth from the sun. His amber eyes, with flecks of green, darkened with surprise.

"That would be most ungentlemanly, and I would never do such a deplorable thing."

But abducting the brother of a duke was apparently acceptable. Though Caitrin kept that thought to herself. She didn't want to be put in the position of defending the Westfields again. Their rivalry with Brimsworth had nothing to do with her, and her most pressing concern was getting a certain earl out of her room before anyone knew he was there.

"Ye said ye wouldna stay long," she reminded him.

Lord Brimsworth rose from his seat and stood before the window, peering out at the coaching yard below. She couldn't help but notice the way his trousers hugged his muscular thighs, and she sucked in a surprised breath.

He was a remarkably handsome man who had been very kind to her the night before. If she wasn't careful, she'd lose her head where he was concerned. And despite the way he made her breath catch and caused flutters in her belly, he was dangerous. He was a Lycan.

"I said I would leave before your maid returned," he began quietly. "She never did so."

Was it her imagination, or did he sound angry? "I'm sure she's with my coachman. Ye doona have ta wait for her."

"She abandoned you last night, when you obviously needed someone to stay with you."

Cait was glad his eyes were still on the yard beneath them. It gave her the opportunity to crawl from the bed and tie her wrapper tightly around herself, putting them on more equal footing. "I think ye should leave, my lord."

He glanced over his shoulder at her and nodded. "Very well. It'll give me time to seek out your maid."

"Ye'll do no such thing!" Cait punched her fists to her waist. "Jeannie is *my* maid, and ye doona hold any authority over her."

"Not yet," he mumbled, though she heard him clearly.

"And just what is that supposed ta mean?" she asked, unable to keep the waspishness from her tone.

Lord Brimsworth stalked toward her, reminding her of an approaching beast. Then he halted, very softly brushed his lips across her brow, and continued to the door. "You'll meet me downstairs for breakfast."

Cait gaped at him. No one ever gave her orders, not even her father. Even within her coven, she was the leader. "I beg yer pardon?"

"I told the tavern-keeper that you were my cousin. If you can round up your maid, no one will wonder at all about our sharing a meal together."

He still hadn't *asked* her to join him. "Cousin?"

Lord Brimsworth smirked at her. "I would have said 'wife' if I'd known I was going to stay the night with you. I'll keep that in mind next time."

❧

Dash had loved the look of utter shock on Caitrin Macleod's face. Obviously no one else dictated to her. Her cheeks had turned a delightful shade of pink, and her pretty mouth fell open. It was probably best not to think about that mouth, or he'd storm up the stairs again and make proper use of it.

The previous night had been torturous. Trying to

fall asleep in the uncomfortable inn chair, when he really wanted to climb under the counterpane with her, had been particularly *hard*. Every little sound she made sent the blood pumping to his nether regions. As soon as his mentoring was done, his highest goal would be convincing her to marry him, sooner rather than later, or he might very well explode.

Waiting in the taproom for Caitrin's maid to return to her mistress, Dash noticed a tavern wench across the room batting her eyelashes at him. In the recent past, just last week, in fact, he would have pounced on the chance to bed the girl. She had a nice figure, round brown eyes, and shiny dark hair. Such encounters had been commonplace for him; but now he found nothing noteworthy at all in the girl's appearance or mannerism, so he refocused his attention on the outside entrance.

Now that he thought about it, he hadn't found even one woman remotely attractive since the night he claimed Caitrin in the Duke of Blackmoor's study. He hadn't engaged one stray thought about another woman, except now to note the change within himself.

"Ah, Lord Brimsworth," the tavern-keeper began, stepping across the room while leaning heavily on a cane. "I understand you'd like the private dining room this morning."

Dash inclined his head. "Yes. My cousin will be joining me soon."

"Of course, my lord. I'll show you the way."

Dash didn't budge from his seat. "I'd prefer to await my cousin here." And see how long that useless maid of hers takes to pull herself out of her lover's arms.

"As you wish."

As if on cue, the taproom door slowly opened, and Caitrin's maid stepped over the threshold.

"Excuse me, sir," he said to the tavern-keeper, as he kept his eyes leveled on the mousy brunette who was trying to sneak up the steps to the sleeping rooms. "Miss!" Dash called, briskly crossing the floor. "I'd like a word with you."

The maid turned at his voice, and her eyebrows scrunched together. "My lord?"

Dash towered over the woman and couldn't keep a scowl from his face. The woman had abandoned her duty to Caitrin and his poor angel had been a blubbering mess because of it. "Is it your standard practice to leave your mistress unattended—?"

"Lord Brimsworth!" Caitrin's voice filtered down to him from the top of the stairs. "We've already had this conversation."

"Cousin Caitrin," he replied, turning his eyes on her. She was stunning, with her flaxen locks knotted over one shoulder. Her blue traveling dress was serviceable, but it showed off her curvy form just the same. For a moment, Dash's mouth went dry. "How delightful to see you again. You and your maid really must join me for breakfast."

"How very generous of ye, *cousin*," Caitrin returned, her jaw clenched with irritation and blue fire flashed in her eyes.

The tavern-keeper cleared his voice. "The room is ready, my lord."

"Excellent!" Dash replied, reaching his arm up the staircase to take Caitrin's hand. "Come along, my dear."

When she reached the last step, he tucked her hand into the crook of his elbow. It felt right having her there. He led her down the corridor to the private dining room and held out a seat for her as the maid took a spot beside her mistress.

"Well," he began, "when I reach Glasgow, I plan to call on Mr. Macleod and inform him of the lackluster staff in his employ."

"My lord!" Caitrin hissed, and her cheeks took on a lighter pallor.

"Beggin' yer pardon," the maid gasped.

"You should have been with your mistress last night instead of entertaining some beau. And—"

"I told ye, this isna yer concern." Caitrin leapt from her seat, glaring at him.

"Anything concerning you concerns me," he informed her.

She looked as though she'd smelled something foul, and she folded her arms across her chest. "Ye heavy-handed, ill-mannered Sassenach. I dinna ask for yer help, and nor do I want it."

That was true. Dash nodded. "Well, I'm giving it anyway, lass."

"Ye have no right," she continued.

"I have more than you realize," he answered.

"Come, Jeannie. I've heard quite enough." With that, Caitrin stepped away from the table, sent him one final, scathing glare, and then stomped from the dining room, towing her maid right along with her.

Dash sighed. Was she going to be this stubborn about everything?

Six

How dare he presume to scold her maid! Of all the arrogant, irritating, obnoxious men she'd ever met, he had to be the worst. And on top of that, he'd even threatened to visit her father to tell him about Jeannie's disappearance. And why did he think she lived in Glasgow? Not that she felt obliged to correct his error. Still it was strange. Is that why he was headed to Glasgow? He thought she lived there? He was certainly in for a surprise, wasn't he?

"I'm sorry, Miss," Jeannie sniffled from behind her. "I dinna ken ye would need me. And ye did say ta go," she cried out as Caitrin tugged her back toward the stairs.

"Ye did fine, Jeannie," she said absently, trying to calm the anxious maid. Caitrin called out to the innkeeper as they passed, "Please send our breakfast upstairs and send someone ta collect my trunk."

The startled man began to speak, but no words rolled off his tongue aside from a grunt and a sputter. His cheeks reddened.

"Is there a problem?" Cait asked, using her haughtiest tone.

"No, Miss, but his lordship said—"

"His lordship," she sneered, "doesna make decisions for me."

"Yes, Miss," the man replied, avoiding her gaze.

Caitrin pulled Jeannie up the stairs and stepped into her room. She glanced around and was surprised to see all of her things were gone. Why would her things already be gone? Brimsworth! She hit the wall with the flat of her hand in frustration.

"This is all my fault," Jeannie said quietly as she wrung her hands. "I never should have left ye."

Caitrin patted her hand. "Do try ta calm yerself, Jeannie. Now what do ye suppose that arrogant earl has done with our things?"

Jeannie shook her head. "I couldna say, Miss."

But Lord Brimsworth could say, and Caitrin would make sure he did so. She turned on her heel, stomped back down the stairs, and stumbled straight into the awaiting arms of the man who'd sparked her ire.

Lord Brimsworth's hands came up to catch her, one hand sliding around her waist as the other moved to steady her. She gasped as his hand grazed the underside of her breast. Then all the breath rushed out of her body. She'd love to be able to say it was because of her mad dash downstairs. But, in truth, it was because of his touch. He took her breath away, and he had since the beginning. Blast him.

She lifted her head to look up at the earl.

"That was not intended, Miss Macleod," he said quietly. Then he chuckled as he shook his head with dismay. "Quite pleasurable. But certainly not intended."

"Let me go." She pushed against his firm chest.

"My apologies," he said softly as his gaze continued to search her face, though he made no move to release her.

Cait punched his shoulder with the heel of her hand. "Now!" she snapped.

"Oh, of course." He set her away from him, as though he'd just remembered she was there, or more likely that they were in a public place. He looked behind her. "Where is your maid? Has she abandoned you again?" His eyebrows scrunched together.

"She hasna abandoned me. And she dinna do so last night. I told her ta leave." She leveled her most piercing stare at him. "So stop worryin' her."

He nodded quickly. "She should be worried. I doubt your father would approve of her actions."

"Jeannie's a good maid. She's in love, and ye'll no' go spoilin' it for her."

"Love?" Brimsworth snorted. "It's more like lust."

"Certainly, ye are no stranger ta the baser emotions," she said, and then felt the color creep up her cheeks.

"How would you know what I am or am not familiar with? We've only slept together once—"

"Slept together?" she hissed. "We did no such thing."

"Yes, lass. We did. And I plan to do a lot more of it. Except with a little less sleeping going on next time."

Cait couldn't believe his audacity. She must have truly made a fool out of herself last night for him to think he could say such a thing to her. "And if I have objections ta yer plans?"

"You simply may not object." He shrugged, the epitome of male confidence. She wanted to slug him.

"Do ye always get yer way?" she snapped.

"Do you?" he shot back.

Of course, it would be a battle of wills with her. She was used to being in charge. To doing what she wanted to do. And probably no more than that. She was utterly delightful.

Dash tucked her hand into the crook of his arm and dragged her back up the stairs and down the corridor toward his unused sleeping room. It was the only place he could be assured of some privacy. He pushed the door wide, stepped inside, and pulled her in with him.

"We need to talk," he said, as he closed the door and leaned heavily against it.

"About?" Caitrin squeaked, glancing around the room as though looking for an escape route. There wasn't one unless she could jump as far as he could.

"Us," he said impatiently.

"There is no 'us,'" she scoffed.

"There's obviously something between us."

"Aye, a dog bite," she snorted as she absently rubbed her shoulder. "One that still hurts," she murmured.

So she knew what he was? That was fortuitous. He'd explain about Mr. Forster, the shipbuilder, and ask her to be patient while he went through training. Perhaps he could train with Forster during the day and court Caitrin at night, using all of his time to his advantage.

Dash smiled and took a step toward her. She took a step back. He took another forward. She nearly tripped over a small table that was squarely in the path of her retreat. Dash reached to catch her, but she put up her hands defensively.

"I have been walkin' on my own for years, yer lordship. I doona need yer help with that simple task."

"Dashiel."

"Pardon?"

"My name is Dashiel," he continued. "I would like to hear it on your lips." He'd like that very much.

"Ye'll be waitin' quite a while for that, *Lord Brimsworth*," she replied saucily.

"Dashiel." He couldn't keep the corners of his mouth from turning up at the stubborn look on her face. She was enchanting, his stubborn little angel.

"Lord Brimsworth, this is highly improper," she said. "And I've been alone with ye for far too long."

"And?" he asked, happy now that he'd finally backed her into a corner.

"And I'll be ruined if anyone finds out." Her voice quivered a bit as he lifted his arms and touched the wall with his hands, putting his weight there as he leaned in to her. "No decent man will ever want ta marry me."

"Is that what you want?" he asked, then inhaled her honeysuckle scent. Her heart was beating like the ticking of a clock wound too tightly. "A decent man?"

"Aye," she said, closing her eyes as he let his breath blow over the shell of her ear.

"I don't think you would be well satisfied with a *decent man*." Dash wanted to chuckle but held it in for fear of ruining the moment. "You would tire of him quickly."

"And ye think ye ken so much about me?" she asked.

Then he almost touched his lips to hers, but not quite. After a moment, she moved forward the last inch and closed the remaining space when she shyly kissed him and then winced as though she realized how easily she fell into his hands.

"Yes, I know that about you," he whispered against her lips as he moved one hand and used it to unlace the ties at her throat. The material whispered softly.

Her hand came up to clutch his, but her eyes remained closed. "Stop," she said softly.

"Let me see your shoulder." He tugged at her laces again.

Her eyes instantly flew up to meet his. "Why?" she asked, doubt written across her features.

"I want to see how much damage I did," he said, trying to look properly apologetic. It was a look he'd mastered as a young boy to keep Eynsford's temper at bay. "I wasn't able to see much in the dark last night."

"And that's all?" Skepticism clouded her light blue eyes.

"Actually, I'd like to see more than that." He couldn't help but grin. "But for now, it'll do. I would feel terrible if I hurt you badly." That part was true, at least. He would feel like the worst sort of cad if he'd injured her needlessly.

"Ye never did tell me why ye felt the need ta take a bite out of me, Lord Brimsworth," she said as she removed his hands from the laces of her dress and simply tugged at the collar of her gown, exposing her neck and shoulder to him.

"Dashiel," he repeated. He appraised the wound on her shoulder. It wasn't too bad. A little red around the bite mark. "You truly don't know why I did it?" She knew what he was, after all. In fact, she might know more about being a Lycan than he did.

"I have no clue." She looked completely dumb-founded, and he believed her.

Dash sighed deeply. This wasn't the time or place to tell her about the claiming. He wasn't even sure he knew everything himself. The situation was at the top of the list of questions he had for the shipbuilding Forster in Glasgow.

Besides, Dash needed her to actually like him before he told her the truth about that little bite. Judging by the scent of her, she was quite a bit interested in him now; but it wasn't the same thing. And though she intrigued him more than he'd have ever imagined, that wasn't enough to make him divulge his secrets yet.

All things considered, he could have chosen a worse mate. Caitrin was beautiful. And smart. And stubborn. He grimaced at the last. "I let passion overtake me," he said as he shrugged his shoulders. "You did kiss me back, you know."

"Aye, I did."

"Kiss me now," he urged softly.

Right when his lips touched hers, the door flew open with a bang. Dash tucked her head into his chest and glanced back over his shoulder, where a big, burly man looked ready to thrash him.

"A moment, if you don't mind," he called out.

"I'm ruined," she whispered as she buried her face in his neck, her hands clutching his waistcoat in her fists.

"I'll take care of it," he assured her. Maybe not the way she'd like for him to do so. But he *would* make it right for her, even if he had to kill the interloper.

"Miss Macleod," the burly man began, and Dash couldn't miss the lilt of his Scottish brogue. "Are ye all right?"

❦

Lamont.

Cait cringed and wished she could vanish with a snap of her fingers. Unfortunately, that wasn't a skill she'd ever learned. Her coachman would never look at her the same after this. And what if the man mentioned this to her father?

She groaned. Life had always been complicated, but never more so than it had been since the Earl of Brimsworth entered her life.

Dashiel put her away from him and turned on his heel. "It is customary to knock."

Lamont paid him little heed and stomped over to her. "Miss, are ye all right? Jeannie said the swell was threatenin' ta get her sacked."

Within the blink of an eye, Dashiel had Lamont's jacket in his hands and held the burly coachman against the wall. It happened so fast that Caitrin gasped.

"If Jeannie had stayed at her post," the earl growled, "there wouldn't be any reason for her to be sacked."

"My lord!" Cait tugged on his jacket, but he couldn't be swayed from his purpose.

"B-but—" Lamont stuttered.

"And if you're intent on maintaining *your* post, you will not impugn Miss Macleod's good name."

The coachman's dark eyes widened in surprise. "O-of course no'."

Dashiel released the man and Lamont slid down the wall until his feet found purchase. He pulled at the collar of his shirt, while his gaze landed on Caitrin. "Jeannie says yer trunk is missin' and everythin' else."

The earl turned back to Cait and smiled sheepishly.

"I was going to mention that. As we are headed to the same place, we should ride together. Your coach may follow mine."

Except there was the little fact that they weren't, in fact, traveling to the same place. She should probably mention that, but not while she was unsure of the power he held over her. Not while he behaved like a martinet. Not while he barked out commands and expected her and her servants to obey them to the letter. Besides, she hadn't technically lied. She had never told him she was traveling to Glasgow; he'd just assumed that for some reason, and she had neglected to correct him.

Cait sighed from exasperation. Lycans were all alike. Bellowing bullies. Arrogant arses. She'd seen those same qualities in others of his kind and didn't find them remotely attractive. "So ye *do* have my things, Lord Brimsworth?"

His amber eyes actually twinkled. "Assuming Jeannie can serve as a suitable chaperone, I don't see any reason we shouldn't keep each other company, Miss Macleod. I know it will make my journey more enjoyable."

Cait did wish her heart wouldn't flip when he looked at her like that. "I'm no' so certain Jeannie will want ta spend any time at all with ye, after ye've threatened her livelihood." Besides, she had no intention of traveling to Glasgow with the man. She'd have to find a way to abandon him before they reached the border. But that shouldn't be too difficult for a witch of her talents.

Dashiel grinned rakishly. "If she can prove her

loyalty, I could be persuaded not to mention last night's indiscretion."

Blackmailing blackguard.

Lamont's sigh of relief echoed throughout the small room. It wasn't in anyone's best interest for Cait to chastise the earl at the moment for his heavy-handed behavior. That could wait until later. She pasted a fraudulent smile on her face. "That does seem most fair, my lord."

Who did he think he was to bully her around like that? She was going to teach the Earl of Brimsworth a lesson he wouldn't ever forget. But timing was everything.

Seven

DASH WAS FAIRLY PLEASED WITH HIS SUCCESS. CAITRIN Macleod was traveling in *his* carriage, directly across from him. Before much longer, he would have her in his bed, too. He nearly groaned aloud at the thought, but with the glares her maid continued to shoot at him, that wasn't a particularly good idea.

He leaned his head back against the squabs and his gaze fell to Caitrin. She looked like an angel in the daylight, too, sitting so properly with her hands folded in her lap. He couldn't help but imagine what it would feel like to have her hands on his bare skin. Heaven in every sense of the word.

Caitrin turned her gaze from the window and settled her soft blue eyes on him. Besotted fool that he was, Dash's breath caught in his throat. He managed to pull himself together and hoped she didn't notice. "So nice not to travel alone."

A tentative smile lit her face before she smothered it. "Why are ye headed ta Glasgow, my lord?"

"I already told you, Miss Macleod. My future's there." In every sense.

He really should ask the lass' father for her hand. Do things properly. He hadn't asked for Prisca Hawthorne's hand until it was too late. Besides, he hadn't been in love with Prisca Hawthorne. He didn't quite believe in the emotion, but he'd liked her quite a bit. She would have made the perfect countess. She was beautiful, poised, and could manage a household with no effort at all. He'd even played the gallant. But that hadn't stopped William Westfield from snatching her out from under Dash's nose.

The loss of Prisca had been a blow to his ego, but his heart had been unaffected. Staring at the beautiful blonde across from him, so different from Prisca in almost every way, Dash wasn't certain he could survive if he lost Caitrin. But was that because of the connection that tied him to her, or was it something even more than that?

She was a lady; there was no question about it, with the way she held herself so proudly. But a Scot? He could just imagine the look on his father's face when he found out. If the Lycan news didn't finish the old buzzard off, a Scottish daughter-in-law might do the trick. That thought brought a smile to Dash's face.

"What is so amusin', my lord?" Caitrin asked him.

"I was just thinking about my father." Not that the powerful Marquess of Eynsford was his true sire, but odds were the vicious old man didn't know that. Or maybe he did, Dash didn't care anymore. "I think you'd knock him off his feet."

A pretty pink stained her cheeks, and Dash bit back a smile. She wasn't immune to flattery. He'd keep that in mind. He'd charm her right out of her dress if all else failed.

The irritating maid cleared her throat, so he must have given something away on his face. Dash raised his brow, daring her to say something. After the way she neglected her duties, it was quite something for her to attempt to chastise *him*.

A giggle escaped Caitrin's throat and he returned his gaze to her, which suited him just fine. "Have you always lived in Glasgow, Miss Macleod?"

The maid sputtered.

Caitrin turned her glance back out the window. "Papa has land in Berwickshire, but I've only been there once."

Only once? That was odd. From the time he was young, he'd been shuffled from the ancestral estate in Kent to the hunting box in Yorkshire and to every other Eynsford property in between. It wasn't until his thirteenth year, when he went through *changes*, that the trips stopped.

His father had called him a demon child, a monster. Dash had been locked up every full moon since, either by the marquess' orders or his own. The first time he'd been free, Caitrin Macleod had stumbled into his path. Was that fate?

"I doona like ta travel," she explained, breaking into his thoughts.

That didn't make any sense at all. Dash glanced around the coach. "Then why did you journey to Hampshire? It's not a short trip."

She shrugged. "Elspeth had need of me."

"Lord Benjamin's wife?" he asked, though he

knew he must be right. The red-haired woman in question was Major Forster's daughter and had Caitrin's exact lilt.

She nodded. "We're very close. Like sisters, ye could say."

"And she needed you in Hampshire?"

Caitrin's blue eyes cast downward to her hands. "Ye wouldna understand, my lord."

"You could explain it to me."

Her hands began to fidget in her lap. "I doona think that would be wise."

Dash frowned at her answer. She didn't trust him. He'd change that, as soon as he figured out how.

All day in a carriage with the Earl of Brimsworth. Caitrin sighed. She wasn't doing very well with her pledge to stay away from Lycans, which was more than a little frustrating. After watching the way Benjamin Westfield had courted Elspeth, she would have thought she knew well the arsenal of tricks Lycans used to capture women.

But Dashiel was different from that. Just as soon as she decided she hated him, he'd swoop in and turn her mind upside down, like he'd done the night before. He shouldn't have stayed all night with her, but it was very sweet of him to worry about her, just the same.

Then he had to turn around and do something as despicable as threaten to expose Jeannie and manipulate Cait into his carriage. Her mind was still whirring on that situation, though she was certain a solution would present itself.

Cait heard a slight thump and looked over to find Jeannie sleeping, her head resting against the side of the carriage. Then she heard him chuckle.

"You cannot avoid me any longer, Caitrin," Dashiel said smoothly.

Cait raised a hand to her chest in surprise. "I doona ken what ye mean, my lord."

"You're holding back on me. I want to know all about you. Every detail, but you've been hiding behind your maid's skirts."

Her cheeks warmed at the accusation. "I most certainly have no'," she hissed. "And I dinna give ye leave ta use my given name."

"Ah, yes." He winked at her. "We must abide by the formalities of our rank, Miss Macleod. I nearly forgot. Thank you for reminding me. I tend to forget my manners when I'm with you."

Cait reached up absently to rub her shoulder. "Did ye have any manners ta begin with?" she murmured.

Again he chuckled softly, a sound that almost made her smile with him. Almost, but not quite. Then he shrugged and said, "I was overcome by the moment. There's no other way to justify it."

Caitrin chose to look out the window and avoid his amber eyes, which suddenly seemed to look *into* her instead of *at* her.

"Tell me about last night," he prompted. "I noticed the pair in the taproom, but I never would have known what sort of villain the man was. How did you know about the girl? And how were you already upset about something that hadn't yet happened?" He held up a hand when she was about to speak. "Not that I minded, of course. I like it when you fling yourself into my arms. Feel free to do so at any time."

She didn't remember *flinging* herself into his arms. Not exactly.

"The girl, Miss Macleod. How did you know?"

Now, how could she explain it? "I saw them downstairs, too," Caitrin lied smoothly. She'd been lying about her gift of clairvoyance for years. It came easily to her. "Somethin' dinna seem right with them."

His eyes narrowed as he appraised her face. "I can hear it when your heartbeat speeds up," he said softly. "I can't tell if you're anxious because you're telling me an untruth, or if it's because you like me." He grinned mischievously at her.

"I can assure ye it's neither." She sat up a bit straighter.

He leaned forward with his elbows on his knees. "Then what is it?"

Truth be told, just the look in his eyes made her heart beat faster. He had this way of making her feel naked, despite the fact that she was fully clothed. She squirmed in her seat.

He chuckled once more and sat back, a supreme example of a relaxed male. "That's what I thought."

Caitrin wanted nothing more than to rant and rave about his superior attitude. But her sleeping maid didn't allow her to say what she wanted to say. Instead, she pushed her lips together in an effort to stay quiet.

❧

The more Caitrin pursed her lips, the more Dash wanted to kiss them. Her very existence tortured him, though she seemed oblivious to his plight. If he could get her talking again, he could focus on her words to distract himself.

"Do you have any sisters or big, burly brothers?" Anyone he should worry himself about meeting when they reached Glasgow.

She shook her head. "Nay. I'm an only child, though I have a small group of friends I'm very close ta. Ye could say we're like sisters in a lot of ways."

Dash had a few friends but none so close that he'd consider them family. Of course, he could never trust anyone enough to divulge the dark secret he kept hidden. What he wouldn't give to have been raised in a pack that accepted him.

"Ye look far away, my lord." Her soft, lilting voice reached the recesses of his mind and brought him back to the present.

"Nothing of any importance, I assure you."

"What about ye? Do ye have any siblings?"

"None that I'm aware of," he admitted. Honestly, who knew how many children his real father had sired?

Caitrin's tinkling laugh warmed his soul. "What is that supposed ta mean?"

He probably shouldn't have said that. He wanted to marry the lass. Confessing to being a bastard wasn't the best way to go about convincing her. "One never knows," he answered vaguely.

She cocked her head to one side as though assessing him, and he didn't welcome the scrutiny. What secrets would she uncover, simply by looking at him?

"My father wanted many sons, but he was only blessed with me. Something he's lamented for years." He wasn't certain why he told her that. There was something about staring into her pretty blue eyes that made him want to confess all.

Caitrin bit her bottom lip, the sight of which made his trousers painfully tight. "Yer father's no' a Lycan?"

Dash nearly fell out of his seat. How could she possibly know that? He shook his head, stunned. Then he took a sidelong glance at the sleeping maid. "No. And that fact, according to Major Forster, means he's probably not my father." There, he'd said it. There was no use trying to hide it; her mere presence would pull it from him anyway.

Her pretty blue eyes rounded in surprise. "And yer mother?"

"Dead. She died in childbirth, taking the secret of my sire with her."

"Oh. That must be difficult. A friend of mine never kent her father, and it pained her every day."

Dash released a breath he didn't know he held. "You're very kind not to judge me."

"Ye're hardly responsible for yer own circumstances, my lord."

He reached across the coach and grasped her hands in his. "Dashiel, or Dash, if you'd rather."

She shook her head. "I doona think that would be appropriate."

Probably not, but wanting to hear his name on her lips was nearly driving him mad. "I won't tell a soul."

Her eyes twinkled devilishly, as though they shared a secret. "Dashiel, why do ye say yer future is in Scotland?"

It was heaven to hear her say his name, and Dash nearly groaned. He leaned forward to touch his lips to hers. Her sweet breath encompassed him, and her soft sigh was almost his undoing. She didn't pull back. She didn't balk. She didn't complain. She didn't abhor him or what he was.

"Because you're my future," he whispered across her lips. "Because I'm going to marry you when we reach Glasgow. After I've properly courted you and asked your father's permission, of course." He pressed his lips to hers again quickly and sat back, unable to keep from wiggling his foot in excitement at the very thought.

A startled laugh escaped her. "I doona remember a marriage proposal coming from yer lips ta my ears, my lord."

And she wouldn't, either. If he asked, she could refuse him. It would be better to discuss the situation with her father. "Not to worry. I'll make you a very wealthy countess, Caitie."

"*No one* has ever called me Caitie," she huffed as she leaned back against the squabs, glowering at him.

Dash couldn't help but grin because she was so adorable. "Then it's a great term of endearment, isn't it?" He leaned back against his own seat. "Caitie, my angel," he sighed dramatically.

"Ye are so infuriatin'."

"I could say the same about you, angel."

"Then why on earth would ye want ta marry me, ye fool?"

"There are several reasons, actually."

"And they are?" she prompted.

"For starters, I like you," he said, winking at her. She scowled. "And?"

"And you're beautiful."

She rolled her eyes.

He laughed out loud but soft enough not to awake the sleeping maid. "And you challenge me."

"Ye want my kind of challenge every day for the rest of yer life?"

"I don't have much of a choice, angel."

She scrunched up her face. "Ye doona make any sense."

Dash sighed, took pity on her, and decided to tell her the whole truth, or at least as much of it as he knew. "I already claimed you."

"Well, *un*-claim me." She folded her arms across her chest.

"It's not that easy. Major Forster says when a Lycan claims his mate, it's…" He paused, looking for the right word. "Permanent," he finally said.

Cait narrowed her eyes at him. "Permanent?" she echoed.

"If the situation was perfect, I'd have courted you and you'd have fallen in love with me. I *am* quite irresistible." He grinned.

Cait looked out the window as her heart began to pound rapidly, and he caught a glimpse of a smile she tried to bite back. "Ye really are full of yerself."

"I'll assume your response means you're amenable to the plan?" He chuckled when a blush stained her cheeks.

"Canna I have just one secret from ye? Must ye Lycans ken everythin'?"

"We don't know everything, Caitie," he murmured. "For instance, I'm not sure if you're willing to accept me, just as I am. I know you want me. I've known that since the very first night. But could you love me? I don't imagine so. No one else ever has."

Dash glanced out the window himself. Once again Caitrin had him admitting things he'd rather have left unsaid. He couldn't even look at her for fear of seeing the rejection he was sure was in her eyes.

❧

Cait stared across the coach at the big, strapping Sassenach. Claimed her permanently! How could he have done such a thing? It wasn't supposed to happen that way. It shouldn't have happened at all. She would have seen it, if it was. Blast him for going against the fabric of destiny. And blast him for making her consider everything he had to offer.

She shook her head. What was she thinking? How could she consider such a thing? She had a duty to her coven, and marrying some English lord she hardly knew wasn't in her future.

Jeannie blinked her eyes open, and the very strange conversation came to an end. The three of them rode in silence until the sun began to sink below the horizon.

Finally Cait broke the quiet when the coach rolled to a stop outside an inn. "We're ta change the horses and keep goin'," she informed her maid.

"No." Dashiel shook his head. "We all need some rest. We'll stay here for the night."

His amber eyes danced with something she couldn't quite identify, but it had her belly twisting and panic coursing through her veins.

"We will do no such thing," she declared as he helped her alight from the coach. "Perhaps his *lordship* would like ta rest, and I think that is a wonderful idea. But I plan ta move on."

"Do you have to argue with everything I say?" he asked.

"Do ye have ta dictate ta me as though I'm still in leadin' strings? I made it all the way ta Hampshire by myself. I assure ye that I can find my own way home."

"That will not happen." He suddenly looked dark and dangerous. "I need you, Miss Macleod."

She wasn't prepared to discuss this any further. Especially not in front of Jeannie. "Ye'll no' be permitted ta hound me for the rest of my days, my lord. I'll no' stand for it."

"You're using the word *hound* to prove your point, I assume." He shook his head, a faint smile lingering about his lips. "I've been called worse, Miss Macleod. Much worse." A shadow crossed his face as he clenched his jaw.

"I doona do well in crowded places such as this," she finally admitted. Already, she could see the futures of people she didn't know. She closed her eyes and took a deep breath.

"Don't worry. I'll protect you."

For some strange reason, she trusted that he would try. And that worried her more than the thoughts of a hundred futures clouding her head. She had to do something about Dashiel Thorpe before it was too late. Before she lost her heart and mind completely to the man. And she had to do something sooner rather than later.

Eight

DASH STEPPED INTO THE TAPROOM WITH CAITRIN following closely behind. The woman didn't trust him to care for her needs. He'd never had to care for another person, but he had to admit he liked it quite a bit. If only she'd let him try.

He turned to ask her a question and was quickly taken aback by the wince on her face.

"Are you all right?" he asked as he cupped her elbow.

"Fine," she gritted through her teeth. Her pretty blue eyes were shut tightly for a moment. Then she opened them slowly and sighed. "I'm fine," she said a little more congenially.

"You're not fine," he contradicted as he tipped her chin up with his crooked finger, forcing her to look at him.

"I *told* ye I dinna want ta stop." She swung her head to shake off his attention. "But ye dinna listen, ye beast. If ye plan ta make me stay, ye can at least let me go ta my room."

The innkeeper smiled from behind his counter. "A room for you and your wife, sir?"

"Yes," he started, but Caitrin cut him off.

"Two please?"

"We only need *one*," Dash said, forcing himself not to raise his lip in warning. It took all of his strength to keep from acting like the beast he truly was.

"We need *two*," Caitrin insisted, glaring at him instead of the innkeeper.

Dash scratched the stubble on his chin for a moment. There were bigger battles to win. He nodded his head, slightly. "My wife prefers her space."

The innkeeper smirked as he turned to get another key.

A moment later, Dash motioned for her to precede him up the stairs. He watched the easy sway of her hips and immediately wished she *was* his wife. In every sense of the word. What he wouldn't give to wrap his arms around her and draw her to him with no restrictions. For now, he'd take a smile. *Smile at me, lass.*

Of course, she didn't. She fit her key in the lock and turned it, then slid inside. But before she could close the door, he stuck his boot in the opening to prevent it from closing and then stepped in behind her. He leaned heavily against the door.

"Oh, no, ye willna stay here, Lord Brimsworth," she shot at him, shaking her head as she advanced on him. "My maid will be here any moment, and ye're ta be gone before then."

"I need you," he said, then watched her face to gauge her reaction. Her eyebrows drew together as she frowned.

"Ye said that in the coach," she reminded him.

"But ye refused ta tell me why ye need me. If ye think ye're ta find yer way inta my bed—" He placed a finger to her lips to stop her tirade.

She sputtered, her lips moving against the tip of his finger. And, heaven help him, he couldn't keep from actually circling her waist with his arms and drawing her closer to him.

She didn't make a sound. Perhaps the way to get the woman to be quiet was to kiss her. Or at least make her think he was going to kiss her. Hell, he wanted to kiss her all the time, so he wouldn't be acting the part of a devoted suitor. He truly was one. Perhaps it was time he told her the truth of their situation. Maybe she wouldn't fight him anymore.

"Do you know what it means to claim one's mate?"

"Lord Brimsworth!" she gasped. "I am shocked that ye mean ta be so coarse in my presence." He placed his finger to her lips again. This time she talked around it. "I'll no' let ye distract me."

In truth, he was the one who was distracted. He had planned to tell her about the claiming of one's Lycan mate, what it meant and the little fact that he'd already claimed her as his. But how could he do that when she looked so beautiful? Her lips were full and pouty. Her eyes danced with blue fire. She smelled like honeysuckle and desire all mixed together.

Her lips moved against his finger as she continued her tirade. His trousers grew snug. He chastised himself for his own indecent thoughts. But she was so bloody beautiful. How could he not think of all the carnal delights he could teach her about? The very idea made his mind wander for a moment.

"Lord Brimsworth." She nudged him back into the present.

Dash threaded his hand through her hair so he could cup the back of her head. "I claimed you the first time I saw you," he finally admitted. "You'll not be able to get rid of me. Because I won't let you."

"Ye are more than a little full of yerself, my lord." She wasn't immune to him, no matter how much she tried to be. He could hear her heart race with his touch. "There's a bit more ta claimin' one's mate than a kiss in His Grace's study." She flushed brilliantly when she realized what she'd said.

If only that were true. If so, he'd be able to walk away from her. But would he even want to do that if he could? He wasn't certain.

"We'll have to finish this conversation at a later time, angel." Before Jeannie had the chance to scratch on the door, Dash heard her approach, and he couldn't hide his scowl. The woman was either around when he didn't want her or not there when her mistress had a need of her. He'd have to hire Caitrin a better maid to serve her once she was his countess. "Dine with me again this evening."

Caitrin frowned at that, and her adorable nose scrunched up. "I doona like being ordered about, my lord. It is a distasteful quality found in yer breed."

Then the scratch came at the door. The inept maid had finally come to her post. "Come," he growled, while he kept his eyes trained on Caitrin. "Order a bath, freshen up, and I'll retrieve you in an hour."

At that moment, the door opened and Jeannie stepped inside.

Dash ignored the woman and took Caitrin's hand in his and brushed his lips across her knuckles. "Until then, angel."

     ❧

Caitrin steeled herself for the moment he released her hand, when everyone's futures would come rushing back into her mind. The short reprieves he offered her were the greatest of gifts. Still, he was an overbearing, self-important Sassenach… With the most mesmerizing amber eyes.

She shook the thought from her mind and extracted her hand from the infuriating Lycan's grasp. Immediately, she was assaulted by stray images of strange people's futures. When she walked back through the doors of Macleod House, she would drop to her knees, kiss the floor, and refuse ever to leave her home again.

Once she saw a particular person's future, it wouldn't haunt her again unless she focused on it and willed it into her mind. At home, she'd already seen her father's future, that of the butler, and footmen, cook, and every maid in residence. It would be a relief not to be inundated with unwanted thoughts, like she had been the last several weeks.

"Since ye're the one who wanted ta stop, my lord, I think I'll just get some rest and see ye in the mornin'."

Dashiel shook his head. "I'm afraid I must insist."

Cait scowled at him. Insist, indeed. "Are ye goin' ta blackmail me inta dinin' with ye, now?"

A wolfish smile graced his lips. "If I have to. Will it be necessary, Miss Macleod?"

Blast him for being charming. She really did hate that about him. If he didn't make her knees weak or look so concerned about her, it would be easy to discount him all together. Cait wasn't used to either. Only one other man had ever made her knees weak, but they had no future together, no matter how much Cait wished otherwise. And no one ever looked at her with concern the way Brimsworth did. The other witches in her coven always came to her for advice and reassurances that things would turn out all right.

It was nice to have someone worry about her for a change. A very handsome someone. What a shame that he was a Lycan. And how disconcerting that she couldn't see what the future had in store for him.

"Miss Macleod?" the earl said, a frown marring his face as he took a step toward her.

She must have been lost in thought. Cait shook her head and stepped backward. "Just woolgatherin', my lord."

A look of relief passed over his features, and he smiled. "Dinner? We have quite a lot to discuss."

Doing so would put her heart in danger, and Cait couldn't allow that. Her coven depended on her, and falling head over heels for a Lycan was not in anyone's best interest. She'd have to escape him tonight. "I am tired, my lord. Why doona ye come by after my bath and see if I'm feelin' up ta it?"

"It'll be my honor." And with that, he was gone and took with him all the warmth in the room. Cait heard a shoe tapping against the wooden floor planks and then noticed that Jeannie was frowning at her.

"I doona care for that man," her maid muttered.

Neither would anyone else in her life. Cait flopped down onto her bed and stared up at the water-stained ceiling above her. "Keep yer voice down," she whispered. "He can hear ye."

Jeannie's eyes shot to the door, which was still closed. "He canna hear me." But she lowered her voice just the same.

Cait smiled. "Trust me, Jeannie. He can."

Jeannie rushed forward, clasped Caitrin's hands, and whispered vehemently, "What are ye doin', Miss Cait? He's a villain of the worst sort. Lamont says he's the one who bashed Lord William over the head and chained him ta a bed so he could steal Lord William's wife."

Cait knew all about his crimes against the Westfields, but she wasn't about to discuss the situation with Jeannie. Besides, they needed to do something more important. Escape. Potions were not her specialty—Elspeth and Sorcha excelled at those. But Cait *was* a witch; so she should be able to manage what was required.

"I'll make ye a list of ingredients I need ye ta find in the village for me."

Jeannie blinked at her. "Ingredients?"

"Aye," she whispered. "Somewhere I have Lady Elspeth's recipe for a sleepin' draught." One she'd enhance with chamomile and lavender and a few magic words. When Lord Brimsworth came to take her to dinner, she'd invite him to tea and then make sure the man slept long enough to let her get away. By the time he awoke, he'd be ready to give up this foolish chase.

Jeannie's brow scrunched together. "Sleepin' draught?"

"I think his lordship is in need of a good night's sleep. Make sure Lamont is prepared ta depart this evenin'."

Jeannie's eyes lit up as she seemed to understand Cait's plan. "Aye, Miss."

"I doona want ta waste any time gettin' home, Jeannie."

"I'll see ta whatever ye need."

❧

Caitrin fought not to roll her eyes as her maid wrung her hands and paced back and forth across the room.

"Ye'll never be able ta fool him, Miss. He isna daft. He will ken exactly what ye're up ta as soon as he walks inta the room," Jeannie said, her voice quaking with worry.

"Shh!" Caitrin frowned. "Whisper." How many times did she need to remind the woman? If they kept their voices to a whisper, all Dashiel would hear was a low hiss. Something she'd learned in dealing with Benjamin Westfield. She'd never known until now how handy that little bit of knowledge would turn out to be.

"He'll no' taste a thing, Jeannie. Everythin' will be just fine," she assured her maid, barely making a sound.

"Ye're underestimatin' him, I think." Jeannie's voice dropped to the level of Cait's. "But I've kent ye long enough ta be aware that once ye get an idea inta yer head, ye'll no' leave it 'til it's done." Jeannie sighed and sank down on the edge of the bed.

"Lamont is ready?" Caitrin glanced over her shoulder at her maid, who still looked worried.

Jeannie nodded. "Aye. He and Boyd said they'd be ready ta go when ye are."

Caitrin tried to hide the grin that crossed her face. Overconfidence had caused more than one good potion to fail, and this was too important.

"Ye'll be meetin' his lordship for dinner, I assume?" Jeannie asked, a frown marring her brow.

"No, I'll no' be leavin' this room. He'll be wantin' ta sleep within moments of drinkin' the draught. If I gave it ta him downstairs, someone would want ta know why he slept so heavily."

"Ye hope," Jeannie snorted.

"Aye, I do." She had to stop him. To escape while she had the chance and the means to do so. "I'll invite him in for tea when he comes ta escort me ta dinner."

Jeannie just sighed heavily.

"Just make sure the coach is ready ta leave. We'll need ta be off as soon as he sleeps."

"The trunks are already in the coach, Miss. But I'll go and check with Lamont and Boyd again."

Perfect. She needed Jeannie to leave the room so she could add the magic to her potion. Once the maid stepped out the door, Caitrin hurried to enchant the tea leaves.

Ordinarily, lavender and chamomile tea would simply help to relax a person. She drank it herself when she found it difficult to rest. But she needed it to do more than simply relax his lordship.

He was arrogant. He was obnoxious. He was annoyingly persistent. She let those thoughts build her ire as she rubbed dry chamomile leaves and lavender flowers between her hands until they warmed from the friction of her movement. Her fingers began to warm even more as she let her anger and irritation infuse the flowers.

He made her feel things she had never felt before, dangerous things. Behind her eyelids, she could see the dried plants as they turned red like embers. Showers of sparks fell from her hands into the bowl as she released the ingredients and let them fall.

"*Cadail, madadh-allaidh, cadail.*"

Caitrin opened her eyes and smiled. She'd never had the impetus for such a strong potion in the past. But his lordship inspired her. She held back a giggle as she imagined her anger-infused potion doing its work by sending him into a deep slumber. Deep enough for her to be able to slip away from him.

Deep enough for her to win this one small victory.

Caitrin made arrangements for the special tea to be steeped and delivered when she was ready for it. Then she sat back with a smile on her face and waited.

Dash paced from one side of his room to the other like a caged animal. She was right next door. She was so close that he could hear her moving about her room. She'd taken to whispering for some reason, which was slowly driving him insane.

What was she doing over there?

Dash lifted his head and sniffed. The odor of lavender touched his nose. Perhaps she'd ordered her bath with a lavender soap. He had to admit he'd be disappointed if she bathed in lavender as opposed to the honeysuckle scent she usually wore. However, the thought of her naked in a bath made him immediately hard. Damn the woman. She was going to ensure his stay at Bedlam. Thoughts of her when she was fully clothed were bad enough. Thoughts of her naked were more than he could bear.

But then he heard her humming and her footsteps moving across the room. If she wasn't in the bath, he could push the thoughts of her unclothed from his mind. He *wished*, anyway.

Her door opened. Dash's ears immediately perked up. Certainly she didn't plan to dine without him. He heard her speak softly to someone at the door. He opened his own door and stepped into the hallway. He didn't care if she knew he was listening. He had to know what she was up to.

A maid stood at Caitrin's door, and she motioned her inside with a tray. Tea? She'd called for tea. So she was avoiding dinner with him then.

Dash stepped into her open doorway just as the servant left the room. Caitrin was beautiful. Her curls hung loosely down her back, daring him to touch them, to bury his face in them.

"Dash, what are ye doin'?" she gasped, tugging her wrapper tighter about her body.

"You're not dressed for dinner."

Caitrin smiled slowly, which completely disarmed him. She was positively enchanting. No wonder he had claimed her that night. Between her and the power of the moon, he'd been completely helpless. He still was.

"I'm no' feelin' quite up ta it. So I ordered some tea instead. Would ye care for a bit?"

"Beg your pardon?" Had she truly just asked him to come *into* her room for tea? His heart soared a bit.

"Tea, Dash." She giggled. "Would ye like some tea?"

He stepped into the room and quickly closed the door behind him before she changed her mind. Cait turned to pour, and he stepped closer to her, his front to her back. If he stepped any closer, he'd have her bottom in the saddle of his hips. He inhaled deeply and smiled. She still smelled like honeysuckle.

She glanced over her shoulder as he heard her heartbeat speed up. He took two steps back. "Are ye all right?"

He nodded. "What is that smell?"

"Oh, it's the lavender and chamomile in the tea," she said as she turned and offered him a cup. Then she took her own and sat down on the bed, scooting over to where she could lean against the wall. She tugged the counterpane until it covered her feet. "Again, I find myself in an improper situation with ye, Dash."

He loved the sound of his name on her lips. "I promise never to tell a soul." He sank into a chair across the room and tried to appear the perfect gentleman. Only he wasn't. He knew it even better than she did.

Her lips pursed as she blew across the rim of her teacup. He'd never aspired to be a teacup, but at that moment…

"Ye doona like the tea?" she asked, her heartbeat quickening.

He took a sip of the tea. "It's quite good, actually."

"My own special recipe." She smiled at him again.

"You're quite talented."

"Oh, ye have no idea," she remarked absently as he took another sip and then laid his head back against the high-backed chair.

"I'd love the opportunity to discover all your hidden talents."

"Ye flatter me, my lord."

He'd do a lot more than that, if given half a chance. "I can't be the first man to flatter you." He took another sip of his tea. Truly the flavor was remarkable, like nothing he'd ever tasted before.

"There might have been one or two who tried."

Dash would thrash anyone who did so in the future. "Is there someone waiting for you in Glasgow?" It was best to know what he was up against.

Caitrin glanced into her teacup. "That's really none of yer concern."

It was worse than he thought. Dash tried to keep the growl from his voice. "Who is he?"

"I doona like for dogs ta bark at me, my lord. Ye'd do well ta remember that."

"For the love of God, Caitie, answer the question. Is there some Scottish lad waiting to haul you in front of an altar when you return?" Dash took a large gulp of tea to deflect how important her answer was to him.

Caitrin shook her head. "There was someone," she admitted softly. "But it wasna meant ta be."

How was that even possible? She was the prettiest girl he'd ever laid eyes on. Anything less than droves of men waiting for her return would be ludicrous. "Who was he?" The vision of her before his eyes began to blur. Strange. Could jealousy cause dizziness?

"Dash?" He heard her voice as though she was suddenly a great distance away. "Dash?" This time, she was even farther.

He opened his mouth to respond but found himself unable. He didn't even care. He was so tired. So, so tired. He closed his eyes only briefly, annoyed to find that they refused to open when he willed it.

And, before he knew it, he was dreaming of a girl with flaxen hair who smelled like springtime and honeysuckle.

❧

Cait stood and crossed the room to look closer at him. He'd looked dazed and confused, and a bit of guilt crossed her mind. Was this really the right thing to do? Of course it was. She couldn't let the man keep assaulting her senses. And the fact that he cleared her mind before he did it made it even more disconcerting, more powerful.

"Dash?" she asked cautiously. He looked to be deep in slumber. Dare she hope? "Dash," she called again as she shook his shoulder. He didn't move. She placed a finger below his nose, happy to feel his breath move in and out. She had no idea how long he'd sleep. So, she quickly donned her traveling dress, tucked her nightrail and wrapper into her bag, and was ready to slip out the door.

But at the last minute, she looked back at him. A lock of golden hair fell across his forehead. She crossed the room and brushed it back, then pressed a kiss where the stray lock had been. "Sleep well, Dash," she murmured, and then slipped out the door.

She met Jeannie in the taproom and called for her coach.

"This is a bad idea, Miss," Jeannie whispered vehemently. "I doona think he'll take too kindly ta bein' tricked."

"Aye, ye already said that," Cait hissed back. "But it's done. Let's be off."

Cait allowed Lamont to hand her into the coach, and Jeannie followed. The coach leapt into motion. She was nearly free. Almost! Then the coach slowed. She groaned. What now?

Jeannie lifted the curtain and looked out. "Looks like it's his lordship's coachman," she muttered. "I told ye this wouldna work."

She heard Dash's driver call to her own but couldn't make out the words. Then she heard Lamont call back. He laughed and said, "No need ta worry. It appears as though his lordship has decided ta stay the night, but my mistress needs ta continue on."

Some muffled words came again. Then Lamont said, "I doubt he'd like it if ye bothered him now. He was above-stairs with two wenches when I last saw him."

Dash's coachman chuckled. "Back to his usual pursuits. It's about time."

Caitrin gasped. Entertaining *two* wenches was his normal practice? The cad! She suddenly felt much better about her decision.

The coach lurched back into motion. *Good riddance.*

Nine

WHAT WAS THAT INCESSANT POUNDING? DASH LEANED forward and rested his elbows on his knees. He blinked his eyes open to find the room flooded with daylight, which sent pain shooting to the back of his head. He closed his eyes tightly.

"Milord?" Renshaw's panicked voice filtered into the room.

Dash's head throbbed. He couldn't remember it ever hurting like this, as though his brain was being squeezed in two. Not even after his most debauched nights of carousing and imbibing did he ever feel this miserable.

The pounding started again.

Dear God, what was that sound? And where the devil was he?

"Lord Brimsworth!" his coachman bellowed.

Must the man scream so loudly? Then he heard a jingling sound that echoed painfully in his brain. He groaned. A moment later, he felt a hand on his shoulder.

"Lord Brimsworth," Renshaw's voice came again, only this time much closer, booming in his ear.

Dash managed to open one eye. This was the most bizarre dream. He'd never experienced anything like it. He was quite ready to wake up now and be done with the fog that encompassed his brain.

Renshaw's face was ashen, but he sighed with relief. "Thank heavens, milord. I thought something had happened to you."

Dash opened his mouth to speak, but no sound came out. His tongue felt heavy and dry.

"Are you all right?" The heavy-set innkeeper stepped around the coachman and pocketed a ring full of keys. Ah, that must have been the jingling sound he'd heard.

Dash opened the other eye and focused on the two men in front of him, since they were blocking out the blinding light. "Water," he rasped.

"Of course." The innkeeper bustled from the room, leaving Dash with his coachman, who bent over him, frowning.

"What happened, milord?"

Dash wished he knew. "I don't know." It hurt to speak. "Where am I?"

"Northampton," the driver answered. "Where we stopped for the night with Miss Macleod's party."

Caitrin. His heart lurched. Was she all right? The evening came back to him in a flash. She'd invited him to tea, and he was intent on behaving. He glanced around the room but couldn't see any sign of her. "Where is she?"

Renshaw frowned. "She left that night, milord."

Something about that made his stomach tighten. "I told you we needed to travel with them, Renshaw."

His voice was growing stronger as his memory started to clear.

The coachman shuffled his feet. "Well, her driver said you were occupied with a couple of wenches and you changed your mind about going to Scotland."

"Your orders come from me, not some damned Scottish coachman!" Fury began to build inside his chest. The whispered conversations. The invitation to tea. The headache that still pulsed in his brain. He'd smelled lavender in her room long before her tea had arrived.

She'd poisoned him!

He clutched the arms of the chair and realized his back was sore from sleeping the night away in the high-backed chair. When he caught up to Caitrin Macleod, he'd toss her over his knee and be certain she knew which one of them was in charge. "Make sure the coach is ready."

The innkeeper bustled in with a tankard of water. "Here ye are, milord."

Dash took the proffered cup and downed the contents in one gulp. He rose only to find his legs were shaky as a newborn colt's and the room spun a bit. Renshaw stepped forward to steady him. "Back to London, Lord Brimsworth?"

"No!" he roared, which was a mistake, as the roar echoed in his ears. "I have to get to Glasgow. And we have to catch her before she gets there." For God's sake, was the man deaf?

The coachman's dark eyes dropped to the floor. "Of course, milord, but they have such a lead that we'll never catch them."

"It's only a few hours," Dash ground out. And his

coach was lighter. There were just two of them while Caitrin's carriage was loaded down with people and heavy trunks of clothes and whatever else she traveled with. Her vanity would be her undoing.

Renshaw lifted his gaze, wincing as he said, "Not hours, milord. She's been gone two days."

Two days! How could he have possibly been out so long? Dash's heart sank as his ire rose even higher. Did she plan to kill him with her poisonous tea? Certainly she didn't think she could murder an English lord and get away with it. It was just his luck to be connected for life to a lass who would like to see him six feet under the ground.

"I have all the faith in the world in you, Renshaw. Just do be careful."

❧

Rain pounded the countryside, and lightning lit up the darkened sky. More than once, Cait's coach slid on the muddy lane. They had to stop; the only question was *where*.

Cait closed her eyes and concentrated on her coachman's future, but she couldn't see anything. The thunder rattled her nerves, and all she could do was pray that the driver would find shelter for them soon. This was the last time she would travel without the climate-controlling Rhiannon. Good weather was a must for any future excursion.

Jeannie peered out the window, her hands shaking in her lap.

"We'll be fine," Cait tried to reassure her.

"Are ye certain?" Her maid's eyes shot to her.

Jeannie never came right out and asked things like that. She never openly acknowledged Cait's powers, generally ignoring anything that would be difficult to explain. She must be terrified to do so now.

Cait forced a smile to her lips and nodded. "Lamont is an excellent driver. He's fared worse durin' many a Scottish winter."

"Ye're right." Jeannie sighed and appeared more at ease.

Cait wished she could be appeased as easily. She'd had a gnawing in her stomach ever since they'd left Northampton four days ago. It was silly, but she missed the comfort Dashiel Thorpe offered.

She rested her head against the side of the coach and wondered for the hundredth time if she'd made a mistake where the earl was concerned. She barely knew the man. How could she possibly miss him?

A flash of lightning lit up the interior of the coach at the same moment thunder boomed overhead. Before Caitrin could gather her wits about her, she heard a splintering crash and the carriage jerked to a stop. Both Lamont and Boyd bellowed one Scottish curse after another. Cait's ears were nearly burning.

The coach door was wrenched open, and the driver looked inside. Rainwater poured from him in sheets. "A tree's blockin' our path, and the back wheel is stuck in the mud. We canna stay here, or we'll be washed away."

Cait closed her eyes and took a steadying breath. "There's an inn just a mile away." She could see it clearly in her mind now that they'd stopped moving. "We can make it on foot."

Jeannie gasped. "We'll drown if we go out there."

But they wouldn't. Cait could see a warm hearth and a kindly faced innkeeper and something... comfortable, though she couldn't quite see what that was. But, if she could see herself inside the inn, they'd make it. "Ye'll just have ta trust me."

She wrapped the Macleod plaid over her head and stepped out into the rain. Her half boots sunk into the muddy road, but she paid that no attention. She needed to keep her mind focused on finding the inn.

As Lamont and Boyd struggled to calm the horses and secure the coach, Cait started off toward civilization. Jeannie slogged behind her as they fought against the wind and pounding rain. Cait finally spotted a warm glow on the horizon and could make out a sign swaying in the distance. Just a little farther.

Freezing and drenched, they pressed forward. Cait could now make out the sign and hear laughter escaping the inn. The Black Swan was just a few feet away. She threw open the door to the taproom and rushed inside.

All sounds of merriment stopped, and water began to pool at her feet. A cheery looking fellow, the man from her vision, rushed forward. "Heavens, Miss! Are you all right?"

Cait wanted to cry, she was so relieved to have found the place. "My coach is stuck in the mud." She sneezed. "I am hopin' ye have an extra room here."

She saw movement out of the corner of her eye and turned toward a group of men playing cards in the corner. Comfortable. The feeling rushed back to her. Then Alec MacQuarrie, as handsome as ever, rose from his seat. "Caitrin Macleod, is that you?"

Ten

DASH SINCERELY DOUBTED HE'D EVER BEEN AS ANGRY in his life as he was at that very moment. He'd been chasing after Caitrin Macleod for days. Every day, he followed her honeysuckle scent, the trail leading him closer and closer to her and the Scottish border.

The rain had obscured the scent for the past several hours, but it would be foolish to leave the Great North Road on which they'd been traveling. He'd catch up to her sooner or later. However, he would really like for the rain to stop so he could catch her scent again, just to be sure.

His carriage was light. And fast. And he'd pushed each set of horses far beyond what he normally expected of such creatures. In fact, he'd pushed his coachman to the point where Renshaw did nothing but glower at him.

Dash looked up at the clouded blackness of the storm-laden sky and let the water rush over him. He'd given up his futile efforts to stay dry after being pelted with heavy rain until his Hessians pulled at his feet like anchors stuck in the mud.

He'd felt a supreme sense of satisfaction when he'd seen Caitrin's coach stopped on the side of the road, its wheels sunk so deeply in the mud that he doubted a team of six could pull the conveyance free.

With a preemptive look of scorn on his face, he'd jumped from his own carriage and stalked toward Caitrin's. Her servants were attempting to unharness the horses as the frightened beasts stomped and danced from side to side.

He ignored them and strode toward the door. He opened it and stuck his head inside, expecting to see Miss Caitrin Macleod sitting in relative comfort. But the coach was empty. Blast it!

"Where is Miss Macleod?" Dash called to her drivers.

The one who'd caught him kissing Caitrin turned and pointed down the road. "Walkin' toward the inn."

"There's an inn near here?" he yelled back, struggling to be heard over the rain.

"She said there was," the man replied as he finally freed the horses and the two coachmen jumped atop them.

"You let her go off alone?" Dash growled, the hair standing up on the back of his neck. If she was hurt, he'd do serious harm to her incompetent servants.

"No, she has Jeannie with her," the coachman called back before he turned the horse and disappeared into the darkness, the other man following. They were swallowed up almost immediately by the noise and heaviness of the storm. And Caitrin had gone that way.

Dash stalked toward the fallen tree that made the road impassable and lifted it nearly effortlessly, happy that Renshaw couldn't see into the darkness. When the way was clear, he stalked back to his coach.

"There's an inn up ahead. That's where we'll stop." He thought he saw the man nod beneath the soggy brim of his hat. He climbed into the coach and tapped his fingers in consternation. When he got to the inn, he would find Caitrin, be sure she was all right, and then drag her to a private room where they could talk. He would make it very clear that he did not appreciate being poisoned and left for dead. He would demand an explanation for her behavior. And an apology. And her hand in marriage. Perhaps not in that order.

His coach stopped in front of The Black Swan. He stepped out and jumped down, immediately sinking into the mud until it sucked his boots right under. He pulled his feet free with a curse.

He stepped into the inn and stopped short. Her honeysuckle scent obliterated the smell of ale and wet bodies. She was most certainly there. Somewhere. He shook his head, flinging water droplets in every direction.

Then he saw her. Even soaked to the skin with her hair plastered to her head, she was radiant. He snorted. God, he was a besotted fool even after what she'd tried to do to him.

But then he saw *it*. Her hand was pressed into a man's, and he had his lips to her knuckles. His look was much too familiar for Dash's comfort. He took two large steps forward so that he stood beside Caitrin.

"If you'd like to keep those fingers, I'd suggest you remove them from Miss Macleod's person," he growled.

The man's eyes shot up and the grin disappeared

from his face, but he didn't loosen his hold on Caitrin. "The lips, too," Dash barked. "You'll find it quite difficult to smile at her without them."

"A friend of yours, Miss Macleod?" The stranger's brow rose with mild amusement.

"Her fiancé," Dash broke in before Cait could respond. Then he took her forearm in his grasp and turned her toward him. "And we need to talk."

Caitrin's eyes narrowed at him, but his gaze was more focused on the bluish tint to her lips as she chattered out, "I am busy at the moment, Lord Brimsworth." She jerked free of his hold. For someone so small, she was quite strong. But of course, she was no match for a Lycan. He let her pull away. "And I doona recall acceptin' yer proposal of marriage. Nor do I remember ye *askin'*." He didn't miss how she stressed that last word. Yet asking her was not on his agenda.

The man snickered. "She won't accept mine, either," he said, and extended his hand toward Dash. "Alec MacQuarrie," he introduced himself. "I'm an old friend of Miss Macleod's from Edinburgh."

Edinburgh? Dash didn't even consider reaching to accept the man's offered hand.

Caitrin elbowed him hard enough in the stomach to make him grunt. "Pretend like ye have some manners," she hissed.

He begrudgingly took Mr. MacQuarrie's hand, but huffed as he did so.

"This obnoxious oaf is Lord Brimsworth." Cait wrapped her arms around herself, shivering indelicately.

"The two of you are traveling together?"

MacQuarrie asked. His eyebrows scrunched together with concern.

"Yes," Dash started.

But Cait said, "No," at the very same moment. "Just because we're travelin' the same road doesna mean we're travelin' together."

"I'll have that word with you *now*, Caitie," Dash said slowly, perfectly sounding out his words. He would not be rebuked, and certainly not in front of MacQuarrie, who seemed entirely too interested in the situation.

"Caitie?" MacQuarrie muttered, scratching his chin. Obviously the man was trying to figure out how close they truly were after hearing Dash use her given name.

Caitrin sighed. "I'm goin' ta my room ta dry off," she said. "I'll see ye a bit later, Mr. MacQuarrie? Ye're no' leavin', are ye?"

"Not now I'm not," he said, smiling at her as she disappeared up the stairs. "Join me for dinner?" he called to her retreating back.

"We'd be delighted," Dash growled. "Thank you so much for the offer."

❧

Caitrin stepped into her room, happy to see a fire blazing in the hearth. Her teeth chattered so loudly she feared she'd wake her neighbors as she lifted her shaking hands toward the flames. She plucked at her sodden garments, wanting nothing more than to take them off. But Jeannie hadn't yet come upstairs since she'd wanted to wait for Lamont to arrive.

But if she didn't get out of her wet clothes, Cait

was afraid she'd catch her death. She stood up and tugged at her laces with shaking fingers that refused to work.

A loud knock sounded on her door. "Caitrin," Dash called.

"Go away," she replied, her jaw shaking so much she doubted even he could hear her. How dare he show up at her door after the spectacle he'd made of himself in front of Alec?

"Cait?" he called again. "Are you all right?"

"I'm fine," she forced through painful lips.

"You don't sound fine," he replied. Then the door opened a crack.

"Go away!" Cait snapped. But he just pushed the door open and stepped inside, closing it behind him. "Ye shouldna be here. It isna right."

"It's perfectly right, and you know it," he said brusquely as he stalked toward her and tipped up her chin to look her in the eyes. "What's wrong?"

"N-nothin'," she stuttered out. "I'm just c-cold."

Dash ran his hands up and down her arms. "You have to get out of your wet clothes."

She held up her fingers and said, "I canna work the laces. Can ye go find Jeannie for me?"

Within seconds, his agile fingers tugged at her dress until he'd undone all her fastenings, grumbling something about her inept maid. The front of her gown fell loosely forward. Cait clutched it to herself, but she wanted nothing more than to let it fall to the floor.

"Can ye go now?" she asked.

"Not until you're warmed up."

"I can manage by myself," she said, wishing for

nothing more than for him to vanish so she could shed
the weight of her sodden traveling dress.

"I won't look," he said quietly as he took her hands
from her bodice and let the gown fall over her hips.
She closed her eyes to avoid the intensity of his stare.

"Do I l–look daft ta ye, Dashiel?" she chattered, her
jaw aching from the cold.

His voice sounded a bit more gravelly when he
replied. "I'd never accuse you of being daft. Beautiful,
yes. Gorgeous, absolutely." His eyes roamed across
her. "Delectable, most definitely." Beneath his breath,
he said one last word that sounded like "mine." But
she couldn't be certain.

"Pretend ta be a gentleman, will ye?" she said. But
she was so happy for his assistance that she couldn't
send him away. Already the warmth of the fire was
heating her skin. Or was that his gaze, which made
him look almost as though he could devour her?

When she stood there in her chemise, he paused,
his hands gripping her hips as he knelt before her, his
eyes skimming her body until her traitorous nipples
responded. But then he simply slid his hands below the
sheer fabric and pulled it over her head.

Cait immediately crossed her arms over her breasts
and turned away from him.

"Jesus Christ," he murmured from behind her. A
groan followed. One that was laden with… something.

Cait squeezed her eyes shut tightly. "Ruined and
mortified, all at once," she said. Her teeth chattered
loudly. A blanket dropped around her shoulders, and
she clutched it to her.

"No need to be mortified, angel," he said as he

spun her to face him. He grinned sheepishly at her. "Pardon me for commenting. I'm nothing more than a man. A man who just had a glimpse of everything he wants in life."

"Me? Naked?" she gasped.

"Absolutely." He leaned down quickly and kissed her cheek.

"Thank ye," she said, finally meeting his amber stare. "For helpin' me off with my things," she clarified.

"I'll play your lady's maid any day, angel."

There was a fire brimming below the surface of the man, she was well aware. His lids were half closed with desire and she saw a pulse jump in his neck.

He shrugged out of his jacket and tossed it across the room as he drew in a deep breath. "Lycans have an amazing amount of body heat," he explained as he undid the buttons on his waistcoat.

"I'm glad someone does," she chattered as he finally tugged his shirt over his head. She couldn't draw her gaze away from his chest. His shoulders. His stomach. The little line of hair that disappeared into his trousers. He chuckled lightly before he picked her up and sat down in a chair close to the fire.

Tucking her into his lap, he said, "You probably won't like this, but you have to touch my body, Caitie. My skin against yours."

Oh, she liked it very much. But instead said, "Ye wish," and moved to get up from his lap. But he tugged her back down with one arm wrapped around her waist.

"I just want to take care of you," he said softly as his hand moved to cup her face. He looked so sincere that she let her body soften against his. He tugged the blanket until it was pulled from between them, and then he readjusted it around her shoulders. He was nearly as warm as the fire in the grate.

Her breasts pressed against the hard wall of his chest.

"I should get a commendation for this," he murmured. "Valor in the face of confrontation. Cait—" he started. But she interrupted.

"Take care of me," she whispered.

"As long as you'll let me," he said as his hand moved in a slow circle against her naked back.

Cait closed her eyes as she rested her head against his bare shoulder, and a contented sigh escaped her lips.

He chuckled. "I missed you, too."

"Arrogant as ever," she replied, letting her fingers trail across the expanse of his shoulders, letting his warmth heat every part of her.

"Is that why you left me for dead?"

Cait must have misheard him. She raised her head to look in his eyes. She saw pain reflected in his face, and her heart ached at the sight. "Left ye for dead?"

"You poisoned my tea. Perhaps you remember that?"

Comfortable as she was on his lap, she wasn't about to let him call her a murderess. "I most certainly did no' poison yer tea."

He raised one brow indignantly, his eyes boring into hers.

Cait cringed from the intensity. "I dinna poison yer tea," she repeated. Then she gnawed on her bottom lip. "I-I gave ye a sleepin' draught."

"I slept for *two* days!" he growled.

"It might have been a strong sleepin' draught," she

admitted as she squirmed, trying to remove herself from his lap.

His hold tightened. "You're not going anywhere until we get a few things straight, Caitrin."

"Let me go, ye ill-mannered English dog."

"Stop moving," he ordered. "You need my heat."

"I'll manage."

His amber eyes darkened. "You're not going to push me away, Caitie. No matter how hard you try. And you're not going to poison me again. And you're not going to run away from me again."

She could hear the determination in his voice, and Cait shivered. "I dinna poison ye."

His face softened and his clever hands moved across her body, warming her. "No more sleeping draughts either. Is the thought of being with me so terrible that you had to run away?" Dash shifted her in his arms and very gently touched his lips to hers.

Cait felt his heat encompass every part of her, and she tingled with awareness, wanting more, wanting every part of him to touch her.

"What are the odds," Jeannie's voice preceded her into the room, "that ye'd run inta Mr. MacQuarrie *here* of all—" The maid's eyes landed on Caitrin in Dash's arms and her mouth dropped open.

"Please, Jeannie!" Cait begged, "Doona scream."

Eleven

DASH GROANED WHEN THE MAID SLAMMED THE DOOR. Blast the woman. Nothing had changed. She *still* was never around when Cait needed her and *always* showed up at the most inopportune times.

At that very moment, the soft fullness of Cait's breasts pressed against his chest. He wanted nothing more than to taste the rosy nipples he'd briefly glimpsed through her wet chemise.

"Miss Macleod!" Jeannie hissed.

Caitrin started to scramble from his lap, but Dash wrapped his arm around her waist. "It looks bad," he whispered. "But if you stand up, it'll look worse."

Her light blue eyes focused on him, and she nodded. "Jeannie, give me a moment, will ye?"

The maid punched her hands to her hips and shook her head. "I doona even ken what ta say."

"Your mistress will call when she's ready for you." Dash speared the irritating maid with his gaze. "I suggest you be available to see to her needs, for once."

"Miss—"

"Jeannie, please," Caitrin begged. "Just a moment."

The maid huffed her displeasure as she stomped out of the room, leaving them alone. Dash let Cait slide from his lap and wrap the counterpane tightly around herself. "Ye've got ta stop all this, my lord."

He leaned forward in the seat, not wanting to display the tightness of his trousers. "Once you're my wife, Caitie, it won't matter."

She shook her head. "I do wish ye'd stop sayin' that. Ye're no' my future. I gave ye that sleepin' draught because I thought it would help ye come ta yer senses about all this."

All it had done was made his resolve stronger. She was his mate, by chance or design. Being separated from her was physically painful. All he could think of as he raced north was bedding her, making her his in every way. It seemed the only thing that would assuage the ache in his heart and loins.

"And I'm waiting for you to come to yours. I'm not like other men. I can hear your heart race when I touch you. I can smell your body and know it craves mine. I'm not going anywhere, Caitie."

"Miss Cait!" Jeannie wailed from outside the room.

Dash growled. He could hardly wait to replace the bumbling servant with someone dependable.

"Ye need ta leave." Caitrin frowned.

"For now." Dash rose from his seat and pulled his shirt back over his head. "I'll be awaiting you along with Mr. MacQuarrie." He snatched up his waistcoat and jacket. "Don't keep us waiting."

⁓

Cait wasn't sure if it was a blessing or a curse that

Lamont and Boyd had managed to lug one of her trunks to The Black Swan. Not having anything dry to wear would have given her an excuse to avoid dinner with the two men who had both been adamant that she would marry them.

She'd wanted to accept Alec MacQuarrie each and every time he'd asked her. *At least he'd asked her, unlike that boorish Sassenach.* But she couldn't marry Alec then, and she couldn't marry Alec now. His future hadn't changed, and she wasn't a part of it.

And how was she supposed to sit down to dinner with the man? Especially with Dashiel Thorpe present. Who knew what he'd say. The blasted earl made everything complicated. Her emotions were a jumble, thanks to him.

"Miss Cait, ye canna ask me ta keep all this from Mr. Macleod. If he finds out from someone else what's happened on this journey, he'll sack me for sure."

"Ye're the only one who saw anythin', Jeannie. And since Lord Brimsworth is headed ta Glasgow, no one else will say anythin' ta Papa," Cait said, trying again to reassure her maid.

Jeannie straightened Cait's blue wool skirt. "It's no' the earl I'm worried about, Miss. Mr. MacQuarrie has seen the two of ye together. He's bound ta say somethin' ta yer father when he sees him."

Cait's shoulders sagged forward. Alec hadn't been in Edinburgh for months. After suspecting she was a witch, he'd taken off for England without a word.

Would Dashiel Thorpe respond the same way? Cait frowned at the thought. It was no matter. He'd eventually tire of the chase, the way all the others did.

A knock sounded on her door. Cait nodded for Jeannie to answer it. Alec MacQuarrie stood in the doorway, his warm brown eyes focused on her. "You are a sight for sore eyes, Cait."

She smiled and walked toward him. "Ye have no one ta blame for that except yerself, Alec MacQuarrie. One day ye were in Edinburgh, and the next ye vanished without a word."

He offered his arm, which Cait eagerly took. He towed her toward the staircase and lowered his voice. "You're one of them, aren't you?"

Her mouth went dry. "One of them?" she echoed. "I doona ken what ye mean."

"The *Còig*," he answered.

The *Còig*. The five mythical witches in her coven, with powers passed from mothers to daughters for generations. But the membership was a secret.

Cait grinned, as though he was a foolish child. "Do ye believe in faerie tales, Alec?"

"You're the seer," he said quietly. "And Elspeth's the healer, and—"

Cait's foot faltered on the steps. They weren't allowed to discuss their coven except with their families, who already knew the truth. She shook her head. "Ye're bein' ridiculous."

He looked down on her with a dark intensity. "That's why you said you didn't see a future for us. No matter how hard I pressed, you wouldn't budge."

Cait could only stare at him.

"But I prefer to make my own destiny, Cait."

"I—um—I'm certain Lord Brimsworth is waitin' for us," she mumbled.

Alec's hold on her arm tightened. "Have you seen *him* in your future?"

Cait shook her head. "No," she answered honestly.

He heaved a huge sigh. "Good." Then he continued to direct her down the steps and into the overflowing taproom. "Brimsworth has secured a private room."

Cait's head swam, and no words came to her mouth. Everything was spiraling out of her control. Alec couldn't renew his suit of her. His destiny lay along another path, and then there was—

"Caitie." Dash stepped from a private dining room at the other end of the room. His amber gaze drifted across her and left Cait feeling slightly breathless. He frowned as his eyes landed on her hand tucked into the crook of Alec's arm.

"Where did you meet *him*?" Alec grumbled under his breath.

Cait tilted her head to better see the man whom she'd foolishly fallen for as a young girl. "Westfield Hall."

Alec scowled. "And I thought Ben was my friend."

Before she knew it, Dash was before her, taking her other arm with his hand. Heat radiated from him and tingled across her skin. "I am glad to see you're not so cold anymore, angel."

Alec looked down at her, a question upon his face. "Cold? Angel?"

"Aye, after walkin' in the rain," she admitted, shooting a look at Dashiel. She had a feeling she was in for a long night.

Twelve

DASH HAD NEVER BEEN IGNORED QUITE SO WELL IN HIS life, unless he counted interactions with his father into the number. The marquess had a way about him that made Dash feel insignificant, something he'd grown accustomed to in the years after his Lycan traits had become obvious.

But he'd never wanted to be a part of a group as badly as he did over dinner at The Black Swan. Most importantly, he wanted to be a part of Alec MacQuarrie and Caitrin's group. He wanted to be a trusted friend. He wanted Cait to look at him with fondness as she did MacQuarrie.

"Do you remember the time Sorcha talked you into climbing the tree in the garden and you fell out of it?"

Caitrin laughed softly. "Aye, I remember I thought I'd tumble ta my death."

"Then, at the last minute, you were falling through the air and the next, you lay in a soft bed of leaves. It was almost as though they'd been placed there just to cushion your fall."

Dash noted that she refused to meet Alec's eyes

when she responded, pretending interest in her meal. "Aye, it was a miracle."

"A miracle?" Dash asked slowly. Cait raised her eyes and looked into his. There was a subtle warning there. He just wished he knew what it was.

"Aye," she said as she took a sip of her wine and avoided discussing the topic any more.

"So, Brimsworth," MacQuarrie said as he focused his dark eyes on Dash. "What are your thoughts about predetermined fate?"

Dash gulped. What the devil did the man mean by that? Did he know of his connection to Caitrin? "I believe things happen the way they are supposed to," he answered enigmatically.

The cultured Scot smiled wickedly. "How unfortunate for you, then."

"What does that mean?" Dash asked as he stabbed a piece of mutton.

MacQuarrie shrugged. "Just that I think a man ought to make his own future. I don't believe my life is mapped out regardless of my wants and desires."

Cait's face turned a bit purple, which made Dash feel sure he was missing something important. He'd make her tell him later. He wished he could take her hand in his and soothe her, though that was impossible with the Scot sharing their table.

"So, tell me, Mr. MacQuarrie," Dash began, "have you known Cait all her life?"

MacQuarrie nodded. "Most of it. I left Edinburgh as a boy to attend Harrow, but I've been home often enough over the years."

There it was again. Edinburgh. Dash turned his

gaze on Caitrin. "I was under the impression Glasgow was your home."

She shifted a bit uncomfortably. "I'm no' sure where ye got that idea, my lord. I certainly never said such a thing."

No, but she'd let him go on believing it. And the whole thing turned his plan upside down. How was he to court her in Edinburgh and train with his mentor in Glasgow at the same time? "Major Forster's family is from Glasgow. You and Lady Elspeth are close, so I just assumed…"

"Lady Elspeth also hails from Edinburgh," MacQuarrie informed him rather smugly.

Dash needed all of his self-control to keep from knocking the self-satisfied look off the man's face. "Does she indeed?" he ground out.

"Aye. Lived her whole life on the outskirts of town until she married my good friend Benjamin Westfield."

Perfect. The damned man was a friend of the Westfields'. Could his luck get any worse?

"Though my eyes have only ever been for Miss Macleod." The supercilious Scot reached to cover Cait's hand with his own and Dash grunted, forcing himself to maintain his control.

Cait tugged her hand from beneath MacQuarrie's, and the man laughed. "A bit too stubborn for anyone's good, I must admit."

"Alec!" she gasped.

Dash bristled at the sound of the other man's name on her lips. It was as though she'd known him a lifetime, which in truth, she probably had.

The man had a decided advantage over Dash. He had an entertaining list of memories he could rattle off at a moment's notice. Dash only had a few stolen moments of passion. There was no comparison. It was like watching Prisca with William Westfield all over again, only worse. He'd never felt the connection to Prisca that he did with Caitrin. He wouldn't recover if he lost her.

"All right," Cait laughed. "I'll admit it. I can be a bit stubborn."

"A bit?" both men said at once. Dash couldn't hide his grin at her over-reaction when she sat back suddenly and huffed as though she'd been affronted.

"A lot," she finally acquiesced. "And yet ye both still want ta spend time with me. So I must be doin' somethin' right."

There was his Caitie. Mouthy as the day was long. He loved her gumption.

"It certainly helps that you're beautiful," Dash said, smiling softly at her. A pretty blush crept up her cheeks. One point for the Brimsworth team. It was all he could do not to smirk.

"Beauty fades," MacQuarrie stated blandly. "What Caitrin has will last forever. It's part of her. And part of what makes her so perfectly lovable."

Lovable. Dash nearly choked on his wine. He had never loved a woman in his life. He'd been in bed with more than he could remember, but he'd never truly loved one. What would the emotion even feel like if it were to happen?

"Alec, what are ye doin' in Leeds? I thought ye were in London. Elspeth said she and Benjamin dined with ye no' long ago."

The Scot leaned back in his chair and regarded her. "Aye, I did. Lord Hallam has a hunting box in the area, and he invited me up last week. Elspeth seemed happy."

Caitrin smiled. "She is. Benjamin finally finished that monstrosity of a home he was buildin'. Ye'll have ta see it."

MacQuarrie turned his attention to Dash. "Have you met the other w—?" He grunted and abruptly cut his words off as he reached to rub his shin. "You don't have to kick me, lass," he said under his breath. But Dash heard every word. "Your secret is safe with me."

"What secret would that be?" Dash hated the idea that they were keeping a confidence from him.

"There is *no* secret, my lord," Cait said. "He's referrin' ta my friends, the young *women* I spend most of my time with."

The friends who were like sisters she'd mentioned earlier. He'd obviously missed something important. "Tell me about them again."

She opened her mouth to speak, but before she could utter a sound, MacQuarrie spoke. "You've met Elspeth?"

Dash nodded. "Benjamin Westfield's wife."

"Aye, just being in the room with her can make one feel better, tenfold. Then there's Rhiannon Sinclair. And Blaire Lindsay. And Sorcha Ferguson. Rhiannon can almost always be found out of doors. She's daft enough to stand outside in the pouring rain."

"She's no' daft," Caitrin broke in. "Just because she likes the elements doesna mean she's meant for Bedlam."

"And Blaire can shoot an arrow straighter than even I can. Or any of the other men in Edinburgh. We finally had to stop inviting her to affairs with sporting events. Or she'd make us all look like weaklings."

"Maybe ye are weaklings?" Caitrin said prettily, obviously goading the man on.

"And Sorcha?" Dash asked.

"Sorcha is but a child," MacQuarrie said wistfully.

"She's the youngest of my circle of friends. But she's no longer in leadin' strings, unlike what Mr. MacQuarrie implies. Many women are married by her age," she reminded the Scot.

"Sorcha makes anyone around her want to be a better person." MacQuarrie shrugged his shoulders. "Everyone who knows her loves her."

"And if they doona love her yet, they will soon enough," Caitrin sighed out, a bit of sorrow in her tone. Though why that made her sad, Dash had no idea.

❧

Caitrin tried to keep the tone of melancholy from her statement. But, in truth, she'd always had a fondness for Alec MacQuarrie, and, at some point, a mutual understanding had been made apparent, one that placed him with her for a lifetime. But no matter how well they rubbed along, Cait already knew he was meant for someone else. He wasn't, and never would be, hers.

She glanced across the table at Dashiel Thorpe, who had amazingly maintained impeccable manners throughout the meal. He was an intelligent man, one whose wildness must surely be his handicap. It was gratifying to see that he could shed it when he needed to do so and become a perfect gentleman.

"What are your plans for the future, Mr. MacQuarrie?" Dash asked.

Alec shrugged. "I have no plans for the time being. I'll return home soon, I imagine, and resume management of my estates. I'm only taking a short respite from reality at the moment."

"Respites from reality usually indicate that one is unhappy with his lot in life."

Alec's eyes narrowed, and he lowered his wine glass. "Not unhappy with my lot in life. I'm unhappy not to have an opportunity for the life I want."

"But ye'll have one so much better, Alec," Cait said, stopping him. "Trust me on this."

"How could it be better if you're not in it?" Alec grumbled.

Oh, dear. This was a really bad time for *this* conversation. Particularly with Alec suspecting her of being a member of the *Còig*.

"I'll be in it. Just no' in the way ye want right now."

"And what if I don't want you in my life, aside from in that capacity?"

Caitrin gasped and sat back. "That is the most unkind thing ye've ever said ta me." She felt tears sting the backs of her eyelids and stood up quickly.

Alec stepped toward her, pain etched across his brow. She could immediately tell he regretted his words. But he'd already said them. And there was no taking them back.

Before Alec could touch her, Dash stepped between them. The man was very fast; it must be a Lycan trait. He tipped her face up to his by gently cupping her cheek and tipping her head up. "May I see you to your room?"

"Cait," Alec tried.

But she wasn't in the mood to hear anything more from him. Not at that moment. "Yes, please," she said to Dash, who immediately slid his arm around her and escorted her from the dining room.

Dash's hand on Caitrin's waist warmed her all the way through her dress as they walked past the patrons in the taproom toward the stairs. "You're obviously keeping something from me," he whispered.

Cait whipped her head up to look at him. She wasn't about to do *this* now. Not again. Not here. Not after the conversation with Alec.

"And what if I am?" she asked tartly. "I doona owe ye a thing, my lord. My life is just that—it's *mine*. Stop behavin' as though ye have a say in it."

Thirteen

THAT WENT WELL. DASH BERATED HIMSELF AS HE watched Caitrin stomp off toward the steps alone. He shouldn't have pushed her. After all, he was the one escorting her to her room. He should have kept his bloody mouth shut.

But so many questions were nagging him after that uncomfortable dinner that he was apparently incapable of holding them in any longer.

"Caitie," he called after her, though she refused to turn back to look at him.

He had to *claim* a Scottish lass with a temper, didn't he? He couldn't have sought out a mild-mannered English girl who would follow his every dictate and make his life easy. He had nothing except his own impulsiveness to blame for his predicament.

Dash wasn't even sure if it was a predicament. Every time his eyes settled on Caitrin, he felt a tug at his chest. Was it because he'd claimed her, or was there something more to it? Something predetermined? He didn't feel like he was here because of some accident, some momentary loss of control. He felt as if he'd always known her. Yet he didn't know her at all. He didn't even know until this evening that she lived in Edinburgh, for God's sake.

Dash heaved a sigh and turned back toward the private dining room. He might not know her at all, but Alec MacQuarrie most assuredly did. He could get answers from one source or another.

He found the man throwing back a whisky. MacQuarrie lowered his glass and leaned forward in his seat. "Well, that was faster than I expected."

"Oh?" Dash closed the door behind him. "What did you expect?"

MacQuarrie shrugged, and then he poured himself another drink. "She doesn't see you in her future either, you know?"

Dash ground his teeth together. How the devil did the scoundrel know that? "She has no better idea of what'll happen in the future than you or I. You speak as though she's a soothsayer."

The Scot snorted. "You might be surprised."

Dash frowned at MacQuarrie, who obviously wasn't the sort who could handle his liquor.

The Scot raised his glass in a mock toast. "I'd wish you good luck with your pursuit, but I'd rather not."

Well, that was honest. Dash pointed to one of the empty chairs. "Do you mind?"

"Help yourself."

Dash slid into the seat and regarded the man across from him. Alec MacQuarrie looked positively tortured. Was this an eerie prelude of his own future? The idea sent a chill down his spine. "You know something she's keeping from me."

MacQuarrie leveled him with an icy stare. "If you're asking me to divulge her secrets, you can save your breath. I'd sooner die."

Well, that was an option and not one Dash was particularly opposed to. "Hurting her is not part of my agenda."

"And what is your agenda?"

Dash sighed. It was changing by the moment. "I plan to meet with Mr. Macleod and ask him for Caitrin's hand." And learn how to be a good little wolf, not that MacQuarrie needed to know that last bit.

The Scot scoffed as he raised his glass to his lips. "Angus Macleod gave me his blessing. You can see the good it did me. Cait'll make her own decision. So you might as well cut your losses. She won't change her mind."

Of course, Dash couldn't give up. His life was doomed unless he could convince her to marry him. "Macleod gave you his permission, but she refused you?" Stubborn chit. He'd thought for sure if he could get her father's approval, she would have no choice but to accept his suit.

MacQuarrie nodded. "She has her father wrapped around her pretty little finger. He lets her make her own decisions."

Damn! This was getting worse by the moment. She'd told him time and again they didn't have a future. What could he do to get Caitrin to change her mind? Or what could he do to get Mr. Macleod to put his foot down and make her listen to reason? The answer leapt to his mind, and he winced.

He hadn't wanted to take her innocence. It seemed like such a cowardly act and was completely ignoble without his ring on her finger. But the rest of his future lay in the balance. Given the right situation, he *could* seduce her. She couldn't continue to refuse him after that. Then he'd make it up to her for the rest of his days.

It wasn't much of a plan. But he didn't have a lot to work with. And looking at the pained expression on Alec MacQuarrie's face made him even more wary about ending up like the Scot. But MacQuarrie could find another woman of some sort. That wasn't a possibility for Dash.

"You look very serious all of a sudden." MacQuarrie broke into his thoughts.

"It's just been a long day of travel." In truth, he'd had several long days of travel, racing across England to catch up to his Scottish angel. "I think I'll retire early."

MacQuarrie lifted his glass again. "Sleep well, Brimsworth. I may just follow you to Scotland, and you'll need your wits about you."

Dash didn't even bother to keep the growl from his voice. "Get in my way, MacQuarrie, and you will regret it."

❧

"Lamont says the axle is cracked on the coach, Miss," Jeannie said as soon as Cait stepped over the threshold.

Her heart sank. A cracked axle. That didn't sound good at all. Cait sighed. "Help me get out of this dress, Jeannie."

"But the coach, Miss—"

She shook her head. "The problem will be there tomorrow. I'll think about it then."

Jeannie made quick work of the dress and helped Cait into her nightrail. "Perhaps Mr. MacQuarrie could be of assistance," her maid suggested.

"Perhaps," Cait replied to appease the woman. But she wouldn't ask Alec MacQuarrie to help her cross Queen Street. He made it seem as if this situation they were in was her fault. He was the one... He was the one who was destined to fall in love with someone else. At least he had a future. She had no idea what was in store for *her*.

"I told Lamont—"

"Go on," Cait told her. "I'll be fine."

"But the earl—"

"Do no' concern yerself with Brimsworth. I doona intend ta."

Jeannie didn't need much persuasion, and she was out the door just a moment later. Cait blew out the lamp, slid into bed, and watched the shadows from the moonlight dance against the wall.

Slumber was elusive, despite Cait's exhaustion. As usual, she was assaulted by the futures of the patrons who stayed at the inn. But none were particularly worrisome. They didn't overwhelm her senses or make her desire an escape outside herself. Some were even joyous, like the woman who would receive an offer of marriage the next morning. Or the tavern-owner's wife, who would soon be a grandmother.

She didn't even try to contain her smile. Although the futures were joyous, she still had trouble escaping them enough to sleep. Finally, she sat up in bed and wished halfheartedly that she'd not sent Jeannie away, so that she could send the woman for a brandy.

Occasionally, spirits provided ample room for escape from her own mind. Cait sighed and swung her legs over the side of the bed. If she had something to read, that would help. Perhaps Jeannie found her book before they left Westfield Hall.

Cait relit the lamp by the bed, then bent and rifled through her trunk. She pushed aside her clothes and personal items, hoping to find her copy of *Patronage* amongst her things, but to no avail. But then her hand closed around a small leather-bound book. She tugged it free and fell back on her bed.

Havers! The book she'd snatched from the Duke of Blackmoor's study. She hadn't meant to steal the thing. Hopefully His Grace wasn't missing it. She'd have to send it back first thing in the morning.

But in the meantime, perhaps it was just boring enough to put her to sleep. Cait sank beneath the counterpane, opened the book, and was surprised to see in a scrawling gentleman's hand the words "Havens for Harlots and Heretics." Then in smaller print it read, "Brimsworth."

She'd picked up Dashiel's book? The memory of their first meeting flashed in her mind. She'd stumbled into Blackmoor's study and had wanted nothing more than to sneak back out. But she'd gone to find a book and felt it necessary to leave with one. So, she'd taken the first one she spotted. Why hadn't he said anything?

She'd not given the matter another thought until she cracked open the handwritten journal. She turned the page and read the words on the next page.

Though Miss W. has a whistle through her nose when she's close to bliss, she's quite easy to move to that end. A gentleman caller must learn to ignore it, or he's likely to be reminded of a hunt where hounds are used and think he must begin again when the whistle blows. If one can overlook the noise, she's quite well worth the annoyance. For if one provokes her to whistle, she'd do just about anything a gentleman desires.

Cait slapped the book closed. She held it tightly within her hands, which trembled more than a bit. Why in the world would Dashiel have written such a thing? She tossed it onto the bedside table and shook her hand, as she often did when she was offended by the dirt that stuck to her skin when she helped Sorcha pot her plants.

What a horrible thing for him to write! She couldn't help but hope the woman didn't know of his ramblings. If she did, would she care? She was obviously free with her favors.

Still, how could Dashiel do such a thing? Intimacy was supposed to be something sacred, something shared with love and dignity. She huffed. There wasn't much dignity—and she was sure there was no love—in the comments he'd made.

She glanced at the book and couldn't help but wonder if the rest of the pages followed suit. Of course, it would be horrible of her to take a peek. She reached tentative fingers toward the book, then snatched them back and pulled the counterpane about her shoulders, squeezing her eyes shut tightly.

She opened one eye. Then sat up quickly and picked up the book. Glancing furtively about the room, she opened to a page in the middle and began to read.

In a small house on Shelton Street live three sisters. I highly doubt that they're truly sisters, but they live very respectable lives as such by day. But pay them a visit by night, and you will be quite surprised. If there were ever sisters who loved one another as much as these three, I would dearly wish to meet them. For these take great joy in making a ménage of themselves. Initially, I thought I wouldn't even be invited to join in. In truth, just watching the brunette part the thighs of the redhead and dip her face—

Cait slammed the book closed again, and then she tossed it across the room where it hit the wall with a thud. She should have thrown the piece of rubbish into the fire.

A soft knock sounded on her door. Cait's heart leapt into her throat. She scrambled across the room and picked up the book, then dashed back to the bed. She tucked it beneath the counterpane.

Then she ran a hand down her unbound hair and cracked open the door.

Fourteen

DASH HAD DEBATED WITH HIMSELF FOR A WHILE OVER the appropriate course of action to take. But no matter how long he contemplated the situation, it seemed the only way he might be able to win Caitrin's hand would be to seduce her. Though it was very ungentlemanly and he would prefer to actually *win* her, a simple seduction would have to do. He knew she was still awake because he could hear her bustling about her room after her maid had once again sneaked out the door.

He'd originally assumed she was dreaming, since her heartbeat had the speed of a horse at a gallop. Strange. Most people he'd known in his life had a steady heartbeat. If they were angry or passionate, it sped up, and if they were tired, it slowed down. Hers was erratic. Steady when they were on the road or when he touched her, but wild every time they stopped in a new place. It was exhausting trying to interpret all the signals her body gave him.

Then he'd heard her footfalls. What in the world was she doing?

He armed himself with a bottle of whisky and two tumblers, then set out to meet his fate. When he knocked softly on her door, he heard her shuffle about the room for a moment. Then she cracked the door an inch and peered out.

"What is it that ye want, Lord Brimsworth?" she asked, narrowing her eyes at him and looking like a humorless governess.

"I come bearing gifts," he said, unsure how to proceed after her cold reception.

"I've no need of gifts," she said stiffly, blowing her hair from her eyes with a quick breath.

He leaned on the doorjamb, preventing her from closing the door. She would have to shove him from it before she could do so. Unfortunately, she looked perfectly capable at the moment. "You're still angry with me?"

"Oh, ye haven't the slightest idea how I feel about ye," she snapped, the edge of her tone cutting into him like a knife.

"Let me in so you can tell me."

"No."

"Please," he said softly.

"Ye drop yer voice down ta a husky whisper and assume I'll melt at yer feet like all yer other women," she said, her icy eyes meeting his and not wavering.

"I have no other women," he said, standing taller in the doorway. He could say that with the utmost truth. "Nor will I."

She snorted. "For some reason, I doona believe ye."

"Let me in, Caitie."

She didn't even blink an eye at his order.

"Caitrin," he started.

"Don't *Caitrin* me," she laughed, the sound completely without humor. "I ken what kind of man ye are. And I've no desire ta be with ye. No' now or ever. So, good night, Lord Brimsworth."

She moved to close the door, but she was no match for his superior strength. He pushed past her into the room, kicking the door shut behind him.

"What is it, Cait?"

"Well, *now* it's that ye're in my room without an invitation." She crossed her arms beneath her breasts and once again blew a lock of flaxen hair from her face.

"And what made you angry at me *before* I invited myself into your room, Caitie?" He set the tumblers and the decanter of whisky on the table and waited for her answer.

"I doona ken what ye're speakin' of," she replied, her tone haughty and annoying.

"Yes, you do," he said as he poured two tumblers of the strong drink and handed one to her. Perhaps she'd soften some if she was intoxicated. She actually took it from him and downed it in one big, fast swallow.

He stood helpless to aid her as she sucked in a breath and her eyes began to water. "What was that?" She coughed.

He cringed. "I'm so sorry," he said as he took her shoulders in his hands to look into her eyes. "It's whisky. I should have warned you."

"Aye, that would've been nice," she gasped, finally finding her breath.

"I'm sorry, Caitie," he said again.

"Ye seem ta be quite adept at sayin' that," she hissed at him. Then she took the tumbler from his hand and tossed back his drink as well. This time, the strong liquor didn't hit her quite as hard.

"Why did you do that?" he asked as he stared into the empty tumbler she pressed back into his hand.

"Because I felt like it." She shrugged. "Isna that why ye do the things ye do, Lord Brimsworth? Just because ye *feel like it*?" She made the last sound like the vilest of curse words.

"If I did everything I felt like doing, Miss Macleod," he shot back at her, mocking her tone, "I'd be kissing you right now instead of trying to figure out what's going on in that pretty little head of yours."

"Ye would be afraid if ye saw what goes on inside my head, Dash," she said as she crossed the room and poured yet another glass of whisky. This one was much more full than the first two, and she carried the tumbler to bed with her, sipping as she walked.

"Why would I be afraid?" he asked as he walked toward her. Cait's feet were bare, and her nightrail rode high enough that he could see a good bit of her ankle. He nearly lost his breath. Of all the women he'd been with, he'd never had one make him feel completely inept, like an untried lad, until Caitrin.

"Because it isna always pretty." She stared into her glass, which was nearly empty, as though she wondered where the contents had gone.

"Why were you angry with me, Caitie?" he asked as he sat down on the edge of her bed and reached to cup the side of her face.

While she said, "Doona do that," she pressed her face into his hand, absently stroking herself against him like a kitten. Any moment, he expected her to purr. But then her claws came back out. "Ye could never be true ta just one woman."

"That's where you're wrong. I could be true to you. If you'd but let me."

"If I whistle like Miss Whomever, will ye still be true ta me? Or will I become fodder for yer little book?"

"What?" Dash shook his head.

She was obviously inebriated. Her eyes were glassy, and her speech was slurred. She sank back against the pillow. "Yer book, Dash. I read it. 'Havens for Harlots,' or whatever ye called it."

Dear God! His heart sank as he realized what she was talking about. He wanted to knock himself over the head. All of his carnal sins on display. "It's not what you think, Cait. How much of it did you read?"

"Two pages. It was all I could stand." She yawned, her mouth open wide.

"Bloody hell," Dash groaned. How would he ever face her in the light of day? "Where is it?" He'd toss the thing in the grate just to make sure she never read another bloody word.

"Would ye like ta ken the whereabouts of it?" she teased him, a lazy smile crossing her features as her eyes closed.

"Don't go to sleep, Caitie." He shook her shoulder. "Where's my book?"

"Go away, Dash," she said as she rolled away from him. He wanted to scream. He'd made a royal mess of things. He'd planned to make her lose her wits, then her innocence. But the only thing lost was the evidence of his past debauched lifestyle. Lost to him. Not to her. She still had it somewhere. He set out to search her room. Only a goddamn fool would leave without it.

Dash glanced around the room. It wasn't lying out anywhere. He opened the drawer on the bedside table, but it was empty. He dropped to his knees and lifted the edge of the counterpane and peered under the bed. Nothing but dust. He stood up again, knowing he was missing something obvious.

Her trunk! It had to be there. It appeared as though someone had been rummaging around through it. He crossed the room in an instant and dug his hands into her things. Soft kid slippers, wool and muslin dresses, a blue-and-green plaid, fine silk chemises. The latter made him groan aloud. He knew what she looked like in only a chemise. But no journal. What the devil had she done with—

The door creaked open, and Caitrin's maid stood in the threshold. Dash should have heard her coming. Blast it! But there were so many different sounds at the inn that he couldn't have known the soft footfalls he'd heard moments ago would stop at Cait's door.

Jeannie's face contorted in surprise and then rage when her eyes landed on him. "My lord!" she gasped. "What are ye doin' in Miss Macleod's room?"

Dash rose from his spot and realized a moment too late that he still clutched one of her chemises in his hands. He tossed it quickly back into the trunk. "I left something in here earlier. I was just looking for it."

The maid snorted. "Well, I doubt that it's mixed up

with Miss Macleod's unmentionables. Leave at once, or I'll go fetch Mr. MacQuarrie."

Mr. MacQuarrie could go straight to the devil. But Dash wasn't ready for all the world to know about his journal, so he nodded curtly and started for the door.

Behind him, Caitrin sighed softly, and he glanced back over his shoulder to see her. Even in sleep, she was the most beautiful woman he'd ever laid eyes on. And now she knew him for the reprobate he was. For the reprobate he had been, Dash amended. Since Caitrin Macleod had entered his life, he hadn't desired another woman in any way. And he never would.

How could he make her forget about his journal and agree to marry him?

"My lord!" Jeannie hissed, tapping her foot on the wooden planks of the floor.

Brought back to the present, he brushed past the maid without a word or another look back. His plan to seduce and ruin Caitrin had been utterly foiled. He needed to get properly foxed.

Fifteen

CAITRIN WOKE WITH A POUNDING IN HER HEAD. HOW much whisky had she consumed? And her shoulder hurt. She rolled to her back and threw an arm over her eyes to block out the sun. Something hard jabbed her in the back. She groaned and moved again, reaching for the object. A small leather book. She closed her eyes. *Dashiel Thorpe's journal of wickedness.*

She tossed the offending item across the room, and it landed, once again, inside her open trunk. She never wanted to see the blasted book again as long as she lived. Thanks to the dratted thing, she'd gone to bed with images of three women in bed together. She could go the rest of her life without such ideas invading her thoughts again.

A scratch came at the door. "Enter," she grumbled.

Jeannie slid inside, a giant smile on her face. Cait scowled at her maid. What did she have to be so happy about this morning?

"It was so nice of Mr. MacQuarrie ta offer his coach ta take us the rest of the way."

Alec. The broken axle. Cait's head began to throb

even harder. "I have no intention of travelin' as far as the next village with Mr. MacQuarrie."

Jeannie's smile evaporated. "But, Miss Cait, last night ye said—"

"I doona care what I said." In truth, she couldn't quite remember what she'd said the previous evening. But she remembered Alec's unkind words, and, at the moment, the only person whose company she desired less than Dashiel Thorpe's was Alec MacQuarrie's. "Ask Lamont ta find out about rentin' a conveyance, Jeannie."

"Very well, Miss, but it makes more sense for Boyd and Lamont ta stay with yer father's carriage until the repairs are done and then bring it on ta Edinburgh."

Cait cocked her head to one side and leveled an irritated glare at her maid. "I doona care what ye think makes the most sense, Jeannie. I willna accept Mr. MacQuarrie's assistance—and that's final."

After her maid bobbed a halfhearted curtsey and slinked from the room, Cait pulled a heavy wool traveling dress from her trunk. A knock sounded at the door, and she glanced toward it. No vision popped into her head, which could only mean that the Earl of Brimsworth stood on the other side.

Cait ignored the knock and shimmied out of her nightrail. She stepped into her chemise, but the pounding just got louder.

"I know you're in there. I can hear you," Dash's voice called through the door.

"Can ye no' let a lass get dressed in peace?" she mumbled.

His voice softened noticeably, and she could almost

imagine him bending to look through the keyhole when he replied, "You're not dressed yet?"

Cait rolled her eyes. She had nothing more to say to him. She pulled her wool dress over her head and flounced back onto the bed, determined to block out his annoying presence.

"Caitie, if you don't open this door, I'll break it down."

She snorted. "As well behaved as always," she returned. "Go away, Lord Brimsworth."

"You truly are the most stubborn lass, Caitrin. Now open the door and stop being so difficult."

She was difficult? "Arrogant dog," she grumbled beneath her breath.

"I have excellent hearing," he reminded her through the door.

Cait sighed. No matter what, he wasn't going away. She slid from the bed and crossed to the door. She pulled it open and glared at the infernal Sassenach before her. Blast him for being so handsome he nearly stole her breath away! "I doona have anything ta say ta ye, Brimsworth."

"Take my coach to Edinburgh," he said quietly. "I can continue to Glasgow on horseback."

She folded her arms across her chest. So he'd heard her conversation with Jeannie. "Eavesdroppin' is so ill-mannered. Ye are an English lord. One would think ye were somewhat civilized."

"I can't help it." He tapped one ear. "No matter where you are, I hear your melodic voice."

Cait rolled her eyes. "Save yer flattery for someone who wants it."

His brow furrowed as though she'd hurt him. Cait felt a twinge of guilt, but only for a moment. His scandalous exploits were still fresh in her mind.

"The inn doesn't have any coaches for hire, Caitie. At least let me do this for you."

Cait sucked in a breath. She hadn't expected that from him. Since the very beginning, he'd been searching for ways to get her alone. Would he really ride to Glasgow alone, outside in the cold January air? "Suddenly a gentleman?"

Dash took a step toward her and brushed his knuckles across her cheek. "Anything to see you smile in my direction."

She couldn't help the smile that tugged at her lips.

"Ah, there it is," he said softly. "The prettiest girl in all of Britain."

A lock of his golden hair hung in his eyes, and her fingers itched to smooth it back into place. But encouraging him wouldn't do her any good. "I'd hate ta impose, my lord—by confiscatin' yer coach," she clarified.

Dash winked at her. "What's mine is yours, angel."

But something he said niggled at the back of her mind. "Are ye really headed ta Glasgow?"

A shadowy expression settled on his face, and he nodded once.

"Why?"

"Something I need to take care of," he hedged. Then Dash gestured toward the corridor. "Say you'll take my carriage."

What else could she do? Cait nodded, still surprised by his generosity. She couldn't help but wonder what awaited him in Glasgow. She'd been foolish to think he'd traveled this road simply to follow her. She'd been flattered but foolish all the same. It would have been so nice, she supposed, if his journey had been inspired by her. What a silly, romantic notion.

"Thank ye, sir."

❦

Her light blue eyes softened on him, and Dash had to force himself not to howl with joy. He'd gladly brave the frigid air all the way to Glasgow, or to her home in Edinburgh if that's where she wanted to go, if it meant she'd travel in *his* carriage. Blast MacQuarrie to hell for trying to steal her away.

"Will you join me for breakfast?" he asked softly, aware he was pressing his luck.

Caitrin flashed him a beautiful smile. "Are ye actually askin' me, my lord? I've been so accustomed ta ye dictatin' my every move."

Only because he'd been convinced that if he gave her a choice, she'd turn him down. And he didn't know how he'd overcome that obstacle. This morning, however, he felt confident enough in her response to ask. After all, she'd already accepted the offer of his coach. What was a little meal between intended mates?

"It's entirely up to you, Caitie."

She nodded. "I think I would like that."

Dash offered her his arm and couldn't help the grin that spread across his face when she accepted it. Things were certainly looking up for him. If only he could find a way to get his journal back... not that he was about to broach the subject with her this morning. She was smiling at him, and they were going to share breakfast together. He'd have to find it later.

As they started down the steps, Alec MacQuarrie walked in through the doors of the inn. His eyes immediately found Caitrin. "What do you mean, you won't let me take you to Edinburgh?"

She stiffened beside Dash, and he squeezed her arm. He tilted his head to one side and raised his brow in the Scot's direction. "I'm headed to Scotland anyway, MacQuarrie. Miss Macleod has accepted the use of *my* conveyance."

Alec MacQuarrie's face heated up, and it was all Dash could do to bite back a smirk. But he didn't think Caitrin would appreciate that. So he schooled his features, hoping he appeared an innocent good Samaritan.

"Him?" MacQuarrie sputtered. "For pity's sake, Cait!"

She leveled her iciest stare at her countryman. "I'm afraid I canna be in yer life, Alec. No' in the *capacity* ye want, anyway. It's better this way."

MacQuarrie scowled at Dash and grumbled, "I'll never give her up, Brimsworth," but his comment was too soft for anyone other than Dash to hear.

Sixteen

COVERED WITH HER PLAID, CAIT GLANCED OUT THE window of Brimsworth's coach. The earl looked magnificent astride a horse. Virile and strong. Though at the moment, he also looked like he was freezing. The last time he'd turned to smile and wink at her, his eyes had lost their sparkle. Perhaps she should invite him inside the coach. She did have Jeannie to chaperone, after all.

She sighed at the thought. That was probably what he wanted. Besides, he *did* have the warm blood of a Lycan running through his veins. He'd be fine.

It wasn't until a few hours later that she looked for him and noticed the rain. It was a mere sprinkle, but he lifted his cupped hands to blow a warm breath across his fingers and guilt tore at Caitrin's heart. She was making the poor man ride in the cold and the rain when there was plenty of room and warmth in his own coach.

Now she felt terrible. Jeannie must have seen the look on her face because she groaned and said, "I was wonderin' how long it would be before it got ta ye, Miss."

"He looks so cold. I canna make him ride alongside any longer. We'll have ta let him inside."

"Seems everyone would be more comfortable if Mr. MacQuarrie invited the earl ta ride in *his* coach."

"It's obvious MacQuarrie isna goin' ta do that, is it no'?" Caitrin didn't know if she wanted to kick Alec or herself for the situation. "We have ta get him out of the rain."

Jeannie called for the driver to stop, and Caitrin couldn't keep from smiling when Dash opened the door and popped his head inside.

"You've need of me, eh?" He smiled broadly as he pulled his hat from his head and tossed it onto the empty seat beside Jeannie.

"I dinna say that," she started.

He chuckled as he climbed inside, dropped his sodden greatcoat on the bench next to his hat, and settled heavily beside Caitrin. "Admit it, Miss MacLeod," he teased, "you missed me."

"I pitied ye, my lord." Cait fought the grin that threatened to erupt.

"Pity the man with the broken heart who's forced to ride outside his own carriage?"

"One must have a heart before one may claim it's broken," she returned.

"Oh, you wound me, angel," he laughed.

Jeannie coughed loudly from her side of the carriage, as though to remind them of her presence.

Dash lowered his voice dramatically. "I vote that we make *her* ride with Mr. MacQuarrie. What do you say?"

Cait couldn't hold back her giggle when she saw the mortified look on Jeannie's face. She reached over to touch her maid's knee. "He doesna mean it," she said.

"I highly doubt that, Miss," Jeannie spat as she glared in his direction.

Dash winked at her, making the woman flush. Then he reached over and touched his frigid hands to Cait's cheek. She jumped back and squealed. "Oh, ye *are* cold."

"And sore. I've been astride a horse more today than I have been in quite some time," he groaned, stretching out his legs.

"Ye mean ta make me feel terribly guilty, do ye?" Cait shook her head. "Ye *did* offer…" She let her sentence trail off.

"I'm just glad you came to your senses," he said before he ducked his head quickly and kissed her cheek.

Cait felt the heat rush up her face. "Ye shouldna have done that," she scolded him.

"I couldn't help it. You can punish me later." He wagged his eyebrows dramatically.

"Ye're terrible," Cait laughed.

"And you love it."

"I wouldna go that far."

He bent his head and whispered in her ear. "Then how far will you let me go?"

Jeannie crossed her arms and stared out the window, shaking her head, her lips pressed so tightly together that white lines appeared around them.

"I thought we might eat at the next stop before we settle for the night."

Cait winced. Another horrid night in an inn. She'd rather count all the stones at Arthur's Seat and then arrange them by shape and size.

"What's that look for?" Dash asked, concern lacing his voice.

Cait shrugged, knowing she couldn't actually tell him about the visions and futures that plagued her in such places. "I'm just in a hurry ta be home is all." That much was at least the truth.

"You want to drive through the night?" He absently rubbed his thighs quickly, creating friction and heat against his leather riding breeches. He still looked a bit blue.

"Only if ye think yer driver is capable."

Dash laughed. "If he thought you questioned his abilities, Renshaw would consider it a matter of pride." His grin faded and he nodded in her direction. "If you want to ride through the night, I'll see to it, Caitie."

"That sounds wonderful," she sighed. Cait lifted the edge of her plaid and settled it over his lap.

He stilled and looked at her. "Thank you."

"For what?"

"For showing me such kindness, angel."

❦

Dash couldn't remember a time when anyone else had ever covered him with a blanket or even tried to see to his comfort. His mother had died at his birth, and his father had taken great pride in seeing to his *discomfort* by hiring nurses, governesses, and tutors who didn't have a nurturing bone in their bodies.

So, he wasn't surprised to find that she touched his heart a bit when she'd offered him the corner of her plaid.

Cait turned to him with a furrowed brow. "May I ask ye a question?"

Her hand slid to touch his leg under the plaid, and Dash tamped down the lust her gentle touch sent racing through him. Traveling through the night suddenly seemed the best idea he'd had in a long while. If Cait wasn't careful, he'd toss up her skirts right then and there. Jeannie be damned. *Move it just a little to the left, angel.*

"I beg your pardon?" he managed.

"I want ta ask ye a question."

"Anything," he answered. And was surprised to find that he meant it.

"What did ye love about Prisca Hawthorne?"

Dash winced, and his ardor vanished. She couldn't have picked a worse topic. Well, she could have asked about his journal. That would have been worse, but not by much.

"Ye asked her ta marry ye," Caitrin prodded. "So, I assume ye must have loved her."

"I wouldn't go that far…"

She nudged him with her elbow when he stopped talking, and Dash nearly growled. He should have stayed on the horse, no matter how bloody cold it was.

"How did ye meet her?"

"One of her brothers is a friend of mine. I met her when he invited me to spend the holiday in Hampshire."

"Ye say it as though ye hail from someplace else."

"Kent," he replied. "Though it has been years since I've been home." And he had no intention of returning until the old buzzard was gone.

"I see," she said, and for a moment he thought that perhaps she really did see through him. "And are ye sad that Prisca married Lord William?"

"Honestly?"

"No, I like it when ye lie ta me." She rolled her eyes.

God, he wanted to kiss her. "No. I'm not sad she married Lord William. I was angry and jealous for a while. And I didn't like losing. But I'm not sad."

"What did ye like about her?"

Dash scrubbed a hand across his face. How could he get back to the horse without looking like an arse? He took a deep breath and told her the truth. "Prisca was beautiful. And she was charming. And smart. She would have made an excellent countess."

"But?"

"But she wasn't meant for me." He shrugged. "Do you always ask so many questions?"

"Aye, she does," the maid mumbled from her side of the coach.

"Why wasn't she meant for ye?"

"Well, that's fairly obvious, isn't it?"

"No." Her eyebrows scrunched together. "What are ye talkin' about?"

"*You* are meant for me, angel."

"We'll see about that," was her only reply. Then she removed her hand from his leg, quieted, and simply gazed out the window.

Dash wasn't certain what to make of her questions, but he figured it was a good sign she was curious about him. As the coach slowed at the next inn, he found himself quite pleased with his circumstances. He alighted and handed her out.

"I need to make some preparations. Will you be all right?" he asked.

"Aye, I just need ta stretch my legs a bit."

She smiled at him, and Dash felt it all the way in his soul. He shook his head as he walked away. She was a bit of a challenge. But he was beginning to think she was worth it.

❧

Cait watched him walk away, enjoying the swagger in his walk more than she should, she was sure.

"Well, he didn't chew you to bits, I see," a deep voice said from behind her. She swung around to find Alec walking toward her.

"Aye, I'm still in one piece, Mr. MacQuarrie. No thanks ta ye."

"Me?"

"Ye could have offered ta let him ride in yer coach when ye realized it was startin' ta rain."

"Why would I want to do that?"

"Ta be nice?"

"To him? Have you gone completely daft, Cait? I'd not ride a foot with him. Much less suffer his company for a whole day."

"He was actually quite a gentleman." Cait didn't even realize she was defending him until the words left her mouth. Still, it was true. "He was pleasant company."

"It's not right, Caitrin," Alec said quietly. "You shouldn't be alone with that man."

"I wasna alone with him. I had Jeannie with me."

"Poor help she'd be if he decided to take liberties with your person."

"He'd do no such thing!" Cait insisted. But her mind was flooded with the memory of him holding her completely bare on his lap the night she'd been caught in the storm.

She realized in that instant she craved Dashiel Thorpe in more ways than one, which was a problem. He wasn't hers any more than Alec MacQuarrie was. How had she gotten herself into such a mess?

Alec scoffed as he took a step closer to her. "Don't be a fool, Cait. The man is hardly a gentleman, earl or not. There's something dangerous about him. I can't put my finger on it. But I don't like the way he looks at you."

It certainly wasn't the first time she'd heard that, but she wasn't in the mood to hear it from Alec. Cait narrowed her eyes at him. "How he looks at me is hardly yer concern."

"The devil if it isn't," he retorted. "You know I'll always take care of you. And you know I love you, and—"

"No' for much longer, Alec. And when—"

"Not another word," he growled. "You may see things, Cait, but you can't possibly know what's in my heart."

But she knew who *would be* in his heart, and she couldn't alter the path of Sorcha's future.

Cait turned her back on Alec and started toward the inn. She wouldn't have this conversation again. It always ended the same, with neither of them gaining any ground. If he knew so much about her abilities, why couldn't he just accept that she knew the future better than he did? Blast him for making this more difficult!

As she neared the taproom door, it opened and Dash stepped outside before her. A warm smile graced his lips, and she cursed herself for finding comfort in his amber gaze. Wouldn't it be nice if she saw *him* in her future?

Seventeen

Dash was relieved when they climbed back inside the coach after dinner. Neither Caitrin nor MacQuarrie said two words over the meal, and while he was comforted by the fact that the Scot hadn't made any inroads, he hated to see his angel so unhappy.

Cait pulled the Macleod plaid over herself and curled up in a ball in one corner of the coach. Her sour-faced maid scowled at Dash as he took the spot beside Caitrin, and he returned the look.

He wasn't certain why Cait insisted on traveling straight through the night. She acted almost as though demons were chasing her out of England. The most disheartening aspect of the situation was that their pace didn't allow him the opportunity to seduce her. He had anticipated sneaking into her room each night as they traveled. Hell, he'd dreamt about it. And though Caitrin was within arm's length of him in his coach, he had her inept maid to deal with.

How could he convince Caitrin to marry him if he wasn't afforded the chance to slip between her sheets?

In no time, he found himself listening to Jeannie's snores and Cait's light sighs. His flaxen-haired angel truly appeared to have been sent from heaven, her rosebud lips so kissable and her soft lashes resting on her cheeks. He couldn't have mistakenly claimed a more fitting mate. How lucky that her grim maid hadn't been the one who'd crossed his path that night in the Duke of Blackmoor's study.

Suddenly, Cait's heart began to race and she jerked awake. She gasped for breath, and Dash hauled her to his lap. "It's all right, angel. I'm here," he soothed.

She clutched at his waistcoat and buried her face against his chest.

"Oh, Blaire," she muttered miserably.

"Blaire?" he repeated. "The lass who makes all the men in Scotland look like weaklings?"

She nodded, soaking his shirt through with her tears.

"Caitie," he said softly, stroking her back. "It was just a dream, angel."

"No," she sobbed. "Th-there was a monster."

"Shh." He held her close, ignoring the word "monster," as he'd been called that more times than he cared to count. "Go back to sleep, Caitie. It'll be all right."

She straightened and looked him directly in the eyes. With the waning moon pouring in through the carriage's small window, he couldn't miss the intensity of her gaze.

"I ken ye doona believe me."

"I believe you," he tried to assure her. In the dark with his excellent vision, he could see the terror in her eyes and his heart lurched. He hated to see her so filled with dread.

"Try to sleep."

Cait shook her head. "I doona want ta see those dead eyes again."

"Dead eyes?"

"Aye. Black and dead," she whispered. "I'm tellin' ye, Dash, Blaire's in danger. The creature that stalks her… Is *dead*."

"Caitie, it's just a dream."

෴

Cait wanted to believe that more than anything. But her visions had never been wrong. Her heart was racing as the disturbing images of her friend in grave danger settled into the darkness surrounding her. Getting to Blaire, warning her, was of the utmost importance. Thank heavens, they planned to drive straight through.

Cait closed her eyes tightly, wishing she recognized the forest in which she'd seen Blaire and the stalking monster. But she couldn't place it. She was certain she'd never seen the place before. If she'd ever been there, she would have remembered the rugged terrain and thick woods.

Those thoughts vanished as Dash's warm hand stroked circles on her back in an apparent attempt to comfort her. And at that moment she wanted his comfort desperately, more than reason.

Without giving the consequences of her actions any thought, Cait leaned forward in the dark and pressed her lips to his.

A startled breath escaped Dash, but he quickly recovered, grasping her to him as though he was a doomed man and she was his salvation. Dash's mouth roamed over hers just as his strong hands cupped her bottom and settled her more firmly in his lap.

He moaned against her lips, urging her to open for him.

His warm tongue swept inside her mouth, touching hers, and Cait couldn't get close enough to him. She cupped his jaw and reveled in the taste of him. Everywhere he touched her, she came alive, wanting more and more of him with each movement of his hands on her body.

"God, Caitie," he rasped as he pulled his lips from hers and rested his forehead against her own. "You'll undo me right here."

Across the carriage, a loud snore from Jeannie reminded her that they weren't alone. Cait reared back quickly, startled at her own wanton behavior. "I-I doona ken what came over me," she tried to apologize.

Dash pulled her closer to him and draped her plaid back across her legs. "I don't mind, lass. I'd just rather not have an audience."

Cait hid her face against his chest, glad it was dark so he couldn't see the blush she felt on her cheeks.

"Soon," he promised beside her ear, sending a fresh wave of chills across her skin.

She gulped, unsure what to say. She should correct his assumption, but she didn't have the heart to do so. Again, his hands caressed her back, and she started to relax.

"Try to sleep, angel."

But she didn't want to sleep. She didn't want to see the dead creature again. She didn't want to watch it hunt Blaire. Cait shook her head. Getting a clearer picture of Dashiel Thorpe would keep her mind occupied. She searched for something to say and then remembered his odd expression from earlier when he spoke about his home.

"Why have ye no' visited Kent in years, Dash?"

He stilled. "More questions?" he asked softly. "Aren't you tired?"

Cait shrugged. "I'm curious."

"The marquess and I do not enjoy each other's company. It's better this way."

His father, who wasn't really his father. "Are ye curious ta find yer real father?"

Dash sighed. "I haven't given it much thought. I don't think it's possible to find him."

"Major Forster could help ye," she suggested. "Yer society has records. He might have a suggestion of how ta go on."

"To what end?" he asked.

"So ye can find out who ye are? Where ye came from?"

Dash very nearly pushed her from his lap. He wanted nothing more at that moment than to be far, far away from her questions and the unwanted thoughts they brought with them. But she cupped his cheek in her hand and looked into his eyes, silently refusing to let him pull away.

"I know where I came from," he growled.

But she wasn't intimidated by his blustering. "Where?" she asked quietly, as she relaxed and laid her head over his heart. "Where did ye come from?"

"I came from a whore who gave herself up to a beast," he said bluntly and then swiped his hand across his face in frustration. She raised her head to look at him. So, this was what guilt felt like? "I'm sorry, Caitie. I shouldn't have said that."

"Perhaps ye came from love," she said quietly as a soft smile tipped the corners of her lips.

"Love?" he echoed. He must have misheard her.

"Aye, maybe yer mother loved yer father. And ye are the product of that love."

"Fanciful tales of love and life race through your mind when you think about *my* situation? I'd never have taken you for a romantic, angel."

She nudged him in the belly with her elbow. "I believe in love," she said quietly as she brushed a lock of hair from his forehead.

Dash nearly melted with that touch, so caring and offered so selflessly. "Caitie," he groaned as he tugged her hand down and pressed a kiss to her palm.

"Dashiel," she groaned back, mocking his tone.

"You're one of a kind, aren't you?" he asked absently as he adjusted his body in the seat so that she lay across him. Then he covered them both with her plaid.

"Oh, my father certainly hopes so," she laughed, squirming in his lap for comfort.

She shifted across his groin and he laid his head back, closed his eyes, and took in a deep breath. "Would you be still?" He sighed.

"Sorry," she murmured. "Ye can put me down."

"I like to hold you," he admitted, smoothing a hand down her back. He'd like to do a lot more than that, but telling her that would get him kicked back out of the carriage.

"If Jeannie wakes up, she'll be scandalized."

"Even your maid can't keep me from holding you," he insisted. "I promise my intentions are honorable." Mostly, anyway.

Cait sat up and looked into his eyes. "All of them?"

Her scent swirled around him, and Dash fought his basic instinct to growl aloud. "Not when you look at me like that, no." He patted his chest and encouraged her to lie back down. If she glanced at him one more time like that with her lips parted, he would have to put them to good use.

She sighed as she laid her head back down on his chest. "If ye could have one thing, something that ye wanted above all others, what would it be?"

"You," he said quickly, without even thinking.

"I am no' part of yer future," she said as she nudged him.

"You keep saying that. But I happen to know differently."

"Stubborn lout."

"Obstinate witch."

"Ye have no idea," she whispered.

Eighteen

Caitrin wasn't sure when it happened, but she woke during the night to find the bed beneath her moving. She grasped for the side of the mattress and jumped when someone's fingers threaded through hers.

"Shhh…" she heard him whisper by her ear. She raised her head to look into Dash's heavily lidded eyes. "If you make noise, you'll wake up the guard," he laughed and nodded toward Jeannie, who slept heavily on the other side of the coach.

"I forgot where I was for a moment," she murmured as she inhaled deeply, his warm citrus scent engulfing her.

"I didn't."

She felt his lips as they touched the top of her head. "So tender," she murmured.

"That's a sentiment that has never been used to describe me before." He chuckled lightly.

The sound of raindrops slowly hitting the top of the carriage drew her attention. "Lovely. And I had planned ta push ye out the door at sun-up so ye could enjoy the weather."

The pitter-patter of rain soon became the steady

drumming of a heavy downpour, making his soft comments more difficult to hear.

"That's very amicable of you," he said crisply as he made a poor attempt to look fierce. "I suffer all night with your bottom in my lap, and you want to push me back out into the cold? Do you have a heart in there somewhere?" He playfully tugged at the collar of her gown, as though looking for a hidden place where kindness and caring might dwell.

He stopped tugging when he'd bared her neck and the top of her shoulder where his mark was located. She self-consciously covered it with her hand.

"Does it still hurt?"

She simply shook her head.

"You're wearing my mark. Do you dislike it?"

"No." And strangely, she meant it.

He tugged her hand from where it rested on top of it and very gently pressed his lips there. A shiver moved through her body. A most delicious shiver.

His lips made a fiery path up the side of her neck, his fingers gently pushing the strands of hair away.

"But if ye bite me again, I *will* put ye back out in the rain."

Then his teeth gently abraded the side of her neck. Her belly flipped. The hair on her arms stood up. How did he do this to her? She glanced over at Jeannie, who still slept soundly.

He adjusted Cait so that her back was to the woman, her plaid still covering them both. "I'll tell you if she wakes."

Her head lay on his shoulder, so he had to do no more than tip her chin to kiss her. Cait didn't even think of resisting. She let him coax her mouth open and then received him as greedily as he wanted to take her.

The heat of his hand seeped through her gown when it landed at her waist. His thumb drew lazy circles as his hand crept slowly up toward her breast, which was suddenly heavy and aching. But he was the balm for her pain when he finally cupped her in his hand.

Cait pulled her lips from his when he swiped his thumb across her nipple, the gentle stroke touching somewhere deep within her, a place she hadn't known existed.

"Do you want me to stop?" he asked quietly.

She took his hand in hers and pressed it more firmly to her breast.

There was her answer. The beast inside Dash rejoiced. His bold little angel liked the pleasure he brought her. When she tucked her head beneath his chin and began to make little mewling noises, it was all Dash could do not to howl to the heavens.

He forced himself not to grind his erection into the side of her thigh where it rested across his lap. But it was difficult. He was fully aware that their little game would have to stop in a moment or he would be too far gone to care whether or not her maid slept across the coach from them.

He glanced over at Jeannie, whose jaw was still slack with slumber, the heavy weight of her breaths easy to hear with his Lycan ears.

Cait began to fidget in his lap, her heart beating a frantic rhythm as he toyed with her.

"Dash," she moaned quietly.

"Yes, angel?"

"What are ye doing ta me?" She raised her chin and kissed his bristly jaw. Her words washed over him like the sweet melody of wind chimes.

"I think I'm bringing you pleasure," he laughed. "If not, then I'm doing it all wrong."

"No," she gasped as he lightly pinched the tip of her breast with his finger and thumb. "Ye ken ye are no' doin' it wrong."

"Hmm," he agreed. "Your body tells me I'm doing it right."

She nodded, pressing her face into him to cover her embarrassment.

"I can tell how much you want me," he admitted. "It's in the pounding of your heart, and your honeysuckle scent is even more intoxicating when your body warms with desire."

His hand crept down and began to gather her traveling gown, raising it inch by glorious inch. When he had it up to her knees, he readjusted the plaid over her, craving what lay beneath like nothing else in the world.

Cait didn't protest when his hand trailed up her stockings or when his fingers walked past her garters. But just as he was about to touch her heat, which called to the beast inside him like nothing ever had before, her maid shifted in her seat. Dash closed his eyes and stilled his body, feigning sleep and swallowing an irritated growl.

He could almost feel the maid's disapproval as she looked over at them. In truth, the way he held

Cait was highly inappropriate, despite the fact that the casual observer could never tell he had his hand beneath her skirts.

The maid snuffed and rolled the other way, making herself more comfortable. She closed her eyes and was back asleep in moments.

Dash tugged the hem of Cait's dress back down. He wanted to slap his own fingers for being so bold as to touch her in a coach when they weren't alone. A wild Lycan. That's all he was and all he'd ever be. He'd never, ever be good enough for the likes of Caitrin Macleod.

"I'm sorry," he said.

"Doona be," she said as she closed her hand around his and brought it to her lips, where she pressed a quick kiss to the palm of his hand. He felt the curve of her smile against his skin.

She had no idea what her gentle touches did to him, and she'd probably be terrified if she knew how base his instincts really were. How could he ask her to accept him when he barely had any control of himself?

Niall Forster. The name echoed in Dash's ears. If he had any hope of winning Cait, of being worthy of her, he had to get to Mr. Forster sooner rather than later. There was no other way for Dash to keep her safe from the beast inside him. He needed to learn to control it. He needed Cait.

~❦~

Cait eagerly stepped from the coach when they stopped to change horses in Newcastle upon Tyne. Her legs were stiff and her back ached. She knew she should wake Dash. With his long legs, he had to ache worse than she did. But her mind was in such a jumble; she needed just a little time to herself.

When Alec MacQuarrie stepped in front of her, his dark eyes filled with fury, Cait instantly regretted not waking Dash from his slumber. "Do you care to tell me just why we're moving at this pace? My coachman nearly fell asleep on the road, Caitrin."

She tipped her nose in the air, leveling him with her haughtiest look. "Well, I dinna ask ya ta follow me. By all means, rest a while here and then return ta yer friends in Leeds."

He stepped forward and took her elbow in his hands. "And leave you with Brimsworth? You'd have ta put a ball in my chest first."

"Doona tempt me," she grumbled.

"What are you thinking, Cait? The man shouldn't ride in such close quarters with you, as you well know." He frowned at her, making her feel like an unruly child.

"And ye shouldna manhandle me," she returned, wrenching her arm from his grasp. Then she started off toward the Tyne, ignoring the way the wind whipped at her skirts.

"Cait," he called, chasing after her. "Wait."

But she refused to stop.

"At least take your plaid," he yelled.

Which, truly, she should have done. It was freezing, but she wouldn't look back at him. She wouldn't give him that satisfaction. Blast Alec MacQuarrie! The sooner he gave up this foolish pursuit of her, the better it would be for all involved.

Cait folded her arms across her chest and rubbed her hands up and down, trying to warm herself. She paid no attention to the men milling about the coaching yard as she stomped past them, down a little path to the river. She supposed it was good to have fresh air, though it would be nice if it was a bit warmer.

She stopped at the water's edge and looked across at the village. From her spot, she could see a bridge spanning the river and a sizable castle resting atop a hill.

Thunder rumbled in the distance, and she shivered.

"At this pace," Dash's voice came from behind her, "you should be in Edinburgh tomorrow." She spun around to find him holding out her plaid, which she readily accepted and wrapped around her arms.

She nodded quickly. The sooner she was home the better.

"I opened my eyes and you were gone," he informed her, his eyes boring into her as though he was searching for something.

"I dinna want ta wake ye, since ye were sleepin' so peacefully."

"Just resting my eyes. I can only take so much in the way of the caustic looks your maid sends me."

"She means well."

The wind tossed his golden hair, and his amber gaze warmed her from the inside out as she remembered the intensity of his kiss and the feel of his hands on her breast. Cait had to look away to keep from blushing under his stare. Her eyes landed again on the castle across the Tyne, and she wished that they could reach Edinburgh even sooner.

Dash's hands stole around her waist, and he held her from behind. "Something about the castle has your attention?"

She shouldn't smile. She shouldn't let him hold her like this, but it felt so nice, so comforting. "Have ye ever been ta Edinburgh?"

"No." His warm breath heated her cheek right before he kissed it.

Cait closed her eyes, loving the feel of him holding her as his citric scent enveloped her senses. "Ye'll have ta visit Edinburgh Castle. It puts yer Sassenach imitations ta shame."

He chuckled, holding her tighter. "My proud little Scottish angel."

She liked the way he said that. She liked the way it made her belly flutter, though she knew in her heart that she shouldn't.

"But, Caitie," he continued softly, "Edinburgh is not my destination."

Cait's heart plummeted with those words. She had been playing with fire, and, just like always, she was the one who would be burned by her foolishness. Of course, Dashiel Thorpe was moving on to whatever he was destined to do, and she'd once again be left behind.

She hadn't even meant for it to happen. She'd tried to be smart where he was concerned. Kept him at arm's length, fed him a sleeping draught, and bolted from him in the dead of night. But still, he'd managed to worm his way into her heart only to dash her desire with icy water that might as well have come from the Tyne.

None of it was fair. Wasn't she entitled to some happiness? Since when did fair have anything to do with life? Cait stepped from the comfort of his arms and pulled her plaid tighter around her shoulders.

"Brimsworth!" Alec called from the distance, and Cait groaned. Must she deal with him now too?

Dash stepped away from her and turned his attention to the irritating interloper. "Ah, MacQuarrie."

Alec scowled at the earl. "I wanted to invite you to ride with me today."

Cait resisted the urge to roll her eyes. Civility was most assuredly not Alec's goal. With a charming smile, Dash tipped his head in acceptance.

"How generous, MacQuarrie. I'd be honored to share your conveyance today. However, I must decline."

"Of course you must," Alec grunted.

Nineteen

DASH TRIED TO KEEP THE GROWL FROM HIS VOICE. Leaving Cait with the supercilious Scot was hardly his choice, but it was that or endanger her with his own presence.

"I'm afraid you misunderstand me, MacQuarrie. I'll hire a horse from here and head toward Glasgow. I trust that you can see Miss MacLeod back to Edinburgh safely?"

"Beg your pardon?" the Scot questioned. The man could not have looked more surprised if Dash had grown two heads and sprouted wings.

Cait's icy eyes raked Dash from top to bottom. "No need ta hire a horse, my lord. Yer carriage awaits. I have no more use for it."

She was irritated with him and a little furious, if he interpreted her words and scowl correctly. Still he'd offered her his coach, and he meant for her to have it.

"Don't be rash, Caitie. My coach will take you safely to Edinburgh—"

She shook her head. "I'm certain Mr. MacQuarrie

willna mind my company the rest of the journey. *We* are headed ta the same place after all."

Damn MacQuarrie straight to hell. "I told you from the beginning Glasgow was my destination." And the only hope he had for his salvation.

"Well, I willna keep ye from it any longer. As soon as yer Renshaw moves my bags from yer coach ta Mr. MacQuarrie's, ye can be on yer way."

A growl erupted from Dash's throat. Damn the beast inside him. He wasn't in control of a bloody thing anymore. The previous night spent with her wrapped up in his arms was proof of that. What did she want from him? Surely she realized he was too dangerous to be around her at the moment? He'd proven it when he'd raised her dress. They weren't even alone, for God's sake. She deserved better.

Was she accustomed to being mauled by gentlemen? Dash turned his gaze to MacQuarrie. If the scoundrel touched one hair on Cait's head, Dash would rip his limbs off one by one.

"You'll keep her safe until she reaches her father."

"Caitrin's safety has always been my highest priority."

Dash ignored the look of pure betrayal on Caitrin's face. Once he was a controlled Lycan, she'd thank him for his sacrifice. "I'll see you as soon as I possibly can, lass."

He wasn't sure what she meant to say, but whatever it was, she changed her mind and bit her tongue. Then Cait feigned a smile.

"Well, I wish ye the best on yer journey and hope Glasgow is all yer hopin' it ta be." Then she spun on her heels and stalked back toward the coaches.

"You'll miss me when I'm gone," he called after her departing form.

In fact, if he had to guess, he'd say she was already missing him. Her reaction was proof that she felt *something* for him. He didn't know exactly what she felt, but it was something. That was a start.

"I wouldna wager on that if I were ye," she shot back at him over her shoulder.

"I could love you so easily," he suddenly blurted. He already did. Or at least what he knew of love.

She stopped in her tracks and tilted her head to the side to see him better. "Ye have an unconventional way of showin' that." Her blue eyes flashed with indignation. "Godspeed on yer journey." Then she resumed her path toward MacQuarrie's coach.

The Scot's servants were already transferring her belongings to his coach. Dash gritted his teeth. What was he supposed to do? She refused even to look at him. He had no idea how long his training would take. So, he couldn't make any promises to her. He couldn't even tell her about how irrevocably she was tied to him, not yet.

He had to let her go. And pray she was waiting for him when he finally arrived in Edinburgh.

MacQuarrie was quick on Cait's tail and hauled open the door to his carriage for her. She ducked her head and stepped inside without even a backward glance.

"MacQuarrie," Dash called out.

The man turned toward him, looking a bit too pleased with himself. Dash was in front of him in three steps. He moved so quickly the Scot took a step back in surprise.

"If she's injured or harmed in any way before you deposit her into her father's very capable hands, I'll find you. And I will not be happy when I do. Do I make myself clear?"

"Come now, Brimsworth. If anyone has hurt her, it's you." He dusted his knuckles on his jacket. "I just get the good fortune of picking up the pieces of her heart."

"Just remember that no matter how many pieces you salvage, they all belong to me," he snarled fiercely.

"I think the lady disagrees," MacQuarrie replied. Then he turned and ducked into the waiting carriage, which pulled away as soon as the door closed.

❧

When Dash finally reached the shipbuilder's modest home on the outskirts of Glasgow, he nearly wept with relief. He bounded up the grey stone steps, took a deep breath, then lifted the cold brass knocker and banged on the heavy oak door. It seemed as though he stood there forever, like an awkward schoolboy waiting for admittance. Dash was ready to do bodily harm to whomever answered, simply for making him wait any longer than was necessary.

Finally, heavy footsteps sounded from within and then the door was flung open. Forster's butler looked down his long, crooked nose at Dash.

"Deliveries are made around back," the giant said as he turned and began to close the door.

Dash looked down at himself quickly. He had to admit he looked a bit like a common beggar one might find in the street, though with much more fashionable clothes.

He stuck his boot in the door just before the butler closed it in his face. He only winced a little with pain and only for a moment. Then he reached into the inner pocket of his coat and pulled out the tattered letter Major Forster had written to introduce him to the shipbuilder. He held it out. "I'll see Mr. Forster now."

Again Dash looked down at his clothes and dusted himself off while the butler took the letter and still shut the door in his face. Dash supposed he could have forced his way inside, but that probably wouldn't have made a good first impression. And he needed Niall Forster's help more than he'd ever needed anyone's assistance in his life.

He'd run most of the way from County Durham, once he'd become frustrated by the speed of his own coach. The snow that had begun to fall, combined with the slippery roads, had made travel crawl at a snail's pace. He didn't have time to waste. He needed to get back to Cait. And he had to do it quickly. So, he'd set off on foot, following his instincts all way to Glasgow, all the way to Niall Forster's door.

He had mud spatters up to his knees, and he even felt a crusty line of mud on his cheek when he moved to rub some heat back into his face. Truth be told, Dash probably would have shut the door in anyone's face who appeared at his home looking as he did. He shook his head in dismay. How had he been reduced to this?

The front door opened once more, and the butler motioned him inside. He took Dash's coat, and, when Dash moved to follow him down the hallway, they both noticed the clumps of mud that were falling from his boots. With a frustrated sigh, Dash sat down and tugged the Hessians from his feet. Hell, he'd walk in his bare feet if he had to. He'd never professed to be a gentleman.

"Satisfied?" he grunted.

"Quite," was the man's only response.

With a short growl that didn't seem to bother the behemoth in the least, Dash followed him down the hallway and into a small library. The walls were covered with drawings of ships of all sizes. And the shelves were lined with books and models of large and small sailing vessels.

A grey-haired man stood up from behind the large desk at one side of the room and pushed his glasses back firmly on his nose. He didn't say a word or even reach to take Dash's hand when he extended it. The man simply motioned to the chair in front of him. Dash sank into it like a recalcitrant child.

Just when he thought the man would never speak, he put the letter down and steepled his hands in front of himself. "Gotten yerself inta quite a pickle, have ye no'?"

"'A pickle' would be a very generous description for my current situation, sir." Dash felt quite naked in his stocking feet, with dirt from head to toe. He'd not felt so exposed since he was a very young child. Or at least since the last time he'd seen his father.

"Why are ye here?" Mr. Forster asked.

"It should all be in the letter from the major, sir," Dash said, motioning toward the paper.

"I'm sure it is, but I'd like ta hear it from yer own lips, son," Mr. Forster said quietly.

"What do you already know?" Dash asked, not quite sure where to start.

"Nothin'," Mr. Forster offered.

Dash wasn't quite sure if he believed that, but he didn't have much of a choice. "My name is Dashiel Thorpe, the Earl of Brimsworth, heir to the Marquess of Eynsford."

"Roughly translated, that means ye have more money than ye have sense."

Dash sighed. "Probably, sir."

"What can I do for ye, Dashiel? It is all right if I call ye Dashiel?"

Was that a test of some sort? "You can call me anything you like, as long as you can help me. You see, there's this girl…" Dash began.

"A victim of yer ferocity, yes?"

"I wouldn't exactly call her a *victim*." Dash's hackles finally rose a bit.

"What would ye call her?"

"Well, her name is Cait."

Mr. Forster picked up the letter and scanned it quickly, his eyes widening in surprise, and then he peered at Dash over the rims of his reading glasses. "Ye're referrin' ta Miss Macleod?"

"Yes, sir." He couldn't help but smile a little when he answered. Just the thought of her brought a smile to Dash's lips.

"Well, ye certainly ken how ta get yerself in a spot of trouble, Dashiel."

Which was something Dash didn't need to have reaffirmed.

"This Miss Macleod is a friend of Desmond's daughter, correct?"

Dash nodded.

The old man chuckled. "And a Macleod, no less. Aye, lad, I believe Desmond has sent ye ta the right place."

Dash nearly felt the weight of his burden lift from his chest. Forster's words were the first bit of good news he'd heard in a long time. "I am relieved to hear it, sir."

Mr. Forster sighed. "So tell me, how does the Macleod lass feel about all this?"

"She likes me. Some of the time."

"Ye better hope she does."

"Yes, I do." He took a deep breath. "You see, I'm afraid I'm head over heels in love with her."

The shipbuilder's green eyes twinkled with mirth. "That's a good thing, lad, since ye're tied ta her for a lifetime."

"I need your help, sir, like I've never needed anything else. But I need you to teach me quickly because I have to go to Edinburgh without delay."

"To convince the lovely Miss Macleod of yer love for her?"

"Yes. And I need to do it before someone else beats me to it," Dash explained. "So, I'm in a bit of a hurry. How long will this training take?"

"A lifetime, in most of us," Forster sighed out.

"I don't have that long." Dash stood up to pace, suddenly aware of his stocking feet again, which made him feel like a complete simpleton.

Mr. Forster drummed his fingers across his desk and confessed, "My wife died a few years ago."

"I'm very sorry." Dash could see the pain written on the man's face.

The shipbuilder met his eyes. "If ye doona win Miss

Macleod's heart, ye will be doomed ta be alone until either ye, or she, dies." He took a deep breath. "And now that I've experienced the loss, I wouldna wish it on anyone. So under the circumstances, I think we should go ta Edinburgh together, lad. So, ye have a fair chance ta win the heart of yer lady love."

"Truly?" Dash's heart was about to jump from his chest in excitement. But the memory of holding Cait in the coach had him questioning the wisdom of such a venture. "Will I be safe to be around her? I nearly lost control when I was with her. I'd hoped to go to her once I had complete control of the beast inside."

Mr. Forster tossed back his head and laughed. "Control of the beast?" he chortled. "My dear lad, ye canna control the beast. Ye *are* the beast. It's a part of ye, no' the enemy."

Dash scoffed. What he wouldn't give to kill the beast all together and go to Caitrin as a man, whole and hale.

One of Forster's eyebrows rose in surprise at Dash's quick *harrumph*. "That'll be yer first lesson, then. We can discuss it on the way ta Edinburgh."

He didn't like being laughed at, but if Forster could help him, Dash would accept the slight without complaint. "Thank you for doing this for me."

"Well, yer in luck. I'm in the mood for a good love story. And yer the only Lycan who's knocked on my door today."

If Dash was in wolf form, his tail would be thumping against the floor, he was so excited about the prospect of seeing Cait again.

"Ye canna go ta her lookin' like that." Forster

motioned for Dash to stand and follow. "Ye'll be wantin' ta speak ta her father. And if we travel through the night, we can be there by mornin'."

"That is a relief, sir."

"Well, I just hope ye're no' too late. Ye have a rival, ye say?"

Dash nodded.

"Ye can tell me all about him in the coach. I'm too old ta run all the way ta Edinburgh."

Twenty

At this pace, you should be in Edinburgh tomorrow. Dash's words echoed in Cait's ears. He'd certainly been wrong about that, hadn't he? Just another line to add to his growing list of sins. Not that he could have foreseen the muddy roads that threatened to swallow MacQuarrie's coach along the way, slowing their process by tenfold. It had even been too late for Cait to say anything that would have prevented the situation when that particular bit of future flashed in her mind. It didn't matter. She was still laying the blame at Dashiel Thorpe's feet.

As soon as she saw the Scotch Arms come into view from her window, she breathed a sigh of relief. She was far from pleased about staying the night in another inn, but she was even less desirous of traveling the perilous road at night. At least if Dash had been with her, she could have blocked the uninvited futures from her mind.

She sighed, kicking herself for wanting to be with him so much.

"That's another sigh, Cait," Alec informed her.

She glared at him.

"Don't look at me like that. I'm just bringing it to your attention. You've done nothing but sigh for the last several hours. Are you feeling all right?"

Cait snorted. "Aye, Alec. I love nearly bein' washed off the road, limpin' along in yer coach, and freezin' ta my bones."

The coach rambled to a stop, and Alec himself sighed. The irony was not lost on Cait. Then the man opened the door and helped her out.

"I was hoping to have this time to change your mind, Caitrin."

She didn't even bother to look at him. What was the point of engaging in the same argument yet again?

"Ye've known me my whole life, Alec MacQuarrie. Have ye ever known me ta change my mind once it's been made up?"

Alec didn't have time to answer her before the taproom door opened and raucous laughter filtered out into the frigid coaching yard. Ready to wash the dust of travel from her skin, Cait brushed past Alec toward the entrance. She couldn't wait to stretch out on a bed, not that she dared hope for a comfortable one; but at this point, any bed would be a godsend.

Cait stepped inside the taproom, thankful for the warmth that emanated from a large hearth at the far side of the dark room. Her back and legs were so sore that she felt as though she'd walked all the way from Hampshire. She released a sigh of relief, but then her momentary feeling of comfort came to an instant halt.

Instinctively, Cait took a step backward, bumping

into what felt like a brick wall. She cocked her head to one side and found herself staring up into the dark eyes of one of the most strikingly handsome men she'd ever seen.

A slight grin settled on the man's face, making his chiseled jaw more pronounced. "Madam." His eyes locked on the side of her neck where Dash had marked her. "Forgive me, I didn't see you there."

Cait couldn't quite find her voice. There was something a bit intoxicating about his presence, and she swallowed. Quick flashes of a gruesome medieval battle interspersed with bare flesh in Cait's mind.

She caught her breath and stared at the well-dressed gentleman.

"What are ye?" she whispered, more to herself than to him.

She knew he heard her, however, when one dark brow rose in mild amusement. "The better question, my dear, is what are you?"

In Cait's mind, she saw a trickle of blood on a woman's slender neck, which was arched in pleasure. She instinctively reached up to cover the mark on her own neck as the vision of this man biting a woman of his own flashed through her mind. She should have been afraid. She should have run back out into the chilly night. She should be sent to Bedlam for simply gaping at the man like a dolt.

"Caitrin!" Alec called from the doorway. "Do you think it's possible you could wait for me?"

The gentleman's smile grew wide. "Ah, sir, I believe your wife was simply hoping to chase the chill from her bones."

Cait snorted, which was quite unladylike, but she couldn't help it. "Wife, indeed," she muttered to herself.

The handsome gentleman sucked in a breath at her statement, and Alec's eyes narrowed on Cait. "Must you attract attention everywhere we go?"

A cold finger tipped Cait's chin up to meet the English gentleman's dark gaze. "This man has dishonored you?" His gaze fell again to her neck.

Alec had certainly annoyed her, but he had never been dishonorable. "Nay, sir, he's just an old friend, an irritatin' one."

A look of sadness crossed the man's face. "Old friends can be irritating until they're gone. Then you find you miss them terribly."

Cait wasn't quite sure what he meant by that, and she didn't get the chance to ask. Alec grasped her arm and tugged her away from the stranger. "Have you lost your mind?"

How many times had she been asked that in the last fortnight? "I doona need ye ta rescue me, Alec MacQuarrie."

The enchanting gentleman laughed. "Forgive my manners, sir. Allow me to introduce myself. The Earl of Blodswell at your service."

Alec's mouth dropped open. "Blodswell?"

"Do I know you?" the man asked.

Alec shook his head. "Alec MacQuarrie. The Third Crusade was a particular interest of mine."

With a bashful smile, Blodswell shrugged. "It is often difficult to live in a famous ancestor's shadow."

Cait looked from one man to the other. What were they talking about?

Alec must have seen her confusion, because he smiled and took pity on her. "Sir Matthew Halkett became the first Earl of Blodswell. He fought along-side Richard the Lionheart. He was a brave Norman knight of legends. Those who faced him fled in fear. Even after all his heroics on the field of battle, the man returned home completely unscathed, not even the slightest scratch.

"But blood gushed from his sword each time he took it up. Hence the name King Richard gave him— Blodswell, or blood-swell," Alec explained. "An earldom was bestowed on the knight upon his return to England."

A smile lit Blodswell's face. "I'm certain Sir Matthew would have been honored to know his legend lives on even in this day and age."

"Of course," Alec gushed. "I spent a large part of my time in Cambridge researching the crusades. Fascinating in an academic setting."

"Quite fascinating in a contemporary setting as well," Cait said under her breath.

As Alec turned from them to talk with the innkeeper, the Earl of Blodswell's gaze returned to the mark on her neck. "That is not the mark of my kind."

"If I had knowledge of yer kind, my lord, I could probably formulate a more appropriate reply."

A corner of his mouth lifted in amusement. "I could say the same."

A flash of the future hit her, bringing so much comfort that she sighed with relief. "Ye will ken enough about my kind in time, sir." She turned from him but then threw back over her shoulder, "Enjoy the fine weather, my lord, while ye still can."

◈

Cait tossed and turned in the lumpy inn bed. Visions of bloody broadswords and cudgels flashed in her mind. Then she saw Blaire running beside a frozen loch being chased by a dark figure.

She woke with a startled cry and bolted upright, gasping for breath, dripping in sweat. A dream. It was just another awful dream. But she knew it wasn't. Blaire was in trouble; Cait could feel it in her bones.

She fell back against the threadbare pillow, accidentally banging her head against the wall in the process.

A soft knock sounded at the door. "Caitrin?" Alec's whispered voice filled the room.

She sighed, slid from the bed, and padded across the cool, wooden floor. Cait pulled the door open and folded her arms across her chest.

"Just what do ye think yer doin' knockin' on my door in the middle of the night, Alec MacQuarrie?"

A look of relief crossed his face. "I heard you scream and wanted to make sure you were all right."

She wished Dash was the one standing before her, but Dash was gone.

"I'm fine," she grunted as she rubbed the sore on the back of her head.

"Just a bad dream, then?" Alec asked.

The worst dream ever. Blaire was in mortal danger. Cait was certain of it. She closed her eyes and tried to see Blaire, tried to find her aura; but it was no use. All Cait could envision was sweeping darkness.

No! She grasped the doorjamb to keep from falling. Blaire wasn't in mortal danger; she was dead. If only she herself had been home, maybe then she would have seen this sooner.

"Cait!" Alec's panicked voice barely filtered into her mind, but Cait pushed it back out.

She focused on her coven. She saw Elspeth in Hampshire and knew she was safe and happy with Benjamin and his family. An image of Rhiannon flashed in her mind. She was alone at Arthur's Seat, looking out at Edinburgh under a fresh blanket of snow. And Sorcha. Cait called to Sorcha's aura. The youngest witch slept in her room, warm and comfortable, with a bit of potting soil under her fingernails.

"Caitrin!"

Again Cait tried to focus on Blaire, called her into her mind; but there was nothing. Never before had she been unable to find someone she was looking for.

Alec's strong arms grasped her shoulder and began to shake her. Cait's eyes flew open, and she blinked back tears.

"I just want ta get home," she said softly.

Alec nodded, panic etched across his brow. "We'll leave first thing in the morning."

"No. Now!" she insisted. There was no time to waste. No more stopping, no matter what. "If ye willna take me, I'll do it alone, Alec."

"Caitrin," he began.

"I need ta go home, Alec. Now. No more stops."

He had no idea how much she needed to be somewhere familiar. Somewhere she could curl into a ball and sob. Somewhere she could rest.

"Cait, it's too dangerous. My driver will fall asleep holding the reins if we don't take a break. Ever since we left Leeds, I've pushed him too hard, just trying to keep up with you."

She begrudgingly nodded. MacQuarrie's driver was just a man after all. He would need to rest along the way. "Can we at least leave at sunup?"

"Of course," Alec affirmed. He held a question within his gaze. "Your dream. Did you see something?" he asked. "Something that scared you?"

She shook her head quickly. "It's no' what I see, Alec. It's what I canna see."

"I don't know what you're speaking of, Caitrin. I'm not familiar enough with your gift."

"It's more of a curse than a gift," she bit out.

"Tell me what you saw. Or didn't see." He shook his head in confusion.

"I canna find Blaire."

"She's probably at home practicing with Aiden Lindsay's broadsword. I'm sure she's fine."

"If she was at home, I would be able to *see* it," she whispered fiercely. "I would be able ta feel her. I would ken where she was."

"Truly?"

"Aye. But I canna see her at all, no' in all of Edinburgh." Tears burned her eyes, and she swiped at them viciously as they rolled down her cheeks. "I think she may be dead."

"Has this ever happened before?" He dipped his head low, peering into her eyes.

"Never. Well, with Brimsworth, I canna see his destiny. But it's no' the same thing."

Twenty-One

"Where did ye get the idea that ye need ta control the beast inside of ye?" Niall Forster asked as he leaned back against the squabs of his well-sprung coach.

What a ridiculous question. Dash shook his head. He'd come to Forster for real help. "If I don't have control of the beast, then I could hurt Caitrin. I can't allow that to happen."

Forster's green eyes focused on Dash. "Ye doona get ta decide what ye allow or no' allow in regard ta yer Lycan side. It canna be repressed and hidden away, Dashiel. It is part of ye just as much as yer blond hair and English heritage."

English heritage. Dash held in a snort. Who was to say his heritage was English? His sire might just as likely be a Frog or even an Irish dog.

"This isn't helping me, Forster. I won't be able to trust myself with Caitrin unless I can control that aspect of myself."

"Ye need ta embrace it, lad."

That seemed like exactly the wrong thing to do. "You don't appear reckless. Neither did the major nor any of the Westfield men. But I always feel it right beneath the surface. Masking it has taken years, but it's always there. I know it is."

"Of course, it's there. It's part of ye. And ye're right. I doona feel reckless. I'm comfortable in my skin. And if ye want the same peace, ye need ta accept that part of yer bein'.""

Dash folded his arms across his chest and sighed.

Forster smiled at him as though he was the simplest of simpletons. "I can see ye're goin' ta be a stubborn Sassenach about this. So I'll change tactics for the time bein'. What do ye ken about the Macleod lass?"

That she was the only woman for Dash. "She's gorgeous." He smiled envisioning her cheeky smile. "And she's clever. Has a mind of her own, which no one has a hope of changing without divine intervention."

The old shipbuilder chuckled. "Sounds like her mother."

Dash's mouth fell open. "You know Caitie's mother?"

Forster frowned. "Nay, but Desmond had more than a few encounters with the old witch. Heard about her for years. I hope, for yer sake, the lass is a bit more malleable than her mother."

"Witch" was a fairly uncomplimentary thing to say about his future wife's mother. Dash growled low in his throat.

"Ah, so ye use the beast ta intimidate others." Forester's gaze swept across Dash. "No wonder ye're scared ta accept who ye are. Ye've intimidated yerself as well."

"Major Forster told me you'd help me control the beast."

Forster shook his head. "I highly doubt that. His letter ta me said I was ta mentor ye. That's no' the same thing, Dashiel."

&ce;

Just when Caitrin was beginning to think she would never see the skyline of Edinburgh again, it finally came into view from the small carriage window. She heaved a sigh. For the last two days, she'd searched for Blaire to no avail. The hope she had of saving her friend had slowly vanished.

With a heavy heart, she smiled sadly at the familiar sight of Charlotte Square and her father's home.

Since that fateful night in the inn, Alec had been fairly quiet. He grunted occasionally as he shifted his arms and legs about, trying to stay comfortable as the carriage pushed through the treacherous roads. But for the most part, he'd said very little. Evidently, talk of her gift had scared him into silence.

She berated herself for even saying anything about it. The fact that she was a witch was secret. It was a secret she was only to tell her spouse. The one she was destined to spend her life with. No one else should ever know of her abilities. It was much too dangerous for all the members of the *Còig*.

Finally, the coach slowed in front of her home. She didn't even wait for it to stop moving before she jumped out and ran up the stone steps to the entrance. Findlay opened the door just as she approached.

"Welcome home, Miss," he said as she shrugged out of her pelisse and handed it to him.

"Where is my father?" she asked quickly. She had

to find him. She had to talk to someone who knew everything about her. She had to tell him everything, or she would simply lose her mind. She needed someone safe.

"I believe he's in his study, Miss," Findlay informed her. She took off in that direction, only stopping briefly when he asked, "What shall I do with Mr. MacQuarrie, Miss Macleod?"

"Just… Put him somewhere," she said with a negligent wave of her hand. Then she continued down the corridor.

Her father's study smelled like home, like all things familiar. The odor of a recently smoked cheroot hung in the air. Her father's woodsy-scented shaving lotion greeted her nose, and she inhaled deeply. What a relief to be home.

She flew across the room and into her father's waiting arms before he could even remove his reading glasses.

"Oh, Cait, I've missed ye so much. I'm so glad ye're home," he crooned as he hugged her, his strong arms easing some of the burden she carried.

"I am, too. I need ta talk ta ye."

"Are ye all right?" he asked, a vee forming between his eyebrows as he appraised her from head to toe.

"Why does everyone keep askin' me that?" she breathed as she raised a hand to rub her forehead.

"Because ye look terrible, love. When was the last time ye slept? What's wrong?" He led her over to the settee and sat down beside her. "Tell me yer troubles."

"I canna find Blaire."

"Ye canna find her?"

"Aye, I canna *see* her. No' at all. I think somethin'

has happened ta her. Has it, Papa? Did she die while I was gone?"

"Oh, dear, ye've gotten yerself worked up over nothin'. A sennight ago, Captain Lindsay received a notification from his solicitor about a piece of property near Loch Calavie, I doona remember the name. Anyway, the lad was so anxious ta lay eyes on it, he packed his coach up with Blaire and Brannock and set out ta see it for himself."

"Loch Calavie?" Cait didn't think she'd ever heard of the place before. She felt some of the weight lift from her heart. She wouldn't have known to look for Blaire there, wherever it was.

"Aye." He stood and crossed to his desk, rifling through his correspondence. "A note came for ye just yesterday from her." He held it out to her.

Cait tore into it like it held the moon and stars. She unfolded the paper and smiled at Blaire's bold, fairly masculine script.

Dearest Caitrin,

I do hope that I have returned before you receive this letter, but if that is not the case, I do hope everything went well with Elspeth. I am sure you arrived in time. You always do. Rhiannon is watching after El's stores, and Sorcha is in her own little world, like always.

Aiden was beside himself when he learned of his inheritance. While any sane person would wait for the snow to melt and the ice to thaw before setting out across the Highlands, my brother was quite impatient to make the journey. You should be relieved that you are not here with me. Briarcraig Castle is absolutely dreadful. The entire place reeks of must and decay. I keep thinking something died in here and no one took the time to bury the poor thing. It is easy to understand why the Grants left this crumbling castle to us. No one else would be fool enough to want it.

Brannock and I are quite anxious to return to civilization, as you can imagine. We are waiting for the roads to be safe enough for travel, and then we will leave this place. Whether Aidan returns with us or not, I neither ken nor care.

Missing you,
Blaire Lindsay

Cait pressed the letter to her heart and took deep breaths as she wiped happy tears from her eyes. She'd never been so happy to read a missive before in her life.

Her father poured himself a tumbler of whisky. "Feel better now?"

"Oh, aye," she sighed. "I thought somethin' dreadful had happened ta her. Not bein' able ta see her nearly drove me mad. I've never been unable ta see anyone I wanted, before. Well, no' until my recent travels. But that's neither here nor there."

A small smile tipped the corners of his lips, as though he knew a secret she did not. "Ye met someone whose future ye canna see?" He scratched his chin. "It wouldna happen ta be a man, would it?"

"Aye, a man. It's strange, Papa. I couldna see his future at all. I get nothin' whenever I try ta concentrate on his destiny. It's been quite frustratin'."

"This is a good thing," her father said and then released a long sigh, a full smile now crossing his lips.

Cait frowned at him. She would hardly refer to her dealings with Dashiel Thorpe as a positive experience. "Why is this a good thing?"

"It's the way with those who have yer gift, Cait."

She rubbed her forehead. Why had her father taken to speaking in riddles?

"Let me put it this way." He sat down beside her, still grinning like a fool. "Yer mother couldna see my future, either."

"No." Cait shook her head. He was wrong. "Mama told me that as soon as she saw ye, she kent ye were hers."

"Love at first sight," he agreed, patting her leg. "But she never could see my destiny."

Cait gaped at her father, and the room started to spin just a bit. This didn't make any sense at all. "Are ye certain?"

That seemed a rather important thing her mother left out of her training.

He chuckled. "Aye, lass, I ken for certain."

"Well, why no'?" Cait asked, sure that she was missing some vital detail that would make everything clear.

Her father shrugged his shoulders. "I'm no' sure. And there are no texts ta explain it. We always assumed it was because I was the one who was meant for her. And that what transpired between us was destined ta be natural and no' forced by any visions. A marriage couldna survive one member always bein' angry with the other one for things he hadna even done yet."

Cait ignored the wisdom in that, because it just

wasn't fair. For years, she'd been waiting to meet the man she would marry. She wanted to see their whole happy life displayed before her when she first laid eyes on the man. She saw everyone else's futures, good and bad. She should get a glimpse into her own.

"The man canna possibly be meant for me," she whispered.

"I beg to differ on that," a deep voice said from the doorway. She turned to find Dashiel Thorpe standing there, looking just as delectable as he had when he'd left her. And with his Lycan hearing, he'd heard each and every one of her father's comments. She groaned aloud.

Findlay frantically tried to block Dash as he stepped into the room, but the butler failed miserably. "I told his lordship I'd announce him, but apparently he had a mind of his own."

"A mind of his own, ye say?" Cait's father remarked as he crossed the room and accepted Dash's outstretched hand. "It's a very good thing when yer mind can be yer own. Particularly when ye have someone like Cait around."

She wasn't quite certain she liked the way her father said that.

"Dashiel Thorpe, the Earl of Brimsworth, heir to the Marquess of Eynsford," Dash introduced himself, full of pomp and circumstance, as he offered a slight bow.

Her father's smile vanished a bit. "Ah, English, are ye?"

"I'm afraid so," Dash replied with a mock frown. "Your beautiful daughter berated me over that fact all the way from Hampshire. Until I met Caitrin

Macleod, I had no idea that I needed to apologize for my nationality."

Her father laughed at that. "An Englishman with a sense of humor. How novel. Tell me, Lord Brimsworth, what brings ye ta Edinburgh?"

"Well, sir, I've come to ask for your daughter's hand."

A squeak escaped Cait's throat. She nearly swallowed her tongue. First he abandoned her and then, with no warning, appeared out of nowhere asking for her hand? When she got her hands on his neck…

"I see," her father continued. "And where are ye stayin' in town?"

Dash shook his head. "We were racing so fast to get here, sir. I haven't had time to give it much thought. Is there a nice inn you can recommend?"

Her father seemed to study Dash with his astute eyes. "Did ye truly travel all the way from Hampshire with my daughter?"

Cait gulped, remembering one moment of impropriety after another she'd experienced at Dash's hands along the Great North Road. She turned away to hide the blush she was sure crept up her cheeks. Heaven help her if her father ever learned of her indiscretions.

"Well, most of the way," Dash amended. "We were separated a few days after I was given a particularly potent sleeping draught. And then again when I had to go in search of a friend."

"A friend," Cait echoed. Some whore from his little book, no doubt.

But her father ignored her words, focusing instead on Dash's story. "Ye doona make potions," he flung at Cait.

"I made an exception." She glared at Dash. How dare he bring that up? And how dare he abandon her to search out some trollop in Glasgow?

Her father chuckled again. "Well, in that case, Lord Brimsworth, ye probably should remain here as our guest."

Over Cait's dead body.

"Thank you, sir," Dash replied, and he sounded so sincere she almost believed him.

Her father scoffed as though the offer was nothing. "It is the least I can do ta thank ye for seein' my Caitrin home safe ta me."

"Safely?" Cait scoffed. "Only if ye consider him abandonin' me before the border as seein' me safely home."

Dash's amber eyes flashed to hers, and Cait's breath caught in her throat. Then he turned his attention back to her father. "Your offer is very generous, sir, but I have a friend who traveled with me," Dash started.

Cait was certain her face was aflame. He'd brought some lightskirt to her home?

Mr. Macleod waved Dash into silence.

"Yer friend is welcome as well."

"And if it's not too much of an imposition," Dash continued, "I would like the opportunity to speak with you privately." He said the last quietly.

"I should think so, after ye traveled that far with my daughter."

"Papa!" Cait's cheeks were on fire. She *was* in the room. She wanted to crawl under the settee and die of embarrassment. But it wouldn't do her any good to leave the two of them to plot her future. It was hers, and she should get some say in it. "Would ye mind giving me a few minutes alone with his lordship?"

Her father's gaze raked across her, as though he was looking for something vital. "Ye want ta be alone with the earl? The same man, if I'm no' mistaken, ye drugged ta be rid of somewhere along the way?"

Cait nodded once.

"Well, after spendin' so much time with his lordship, I doona see what harm a few more minutes alone could do." Then her father started for the door and looked back over his shoulder at Dash. "I'll have Findlay take yer things ta one of the guest rooms."

"Thank you, Mr. Macleod."

"Doona thank me until after we've had our private conversation, my lord."

Then he was gone, leaving Cait alone with Dash. And now that she had him all to herself, she wasn't certain what to say to him. He took the choice from her, however, when he said, "Excuse me for just a moment."

Twenty-Two

Dash couldn't understand why Caitrin was frowning at *him*. He'd only stepped away for a moment to ask Mr. Forster how to proceed. The old shipbuilder had smiled, patted Dash on the back, and hastily whispered some words in his ear.

She was the one keeping secrets and, from the sounds of them, they were fairly large ones. He hadn't put all the pieces together yet, and he wasn't quite sure what the pieces made, but he was starting to connect them.

He didn't want to dwell on that too much, however. Mr. Macleod liked him. It was a coup he hadn't even dared hope for. Now, if he could just get Cait to smile at him again, everything would be perfect. Just seeing her soothed his soul, and listening to Forster's instruction would be much easier if he knew Cait would accept him.

Dash crossed the room to where she sat on a small settee and reached for her hand. He pulled her to her feet and wrapped his arms around her waist. She fit so perfectly there that he couldn't help but grin. How he'd missed holding her.

But Cait's frown deepened. Dash sighed at the sight. "What's wrong, angel?"

Her light eyes bored into his. "After ye left me by the side of the road, ye show up out of nowhere. And now ye're goin' ta ask him for my hand."

"As soon as possible," he agreed.

"And he'll say yes."

"That is good to know."

Cait swatted at his chest. "I doona ken what I think about it, and I do wish ye wouldna act so smug about the situation."

He winked at her. "I can't seem to help it. You know that's what I've wanted since the very first day."

"No, I think ye wanted ta gobble me up the very first day."

He laughed, so relieved that he wasn't doomed to a life without her. "No, lass, that was the first *night*. The very first day, I wanted to marry you."

She stalked away from him. "Ye ken what I meant. I doona want ye ta stay here. Go ta the Thistle and Thorn. That's where Benjamin stayed. Findlay can give yer man directions. It's nice and clean and…"

Dash felt the levity drain from him. "Don't push me away, Caitie. I've traveled so long and so hard to get here—"

"I dinna ask ye ta come."

"But I came anyway because you're my intended mate," he growled. "I know it. You know it. Even your father knows it. So stop being difficult."

He hadn't meant to sound so cranky, but it had been a long forty-eight hours, first running across four counties, then suffering through four hours of lectures on being one with his inner beast. And now that Dash was so close to getting all that he wanted, she was telling him to leave.

"Go ahead and bare yer teeth at me, Dashiel Thorpe. I'm no' afraid of ye. And I'm in no mood for this. I spent the last two days thinkin' that one of my dearest friends lay dead because I wasna here ta keep her out of the danger. I'm exhausted and drained, and I doona want ta do this right now."

That didn't make any sense to Dash at all, though he could see the anguish in her pretty eyes. "Caitie, we don't have to do this right now. But I *am* staying here. Your father has asked me to, and I'm accepting his offer."

"Doona ask him for my hand," she said softly.

"Why the devil not?" He felt his temper start to rise, and his blood began to simmer.

"Because I doona ken what I want."

Dash's heart sank. She was refusing him, and he hadn't even asked yet. "I know I'm a bit wild," he confessed. "But, I'm working on that. That's why I had to go to Glasgow."

He didn't even know what he was until a month ago. He'd always been told he was a monster. Chained up during every full moon, save the last one, to protect others from him. Maybe if she understood, it would be different. Then again, maybe not. And he couldn't risk it. He was doomed without her.

"I'll have that talk with your father, Cait. And I'll ask him for your hand."

She pursed her lips. "It willna do ye any good. I willna marry ye. No matter what. No' now."

Dash gritted his teeth. Why did the lass have to be so difficult? He knew she was glad to see him, he could tell it the moment he walked into the study.

"Don't be too sure about that." He started for the door. Hopefully, Mr. Forster would have some advice about how to go on from here.

❧

Cait slumped back down on her father's settee. She was certain her heart was breaking. And she was so confused. She wanted Dashiel Thorpe in so many ways, and she'd missed him desperately, but she didn't know what to make of him.

He was charming, then infuriating. Kind, then domineering. How was she to spend her life with a man she could never read? And what exactly was so important about Glasgow? He never did say.

On top of all that, the insufferable lout refused to give her time even to think about the situation, insisting on speaking with her father immediately. And he *still* hadn't asked her to marry him. During their travels, he *told* her she would marry him, and now that they were in Edinburgh, he was behaving the same way.

Well, she wasn't going to bind herself for life to a man who didn't trust her enough to give the matter some thought.

Cait rose from her seat and held her head high. No matter what her father thought, she had to convince him not to accept Dash's offer. She opened the door, prepared to go in search of her father, but found him in the hallway.

Jeannie was at his feet, tears pouring down her face. "I tried ta stop her, Mr. Macleod, but she wouldna listen ta me. And I ken he spent the night in her room more than once along the way."

Cait sucked in a mortified breath. Never in her wildest dreams would she have ever imagined that Jeannie would go running to her father. That she would betray her in such a way. How had she not seen it?

She watched her father's eyes move from Jeannie's heaving form to land directly on her. His face was hardened, like stone. She'd never seen such a fierce look in his eyes before.

"Doona worry, Jeannie," he said, keeping his eyes level on Cait. "Tomorrow Lord Brimsworth and Caitrin have an appointment with Mr. Crawford."

Mr. Crawford? The vicar? If Cait was the fainting sort, she would have swooned right there. Even still, all she was capable of was gasping.

"Papa!" she pleaded.

"Society has rules, Caitrin. And even ye have ta follow them. I suggest ye find yer earl. We'll be havin' that private conversation now instead of later."

She gulped.

"And ta keep talk down, ye better start sendin' out invitations. It will keep ye busy while I discuss matters with his lordship."

"But, I'd planned ta be there when ye had yer talk with him," she protested.

"I have some things I need ta say ta his lordship that ye willna be a part of," he snapped. "I've let ye have yer way most of yer life, Caitrin. But, in this, I will have *my* way." He motioned for her to pass. "Go ta yer room."

"But, Papa…" She let the words die in her throat as she saw the stormy look on his face.

"Now!" he snapped.

Caitrin turned and ran down the corridor toward the stairs. She heard her father call for Findlay and say, "Find his lordship and bring him ta my study." Then the heavy oak door slammed shut.

Dash settled into the chair across from Cait's father and took a deep breath. In all his life, he never would have expected to be as nervous as a scolded puppy when he asked for a woman's hand. He hadn't felt like this at all when he'd asked for Prisca Hawthorne's hand. He'd been all full of pomp and pride.

Now, he had none whatsoever. His fate was in the hands of this man. Well, sort of. He could always throw Caitrin over his shoulder and make off with her. And no one would ever be able to stop him. Aside from Mr. Forster. He *was* Lycan, after all.

But there was a part of him that really wanted to do this right. He wanted to ask for her hand and be accepted because he proved to her father that he could take care of her. And he always would. He didn't doubt that a bit.

"Do ye love my daughter?" Mr. Macleod boomed as he strode toward the sideboard to pour a drink.

Dash cleared his throat quickly and said, "Yes, sir, I do." If anyone had ever foretold that he would be purging his soul to this man, he'd have taken them to

Bedlam himself. But Mr. Forster had told him to tell the truth.

Mr. Macleod held out a tumbler of liquid, and Dash took it, noting that his hand trembled a bit. He snorted at his own situation.

"A bit dauntin', is it?"

"Well, you've yet to approve of my proposal, sir," Dash admitted. "You hold my future in your hands."

"What would ye do if I said no?" The man sat back and narrowed his gaze at Dash.

"I'd like to say that I'd accept your decision. But I'd be lying, sir," Dash answered with all sincerity.

The man fought back a grin, Dash could tell.

"What do ye love about her?" Mr. Macleod asked as he rummaged absently in a drawer. "Her pleasantness? Her desire to please? Her selfless acts of goodwill?"

"Honestly, sir?" Dash asked. Then waited for Mr. Macleod to nod. "She's obstinate and obnoxious as the devil. And I haven't seen much of her goodwill."

"Then it's her beauty, ye love?"

"That certainly helps," Dash admitted. He was going about this poorly. The frown on Mr. Macleod's face was evidence of that.

"My daughter is no' easy ta get along with."

"I'm aware of that. But, sir, I believe you're being a bit harsh. She's beautiful. But she also has a good heart, and I believe she's the other half of me."

"Do ye, now? I was wonderin' if it was just that she let ye sleep in her room during yer travels that made ye fall in love with her."

After a moment, Dash realized his mouth hung wide open, and he managed to close it.

"Dinna think I was aware of ye defilin' my daughter?"

"I never did—" Dash began.

But the older man cut him off. "Her maid informed me that ye slept in her room on more than one occasion. I dinna raise her ta be free with her favors. But I also may have neglected ta teach her about men such as yerself."

Dash jumped to his feet. He wouldn't let anyone assume the worst of Cait, even if it was her father. "I *did* sleep in her room, sir, but only because she had need of me."

"All women need ye, do they, my lord?"

Dash pinched the bridge of his nose between his thumb and forefinger, trying to push back the ache in his head that was slowly building. This had been much easier when he'd done it with Prisca Hawthorne's father. And when he'd practiced with Mr. Forster in the coach.

"Her maid snuck out every night to go and lay with your coachman, leaving Caitrin alone," Dash finally growled.

Mr. Macleod's eyes narrowed. "Continue." He steepled his hands in front of him.

"And during the night, I could hear her crying through the walls. I'm not sure why, Mr. Macleod, but my presence seemed to bring her peace."

Her father frowned slightly. "Those sorts of places can be very hard on her at times," he conceded.

At least the man was aware of the problem, "Honestly, sir, I went to her to soothe her. Not to defile her."

"And did ye? Soothe her?"

"Yes."

"I doona ken if I should be angry at the fact ye *soothed* her ta begin with or if I should be amazed at the fact that she took comfort with ye. She's typically a solitary soul, aside from her circle of friends."

Dash shrugged and sank back into the chair, then picked up his tumbler of liquor. "My intentions were noble."

"Ye've accepted her, even though ye ken she's a witch?"

"She's a *witch*?" Dash knew his eyes must have rounded with surprise. That possibility hadn't even occurred to him.

Mr. Macleod closed his eyes and shook his head, sighing deeply. "Aye, it's where she gets this power."

Dash felt as though the wind had been knocked out of him. "Power?" he echoed.

Her father nodded. "Aye, just like her mother, she can see the futures of all those she comes in contact with. In an unfamiliar settin', she's assaulted by continual visions of what's ta come. Supposedly, it can be quite painful."

A million thoughts raced through Dash's mind as he replayed their journey from start to finish. That's how she knew about the villain in the room beside hers at the first inn along the way. That's why she wanted to drive straight through, to avoid the horrors of one inn after another. That's why MacQuarrie kept going on and on about predetermined fate.

A witch! Niall Forster hadn't been insulting Cait's mother when he called her that; he was just being accurate.

Then one particular moment from their journey

stuck out, and Dash frowned. "Is that how she was able to make me sleep for days, some magical power?"

Mr. Macleod finally chuckled. "Aye, that's how. She doesna make potions very often. She must have been quite angry with ye."

"She's angry with me a lot," Dash admitted. Dear God, what else was she capable of? He'd *claimed* a witch? His Caitie. It was still hard to believe.

"Is she, now?"

The man's question brought Dash back to the present. "I beg your pardon?"

"Ye said she's angry with ye a lot."

Dash nodded. "Aye, but I think it's because of what's between us."

"And what would that be exactly?"

No matter that Mr. Macleod had laid the truth about Cait at Dash's feet, he wasn't about to tell the man he'd claimed his daughter under the power of a full moon. No man would want such a future for his daughter.

"I love her," he confessed, instead. Witch or not, she was his future, and he did love her. "I want to marry her. I want to be with her forever. I don't care if she can see futures or put hexes on people."

Mr. Macleod chuckled. "She's hardly that sort of witch."

Well, Dash supposed that was good. He wasn't sure. He sighed. "I just want time to make her see that we can make this work. May I have your permission to marry her?"

"Oh, aye," her father said as he waved his hand absently. "Do ye think I tell just anyone that my daughter is a witch? No, Lord Brimsworth, I was goin' ta insist ye marry her as soon as I learned she couldna see yer future. That indicates ye're the one for her. No' yer desire ta have her." He shot Dash a telling look. "And certainly no' that ye're an English lord."

"There's not much I can do about that fact, sir." Dash grinned.

"Ye canna help it that ye were born outside Scotland." Mr. Macleod rummaged in the drawer of his desk until he finally found what he sought. He pulled out a small box and handed it to Dash.

"I'd be delighted if ye used her mother's ring. I'm sure ye have one with yer own crest, but I'd like for Cait ta have this if she wants it. And it might buy ye some of her favor if ye're the one ta present it ta her."

"You know her so well," Dash murmured. Truth be told, he had no ring to offer his future wife. And he didn't have any Thorpe heirlooms on him. His father had never thought him worthy of even looking at the family crest, much less wearing a reminder of it at all times.

He opened the small box and looked at the delicate golden band, adorned with a ruby so dark it was almost black.

"There's a legend about that stone," Angus Macleod told him. "They say it was once the eye of a dragon."

Dash snorted. What rubbish. Lycans and witches were one thing, but dragons were something else.

"Ye can laugh all ye want," her father said. "Fiona's mother, God rest her soul, said her grandmother told her time and again how the *Còig* defeated the fearsome creature."

"The *Còig*?"

"Aye." Mr. Macleod looked directly into his eyes. "I want ta be very clear on one thing. If ye hurt my daughter or make her suffer in any way, it willna only be *her* powers ye should fear. Do ye ken?"

"I understand completely." Though he hadn't a clue what the man meant. Did Mr. Macleod mean that he would have to answer to him? Or to an even higher power?

"Good. Then it's settled. Tomorrow ye'll be married and—"

"But the banns," Dash began.

The older man laughed. "Ye are in Scotland, Brimsworth. Havin' time for the banns would be nice, but we doona have the luxury for such foolishness under the circumstances. It would be better ta see ye and Cait bound by marriage as soon as possible. I'll be fined for havin' an irregular marriage, but it's certainly doable. So Mr. Crawford will marry ye tomorrow, and that's that."

Dash stood and shook Caitrin's father's hand. He supposed, all things considered, it had gone better than he'd expected. What a relief it was not to have to wait an additional three weeks to officially make her his!

"There's a matter of a dowry ta discuss, my lord. But it can wait until tomorrow."

"I've no need—"

"But *I* do. Ye'll understand when ye have a daughter of yer own."

"Yes, sir," Dash acquiesced. He could afford the man that bit of pleasure, if it was truly what he wanted. "I'll need to find Caitrin," he remarked as they stepped out of the study and into the corridor.

"That will be a bit difficult, sir," the butler announced from just a few feet away.

"Why is that?" both men asked at the same time.

"She's gone."

Twenty-Three

CAITRIN HAD ONLY PACED HER ROOM FOR A MOMENT before she'd washed and changed her dress, then went in search of her friends. She was about to be locked in a marriage she didn't want. There was no way she'd be locked in her room, too, like a child who had been scolded and sent to bed with no supper.

The window creaked only a little when Caitrin pushed it open and stepped over the edge. Her foot easily found the rose trellis that hugged the wall, all the way up to the roof. She quickly climbed down and landed on two feet when she jumped over the rosebush at the bottom. Learning to do that had taken years, else she would have come home with a dress full of thorns and scratches on her legs. There could be no proof of her late-night meetings with her coven sisters.

She closed her eyes and immediately saw that Rhiannon and Sorcha were in the Fergusons' orangery. She smiled as she struck out in that direction.

Sorcha squealed and threw herself into Cait's arms as soon as she stepped over the orangery threshold, and Rhiannon smiled softly.

"I'm so glad ye're home. How's Elspeth? Did ye make it ta Hampshire in time?" Sorcha pelted her with question after question, while Rhiannon just smiled. Rhiannon was much more the sort to create a gentle wind to brush across your cheek than to hug you. And Cait had always appreciated that about her.

"Did ye see Lord William?" Sorcha asked, with a dreamy quality to her voice.

Cait sighed. Why Sorcha was obsessed with Lycan men she had never understood, not until recently, however. "Aye, and I met his *wife*."

Sorcha's dark eyes widened at that. "Wife?"

"It's for the best," Cait told her as soothingly as possible. "We have enough Lycans in our midst as it is." That was quite the understatement, but she didn't want to go into those details at the moment.

Sorcha frowned. "I canna agree with that. None of them are in our midst. Even Benjamin isna here."

"Aye," Rhiannon agreed. "But he and Elspeth will be back soon enough, isna that right, Cait?"

She nodded. "Ye ken that she'll deliver their daughter here, in our circle."

"She was worried the Westfields wouldna accept her. Is she all right?" Sorcha bit her bottom lip.

Cait told them all about the trip, or most of it, while they sipped tea in the orangery. Then Rhiannon stilled as she looked over Cait's shoulder toward the door. "Looks like we have visitors," she murmured.

Cait groaned aloud as she heard her father's voice behind her. "See, I told ye we'd find her here," he said loudly. She turned and was surprised to find him standing with Dashiel.

"And I thought I was finally free of them. If only for a moment." She let her face drop into her hands.

"Cait," Dashiel called. "May I speak with you a moment?"

"No' right now, Lord Brimsworth," she called back. "I'm a bit busy."

"I think I'll go visit Seamus Ferguson and leave ye ta face the wrath of the women, Brimsworth," her father chuckled before he abandoned Dash, laughing so loudly he could be heard through the closed door.

Rhiannon said quietly by her ear, "Lightnin'?"

"No' indoors," Cait hissed.

"I can use just enough ta shock him out of his trousers."

Dash approached until he stood directly behind Cait. "I appreciate the sentiment, but the only one who will be getting me out of my trousers is Cait. Tomorrow."

A gasp was Rhiannon's only response, and Sorcha covered her mouth to giggle. Then she flushed and giggled louder.

"Did ye just wink at her?"

"Not me, angel."

Cait stood up beside him. "Behave," she said as she elbowed him in the belly.

"Introduce us ta yer friend," Sorcha suggested.

"Sorcha Ferguson, Rhiannon Sinclair, this is Dashiel Thorpe, the Earl of Brimsworth—and he's *no'* my friend," Cait complained.

"That's right. I'm just her fiancé." He put his arm around her shoulders.

"Fiancé?" Rhiannon questioned, and Cait was certain her hazel eyes couldn't get any wider.

"We're to marry tomorrow," Dash informed her, sounding quite a bit proud of that fact.

"We are?" Cait groaned. But a little piece of her heart leapt at the thought.

He chucked her chin. "We are. So, stop pouting."

"I'm no' poutin'."

"Yes, you are."

Rhiannon leaned over and mumbled something to Sorcha, which made her giggle again.

"What did ye say?" Cait demanded.

"Nothin'." Rhiannon shrugged, a grin pulling at the corners of her mouth.

"What did she say, Sorcha?"

But Dash interrupted. "She said she thinks you may have finally met your match."

"How did he hear me?" As Rhiannon stood, a strong wind whipped at Dash's hair.

"It's nothin' nefarious enough ta require one of yer storms," Cait hissed.

"Then, how?"

"He's a beast!" Sorcha clapped her hands with glee. "I bet he is, just like Lord Benjamin and his brothers! Am I correct?"

Dash raised an eyebrow at Cait, as though asking for permission to answer the younger girl's question. She nodded quickly and shrugged her shoulders. "They do know about the Westfields."

"Ah." Dash smiled, charm oozing from him in waves. "Then yes, it is true. I am a Lycan."

"Oh, a beast of yer very own!" Sorcha cried. "I want one!"

"Ye have ta be careful of this one," Cait informed

her. "He bites."

Dash pinched her on the bottom, and she shot him a look that would have made most men slink away.

"Ladies, I know you've only just been reunited with Caitrin, but it's imperative that I talk with her. Will you be too perturbed with me if I steal her away?"

"Oh, no need ta steal her away." Sorcha laughed, tugging Rhiannon by the elbow. "We'll let ye have some time ta yerselves." As Sorcha walked by them, she reached over and lovingly rubbed a closed rose bud. After it opened beneath her caress, she plucked it and held it out to Dash. He took it with a small smile and a bow, and then tucked it into the buttonhole of his jacket.

When they were gone, Dash just stood and looked down at her. "More witches, I presume?"

So he knew? Her father must have told him. Not that Rhiannon or Sorcha had made much of a secret of their powers. She supposed it was a good sign that he hadn't run for the hills. And it was inevitable, she supposed, that he'd learn everything else, especially since she didn't have any choice about this marriage. "There are five of us."

Dash surprised her by saying, "I'll not force you into a marriage you don't want."

"Ye willna?" Cait's heart fell.

"No. But I do ask you to give me ample opportunity to sway you."

"And how might ye do that?" she breathed when his lips hovered just above hers.

"I plan to seduce you." Then he bent and covered her lips with his, insistently pressing until she opened for him and his tongue could sweep inside.

All conscious thought left her head when he lifted her arms to wrap them around his neck. She gratefully went up on tiptoe to press back against him.

"Easier than I thought," he mumbled, smiling against her lips before he pulled away.

She tugged at his neck to bring him back down to her. *Don't stop now. Seduce me. Please.* "Dash," she complained.

"How big is this orangery?" he asked, smiling broadly. Let the man gloat. She didn't care. "Cait?" He nudged her back to reality.

"It's huge, why?"

Dash swept her up in his arms and turned a corner, winding through rows and rows of plants, trees and other items Sorcha used in her work. When they reached the back wall, the only one not made of windows, he slowly released her and let her slide down his body. He grunted when she slipped across the bulge of his trousers.

"Sorry," she whispered, unsure of what she was sorry for. But the man appeared to be in pain.

"Don't be. You can fix it tomorrow."

"What?"

"Nothing," he laughed as he started to tug at the laces of her dress.

"What are ye doin'?"

"Seducing you." His lips trailed down her neck and across her collarbone, as soon as he'd bared it. He stopped briefly to tenderly kiss the bite mark he'd left on her.

"Ye canna seduce me, here."

Dash tugged at her hair until she tilted her head to

expose more of her neck. He licked and nipped his way down her chest.

"Is that a challenge, Cait?" Even in the shadows of the orangery, she could see the twinkle in his eye.

"No' a challenge," she said as he pulled her dress from her shoulder and exposed the top of her breast. "It's a fact. It isna proper."

"You think I give a damn about proper? If so, you don't know me very well."

His hand cupped her breast, his thumb brushing across the turgid peak until she feared she would melt right through the table. Then he took her a step further and bent to take her into his mouth.

Cait groaned aloud as she cupped the back of his head, her fingers threading through his hair.

"Shhh," he laughed, the sound like warm water over a waterfall, wild and untamed. "It isn't proper to make so much noise."

"Oh, shut up." She drew him even closer. "Dash," she pleaded.

"Yes, angel?"

"What are ye doin' ta me?"

"Seducing you," he said absently as he began to gather her skirt in his hands, his fingers brushing up her thighs, across her garters, and to the slit in her drawers.

"Are ye makin' love ta me?"

He raised his head and breathed across her mouth, "Do you want me to?"

She trembled beneath his intensity.

"I want—" She stopped, unable to put it into words.

"What do you want?" His fingers probed at her

heat, his thumb pressing lightly but insistently against the place that ached the most.

"You!" she cried. "I want *you*!"

"Then you shall have me," he said, withdrawing from her body. Then he righted her clothes and even fixed her hair, which had become untidy. "Tomorrow."

He kissed her forehead and turned, leaving her standing there alone, her pulse still thumping and her most secret of places drumming with a want she couldn't satisfy.

But he could. And he was well aware of it.

Twenty-Four

DASH GRINNED AS HE LEFT THE ORANGERY, QUITE pleased with himself. She wanted him. He'd known it, but hearing her say the words brought more joy to him than he could have ever imagined.

He marveled at his own ability to walk away from her. The smell of her desire and the rapid rhythm of her heart, beating with excitement, would have been a prelude for disaster before he'd met Cait. But, for some reason, he wanted to do everything right with her. He wanted to be respectable. He wanted to be her husband.

So, he'd tamped down his own lust, pushed the beast further away. He wouldn't take her like a common doxy in a public place. He'd tempted fate just by holding her bare breast in his hand as he brought it to his mouth.

Dash adjusted his trousers and reminded himself that tomorrow she would be his.

He started down the corridor, hoping a servant could direct him to Mr. Macleod. Then he heard an unhappy grunt, and a man the size of small ogre stepped into his path. The fellow's arms were the size of tree trunks, and he glared menacingly at Dash.

"Ye're Brimsworth?" he asked.

Shocked into silence, Dash nodded.

"And ye think ta take my Caitrin from me?"

Who the devil was this man? And why did he think he had a claim on Cait?

"Exactly who are you?"

"Wallace Ferguson. And I understand ye've asked for Cait's hand."

Dash nodded once more. He had asked Cait on more than one occasion who was waiting for her back home. Already he'd run into Alec MacQuarrie and now Wallace Ferguson. How many other Scots were there waiting in the wings for her? It was a good thing they were getting married tomorrow.

"Angus Macleod has given me his blessing. Perhaps you'll be invited to the festivities."

Wallace Ferguson growled. And though he was roughly the size of a baby elephant, Dash was a Lycan. The man didn't scare him—not much anyway. Although, the giant might possibly have some sort of power Dash was unaware of.

"Wallace!" One of Caitrin's friends, the pretty dark-haired lass who resembled a wood sprite, emerged from behind the over-sized Scot. Then she floated toward them and heaved a sigh. "I am sorry, Lord Brimsworth, but my brother did have his heart set on marryin' Caitrin. Ye'll have ta excuse his poor manners."

The giant frowned as his eyes raked across Dash as though he was sizing him up.

"I see," Dash replied.

"Wallace, Papa sent me ta find ye. He and Mr. Macleod are in the library. They'd like for ye ta join them there." She shooed him away with her hands and an impatient look. The oversized oaf growled a bit when he turned from them, though Dash was sure it was just a human growl intended to scare him. If the man wanted to hear a *real* growl, Dash would oblige.

With his shoulders slumped forward, Wallace Ferguson stomped down the corridor and rounded a corner, vanishing from view. Dash turned his attention back to the wood sprite. "You're Sorcha?"

Her grin brightened the hallway. "Aye, my lord. It is nice ta make yer acquaintance. Were ye lookin' for Mr. Macleod?"

He nodded.

"Well, ye might want ta wait a little while. Wallace is no' in the best mood this afternoon. Did ye leave Cait in my orangery?"

"Aye."

"Well, I've been sent ta find her, too. We've got invitations ta send out for tomorrow night."

Angus Macleod had told him on the way over that they would invite half the town to celebrate with them the next evening. It all seemed rather rushed. "Do you need help with the invitations?"

Sorcha laughed as she started for the orangery. "Ye are kind ta offer, but ye doona ken anyone in Edinburgh."

"I can still be of help." He followed the girl back inside the orangery, where his eyes immediately landed on Caitrin.

Just the sight of her kiss-swollen lips made him wonder how he'd had the strength to walk out of the room in the first place. She folded her arms under her chest and seemed unable to meet his eyes.

"There ye are!" Sorcha's sweet voice came from beside him. "We're startin' on yer invitations."

"Oh?" Cait said, focusing her eyes on the young witch.

"Of course." Sorcha bustled toward Cait and linked her arm with her friend's. "Ye have ta come and tell us who ye want ta send them ta."

"Do you mind if I tag along?" Dash asked.

When Cait finally looked at him, a pretty pink blush settled on her cheeks. "If ye must."

He winked at her and loved when her blush darkened. "I just met Miss Ferguson's charming brother. I think I'd best keep you in my sights."

Sorcha laughed. "I was almost afraid Wallace would trounce ye. But if you're really as strong as Lord Benjamin, ye have nothin' ta fear from my brother."

"He doesn't have some mystical power?" Dash asked, turning his attention back to the dark-haired lass.

She giggled. "Ye're in luck. He's my half brother, no' that it matters because only the women in my family have had mystical powers. Though I am startin' to wonder about the next generation. Elspeth has Ben, and now ye have Caitrin." She looked up at Cait. "What will yer sons be like?" she wondered aloud.

"I'm sure they'll carry their father's traits, like other Lycan lads."

Sorcha nodded, as though that made sense. "Do ye think this is some sort of pattern? Will we all get our own Lycan?"

Cait frowned as she directed her friend toward the exit. "I doona ken how many times I've told ye, Sorcha. I've seen the man ye marry and he is no' a Lycan."

Dash was quick to follow them into the hallway.

"Are ye certain, Cait? Maybe he is a Lycan, and ye just doona ken it."

She released a long sigh. "He is no' a Lycan, Sorcha. I am sure of it. Now, no more please."

⚬⚬⚬

Cait was aware of Dash's eyes on her backside all the way down one corridor and then down the next. Her heart still pounded wildly from his *seduction*. She wanted to curse him for stopping, even though she knew it was for the best.

Tomorrow, he'd promised.

Tomorrow he would be her husband, though she still wasn't quite sure how she felt about that. She wanted him. She needed him. She was halfway in love with him. But he was a bully, and she didn't appreciate the control he seemed to have over her.

"Here we are," Sorcha nearly sang as they reached the Ferguson's yellow parlor.

Inside, she found Rhiannon seated at a writing desk with a stack of foolscap, an ink bottle, and a quill. Her eyes widened in surprise when they landed on Dash.

"Lord Brimsworth, are ye goin' ta aid us with the invitations?"

Cait looked over her shoulder at him. Dash shook his head. "I just can't seem to tear myself away from my lovely bride-to-be."

Sorcha sighed beside her. "Doesna he remind ye of Lord Benjamin?"

"A bit," Rhiannon admitted.

Cait flounced down on a light yellow brocade settee, while Sorcha chose a seat across from Rhiannon. Then Cait leveled her most regal stare on Dash. "Do ye ken what is the most irritatin' trait of Benjamin Westfield's?"

An easy grin played about his lips, and he leaned his shoulder against the doorjamb. "Do tell, angel."

"We each have our own abilities," Caitrin began, "as ye probably have guessed. Rhiannon can control the weather inside and out. Sorcha can make things spring to life or wither away at will. Elspeth can heal almost anyone, with just the tips of her fingers."

He nodded as though he understood all of that. "What a wonderful gift."

"Aye," Cait agreed. "She has helped many people over the years, but Benjamin doesna approve and he's been a bit of a bully about the entire thing. I wouldna have even had ta set out for Hampshire in the first place, if he'd have simply let her use her powers ta heal his mother. Stubborn lout."

Dash's brow furrowed, and he stepped into the room. He folded his arms across his broad chest. "So I have Lord Benjamin to thank for leading you to me, do I?"

She scowled at him. That was not the point of the story. "What I am sayin', Dash, is—"

"That Westfield is a stubborn lout. Yes, Caitie, I heard you. But I might never have found you if you hadn't come to Hampshire. So I'll have to send him a token of my gratitude."

Sorcha released another wistful sigh, and Cait thought she might scream. How could her friend find such traits charming? "Doona ye have somethin' else ye can do? I think we're goin' ta be busy here for the rest of the day."

"The rest of the day?" He quirked an amused brow in her direction.

"Aye, and most of the night, too. Perhaps I'll be too tired ta even meet ye at the church in the mornin'."

He chuckled. "You'll be there, Caitie. You can deny it all you want, but we both know you want me." Then he bowed to her friends. "Ladies, I trust that I will see you both on the morrow."

Rhiannon nodded as she bit back a smile, and Sorcha giggled. "We wouldna miss it for the world, my lord."

Finally alone, Cait turned to her two coven sisters and frowned. "I doona ken how I'm goin' ta marry that bully."

"He loves ye," Sorcha said, grinning.

Caitrin held in a snort. If he loved her, he'd never told her. She didn't want to admit as much to her friends, however. "So, the invitations?"

"We've got them done," Rhiannon said. "We just need ta address them."

Cait nodded. "The Colsons," she began. "And the Gillespies." Then she stopped as her heart felt heavy. "I hate that Elspeth and Blaire are no' here. It doesna feel right."

Sorcha shrugged. "None of us were there for Elspeth, aside from me."

Cait frowned at her. "I was in bed recoverin' from a wolf attack."

"Ye still wouldna have been there. Besides, Elspeth will understand. She kens all about true love."

Sorcha and her fanciful ideas. Cait felt her ire building by the second. "But Blaire…" Guilt washed over her. She had seen that awful vision of Blaire's future, and, even though she knew her friend to be safe, she didn't know how much longer that would be.

"What about Blaire?" Rhiannon asked softly.

Cait shook her head. "I had a vision. I dinna recognize the place, but it was dark and she was being chased by a creature with dead, black eyes. It seemed as though it was huntin' her." They were in a place Cait had never seen before. Right now, Blaire was at Briarcraig Castle, a place Cait had never been. Her heart clenched.

She had to get to her, to warn her before it was too late. She leapt from the settee and started for the door.

"Caitrin!" Sorcha called after her. "The invitations."

"Invite whoever ye want."

She flew down the steps of Ferguson House to the streets of Edinburgh and raced toward her home. She barely noticed the other pedestrians gaping at her as she ran at full speed. Within minutes, she bustled up the steps of Macleod House. Findlay opened the door for her, and she nearly threw her pelisse at him. "I need a coach, Findlay. And a valise."

"Running out on your husband-to-be?" Alec MacQuarrie stepped into the hallway from a parlor.

Caitrin gaped at him. "What are ye doin' here?"

"I've been waiting to speak with you all day," Alec said.

He hadn't returned to his own home? He'd been waiting *here* since this morning? She owed him better than that, but she couldn't do so now. She had to find a way to get to Loch Calavie. "Alec, I doona have time right now, but—"

"Are you really marrying Brimsworth?"

Cait swallowed. She really was, she supposed. But it would have to wait. The words were stuck in her throat, but she managed to nod.

He stepped closer to her, his dark eyes filled with pain and regret. "Don't do it, Cait. I'll do whatever you want, if you will just call this off."

She couldn't have this conversation with Findlay looking on. So she grasped Alec's arm and dragged him back to the parlor where he had been so dutifully waiting all day. She swiftly shut the door behind her. "Alec, please."

"I'm the one begging *you*, Cait. I don't know what you see for me, but I know what's in my heart, and I love you."

Alec loved her. He'd told her that before, and yet she was marrying a man who had never said those words to her. She thought her heart might break. "I'm no' for ye, Alec. Ye have ta believe me."

"Shouldn't I get a say in that?" he asked, his voice stricken.

Tears started to fall down Cait's cheek. It wasn't fair. "Please. This is hard enough for me as it is, Alec. And I'm worried about Blaire."

"She's not here?"

He was apparently unaware of everything that had transpired today, with the exception of her betrothal. She shook her head. "She's at some crumblin' castle near Loch Calavie. Briarcraig Castle, wherever that is. It's in the Highlands somewhere. I have ta get ta her."

Alec brushed away her tears with the pad of his thumb. "I'll go with you. We'll find her together."

Cait blinked at him. She didn't know what to say, but she knew she couldn't take him up on his offer. It would be the most unconscionable thing she could do.

"Come with me, Cait," he urged. "I'll love you all of my days, I swear it."

She shook her head. "Ye canna go with me. Stop makin' this so difficult, Alec. Ye doona ken what ye're askin' me ta do."

He tipped her face up to look at him. "Do you really want to marry Brimsworth?"

Did she want to marry Dash? She didn't want to be forced into it, but she did want him. Alec deserved her honest answer. Perhaps it would help him move to his intended path. Cait nodded.

His face twisted in agony, and Cait felt a fresh wave of tears trail down her cheeks. In another life, another time, Alec MacQuarrie would have been the man for her.

"You can't go after Blaire then, Caitrin. You're supposed to marry the man tomorrow."

"But I have ta," she stressed. "Blaire is in danger."

Dash would understand. She'd explain it to him and he would… think she was running from him again.

"Did you ever love me?" Alec's strained voice tore at her heart.

"Aye," she choked out. "But no' the way ye need."

He lowered his head and pressed his lips to hers. It was tender and sweet and so far in every way from the all-encompassing passion she felt in Dash's arms. It was a good-bye to what could have been.

Slowly, he lifted his head, and the anguished look in his dark eyes twisted her belly in knots. "I can't stand back and watch you marry him," he whispered. "So, I'll go after Blaire. You should stay here." Then he stepped away from her. "Briarcraig Castle by Loch Calavie?"

She managed to nod.

Alec opened the door and sucked in a strangled breath. Cait looked up to see Dashiel Thorpe standing in the hallway.

"Miss Ferguson said you were upset and left in a hurry," he said smoothly, though his amber eyes seemed filled with rage.

Alec nodded his head toward Dash. "Best of luck to you, Brimsworth."

"And to you, MacQuarrie." Dash answered, but he never took his eyes off Cait.

The door closed softly behind Alec, and Cait turned to watch out the window as he walked away. His stride was strong, but there was a stoop to his shoulders that nearly broke her heart.

She wiped a tear from her cheek.

Twenty-Five

"YOU RAN BACK HERE FOR AN ASSIGNATION WITH MacQuarrie?" Dash demanded. Ire coursed through his veins, and he was having a difficult time restraining his temper.

"Ye doona ken what ye're talkin' about." She sniffed and turned away from him toward a window overlooking the front walk.

He took a deep breath. MacQuarrie was gone, which was what he'd wanted since he'd met the man. Dash walked slowly into the room until he stood behind Cait as she stared blankly out the window. His heart hurt a bit when she brushed a tear from her cheek.

Dash closed his eyes tightly. He couldn't let himself touch her, not until he knew what was in her heart.

"If you love him so much, I'll go and bring him back for you," he said. It would kill him, but he'd do it. He'd suffer the consequences.

She spun around quickly until she faced him, a blue fire lighting her eyes. Then she poked her finger into his chest.

"If I loved *him*, I would have asked him ta stay, ye

beast. But I dinna. Instead, I've doomed myself ta a lifetime spent with the likes of ye."

"If you find me so detestable, Caitie…" He let his voice trail off. "Damn it all to hell," he bit out, running a frustrated hand through his hair. "Do you want to marry me or not? Can you accept who I am?"

Cait turned back to look out the window. She didn't respond.

That was all the answer he needed. He quickly quit the room, dashing up the stairs to his borrowed quarters as quickly as he could. He'd get his things, round up Niall Forster, call for his carriage, and be out of her life forever.

Her quick footsteps beat a rhythm against the wood floor as she ran behind him. But at the last minute, she turned and went in the other direction. It was better that way. He could leave without making a scene. It would rip his heart out, and he would be doomed to live a life alone. But she could find a modicum of happiness, were he not in her life; which apparently was what she wanted.

Dash saw Mr. Forster stick his head out the door next to his own. Then the arse grinned and pulled his head back, slamming his door closed before Dash could ask him what he should do. Some mentor he turned out to be.

He barged into his own room and opened his valise.

"Doona forget yer journal of debauchery, Lord Brimsworth," Cait sneered from the doorway, where she held out his small leather-bound journal.

"I no longer need it. Toss it in the fire." It was of no use to him. If he couldn't be with her, he couldn't be with anyone. But would he if he could? If he really and truly asked himself, he would have to say no. He wanted Cait. And by God, he *only* wanted Cait.

"No more women, Lord Brimsworth?" she taunted from the doorway. "Surely ye'll need yer journal so ye can find the plump actress who has that little trick she does with her tongue."

He closed his eyes and stilled, wincing a bit. She'd obviously read more of his book. "That was in the past," he mumbled.

Then she opened his little journal and flipped through the pages. She read aloud, "Lord Ridgely told me today he plans to pension off his lovely mistress, as he has suddenly discovered he loves his wife and wishes to pursue both lust and love with his one and only, the one who bears his name. I cannot imagine ever feeling such an irrational emotion as love. I believe it's a myth fabricated by those raised on faerie tales and dreams. I may pay the fair woman a visit."

Dash growled low in his throat. It had once been a noise that stopped grown men in their tracks. But Cait just narrowed her eyes, raised her hand, and threw the book at his head with such force he had to duck or she'd quite possibly have taken out his eye.

With that, Dash stepped toward her, caught her around the waist, and drew her quickly against him. She struggled and smacked at his chest until he caught her wrists in his hand and pulled them behind her back, imprisoning her against him.

"I doona believe in faerie tales and dreams, either, my lord." She still held her chin high, meeting his eyes as he looked down at her.

"You let him kiss you?" He knew she did. He'd heard most of the words they'd spoken quietly in the parlor clearly through the closed door. And he could still *smell* MacQuarrie on her. He jostled her when she didn't answer and repeated the question. "Didn't you?"

"Aye, I did."

He growled again. God help MacQuarrie after Dash got his hands on him.

"I had ta ken," she said softly, bringing his attention back to her.

"You had to know what?"

"I had ta ken…" Her words came out broken, choked by a sob. "…if his kisses make me feel like yers do." She sniffed loudly. "A-and I had ta tell him good-bye."

Dash felt physical pain within himself when her eyes filled with tears. He loosened his hold on her hands, and she buried her face against his jacket.

"And his kiss… did it make you feel like mine?" His whole world hinged on her answer to that one question.

"No," she mumbled against his chest.

"No?" Dare he hope?

"Has somethin' happened ta yer hearin', Dash?" she groused at him. "I ken better than anyone that ye heard me just fine."

"Say it again."

"No one makes me feel the way you do," she admitted.

Then Cait stuck out her chin, and Dash couldn't resist the invitation. When he touched his lips to hers, she shivered in his arms and her pulse pounded like mad.

"I want to rip your clothes off and lay you upon the

bed. Then make love to you for hours," he whispered close to her ear.

"Then what's stoppin' ye?"

"You've yet to say your vows to me."

"Ye've yet ta ask me."

"I *did* ask you, you little witch!" Dash growled at her obstinacy.

"No, ye never did, ye beast!" She punched his shoulder.

"I *am* a beast," he muttered. "Bloody hell." She looked up at him, her eyes still wet with the pain that he'd caused. He dropped to one knee before her.

"Caitrin Macleod, will you do me the honor of being my wife?"

"Is that the best ye can do?" she asked, tears shimmering on her lashes but a smile on her face.

"What more do you want of me, Cait?"

She turned her body and sat down on his extended knee. Then she cupped her hand around the shell of his ear, leaned close, and whispered, "I want all of ye."

∾

Cait squealed as Dash swept her up in his arms, kicked the bedroom door shut, and tossed her into the center of the bed.

"Naughty little girls who tease big, bad wolves deserve to be mauled," he said, a half-smile upon his face as he landed on top of her and pushed her toward the headboard.

"Did I ever tell ye about the time I *was* mauled by a wolf?"

He stilled above her. "By a Lycan?"

"No, by a real wolf. Elspeth had ta heal me."

His eyebrows knit together as he rolled from atop her and propped his head on his hand. "What happened, Caitie?"

"It was poor judgment on my part that put me in the situation."

"That I don't doubt," he teased. "Tell me, anyway."

Cait sighed. "At the time, I was wholeheartedly opposed ta Elspeth's relationship with Benjamin Westfield, and I'd gone on a walk in the woods with Jeannie ta clear my mind. I get a little annoyed when people doona heed my counsel."

"I'll keep that in mind." He smiled at her. "What happened?"

"Well, I wasna payin' attention ta where I was, and I stumbled across a wolves' den." She shrugged. "The mother was just protectin' her pups."

A shadow of something crossed his face.

"What is it?" she asked as she smoothed his hair from his brow.

Dash closed his eyes and pressed his cheek against her hand, then turned and kissed the center of her palm. "It's nothing," he said absently.

Cait sat up. "It's no' *nothin'*."

"You'll think I'm daft."

"I already think ye're daft, ye big lout. Now tell me what ye're thinkin'. I canna read yer mind, ye ken."

"That's right. I'm the only man you cannot predict." He playfully tugged a lock of her hair.

"Doona remind me," she grunted. "And stop changin' the subject."

Dash closed his eyes and breathed, as though

steeling himself. "Will you be as protective of our pups as the mother wolf was of hers?"

Cait crossed her legs beneath her, tucking her skirts around her. "We willna truly have *pups*, will we?"

Dash chuckled. "Of a sort, I believe. Although I'm not completely sure. I never even knew what I was until I met the Westfields. I thought I was some sort of monster, an anomaly, a cruel trick of fate. 'Revelations' was a particularly difficult book for me to get through in my theology studies."

Cait tried to work out the problem in her head. "So, the father who wasna yer father never told ye what ye were, either? Ye grew up completely without any idea that ye're a Lycan? With no one ta stand up for yer best interests?"

Caitrin could see that she'd touched a place where no one else had been before with him.

"Think of it as though you had your gift of clairvoyance but you were only permitted to use it every so often. And when you *did* use it, it was uncontrollable. So much so that you had to be bound to prevent you from using that part of yourself. A part you're born with. A gift that is *supposed* to be a part of you, if you could only figure out how to use the bloody thing."

"That would be positively dreadful."

"And when you were permitted to use it, you had no idea how to control it."

"Ye only turn ta a wolf the night of the full moon?"

"Only that one night. Correct." He suddenly looked very serious.

"So, I'll be able ta see what ye look like in yer

wolfen form. Which'll prepare me for our *pups*." She laughed with that last word, exaggerating it more than necessary. "I'll be fine with it. But I'll tell ye right now that ye're the only one who'll be allowed ta nibble on my fingers."

He took her hand in his and squeezed it. "No. It will not be like that."

"What do ye mean?"

"I mean I'll share every part of myself with you, Caitie. And I'll make you happy. I'll be a good father. I might even nibble various parts of you. But I'll not share the night of the moonful with you."

"But Ben and Elspeth are together when the moon is full. And so are the other Westfield brothers and their wives."

"They're not like me." He sat up and took her hands in his. "They're not wild. They're controlled." He peeled back the shoulder of her gown. "Look how I hurt you. And I didn't even intend to."

"Ye just wanted ta seduce me."

"Oh, I still want that. Quite a lot," he growled as he sat up and rolled her beneath him. His knee quickly slipped between her legs and parted them.

"Wait." She tapped his shoulder, forcing him to remove his lips from the side of her neck, where they tickled a path up toward her ear.

"Yes, angel," he sighed as he lifted his head.

"I need ta tell ye somethin'."

"Can it wait? I'm making love to you here."

"Doona brush me off by play-actin' ta change the subject, Dashiel Thorpe. I can see right through ye." She took his face between her hands and forced him to look at her, his eyes like amber pools she could surely drown in.

"I'll love our pups. And I will protect them with my life, if needed. The fact that they could be Lycan will no' make me treat them any differently. Unless, perhaps, it's ta love them more because they're part of ye."

He kissed her softly and tenderly, until he could do so no longer. When he had her panting beneath him, he pressed his forehead against hers and breathed, "If you don't get out of my room, I won't be responsible for what I do to you."

"I dare ye," she giggled.

"No," he said as he rolled from atop her. "I want to do this right." He pulled her to her feet and prodded her toward the door.

"But, Dash," she complained. If anyone had ever told her she would be begging a feral Lycan to make love to her, she'd have thought them daft.

"I've never done anything honorable in my life, angel. Until now. Out."

Their parting was almost painful, and Cait couldn't wait until the next day to marry the big oaf. Dash finally shoved her from his room and firmly closed the door behind him. Then the lock clinked as he put one last barrier between them.

"Dashiel," she whispered softly through the crack in the door.

She heard him chuckle on the other side. "Go to your room, Caitrin, before I forget my vow to wait and do this properly. I'll have your skirts up around your ears, and you won't even remember what happened."

"Promises, promises," she teased back.

She assumed the thunk she heard was his fist hitting the door.

❧

Mentors should be useful, or what was the point in having one? Dash knocked again on Forster's door. Where was the man, for God's sake? Then he heard the old Lycan shuffle up the steps. Dash turned around and watched the shipbuilder stop on the final step, a twinkle in his green eyes.

"I assume everythin' turned out well with yer betrothed."

Dash scowled at him. "I need your help, Forster."

The man shook his head and gestured for Dash to enter his room. Then he joined him and shut the door behind them.

"What help do ye need, Dashiel? It sounded as though ye had everythin' well under control."

Control. He said the word as if it was a curse. "I'm marrying Caitrin tomorrow."

"Aye, I heard. Congratulations."

Dash raked a hand though his hair. How could the man not see his anguish? "What do I do, Forster? When I have Caitrin all to myself?"

The old man laughed. "I'm sure ye'll figure that part out, lad. Do ye really have a journal of debauchery?"

Dash groaned. So Forster had heard every word Cait had said to him, not that he should have been surprised. "That was a lifetime ago."

Forster dropped into a wooden chair by a window and shook his head. "Ye've clearly been with women in the past, Dashiel. I doona ken what ye're askin' of me."

Dash scrubbed a hand across his face. Niall Forster was going to be the death of him. "I have had my share of whores, sir. But Cait…"

"Before, in yer previous lifetime, how did things go with the lasses ye bedded?"

No one had ever asked such a question of him before, and he'd really rather not discuss the details. The old man shook his head, a look of impatience crossing his face. Though Dash didn't think Forster had any right to be impatient about a bloody thing.

"Were ye able ta control yerself, or did the beast inside ye take over?"

That's what he was asking? Dash breathed a sigh of relief. "I struggled to be in control."

Forster nodded his head. "I figured as much, just wanted ta be sure." He drummed his fingers atop the arm of his chair. "Ye have ta accept what ye are, Dashiel. Yer Miss Macleod seems as though she accepts the truth about ye. Try takin' a page out of her book, so ta speak. Doona shield yerself from her. Let her in ta every part of yer soul."

"You're saying to let the beast have its way."

Forster sighed. "Ye talk about it as if it wasna a part of ye. *Its way*. Ye *are* the beast, Dashiel. Embrace it."

The man was daft. Embrace it. What a bunch of drivel. The beast would hurt Caitrin, and Dash could never allow that to happen.

"When was the last time ye had a refreshin' run?"

Dash shook his head. Forster truly *was* daft. "A refreshing run?"

"Aye, just ye runnin' through the forest or across an open meadow, the crisp air whippin' through yer hair?"

"I ran all the way from County Durham to Glasgow."

A beleaguered sigh escaped Forster. "That was no' a refreshin' run."

"Hardly," Dash agreed.

"That's no' what I'm askin' ye, Dashiel. Ye were in a bit of a hurry when ye ran from England. What I'm suggestin' is a wild run through the park. Helpin' ye get in touch with the beast inside ye. Let him loose in a safe place."

"A safe place?"

Finally, Forster smiled. "I ken just the place. Arthur's Seat is the highest point in Edinburgh. It's what's left of some ancient volcano. Anyway, legend has it that the place has magical properties. Healin' ones at that.

"Go ta the base of the hill at Dunsapie Loch, and have yerself a refreshin' run. Doona think about reinin' in yer beast. Doona think about yer impendin' nuptials. Doona think about the trouble ye left behind in England. Just listen ta the breeze. Watch the gentle lap of the loch. Close yer eyes, absorb the nature inta yerself, and run ta the top of Arthur's Seat."

Go for a run. That was his mentor's advice? Dash's shoulders sagged forward. He was truly doomed. He needed to learn to make the beast do his bidding. To learn to rein it in. To learn to control it.

He didn't need to *become one with it*. He didn't need to *accept it as part of himself*. What nonsense. Obviously, Major Forster had sent him on a fool's errand when he sent him to his cousin. Perhaps that was his penance for torturing Lord William and Prisca Hawthorne the way he had. He sighed deeply.

"Stop thinkin'," Mr. Forster urged as he spun Dash around and gave his shoulder a none-too-gentle shove. Dash stumbled forward, a growl in his throat. He turned back toward the old shipbuilder, so frustrated he was ready to bare his teeth at the wizened Lycan. But before he could even raise his lip, the old man raised his hand and thumped Dash right in the middle of his forehead.

"Ow!" Dash cried as he reached up to rub the offended area. "What did you do that for?"

Mr. Forster shook one finger in Dash's face. "If ye think ye can intimidate me with yer scowl or yer snarl, ye have another think comin', pup."

"You didn't have to hit me," Dash mumbled as he absently rubbed his head.

"Ye should be happy I dinna take some rolled-up newsprint ta ye, ye ungrateful little mutt," Forster mumbled to himself as he turned away from Dash. "I come here for a love story, and all I get is a sulkin' Lycan who willna listen ta what I tell him. He's even afraid ta go for a simple run at Arthur's Seat, as I have instructed."

"I'm not afraid," Dash tried to explain.

"Aye, Dashiel," the old man said. "Ye *are* afraid. Afraid of what ye'll find when ye allow yerself ta be all that ye can be." He turned back around, the sadness in his eyes instantly making Dash regret his belligerence. "I can tell ye right now that a Lycan canna love another until he learns ta love himself, Dashiel."

He loved himself. Didn't he? And he loved Cait. He knew he loved Cait. If he didn't, it wouldn't hurt nearly as much when he wasn't with her, would it?

"Ye can stand there and lament about what a daft

old man I am, or ye can go and follow my instructions. The choice is yers."

Dash groaned inwardly as he turned and slunk from the room, feeling like a scolded puppy with his tail between his legs. Mr. Forster was disappointed in him. Just like his father had been his whole life.

The difference was that he actually *cared* if Mr. Forster was angry at him or not. Unlike his father, the old man *had* tried to help him. He owed it to him to at least heed his advice. Dash had no doubt that it was a fool's errand. But it was the old man's request. And he'd do it.

Dash stepped out into the cold and tugged his cloak tighter about his body. "Become one with the beast," he chanted to himself. "Enjoy a refreshing run." He snorted out loud at the last.

Dash focused on not reining himself in and just let his body move. He had a fairly good idea of where Arthur's Seat was located, though it was impossible to see through the dense fog that clouded the area.

As he ran, the coolness of the night crept across his skin. Rather than curse the cold, he embraced it. He let it buoy his senses. The air smelled cleaner. The sounds of the night were the innocent sounds of water lapping against the loch. They weren't his own thoughts of what a disappointment he was. It was somewhat freeing just to enjoy the quiet of the night, he had to admit. He took a deep breath. The beast within him calmed, just as he did.

The fog grew even thicker as he reached the base of Arthur's Seat. He'd never seen a mist so heavy and all encompassing, as though it wrapped around the base of the hillside, hiding it from view. Dash blindly searched for hand- and footholds as he climbed the side of the small mountain.

The wind picked up, buffeting him as he continued to scale the wall. It was a matter of pride at this point. He *would* find the tip of Arthur's Seat. Dash closed his eyes and took a deep breath, then quickly and stealthfully ran toward the peak.

He embraced the strength that came with being Lycan, for it allowed him to heave his body up the craggy mountainside. He reveled in the sinewy cords of his body, for his muscles did not fail him.

When he finally reached the top, he turned to look down at the city of Edinburgh. Yet the fog was so thick that he could see nothing. He couldn't even see the ground beneath his feet.

He stepped forward and was surprised to find himself suddenly in an area clear of fog where a toasty fire burned slowly. He cocked his head to the side and listened as he heard a soft voice chanting nearby.

And that was when he noticed the heap of clothing lying on the ground by the fire. A woolen gown. A chemise and drawers. Stockings. He turned to look around, completely bewildered. Had he stumbled upon an assignation? A tryst between lovers?

"I should have guessed that ye would no' pay heed ta the heavy fog I laid in yer path, Lord Brimsworth."

"Beg your pardon?" he called back toward the sound.

"The wind that nearly knocked ye from the side of the hill. And the fog that obscured yer path. That was all my doin'. I wasna in the mood for company. But ye were relentless."

Dash glanced down at the pile of clothing. "It

would appear that you were not expecting company," he agreed. Then he turned his back to the pile of clothes. "Which one are you?" he asked, fully aware that he must be talking to one of Cait's coven sisters. If only he could remember which one had which power. One of them could control the weather. Not the wood sprite. The other one.

"Rhiannon," was all she said. He heard the dress as she snapped it, shaking the wrinkles from it. There was a naked witch behind him. At one time, he'd have been beside himself with lust. The beast would have tried to take over and consume her. Yet the beast wanted no part of this witch. Dash only wanted Cait. And he felt an instant sympathy for the weather-disturbing witch. It discomfited him a bit.

He took a deep breath. "Miss Sinclair," he began. "Do you often stand naked at the top of Arthur's Seat?"

"Only when I'm feelin' particularly sad, honestly," she admitted on a sigh. "When I'm in the doldrums, I like ta come here and let my emotions wreak all the havoc they like. Do ye ken the townspeople think there was a volcano inside the mountain?"

"There's not?"

"There may have been at one time," she shrugged. "But the disturbances here are usually mine."

He turned to face her, happy to find that she was now clothed. "Would you care to discuss the cause of your melancholy mood?"

"No' particularly," she sighed again. A cold rain instantly drenched him. "Oh, drat," she said as she wiped a tear from beneath her eye. "I'm sorry. I dinna intend ta do that."

Dash shook his head, flinging cold water droplets in every direction.

"Come closer ta the fire. I'll send a warm breeze ta dry ye off, Lord Brimsworth."

The fog stirred, pushed by a gentle wind that did warm his bones a bit.

"I would offer ye some tea, but I'm no' quite prepared for guests," she said as she motioned toward a log by the fire. "But ye may sit, if ye like."

"I should be going back," Dash remarked absently. He was quite out of his element, stuck on a mountaintop in a circle of fog with a melancholy witch who controlled the weather.

"I'll clear the fog for ye in a moment," she said quietly. "I only want a few more minutes."

Dash sat down cautiously on the log and held his hands out to the fire. The flames leapt toward him, coming just close enough to warm him but not singe him. That is, if he held very still.

"They willna harm ye. Ye can relax."

"That's not very easy to do around you, Miss Sinclair. I have a feeling I've only seen a small sample of your powers tonight."

A smirk crossed her lips. "Quite true."

"Why so sad?" he finally asked. He felt a great sympathy for this witch. Her pain was great. And he could nearly feel it in the wind, the rain, the cold.

"It's difficult to say good-bye to good friends," she said quietly. Then she blurted out, "Cait has seen a future for Sorcha. A happy one."

"Has she not seen one for you?"

"No' yet." She shrugged. "If she has, she hasna told

me. She hasna seen one for Blaire, either, so I'm no' too worried." Lightning cracked across the sky. "Blast it all," she cursed.

Dash raised his brows and looked toward the heavens, then shot her a telling glance.

"Aye, that was mine."

"I would wager you can throw a devil of a temper tantrum if you ever have the right provocation, Miss Sinclair."

She finally smiled. "Doona tempt me." She stood up and shook the dust from her skirts. Her delicate little hand rose to lie flat in front of her pursed lips. She blew gently, and the fog began to stir. Within moments, it had completely dissipated. The city of Edinburgh lay below them. He could even see Charlotte's Square and Cait's fashionable townhouse. He imagined her snug in bed, the counterpane tucked beneath her chin. Then he imagined himself wrapped around her.

"Make her happy, Lord Brimsworth."

"Never doubt it," he guaranteed. And, for once, the beast within him wasn't demanding that he do the opposite of what his heart desired.

Twenty-Six

TOMORROW COULDN'T COME SOON ENOUGH. DASH needed Caitrin like he needed the air he breathed. Just a few more hours. He'd been waiting for nearly a fortnight. A few more hours wouldn't kill him. It just seemed like it would.

Actually, he could use a strong whisky. That should take the edge off and help him sleep. The entire house was silent. So he quietly made his way to the first floor and down the corridor toward Angus Macleod's study.

Dash could see a warm light under the door and cocked his head to one side. Had Caitrin's father left a fire blazing in his grate? He knocked lightly.

"Come," his future father-in-law called.

Dash pushed the door open and poked his head inside to find the older man poring over papers on his desk. "I hope I'm not disturbing you, sir."

"Ah, Lord Brimsworth, come in, come in. I stayed at the Fergusons' for dinner tonight. I hope ye dinna miss me."

Dash shook his head and then shut the heavy oak door behind him. "I actually took dinner in my room."

"Nervous?" the Scot asked, gesturing to one of the dark leather seats in front of his desk.

"A bit," Dash affirmed. But only because he would have Caitrin all to himself the next day. She'd be his. And all he could think about was their wedding night. It wouldn't do for him to tell the man that all he could think about was rolling his daughter beneath him and taking her as a husband takes a wife.

As Dash dropped into the chair, Mr. Macleod rose from his. "Would ye care for a drink, my lord?"

He nodded, hoping he didn't appear too eager. He didn't want the man to think he was a drunkard. When did he start to care what others thought about him? "Thank you. That would be nice."

Angus Macleod began to pour some whisky from a decanter on his sideboard, and then he raised his gaze to Dash. "Caitrin tells me ye're of the same variety of beast as Benjamin Westfield and Desmond Forster."

"Does that bother you?"

His future father-in-law smiled, stepping forward and offering Dash one of the snifters. "Who am I ta judge, Brimsworth? I married a witch, and I sired one."

Well, that was generous of him, though it wasn't quite the same thing. Dash relaxed just a bit.

"Since ye're awake," Angus Macleod began, "we might as well finish our earlier conversation."

"Sir?"

"Caitrin's dowry."

Somehow, with all the events of the afternoon, he'd forgotten about that. "Of course."

"What lands do ye possess?"

Dash shrugged. "*I* have a set of rooms in London. Everything else is part of the marquessate. Eynsford's holdings are extensive. There's the family seat and manor in Kent. A hunting box in Derbyshire. A home in Mayfair. Cottages in both Gloucestershire and Cambridgeshire."

"Well, ye can add a home in Berwickshire ta the list."

Dash sat back in surprise. He hadn't expected that. Honestly, he hadn't expected anything save a few hundred pounds. He'd have given up his entire inheritance for Caitrin. "Your daughter doesn't like to travel."

"Ah, well," the man laughed, "ye'll have ta wait for me ta stick my spoon in the wall before ye can take Macleod House from me."

A rare warmth rushed up Dash's neck. "That's not what I meant, sir. I—"

Angus Macleod just laughed some more. "Doona fash yerself, Brimsworth. I ken ye dinna mean that." Then his smile vanished as he resumed the seat behind his desk. "Anyway, the Mordington property is Cait's. Really, it was her mother's dowry, and someday it'll belong ta yer daughter.

"It's the ancestral seat of the seers, though only Cait's line has survived the witch hunts of the last few centuries, at least as far as we ken. Since ye have a secret of yer own, I doona think I have ta tell ye how imperative it is that no one outside the family discover what she is."

Then why did it seem as if Alec MacQuarrie already knew that piece of information? Dash shook the errant thought away and swallowed the rest of his whisky.

Cait chose him, not MacQuarrie. "I'd protect her with my life, sir."

Angus Macleod nodded. "I am glad ta hear it. It sounds as though yer firstborn son will be quite taken care of. On the other hand, daughters are often ignored. As Cait is my only child, that isna the case for her, and I'd like ta ensure that it willna be so for her daughters. Upon my death, I'll leave everythin' else ta my granddaughters ta be split evenly among however many ye have."

Dash didn't quite know what to say to Macleod's unorthodox idea. So, he grunted out a quiet, "Thank you."

"What does yer father think about this marriage?"

"He doesn't know about it yet, Mr. Macleod. It's been quite some time since we've exchanged correspondence."

Caitrin's father rose from his desk and looked down at Dash. "Well, ye'll need ta fix that, lad."

Dash bristled at the censure. Angus Macleod didn't know the first thing about his life.

"There are all sorts of circles within the *Còig*, Brimsworth. The first is between the witches themselves. If they are not in harmony with each other, it can play havoc on their powers. And the second circle is within their family. Repair whatever rift ye have. Cait needs her family circle ta be strong."

Then the man started for the door. "That's all the unsolicited advice I have for ye tonight. I'm goin' ta bed as I have ta give away my only daughter inta yer keepin' tomorrow."

Mr. Macleod slid into the darkness of the hall, leaving

Dash to gape at his disappearing form. Repair the rift with his father? He'd honestly hoped never to see the old man again. Dash shook his head at the thought. It would be a cold day in Hades before he'd send as much as a couple of lines to the vindictive buzzard.

He rose from his spot and made his way back to his room. The whisky had helped dull his senses, and he prayed that sleep would find him soon.

Caitrin glanced in the mirror at her reflection. Her light blue silk gown was nice, but *just* nice. It wasn't exactly what she would have wanted as a wedding dress, but it would have to do. She didn't have time for something new. A wide white ribbon rested beneath her breasts and made them appear a bit larger than they actually were. Hopefully, Dash wouldn't be disappointed. Of course he'd already seen them through her wet chemise. He had some idea of what he was getting.

Behind her, Sorcha gasped. "Oh, Cait! Ye look beautiful." The young witch dropped a small valise on Cait's bed and then rushed forward to kiss both of her cheeks. "Such a pretty bride."

"Ye are a bit partial. I hope his lordship likes this old dress."

"Doona frown," Sorcha ordered. "Only smiles on yer wedding day. Ye doona want lines across yer brow. And the dress isna old. Ye wore it only once right before ye left for England. And I'm sure Lord Brimsworth will love it. Ye are radiant." She paused only to take a breath. "He's already gone over ta the church. I think he's quite anxious."

Cait nodded. "I suppose I'm fairly nervous myself."

Sorcha's dark eyes lit up. "Oh, Cait! Promise me ye'll tell me what ta expect on my weddin' night. I doona want ta get the talk from my aunts."

Cait's mouth fell open. She hadn't had any sort of talk with anyone, and the only person she'd feel comfortable asking questions of was Elspeth, though she was still in England. Cait figured she'd have to make do on her own. After all, Dashiel knew what he was doing.

"I promise," she somehow managed to say.

Sorcha laughed. "A pretty blush. That is nice." Then she returned to the bed and opened her valise. "I brought armfuls of honeysuckle for yer hair. I think ye should wear it up. Rhiannon promises an unseasonably pleasant day."

>∞<

The church was sparsely populated with only the Macleods' closest friends. Dash figured that was good; the fewer people he met, the fewer he'd have to remember—and his mind was already preoccupied.

He paced a path in front of the altar of the small church, trying not to focus on the vicar, Mr. Crawford, who sat in the front pew rehearsing his lines. The vicar rubbed his balding pate more than once, and just watching the man made Dash's nerves even worse. Where the devil was Cait? She wouldn't run out on him again, would she?

Mr. Forster patted Dash's arm. "She'll be here soon, lad."

Angus Macleod walked in through the door at the

back of the church, a large grin upon his face. "Ye all right, my lord? Ye look a bit queasy."

"Fine." Dash managed to nod.

"Ah, Angus." Mr. Crawford rose from his spot. "It is surprisingly warm today. That's a good sign for a long and happy marriage, is it no'?"

Dash noticed Rhiannon Sinclair smother a smile as she sat in the second row of pews. So this was her handiwork? What an intriguing lass.

He didn't have long to contemplate that before the back door opened again and Caitrin stepped into the church with Sorcha Ferguson following closely behind her.

Dash's mouth went dry. Cait was breathtaking, even more so than normal. Her blond hair was piled high on her head, and she wore a crown made of honeysuckle.

Sorcha took Cait's pelisse from her and handed her a bouquet of pink and white roses. Dash couldn't help the smile that crossed his lips. As soon as the ceremony was over, he was going to peel that blue dress off his bride. She blushed, as if she could read his thoughts, and Dash wished for a moment she could see what he had in store for her.

"Caitrin is here, Mr. Crawford," Mr. Macleod said, bringing Dash back to the present. "Are ye ready ta begin?"

The vicar nodded and retrieved his bible from the front pew. Dash held his breath as Caitrin walked up the aisle, never removing her eyes from his. Mr. Macleod met her halfway and offered her his arm.

"My darlin' girl," he whispered, "ye are beautiful."

She smiled at her father and then turned her attention back to Dash. Cait stopped before him, and Mr. Macleod placed her hand in Dash's. Then he slid behind them and took his seat.

"I'm glad you made it," Dash said beneath his breath.

"I was right on time," she informed him.

He sighed, knowing he was foolish. "I'm just anxious, angel."

Mr. Crawford cleared his throat, garnering everyone's attention. "*Slainte mhor agus a h-uile beannachd duibh.*"

Whatever the devil that meant. Dash glanced down at Cait who smiled beatifically at him.

"Repeat after me, Lord Brimsworth. 'I, Dashiel Jameson Aberdare Thorpe, take ye, Caitrin Louisa Macleod, ta be my wife before God and these witnesses.'"

Dash took a deep breath. A month ago, he'd never have envisioned he'd be in Scotland, holding the hands of the one girl who knew all his secrets and who somehow wanted him anyway. "I, Dashiel Jameson Aberdare Thorpe, take you, Caitrin Louisa Macleod, to be my wife before God and these witnesses."

Beside him, Caitrin sighed and he squeezed her hands, loving her more than he'd ever thought possible.

Mr. Crawford looked down at Cait and smiled warmly. "And now ye, Miss Macleod. Repeat the words: 'I, Caitrin Louisa Macleod, take ye, Dashiel Jameson Aberdare Thorpe, ta be my husband before God and these witnesses.'"

Her voice only shook a little as she repeated the words, her light blue eyes boring into his. Dash's heart leapt at the sound. She was his.

"Do ye have a ring, my lord?" the vicar asked, breaking him from his quiet celebration.

Caitrin's gaze shot up to reach his, her eyebrows drawn together. "It's all right if ye doona have one," she mumbled.

Dash patted his pockets until he found the bulge of the ring box. Then he pulled it out and said, "I have everything you need, angel." He opened the small box and showed her the contents.

Her gasp could be heard around the church as she raised her fingertips to her mouth and her eyes filled with tears.

"May I put it on you?" Dash didn't even care if the smile on his face was as juvenile as a puppy who received a treat.

She nodded swiftly, holding out her hand.

"Fits you perfectly," he whispered as he slid it onto her finger.

"So do ye," she whispered back.

Twenty-Seven

CAITRIN STOOD ON TIPTOE TO PRESS HER LIPS TO HIS, expecting a quick kiss before they greeted their guests and headed off to their celebration with friends and family. But Dash obviously had other ideas, because when she kissed him, his hands grasped her elbows, encouraging her to wrap them around his neck before his hands slid around her waist and he drew her to him.

Gone was the teasing exploration of her mouth that she'd become used to. Gone was the gentleness that he'd shown when he held himself in check. In its place was a fiery passion that took her breath away. His lips immediately parted hers, his tongue sweeping inside. She nearly felt the need to weep with passion when he groaned and began to move his hands down toward her bottom.

Suddenly Dash jumped and pulled back. "Ouch," he grunted as he released her.

"What is it?" Cait asked, reaching up to touch the side of his face.

"I don't know, but it hurt," Dash mumbled.

"Ye're in a *church*," Rhiannon said, smiling as she walked by them.

"Rhi!" Cait hissed. "Tell me ye dinna!"

"Oh, it was only a tiny bit of lightnin', and it was for yer own good," she whispered back then had the audacity to wink at Dash.

"Did she just…?" Dash let his voice trail off, shaking his head with wonder.

"Aye, she did. I'm so sorry," Cait hastened to add. "She should behave like she has some manners."

"He deserved it, Caitrin," her father said from behind her. "He may be yer husband, but he needs ta behave in polite company." He leaned closer to Dash and said, "Be very happy she only hit ye with a little of it, lad. She has a lot more she could have thrown at ye."

Dash coughed into his hand, hiding the smile upon his face. At least he hadn't offended Caitrin's father terribly when he'd tried to devour her without thinking. "My apologies," he offered.

Cait's father held his arms open to her, and she fell into them. "I'm so proud of ye," he whispered. "And yer mama would be, too." He raised her left hand and pressed a quick kiss to the ruby ring.

"Are ye sure ye want me ta have this?" she asked, praying he would say yes.

"I dinna give it ta ye. I gave it ta yer husband." He placed Cait's hand in Dash's. "And I canna think of a prettier place ta display it."

❧

If Dash didn't get inside her soon, he would surely

lose his mind. He'd spent the last two hours socializing with her friends and her father's friends. It was the only time he'd ever appreciated anything his father had done for him, since he *did* know how to socialize in polite company. He just didn't practice it often.

But he wanted Cait. He wanted her with an intensity that even he didn't understand. He'd had women beneath him, on top of him, and in every position in between since the first time he'd tupped a servant girl at the age of fourteen. But he'd never felt the desire to *hold* a woman. To stroke her. To bring her pleasure. Then to do it again and again until they were both sated. Then sleep and do it some more.

Several times, she'd been dragged away from him completely by her friends or one acquaintance or another. And each time, he felt physical pain at her departure. He wanted her. In the worst way.

Dash made his way across the Macleod drawing room to get her. It was time for them to be alone. It was time for him to love her. She leaned into him and tilted her head back to smile at him when he slid his arm around her shoulders. She felt like *home*, or at least what he imagined a home and family should feel like.

But then a strong wind whipped at his hair.

"Is that a warning?" he asked, forcing a congenial smile he didn't feel to appear on his lips when he addressed Rhiannon Sinclair.

"Only a reminder, my lord," the girl said quietly. She stepped closer and leaned in as though she was telling him a simple secret. "If ye ever hurt our sister, there are four of us ye'll have ta deal with. And Blaire isna even here so ye canna get a taste of what *she* has ta offer."

"I'm positively shivering in my boots," Dash remarked, trying to keep the growl from his voice. If the witches thought they could keep him from Cait, they were sadly mistaken.

As casually as possible, he turned Cait away from them and said quietly by her ear, "Do you think we can be alone, soon? I would like to make love to my wife."

She swallowed so harshly he could hear it. "Now?"

He tilted her chin up until her blue eyes met his. "Please?" he asked. *Please, save me from this torture.*

"Aye, we can go," she said, and then she turned to hug Rhiannon and Sorcha. The younger girl was giddy with excitement.

"Doona forget yer promise. Ye have ta tell me about it."

"Shh!" she said, attempting to quiet the wood sprite.

Dash tugged her fingertips as gently as he possibly could until he finally had her moving toward the door. "If one more person stops you, I'll not be responsible for my actions," he growled.

"Oh, such a beast," she teased, a watery smile upon her face.

"Are you all right?" Her tears tugged at his heart.

"Aye, I'm all right." She sniffed and then climbed into the waiting carriage.

"What is it that you're supposed to inform the littlest witch about?"

Cait waved nonchalantly, but her hand shook a little in the air. "She wants ta ken everythin' about the marriage bed." A pretty blush crept up her cheeks.

Dash tugged her into his lap. "You'll have to learn a bit about it yerself, angel, before you can tell her *all* about it." He tucked her tightly in his lap and looked down into her warm blue eyes. Then he whispered to her. "But don't worry. I'll try to be a good teacher."

She shivered in his arms.

Cait nearly jumped when he brushed his hand across her cheekbone. "Why so skittish, angel? I can tell you want me. Your pulse is pounding like mad." He pressed his lips to the side of her neck and then groaned aloud, "If we don't get to wherever we're going soon, I'll disgrace myself and take you in the carriage." He glanced out the window as the coach slowed. "Where *are* we going?"

"It was supposed ta be a surprise. But ye'll find out soon enough. Elspeth's cottage is empty, ever since Westfield built his massive estate. And since they're in Hampshire anyway, Rhiannon and Sorcha fixed it up a bit and we're ta stay there tonight."

Dash's heart swelled just a bit. She'd made plans for them to be alone. "Alone with you? How'd I ever get so lucky?" He couldn't remember anyone else ever having planned a surprise for him. No one had ever cared enough.

❧

The coach slowed and Dash opened the door, stepping outside. He handed her out, pulled her hand into the crook of his arm, and surveyed the small cottage. "Charming little place," he remarked.

Cait turned the door latch and stepped inside. The interior took her breath away when she was immediately assaulted by the pleasing aroma of flowers. A fire roared in the hearth where soft blankets had been thrown down upon the rug. The windows were shrouded with hanging vines that twisted and turned, their leaves and flowers blocking all of the sunlight from the room, leaving them in darkness, aside from the glow of the hearth and candles placed about the room.

"Sorcha's handiwork, I presume?" Dash laughed, his mouth hanging open as he took in all the girl had done. "I had no idea she was so talented."

"Oh, she just tells the plants what ta do and they do it." Cait shrugged and then busied herself worrying one of the flowers that hung on the wall.

Dash put his arms around her from behind, drawing her slowly to him. "Why so fretful? Scared?"

She sniffed. "I'm no' afraid."

"Then why are you shaking?" he asked as his hands crept up her belly to cup the fullness of her breasts. She raised an arm and hooked it behind his neck, allowing her head to fall back on his shoulder.

His warm breath blew across her neck, and she said in a choked gasp, "I'm no' shakin'."

He turned her in his arms to face him, tipped her face up to his, and said, "I'll not hurt you, Caitie." She nodded quickly before Dash scooped her up and crossed the room, laying her on the soft blankets piled in front of the fire.

"Dash," she said, pressing her hand against his chest to stop him.

"Yes, angel?" he asked absently as he slowly untied the laces of her gown, apparently taking great pleasure in drawing out the moment.

"I canna see the future."

"I know you can't see ours. That's a good thing, Caitie."

"No' for me," she protested, but she lifted her arms when he had her gown loosened so he could tug it from her shoulders. Then she lifted her bottom when he tapped her hip so he could slide her dress down over her hips and toss it to the side, leaving her in nothing more than her chemise and stockings. How had he done that so quickly? She immediately crossed her arms over her breasts.

"Ye have done this with a lot of women, Dashiel?" she asked, watching his face closely for a reaction. His eyes narrowed slightly.

He stilled, no longer even touching her, his amber gaze nearly swallowing her whole. "I need you to know, Caitrin, that I have *never* done *this* with anyone before you."

"I doona ken what ye mean, Dash. Yer book—"

He stopped her with a finger to her lips. "*That* was nothing like this." He raked a hand through his hair.

"Ye are vexed at me. I should have kept my big mouth closed." Tears pricked at the backs of her eyelids.

"I'm not angry at you, Cait. You have a good reason to be doubtful. I'm a Lycan. That's enough to make any sane woman afraid. Not to mention that you've never done this before."

He leaned against the front of the settee and spread his legs, then gathered her and set her in between, his front cradling her back.

"Close your eyes," he said quietly.

Cait let her lids drift shut, sighing as she rested her

head on his shoulder and relaxed into him. "I doona ken what it will be like," she finally admitted.

"You have to let some things just *happen*," Dash said as his hands moved up to cup her breasts once again. Without preamble, he stroked across her nipples. She fought back a gasp. "Just like that." His breath brushed across the shell of her ear.

"Stop trying to predict how well I'll love you. Because, if I don't do it well enough the first time, I plan to do it again." Another stroke across her nipple made her back arch. "And again." His hand walked down her stomach toward the curls at the juncture of her thighs. "And again," he growled as his fingers finally dipped into her heat.

He stroked her, the sensation not unpleasant, not nearly what she'd expected. "That all right?"

"Aye," she gasped as one finger stroked across her pulse point and then slipped inside her. She arched her back, completely ashamed of the way he made her react to him.

"So wet for me." He panted with every breath.

"Dash, please!" she cried.

"Please, what?" he teased as his fingers moved from inside her to stroke her folds and back again.

"I doona ken!" she finally cried. "I doona ken what happens next!"

"Don't worry, angel. I'll show you," he said as he turned her in his arms and began to work at his own clothing, tugging his shirt over his head.

She'd seen his chest before, but not close enough to touch him. She reached out one tentative hand. His chest pulsed against her fingertips before he closed his own hand around it and placed it back in her lap.

"If you touch me, I'll be done for, lass."

"But…" she protested.

He coaxed her into lifting her arms so he could pull her chemise over her head. Then she sat before him completely and totally naked, aside from her silk stockings with the pink garters Sorcha had insisted she wear. "Shall I take them off?"

He shook his head. "No. I like them on." He smiled at her softly. "Do you need for me to slow down?"

His tenderness and thoughtfulness touched her heart. She lay back and held her arms out to him. The touch of his bare chest moving across her own as he covered her was sublime. She wiggled beneath him, urging him to move a little faster. Toward what? She had no idea. He trailed a kiss down the side of her neck, and she reached up to thread her hands through his hair.

"I never expected you to be so complacent, Caitie," he teased. "You normally have such fire."

"I'm a little bit preoccupied, ye beast." She couldn't help but giggle at him. Was she the kind of person to just lie beneath him, even if this was her first time? Absolutely not. "But if ye insist… Off with yer trousers, Dash," she ordered.

"I'm not ready to take them off," he chuckled, bending to take her nipple into his mouth. She arched her back, tugging his hair to bring him closer. "If I take them off, I'll have to be inside you. And you're not quite ready."

"I think I am." The man was speaking in riddles, and her head was already spinning with the way his rough tongue abraded the sensitive tips of her breasts as he went back and forth, back and forth. "What should I do?"

"Nothing. You can be quiet so I can work."

"Quiet? Ye want me ta be *quiet*?"

"Make all the noise you want, angel. But, please stop talking." His hand ran down her belly and over her mound, where he pressed and rocked the heel of his hand against her as his fingers trailed through her heat.

"You can make a noise when I do this," he said as he parted her folds and touched the center of her.

She gasped and rocked herself against him. She cried out when he moved his thumb across the nub that was her pleasure center, his mouth still devouring her breasts.

"Ye doona play fair."

"Never said I did." He raised his head briefly to respond.

"Out of yer trousers, Brimsworth," she growled, the noise foreign to her own ears.

"As the lady wishes," he breathed. Finally. Finally, he would ease this ache. Finally, he would take her and make her his.

When he came back to her, he eased her legs apart with his knee and then settled himself fully between her thighs. Something hot and hard pressed at her most secret place.

"I've never wanted anything more than I want you," he breathed.

"Then take me, ye big wolf."

"Witch," he grunted when she ran her hand down his chest.

"Ye say that like it's an insult."

She could barely breathe the last word as he probed at her center, pressing at her insistently until she rocked back.

"That's it, Caitie. Tell me when you're ready." He held himself above her, looking deeply into her eyes. His amber depths called to her.

"Make me yers," she pleaded. Then he thrust himself fully inside her in one swift stroke. A brief moment of pain jolted her from her passion-filled haze.

"I love you, Caitie," he said, his forehead touching hers as he breathed heavily in and out, in and out, remaining completely still within her. His fingers slipped between them so he could stoke the fire within her. Up, up, up she went. He began to move slowly within her, his slow strokes driving her mad, combined with the slow and steady movement of his fingers.

"Doona hold back," she commanded, tugging harshly at his hair so he looked at her. "I want my beast," she cried.

At her command, his strokes deepened, his rhythm increased, and his breaths blew harshly across her skin. He grunted, his arms sliding beneath her as he pressed farther and deeper than she ever would have expected. Up she went, farther and farther, the rhythm of her body matching his, thrust for thrust. Pressure for pressure. Pleasure for pleasure.

"Dash!" she cried when the passion swept over her in a sweet release, pushing her into the pleasure-filled promise she hadn't even known would be there. He followed while she was still fluttering around him and then stilled so she could pull the last of his pleasure from him. He remained inside her for a moment, his weight heavy upon her. Right. Heavy and right.

Then he lifted his head and looked down upon her, wiping her hair from her sweaty brow. Her Lycan tried to be calm and complacent, but beneath it all, he was still a bit wild, and she would have him no other way.

"I doona ken what comes next. We do it again?" She giggled at the stricken look on his face.

He chuckled. "I'll need just a moment, angel."

Cait liked the sound of that, and she rested her head against his chest, reveling in the feel of his arms holding her tightly.

Twenty-Eight

DASH ROLLED CAITRIN BENEATH HIM AND MADE LOVE to her all over again. He tried to keep in mind that this was new for her and to be careful with her, but she had other plans. She begged him to take her harder and faster than before, and Dash needed all of his control to keep his wildness in check. If he hurt her, he'd never forgive himself.

His little witch finally seemed sated and dropped her head upon his chest. Dash pulled a blanket up over her to keep the chill off them during the night. Then he cradled Caitrin against him and released a sigh of relief as warmth spread over every part of him. He'd never have his fill of her. She was everything he'd ever wanted and more, all wrapped up in the prettiest bundle. "Try to sleep, angel."

"Orderin' me about again?" She covered a yawn with her delicate hand.

Dash chuckled. "I am your lord and master now, Caitrin." She poked him in the side, and he laughed harder. "Besides, you're going to need your strength tomorrow."

"Oh?" She ran her delicate hand over his chest, making him hard all over again.

"Mmm," he agreed, tightening his hold on her. "I may not let you out of bed for a sennight."

Caitrin giggled softly. "We are no' even in a bed, Dashiel."

He smiled into the darkness as he watched her eyes flutter shut. "Good night, lass."

Dash knew the minute she fell asleep, as her breathing became rhythmic and her body went limp against his. Tired as he was, Dash wasn't able to nod off. He was too amazed at his good fortune. For the rest of his life, he'd get to make love to Caitrin and wake up every morning with her in his arms.

He'd never been responsible for anyone other than himself before. She was his, in every sense of the word. And every sigh she uttered, every breath she took, fascinated him. He didn't want to miss a moment of it.

"Come home, Dashiel," she whispered in her sleep, clutching him tighter.

But he was home. "Shhh, Caitie, I'm here." He ran his hand over her back, soothing her.

When she relaxed, he glanced around Elspeth Westfield's cottage. He wasn't *home* exactly. But wherever Caitrin was, he'd be at her side, and he had a feeling that meant Edinburgh. Her life was here, and he couldn't envision her leaving.

Dash sighed. He probably should locate a house for them as soon as possible. Accommodating as Angus Macleod was, Dash didn't want to live with the man. But he didn't know the city well enough to find a place himself. He'd have to hire a broker in the morning to start his search.

Caitrin's heart began to race, distracting him from his thoughts. Then her breath came in quick spurts, and before Dash could respond, his wife bolted upright and gasped as though she desperately needed air.

"Caitrin," he crooned to her. "You're all right. I'm here." He wrapped his arms around her.

She sucked in an anguished breath and trembled against him.

"Caitie, what is it?"

She shook her head. "I-I doona ken."

"Were you dreaming?" he asked. "Is it your friend again?"

"No, no' Blaire." Her heart began to slow to its normal pace. "It was a man."

"A man?" He wasn't at all happy about the prospect of other men visiting her in her dreams.

"In my dream. I think I saw the past," she explained. "Which isna right. My gift is to see the future, not people or events that have already happened."

"You saw the past in your dream?"

She nodded against his chest. "The man, the old man," she clarified, "he had powder in his hair."

An uneasiness started in the pit of Dash's stomach, but he let her continue.

"He was in pain and..." She sat up and looked directly in his eyes. "He was callin' for ye."

Dash closed his eyes. He didn't want to hear any more.

"But why was he callin' for ye? Do ye ken who he was?"

Dash had a fairly good idea. "You've been very vague," he evaded. "How would I know who that was?"

Cait frowned at him. "Ye do ken. I can hear it in yer voice. Who is it, Dash?"

He winced when he asked, "Does he have a crooked nose? Strong chin?"

She sighed with relief. "Yes. Who was he? What did he want with ye? So strange ta see the past."

Dash shook his head. "I don't think it was the past, Caitie. It sounds like my father—Eynsford, I mean."

A look of confusion settled on her face. "But he looked like—"

Dash well knew what the man looked like. "A page from the last generation," he finished for her. "He still wears a wig and powders his hair. He thinks current fashion is undignified and rather common."

Caitrin threaded her fingers through his hair. "He was calling out for ye, Dash."

"Won't he be surprised that I'm not in England?" he replied dryly.

"Ye shouldna say that," she said softly. "I doona ken what there is between the two of ye, but there's a reason I had my dream."

"And why is that?"

"I'm no' sure, but ye have ta go ta him."

Dash turned his head and kissed the palm of her hand. "I said my vows this very day, Caitie. You're not getting rid of me that easily."

"I'm no' tryin' ta get rid of ye. But ye have ta go ta him. It's important."

"Nothing is more important than you. I'll not leave you the day after our wedding and certainly not to rush to *his* miserable side."

"He's dyin'," Cait said softly.

Dash couldn't bring himself to care. During his entire life, the marquess had berated him and looked down on him, locked him up and cursed his existence. Dash didn't care if he ever laid eyes on the old man again. "Not soon enough."

She smacked his chest. "That's awful."

"Caitie," he began, but she poked her finger into his chest.

"Listen ta me, Dashiel Thorpe. Ye have ta go see the man. I doona ken why it's important, but I wouldna see it if it wasna."

"I'm not leaving you," Dash insisted. He'd spent his whole life needing someone who understood him, someone who cared for him. Cait hadn't admitted to loving him, but her affection was the closest thing he'd ever had. And he wasn't about to rush all the way to Kent to see the man who had made his existence miserable.

"I'm goin' with ye," she said determinedly.

Dash snorted. "The devil you are. I saw you at each inn along the way here, Caitie. You can't be around all those strange people. I won't torture you that way. I won't ask it of you. And since I have no desire to return to Eynsford Park, it doesn't matter anyway."

"As long as ye're with me, I'll be all right," she whispered, touching her lips to his chest.

"Cait!" he groaned. "Don't try to persuade me. I'm not going."

"As long as ye're touchin' me, it blocks out all the other images," Caitrin admitted.

Dash reared back and looked at her, silhouetted in the dim light from the grate. "Blocks out the other images?" he echoed. "What do you mean by that?"

"I mean," she sighed, "yer touch is the remedy ta the pain of all those strangers' feelings when I travel. I am no' plagued by the futures of those around me when ye touch me." She threaded her fingers with his. "We have ta go see the marquess, Dash. I wouldna have dreamed about it, otherwise."

She seemed unwavering, and Dash heaved a sigh. He couldn't believe she was making him do this. He was indeed a besotted fool even to consider it.

"I can't imagine what we'll gain from this."

Cait shook her head. "Whatever it is will be revealed." Then she smiled brightly. "Oh, and if we time ourselves properly, we'll meet Elspeth and Benjamin along the way. They've just started for home."

Bloody wonderful. A Westfield brother *and* his father all in the same journey. Dash didn't even try to stop the growl that escaped him.

❦

Caitrin seemed to be enveloped in a dark cocoon of all-encompassing heat. The sensation was completely unfamiliar as she was often so cold in Scotland. She sighed, perfectly content to stay wrapped up like this forever.

"Caitie." She heard her name from so far away. "Caitie." Dash's voice was suddenly much louder, beside her ear.

"Hmm?" she lazily managed.

Then her warm cocoon shook. "You make the most enchanting little sounds when you sleep, angel," Dash chuckled.

She blinked her eyes open to find herself staring

at her husband's sculpted chest, lightly dusted with golden hair. Cait smiled as memories of the previous night flashed in her mind, and she couldn't recall ever being so happy. She pressed a kiss to his collarbone.

"Good morning, my lord."

Dash's fingers traced circles on her back.

"Good morning, my lady. How did you sleep?"

Cait lifted her head to look at him. "Ye are very warm. I doona think I'll have need of a blanket ever again."

A grin tugged at his lips, and he rolled her beneath him. "Are you suggesting I cover you day *and* night?"

Cait giggled.

"That can be arranged, lass." He nuzzled against her neck, making tingles race across her skin. "How long can we stay here in Westfield's cottage?"

"By the time we return from Kent, Elspeth will already be back."

Dash stilled, and then he lifted his head and pierced her with his amber gaze. "You're not really serious about that, are you?"

Cait frowned at him. Did he think her power was something to make light of? "Of course I'm serious about it, Dashiel. We have ta leave today."

His brow furrowed. "Today? Caitie, I want to locate a broker today to help find us a place of our own. And we just finished a long journey. I'd like a sennight or so to recover from that, and—"

"Today," she insisted, pushing at his chest. "I had my dream *last* night. We need ta start for Kent today."

He groaned and rolled off her. "I don't want to do this, Cait. I don't want travel all the way to Eynsford

Park and visit with my father. I want to build our life here and look to *our* future."

She could hear the pain in his voice, and her heart ached for him. The marquess must be an awful man, but her dream meant something and they couldn't ignore it. Her mother might have been remiss by not mentioning certain things like not being able to see her husband's future, but she had been very clear about following premonitions.

To ignore one would have dire circumstances. Cait wasn't quite sure what that meant, but there was nothing in her life she was willing to jeopardize to find out.

"We have ta go, Dash," she said softly. "I wish we could stay, too, but my dream…"

He pushed up on his elbow as though to see her better. He nodded slightly in assent. "If you feel it's necessary, we'll leave today."

Cait sat up and threw her arms around him, relieved that he understood the importance of her power. She couldn't help but smile. Dash wouldn't be the same dictatorial prig Benjamin Westfield was over Elspeth. He respected her gift. She wanted to weep with joy.

Twenty-Nine

As Dash descended the steps of Macleod House and approached his coach on the drive, he could hardly believe he'd agreed to this journey. The conveyance was already loaded with his wife's trunks, and Renshaw looked as though he was ready to quit his post. The poor man had driven through brutal winds and storms just to get here, and now Dash was making him turn around and do it again.

At least only Dash and his bride would be going south. No supercilious Scotsmen trying to steal Cait from under his nose. No hulking coachmen with threatening glares. No irritating maids to deal with this time around. This time, Dash could touch Caitrin anytime he wanted without fear of discovery.

At the front of his carriage, Sorcha Ferguson and Rhiannon Sinclair huddled around Caitrin, saying their good-byes. As his wife assured her friends that they wouldn't be gone long, a hand clapped Dash on the back. He spun around to find Angus Macleod smiling at him.

"Ye'll take care of my little girl, right, Brimsworth?"

"With my life," he assured his father-in-law.

The old Scot winked at him. "Well, let's hope it doesna come ta that. She says ye want ta find a home of yer own here when ye return?"

Dash nodded. "I don't want to take advantage of your generosity, sir."

Angus Macleod tossed back his head and laughed. "Ye are a bad liar, lad. Ye want my daughter all ta yerself."

Was he that easy to read?

"I was the same way with Fiona all those years ago," Macleod continued. "When ye return, I'll have ye a broker and ye can search Edinburgh for a proper home ta yer heart's content. Just watch after her, will ye?"

"Yes, sir." Dash shook his father-in-law's hand. Then he looked over his shoulder to find Niall Forster regarding him with a look of mild amusement. What the shipbuilder had to look amused about was a complete mystery.

Dash nodded his head in the man's direction. "Sir, thank you for all of your advice."

Forster stepped forward and shook his head. "Ye mean all that advice ye paid no heed ta, Dashiel?"

Somehow, Dash was able to keep a growl from escaping his throat. The old man simply didn't understand. Forster had been raised knowing what he was, raised knowing how to control himself; Dash had not.

If he allowed the beast inside him free reign, Caitrin could be in grave danger. No matter the menace that called for freedom from within, Dash was enough of a gentleman on the outside to keep the beast at bay. "On the contrary, the run was quite refreshing."

The shipbuilder lowered his voice, so only Dash could hear. "If ye doona heed everythin' I've said, Dashiel, there's no tellin' the harm ye can cause. Accept who ye are, embrace all of yerself, or yer doomed."

What a cheery thought. Dash scowled at the man. "I believe I have everything under control, sir."

"Aye," Forster remarked. "That's the problem, lad."

Dash was in no mood for any more of Forster's words, so he bowed, letting the man know the conversation had come to an end. "Do have a safe journey back to Glasgow."

Then he caught Caitrin's attention at the front of the coach, where she was still chatting with her friends. "Lady Brimsworth, are you quite ready?"

Cait smiled at him and stepped around the side of the carriage. Dash opened the door for his wife and helped her inside. Before he could climb in himself, he felt someone tug at his jacket.

Dash turned back around to find Sorcha standing behind him, tears trailing their way down her cheeks. "I'll take care of her, lass. There's no need for worrying. We'll be back before you know it."

He ignored the groan of his coachman at those words. He was going to have to increase the man's pay considerably if he wanted to maintain his services.

Sorcha stepped closer to him and handed him a sprig of a purple flowers. "Wisteria," she said quietly. "It's for safe travels."

Dash accepted the flowers and raised Sorcha's gloved hand to his lips. "Thank you, Miss Ferguson. That was quite thoughtful."

Then he climbed into the coach and rapped on the ceiling for Renshaw to depart.

The coach lurched forward and Caitrin settled beside him, resting her head against his arm. Her hand landed softly on his chest as she sighed. He'd once scoffed at love. But, no longer. There was no doubt it existed, because it nearly overwhelmed him with every breath he took.

"How long has it been since ye've seen yer father, Dash?" she asked quietly as her fingertips began to move slowly across his chest.

"Not long enough."

"I hope he's still alive when we get there. I'd like ta meet the man who's made yer life so miserable."

"Planning to boil him in oil, angel?" He couldn't help but laugh at the image. "Or poison him with one of yer potions?"

Cait sighed sadly.

He nudged her with his elbow. "What's wrong?"

"I canna help but think about how lonely he must be. He never remarried after yer mother died?"

"No woman of sane mind would have him." He picked at an imaginary piece of lint on his trouser leg.

"Yer mother married him."

"She also let herself be seduced by a Lycan. Her mental standing is still in question for me."

She punched his shoulder and sat up, her mouth open wide with outrage. "How can ye say such a thing?" she gasped.

"Oh, come now, Caitie," he said, trying to soothe her as she removed herself from him completely. "I didn't mean it," he finally groaned, though he had no idea why she was suddenly so put out with him.

Cait ignored him and just stared out the opposite window.

"What did I do?" he finally asked when the silence became deafening.

"Nothin'." She turned up her nose.

"Angel," he began.

"Don't *angel* me, Dashiel Thorpe. Ye canna insult me and then expect me ta fall right inta yer arms just because ye're charmin'."

"When did I insult *you*?" Damn women. He'd never understand them.

"Ye said yer mother's mental status was in question because she allowed herself ta be seduced by a beast." She raised one eyebrow at him and then raked her gaze down and up his body.

"Oh." He sighed loudly. "I didn't mean you, Caitie. *You* had no chance against *my* charm." He glanced at her out of the corner of his eye.

A smile tugged at the corners of her mouth, though she fought it. Then she pulled at the neck of her gown, exposing her shoulder. "Fight yer bite, ye mean? Once ye had sunk yer teeth inta me, I was done for? It's no' as though I had much of a choice, is it?"

"Oh, you had a choice. You could have chosen MacQuarrie. You could have moved on." He picked her up and set her in his lap, despite her struggles. He lowered his voice. "But you didn't. Because you love me. Even if I say the wrong things at times and am completely inappropriate."

She stopped moving in his lap, thank God. If her bottom had wiggled against him for one more moment, the beast would have been under her skirts, even if she was angry at him.

"Ye're a boor," she said as she quieted and laid her head against his chest.

"I know. I'm sorry." She let him brush the hair back from her brow. "Forgive me."

Forgive him? And let the big lout get off that easily? Not very likely.

"Perhaps tomorrow," she said, unable to stop the giggle that erupted.

"Do you have any predictions about what will occur when we reach Kent?" His brow was marred by concentration.

"Ye ken I canna tell the future where ye're concerned." If only she could. She could make this so much easier for both of them. "Are ye worried?"

"We didn't part on good terms, angel. My father probably will detest my very presence, just like he's done every day since I was born."

"That wasna the sense I got in my dream, Dash. He needed ye. I just doona ken why."

He tucked her closer to him, and she was content just to let him hold her for a while with her head tucked beneath his chin.

"He knows I'm not his son," Dash finally said quietly. "He told me so himself. I didn't believe him at the time. I thought it was his disappointment speaking."

"Do ye think he kens who yer real father is?"

She felt his head move from side to side. "No. If he does, he didn't tell me."

"Do ye want ta ken?"

He shrugged.

"Of course ye do," she mumbled.

"It would be nice to know," he finally said, though he'd never given it much thought. What good would it do now? "But it isn't important. I wouldn't be making this trip, if not for you." He nudged her playfully. "The things I do for love."

"Ye just hope ta get beneath my skirts again," she said, feeling the color in her face rise as he reacted to her comment. She took his chin in her hand and kissed him quickly.

"Don't try to distract me with your kisses, angel," he growled. "I like that idea, the one you just had. Let's go back to that."

"Ye are incorrigible." But, truth be told, she liked being one with him. She liked the closeness. Having him inside her was more than she'd ever dreamed it would be. "Ye canna do that in a carriage."

He looked down at her with his eyebrows raised. "And just why not?" His voice dropped to a low hum. "I can take you anywhere I want."

Cait could already feel the mad dash of her pulse and knew he could hear it. And the one at the juncture of her thighs began to pound as well. The man just had to mention taking her, and she warmed like a stoked fire on a cold winter day.

"I love the way you react to me," he murmured as he picked her up and put one leg on each side of his, so that she straddled his lap. His hands cupped her bottom, drawing her closer so she could feel the bulge of him against her thigh.

"We canna do it like this," she whispered, slightly scandalized but highly aroused at the same time.

Dash distracted her by talking as he loosened the bodice of her gown. "We can do it anywhere, angel. We can do it standing up." They could? "We can do it lying down." She nodded, more and more distracted by his movements as he deftly pulled her bodice down and exposed her breasts to the cool air. The peaks of her breasts immediately hardened. "And we *can* do it in a carriage."

"Aye, I'm startin' ta realize that," she gasped out as he lifted her breast to his mouth and slowly drew the peak inside, his eyes never leaving hers. She inched forward on his lap, trying to get a bit closer to him.

"Easy," he said quickly, when she made a wrong move.

"Sorry. I dinna mean ta hurt ye."

"It's a most delicious pain, angel. No worries. Just trying to keep the beast in check." He unbuttoned his trousers, and she reveled in the velvet feel of the soft skin that covered his hardness against her thigh.

"Soft?" she asked.

"Pardon?" his head snapped up. "Angel, there is nothing soft about me right now," he chuckled.

"May I touch ye?" She was suddenly curious to see and feel the part of him that filled her so well.

He lifted his hands up behind his head and lay back against the squabs. "You may touch me anywhere you like." A naughty smile played around his mouth.

Cait sat back to put enough room between them that she could take him into her hand. He drew in a quick breath, and she released him even quicker. "Did I hurt ye?"

"That was a gasp of pleasure. Not pain. But I'm not sure how much more pleasure I can take, to be quite honest. Might we finish this exploration later?"

His hands slipped back beneath her skirts so he could cup her naked bottom and pull her forward, to where she rested over him. Then he nudged at her center, kneading her bottom as he tugged her close and filled her in one swift stroke.

Cait raised her arms around his neck and let him lead their dance, rising and falling as he lifted and lowered her with his hands on her hips. A most curious look crossed his face as she neared the apex of her pleasure and gazed into his eyes. His hand slipped between them and sent her over the top. Cait allowed her eyes to flutter closed as she pulsed around him, and he immediately followed.

She lay on top of him for a few precious moments, her heart pressed close to his. Then she sat up and peeled back his shirt at the neck. "Ye wear the mark of the beast."

He looked down to see what she referred to. "My birthmark?"

"Aye, it's just like Elspeth's. I've seen it my whole life. See how it's shaped like a moon?"

"I've never paid much attention to it," he said, brushing her hands away gently.

"Doona do that," she protested, bending to place her lips to his mark. "I like it. But others may say I belong in Bedlam for loving a Lycan," she giggled against his neck, where she bent and pressed a quick kiss.

"I heard that," he growled.

"I meant for ye ta hear it."

Thirty

"THIS IS IT!" CAIT NEARLY SQUEALED AS SHE LOOKED OUT the coach window at the Cat and Fiddle Inn.

Dash sighed. For the last week, he'd watched his wife grow more excited at the prospect of being reunited with Elspeth Westfield. Now, it seemed, the time was upon them.

"And you're certain they're here?" Dash asked. He wouldn't take her joy from her, but he was not anxious to meet back up with Benjamin Westfield, nor his wife. He hadn't exactly been a welcome guest when they'd last seen each other.

Cait turned back to him and smiled radiantly. "Of course, I'm sure. Look, there's Benjamin's coach."

Dash peered out the window. Sure enough, there in the coaching yard against the setting sun, the Westfield crest was emblazoned on the side of a carriage. A proud wolf, golden against blue. "It does indeed appear as though they're here."

She cupped his jaw in her hands. "Doona worry, I'm sure they've forgotten all that business with ye abductin' Lord William and…"

That he highly doubted. Dash winced. It hadn't been his finest moment. The Westfields were a loyal bunch. He wasn't part of their pack, and he never would be. Still, he wasn't a coward. He pushed open the coach door and helped Cait alight from the carriage. As they approached the taproom, Dash snaked his arm around her waist.

He opened the door and directed Caitrin over the threshold. Then she darted from him toward the innkeeper so quickly that he lost his hold on her. Cait reared back and Dash rushed forward, placing his hand on her back, hoping to take her pain away. As long as he was touching her, she wouldn't be assailed by unfamiliar futures.

She took a staggering breath and then looked up at him. "My fault. I wasna thinkin'."

"You're just excited." Dash hooked her arm with his, determined not to let her slide past him again. Seeing her in agony tore at his heart. It was a matter of pride to him that he, and he alone, could keep unwanted images out of her head. Predetermined fate. If he hadn't been a believer before, he certainly was now.

He led his wife toward the slender, pit-faced innkeeper behind the bar. Dash nodded in greeting. "My wife and I require accommodations, sir."

"Of course," the man replied.

"And I believe my friends are here as well," Caitrin broke in. "Lord Benjamin Westfield and Lady Elspeth."

The man scratched his chin. "Indeed, ma'am. His lordship has reserved one of our private dining rooms this evening."

Caitrin nearly glowed. "Which one, sir?"

But there was no need to ask. Benjamin Westfield had hearing that matched Dash's, and the sound of his name had obviously caught his ear. The Lycan stood at the end of the taproom, the door to a private dining room held open by his hand.

"Caitrin Macleod?" he asked, though his hazel eyes were leveled on Dash. "What are you doing here, lass?"

Cait started to move toward the man, but Dash kept his hold on her this time. "Careful, angel," he whispered to her.

Westfield still caught the words. Dash could tell by the way his brow furrowed a second later. Cait looked up at Dash, then back across the taproom at the other Lycan.

"Benjamin, I'd like for ye ta promise ta behave yerself."

A moment later, Elspeth Westfield poked her head out into the taproom. Her fiery curls swayed from the motion, and her face lit up in joy. "Cait!"

The expectant redhead darted from the room and threw her arms around Caitrin's neck. "Good heavens! Ye're the last person I expected ta see here. What are ye doing? Why did ye flee Westfield Hall in the dead of night? And what…" Her green eyes finally landed on Dash. "Lord Brimsworth."

"Lady Elspeth," he said smoothly. "How nice to see you again. Cait was certain we'd run into you here."

Lady Elspeth blinked at him, apparently at a loss for words. However, that ailment did not afflict her husband who crossed the floor in a few strides to drop a protective hand on his wife's shoulder. "Perhaps you should join us for dinner," Lord Benjamin suggested.

Cait squeezed Dash's hand, and no matter how

awkward he felt at the moment, the love and affection in her gesture warmed his heart. "Thank you, Westfield. Lady Brimsworth and I are quite tired from our journey."

He wasn't certain whose gasp was louder, Lord Benjamin's or his wife's. Lady Elspeth recovered from the shock first, and she quickly kissed Caitrin's cheeks. "Well, congratulations! Do come join us. It sounds as though ye have a tale ta tell."

❧

As Cait stared across the table at her dearest friend in the world, she hoped with all her might that Elspeth and Ben would find a way to accept Dash. As members of the *Còig*, they would be in each other's lives until the end of time. It would be better for everyone if they got along.

"So," Benjamin began as he pushed a goblet of wine toward Dash, "you've married Caitrin?"

She watched her husband nod and noted the muscle twitching in his jaw. "I was lucky enough to convince Caitrin to accept my proposal."

"When did this happen?" Elspeth asked, nervously moving the food around her plate.

"Ye should eat, El," Caitrin reminded her.

Her friend shook her head. "Later. I want ta hear all about it."

"Well," Cait began, "we met at Westfield Hall, and then Dash and I met up on the way ta Scotland. By the time I arrived home, he'd won me over."

Elspeth would never accept that version of events, but hopefully she wouldn't question it with the men present. Later, when they were alone, Cait would confide all to her friend. The other witches knew the truth, anyway.

"The major said he'd sent you off to Glasgow," Ben said, narrowing his eyes on Dash.

"He did. Mr. Forster accompanied me to Edinburgh, not that it's any of your concern," her husband growled.

Elspeth put a hand over Ben's. "It's clear Cait is happy. We should just wish them our best."

Ben Westfield grumbled something under his breath, but Cait was certain it wasn't his best wishes. She ignored her friend's husband, like she usually did.

"Ecstatically happy," she confirmed, smiling at Elspeth. "In fact, we are on our way ta visit Dash's father in Kent."

After they finished dinner, Elspeth stepped around the table and squeezed Cait's shoulder. "Do ye want ta go for a walk with me?"

So she could get to the truth. Cait felt Dash stiffen at her side, and she flashed him a smile. "I'll be fine. The further we get from the inn, the less the visions bother me."

"That doesn't exactly make me feel better." He heaved a sigh. "Be careful, will you?"

Cait nodded. Dash slid his arms around her waist and pressed a kiss to her brow. "Love you."

"Love ye, too. We'll be back soon."

Cait followed Elspeth through the taproom and out the front door of the building. The side of her that was incredibly happy to see her sister witch warred with the side that held allegiance to Dashiel.

"Why do ye look so worried, I wonder," Elspeth said absently as she fell into step beside her.

"Elspeth," Cait began. Then she stopped and shook her head. "I ken ye doona approve."

"I wasna aware we had ta approve of one another's spouses, Cait." The red-haired witch's eyes danced with something Cait couldn't quite identify, but possibly there was a bit of smugness in her gaze. "I vaguely recall that ye were wholeheartedly opposed ta my marriage ta Ben. Ye had Rhiannon shake the town with an angry storm." Then she laughed and broke the tension. "But at least ye had an opportunity ta object ta my marriage. I dinna even ken about yers. Ye're my very dearest friend."

"There wasna time," Cait muttered, hoping Elspeth would understand.

"Why no'? What was the hurry?"

"What was the hurry with ye and Benjamin?" Cait shot her a pointed look.

"I'd been ruined, if ye remember correctly."

Cait just raised her eyebrows at her and planted her hands on her hips.

Elspeth caught on immediately. "He ruined ye? Was it on purpose? I've always suspected that Ben ruined me on purpose." She laughed.

"Westfield never cared if he ruined ye or not. He simply wanted ye."

"No more than I wanted him," Elspeth said softly, a light smile upon her face. "But Ben and Brimsworth are no' cut from the same cloth."

Elspeth must have seen the fury that screamed through Cait's body at that comment because she hastily added, "I shouldna judge him since I havena spent much time with him."

Furious, Cait wanted nothing more than to rail at her friend. Comparing Benjamin Westfield to Dashiel Thorpe was comparing apples to oranges.

"Why did ye leave Westfield Hall in the middle of the night without even a backward glance?"

Now, they got to the meat of the matter. "It's a long story," she hedged.

"Then ye should start with the tellin'."

"I met Dash," Cait shrugged. "The rest of ye were frolickin'," she shot Elspeth a telling glance, "in the woods. No one else was about. And we just bumped inta one another."

"And it was love at first sight?"

More like love at first bite. Cait didn't answer and just kept walking.

"What happened, Cait?" Elspeth asked quietly. "I always assumed Alec…"

Cait sighed. "El, ye ken Alec MacQuarrie and I werena destined ta be together."

"So ye said. But I never understood why. The man has been in love with ye for a lifetime. And I thought ye were softenin' ta him."

"I dinna see him with me."

"Ye mean ye couldna see him in yer future? Ye ken that ye canna always see what'll happen. Just because ye dinna specifically see the two of ye with a bairn or two doesna mean it wouldna happen. I hope ye dinna let yer lack of a vision entice ye inta marryin' the wrong man."

The wrong man. Cait winced. It would be nice if

Elspeth had a bit of faith in her. Still, her friend knew her better than anyone in the world, and Cait couldn't lie to her. "I saw Alec with someone else. And they were so happy. I had no choice but ta let him go."

Elspeth gasped. "Who was he with?"

"I canna tell ye," Cait moaned. "Ye ken I canna. I canna change the events in the future. I canna chance it."

"Can ye see yerself with Dashiel Thorpe in the future?"

"No." Cait turned away and plucked a tall stem of grass from the trail where they walked. "I can see no future with him at all."

"Oh, Cait," Elspeth sighed pitifully.

"It's no' what ye think," she explained. "My mother couldna see my father, either."

"Truly?"

"Aye, truly. It's the way of things, my father says. Ye ken how it is with me. I'm assaulted by every future that exists but, even if I search, I canna find his. In fact, he clears my mind and makes me feel more at ease than anyone before. All he has ta do is touch me. It's right, El." She took her friend's hands in hers and squeezed. "It's right, I tell ye. He's right for me."

Elspeth squeezed back. "The earl has a bit of a past, and that makes me worry. But if ye can be happy with him, I'll be happy for the both of ye."

Cait pulled Elspeth close for a hug.

"I'm so glad he claimed me as his own," Cait sighed.

Elspeth froze. "What do ye mean claimed ye as his own? We havena had a full moon since the night ye left Westfield Hall. How could he have claimed ye?"

Thirty-One

DASHIEL THORPE HAD NEVER BEEN AS UNCOMFORTABLE in his life as he was sitting across the table from Benjamin Westfield. The man's shrewd hazel gaze raked him from top to bottom. The hair on the back of Dash's neck stood up.

"Miss Macleod means a lot to my wife, Brimsworth," the man finally said as he raised a glass of whisky to his lips.

"You mean my countess, don't you? She's not Miss Macleod any more, but Lady Brimsworth, and I would appreciate it if you would remember that."

Dash knew he was acting a bit high in the instep, but he was an earl, after all. If anyone was entitled to behave in such a way, it was he.

"It's a very difficult thing for me to reconcile in my mind. My apologies," Westfield said as he tipped his head toward Dash and reached to refill his glass.

"Accepted," Dash grunted.

Westfield drew in a deep breath. "I do feel like I have to tell you—you seem like a changed man. Perhaps she's good for you."

"I'm not sure what you mean." Though Dash had a fairly good idea, he just wanted to hear the man say it.

"Perhaps Caitrin brings out the best in you," Westfield clarified. "You've lost a touch of the wildness that used to tail you like a hound tails a fox. Not completely, mind you; but a touch."

"Hard to shake the hound, isn't it, Westfield? Particularly when we're born with it in us, whether we want it or not."

"Whether we want it or not?" Lord Benjamin echoed. "That doesn't sound like you've accepted who you are."

The man sounded like Niall Forster, and Dash wasn't anxious to hear again how he should embrace the beast inside him. He downed the rest of his drink in one big swallow and pushed the glass back toward Westfield for a refill. "I'm a Lycan, as are you. There's nothing else to discuss."

Benjamin Westfield bristled visibly. "Well, not all Lycans are the same, obviously."

Before Dash could respond to that fairly uncomplimentary remark, Lady Elspeth burst back into the private dining room, with Cait following close behind and calling to her.

"El, wait," his lovely wife begged.

He heard the torment in her voice and immediately jumped to his feet. "What is it, Caitie?"

Elspeth flew across the room and into Westfield's arms, and then said vehemently, "Ye willna believe what *he* did, Ben. He claimed her that night. The night of the last full moon. He claimed her after knowing her for no more than a few minutes."

"You mean he…?" Westfield let his words trail off, as his hazel eyes took on a murderous glint.

"Aye, he *claimed* her."

"Bloody hell," Dash muttered before he pushed Cait safely to the side and took the first punch Westfield threw across his chin. He crashed into the sideboard, and the unlucky piece of furniture splintered under the force of that momentous blow.

Cait's gasp echoed in his ears.

Dash lay there for a moment, rubbing his jaw, as the enraged Lycan looked down at him. Then he said, "I'm sure I deserved that, Westfield." He climbed to his feet as Cait came to assess his injuries. He met his attacker's gaze without flinching and growled, "I've not always been an honorable man, but if you ever do that again, I'll do my best to flatten you."

"I canna believe ye told him that, El," Cait hissed at her friend.

Dash put her arm around Cait's shoulders and pulled her to him. "It's all right. I had that one coming, angel."

"He had no right ta hit ye like that," Cait insisted, standing on tiptoe to kiss the side of his jaw, which was already healing.

"Yes, he did, angel. He had a right." A smile tugged at the edges of his mouth. "He has your honor in mind, but I believe he's thinking I claimed you a bit differently than I actually did."

"I doona ken what ye mean." She blinked up at him.

He kissed her forehead. Still his little innocent.

Dash addressed Westfield with a softly breathed

comment that only another pair of Lycan ears could hear. "I didn't do *that* until I married her."

"Then what *did* you do?" The man looked totally flummoxed.

"I claimed her as my Lycan mate. Without any of the benefits." He arched his eyebrows at the man, still speaking under his breath.

Westfield's eyes widened in surprise, and he looked a bit ill. "I didn't know you could do that."

"Neither did I," Dash chuckled. "But I'm lucky I did." He pulled Cait close again and dropped a kiss into her hair, squeezing her tightly. "So lucky," he finally said in a voice she could hear.

She simply caressed his jaw, love for him shining in her pretty blue eyes.

"I doona understand," Elspeth said, her eyes flashing fire. Westfield probably had his hands full with that little redhead.

"I'll explain it to you, later," her husband answered as he held out a chair for her at the table. Then the man's face lit up, and he rubbed his chin. "This really is quite fitting, actually."

Dash followed suit, holding Cait's seat for her. Then he dropped back into his own chair as Benjamin Westfield passed him the whisky bottle. "Thank you."

The other Lycan grinned as though enjoying a private joke. "You do know that your wife has taken special delight in antagonizing me?" Westfield asked. "I've been called dog, hound, and mutt, among more unsavory things."

Cait stiffened at his side. "Aye, and in yer case, Benjamin, they're all accurate."

Westfield tipped back his head and laughed. "I do believe you deserve each other. I'm thoroughly going to enjoy watching this play out." He moved his hand, gesturing to encompass both Dash and Cait. "I assume she strong-armed you into residing in Edinburgh?"

Dash shook his head. "Caitie hasn't made any demands on me." Not that he wouldn't have done whatever she asked.

Westfield's eyes grew round. "Indeed?"

Caitrin sat forward, leveling the man with her haughtiest glare. "Dashiel didn't need convincin'. *He* would never dream of takin' me from my coven, unlike some other flea-ridden mongrel I could mention."

"Ah, yes." Westfield turned his attention to Dash. "I do believe Caitrin will punish you more than my brother could ever have hoped to."

Dash squeezed Cait's hand. "I hardly find marriage to my beautiful and clever witch to be a punishment. More like a reward I don't deserve."

The concerned look on Lady Elspeth's face vanished, and she actually smiled at him. "In that case, Lord Brimsworth, welcome ta our circle."

Dash winked at her. "A much nicer welcome than the one I received from Miss Sinclair."

Cait sighed dramatically. "Rhi shocked him, right in the middle of the church. Can ye believe that?"

Westfield nodded. "You're lucky that's all you got. I was attacked by some very determined ivy, my coach was destroyed by lightning, and fireballs were thrown at my head."

"Please." Cait's pretty blue eyes twinkled wickedly. "It was *one* fireball, Benjamin. Ye are such a bairn."

It was Dash's turn to laugh.

⊷

It was hard not to join in with Dash's laughter, though Caitrin managed to hide her smile. Goading Benjamin Westfield was one of her most favorite pursuits. But the fireball had made her think of Blaire. She looked across the table at Elspeth. "When ye get home, check on Blaire, will ye?"

"Is she ill?"

The look of mild annoyance on Benjamin's face quickly became a scowl, and Cait wished she had the power to throw fireballs herself. If one of their sister witches *was* sick, Elspeth would want to heal her, yet her annoying husband would try to stand in her way. Besides, Elspeth wouldn't have been given the power to heal if she wasn't supposed to use it.

"She's no' ill." She sent Benjamin a scathing look. "I havena seen her. She was at some crumbling castle in the Highlands when we left, some monstrosity Aiden inherited, apparently. Anyway, I've had a series of frightenin' visions about her, so Mr. MacQuarrie went ta check on her for me."

Elspeth sat forward, immediately concerned. "Frightenin' visions?"

Cait nodded. "It was as if something, someone evil was hunting her. He doesna feel like a regular man ta me. There's no life within him." She laughed at herself. "I ken that sounds like the ramblings of a madwoman, but I doona ken how ta explain it any better than that."

"Alec MacQuarrie went after her?" Benjamin asked.

Cait ignored the low growl that came from her husband at the mention of Alec's name. "Aye."

"Well, I'm sure she'll be fine, then," Ben assured her. "There's not a more honorable man to be found."

Dash rose from his seat. Apparently the talk of Alec MacQuarrie didn't set terribly well. "Well, it's been a long day. So nice catching up with you, Westfield, Lady Elspeth."

Caitrin slowly stood as well and hooked her arm with Dash's. "I am quite tired." She looked across the table at Elspeth. "I'll see ye in the morning."

As soon as they retrieved their key from the innkeeper, Dash directed Cait up the stairs toward their room. "Did you really try to keep Westfield from marrying Lady Elspeth?"

"Aye. Ye see the good it did me."

His amber eyes bored into hers as he turned the key in the lock. "Did you not see him in her future?"

Cait cringed and shook her head. "Nay, I saw him. I just wasna happy about it." She entered the room with Dash's hand at her waist. He'd been very careful not to let any stray visions encroach upon her mind, for which she was very grateful.

"He seems like an all right sort, when he's not knocking one to the ground or lauding the many virtues of Alec MacQuarrie." He shut the door behind them.

Cait rose up on her tiptoes to press a kiss to his jaw. "Ye ken there's no need ta be jealous, Dash. My heart is yers."

He slid his arms around her and pulled her flush against his hardness. "I don't plan on ever giving it back." His lips descended on hers.

"I doona want it back, and I would force ye ta keep it, even if ye tried," she said when his lips left hers to trail down the side of her neck.

"Saucy little witch, aren't you?" he murmured as his fingers went to work on the fastenings of her dress. Within moments, she stood naked before him, aside from her garters and stockings.

"Why is it that ye always strip me bare but leave these things on?" she asked absently as he stepped back to work at his own clothing.

"To give you something to complain about?" he said with a big grin.

"Oh, ye are no' humorous in the least!" she groaned as she looked around for something to throw at him. But before she could pick up any weapons, he'd scooped her up and deposited her on her back in the middle of the bed. He held her foot in his hand as he looked down at her.

"I leave them on you, angel, because if I took them off, I'd have to kiss you in the most inappropriate places."

She sat up on her elbows. "Such as?" She felt the color creep up her cheeks as he raised an eyebrow at her.

"Shall I show you, my little innocent?"

She was quite happy to hear her voice only quiver a bit when she said, "If ye insist."

Dash tugged at the ribbons of her left garter until he'd loosened it. Then he began to slowly roll her stocking down her leg. She sighed loudly.

He tilted her leg enough to expose her bottom, which he popped loud enough that it could be heard around the room. The swat didn't hurt Cait; it surprised her more than anything and she sucked in a breath.

"Patience," he said, his eyes very intent upon his project.

"Patience is no' a virtue I have, Dash. I'm very sorry ta tell ye, but ye would find out soon enough, anyway."

He chuckled out loud.

But then her foot was bare and his lips touched the inside of her ankle. A shiver tingled up her spine.

Dash made his progression up her calf a lovely experience, his lips adoring every inch of her flesh and raising goose bumps along her skin.

"Dash," she said, trying to get his attention. His slow torture would drive her mad.

"Yes?" he breathed against the inside of her thigh as he opened her legs a bit with his hands.

Cait gasped as he very tenderly scraped his teeth across the sensitive skin of her inner thigh. "Nothin'."

Cait found herself gripping the bedclothes fiercely in her hands as his lips traveled farther and farther up, alternating between teasing licks and tantalizing nibbles, until her blood was ready to boil.

Then he did the unthinkable. He touched his lips to the very center of her. Cait jumped and tried to scoot back on the bed.

"Ye shouldna be doin' that."

But he wrapped his arms around the outside of her thighs to draw her back down, firmly holding her in place.

"Why not?" he asked, intent upon his task.

"It's no' proper," Cait said, followed by a moan of pure delight as he licked across her center.

He raised his head for a moment and said, "I did warn you that I would have to do things that were completely inappropriate if I took off your stockings.

Your only comment was 'if ye insist.'" He mocked her accent.

His slow licks across her folds quickly became more and more vigorous until he put his fingers inside her. Cait lay her head back against the counterpane and let him take her higher, until she was arching against his mouth and hands and calling his name.

Then one quick suck at the pulse point between her thighs took her over the top, to a place where she soared above him, where he was her anchor to this wondrous sensation.

When he'd wrung every bit of pleasure from her, and only then, he crawled up the bed and looked down at her.

"Are you all right?" he asked as he brushed her hair back from her face.

"I *like* inappropriate," she sighed, still quivering on the inside.

He laughed as he drove within her in one stroke. "I know you do." Then he took her back up, until she wrapped her feet around his back so she could take him even deeper.

Once he'd taken her back to the top of that beautiful precipice, he joined her, which was the most wondrous sensation of all.

Thirty-Two

FROM THE COACH, CAIT WAVED GOOD-BYE TO ELSPETH and Benjamin, and then brushed a tear from her cheek as the conveyance lurched forward. Dashiel enveloped her in his arms and pressed a kiss to the top of her head. "It won't be long before you see her again, angel."

Though she couldn't see what the future held for her and Dash, she somehow knew that he was wrong. This journey they were on would last longer than either of them expected. Cait wished she had some inkling about what was in store for them.

Two days later, their coach crossed over the invisible border that marked the boundary of Eynsford Park. Cait sensed the change in her husband almost instantly. Gone was the loving and considerate man she'd married. If she hadn't known better, she would have thought someone had replaced him with an irritable duplicate.

He gazed out the window, watching the manor house grow larger as they approached it. Dash's arms were folded across his chest, and his back was stiff. He appeared to be preparing himself for a most unpleasant encounter. Cait swallowed nervously. His apprehension only made her more anxious.

Cait slid closer to him on the bench and touched his arm. "Dash, are ye all right?"

He grunted noncommittally. Then the coach rumbled to a stop on the drive. Dash didn't hop out as he generally did. Instead, he took a deep breath and allowed Renshaw to open the door for him. After he stepped from the carriage, he turned back and offered his hand to Cait.

As she stepped out into the sunlight, Cait stared up at the large baroque manor of sandstone that loomed before them. She gulped as she saw a frail old man in her mind, lying in bed. Aside from his nightshirt, he wore only a powdered wig and a scowl.

Dash tucked her hand in the crook of his arm, and the vision vanished as though it had never been. That did nothing to relieve her fears, however.

They walked up the steps, between large stone pillars, and Cait gaped at the size of the place. It was larger even than Westfield Hall. As they approached the massive door, it was pulled open, and they were greeted by an ancient butler who looked as though he might have been in service during James II's reign. How the man had the strength to open the door was a complete mystery.

Cait glanced around the front hall. Marble floor and pillars. It was as grandiose as any place she'd ever seen.

"Price," Dash said in greeting.

"M-my lord!" the butler stumbled over his words. "We weren't expecting you, Lord Brimsworth."

Dash directed Caitrin over the threshold, though his eyes never left the old servant. "Please prepare a room for my wife and myself. I do not know how long we will be staying."

Price bobbed his head. "Of course, my lord."

"And, Price, I would like to see my father." He led Caitrin further down the corridor and into an immaculate parlor that was stark white with golden accents.

Cait didn't even want to sit down on the elegant divan for fear of disturbing the pristine nature of the room. "This place is—"

"A bloody prison," Dash grumbled under his breath.

"I was goin' ta say spectacular." Cait's eyes flashed up to him. His jaw was tight, and his amber eyes were so cold that she shivered.

"Hmm," he grumbled. "Never thought of it that way."

"Dash," she began, touching his chest. "I'm sure it will be all right."

A twisted smile appeared on his face. "You cannot know that, Caitie, and I highly doubt it."

"Why doona ye go up and see yer father, Dash? I can entertain myself for a bit."

Dash visibly shivered, and then she watched him straighten his spine and shake his head. "You afraid to meet the old buzzard?"

Cait sighed. "I'm no' afraid. If ye need me ta go with ye, I will. I just thought ye might want some time ta be alone with him."

"Why would I want to see him alone? If you hadn't insisted on this journey, I wouldn't even be here." He fidgeted nervously and drew his eyebrows together.

Cait stiffened her own shoulders. "I should like ta

meet him, then." She tucked her hand in the crook of his arm. His muscle bulged beneath her fingertips. She tugged him to a stop when he began to move.

"Dash," she whispered.

"What is it, Cait?" he sighed.

"I just wanted ta tell ye I love ye." She stood on tiptoe to press her lips to his quickly. He immediately drew her into his arms and sunk his face into her hair, inhaling deeply.

"I can do anything with you beside me," he finally said, then pulled her up the stairs.

∼⁂∼

Cait believed in him. She believed there was goodness in him. She believed he could be worthy of her. He was determined to prove her right.

He rapped quickly on his father's door. A mousy little maid immediately cracked the door an inch, just enough for him to see her.

"Move aside," Dash said. Cait punched him in the arm.

"What?" he asked, not understanding the reason for her censure.

"Ye ken *what*," she grunted, folding her arms beneath her breasts. "Behave yerself."

The door opened quickly after his bark. Dash led her into the room with his hand at her back. The maid curtsied with a quick, "Milord, milady," her gaze pointed toward the open doorway, as though she ached to flee.

The odor of an unwashed body immediately met Dash as they stepped through the door. He fought to keep from covering his nose. He took Cait's upper arm in his grasp and turned her. "You should go. This isn't a place for you."

She pressed a hand to his chest and smiled softly at him. "I'm here for ye, Dash. No' for anythin' else. The rest I can ignore. All of it."

"Who's there," a scratchy voice called. "If it's that bloody physician, tell him he can go to the devil. I'll die in good time, when I'm goddamn ready. And not a moment before."

Cait stood back as Dash approached the bed.

"You do everything in your own time, don't you, Father? Why should dying be any different?" Dash tried to modulate his tone, showing no emotion, whatsoever. Eynsford did not appreciate displays of emotion. A lesson learned many years ago.

"Who's there?" his father called from the bed.

"The Monster of Eynsford has returned," Dash said as he stepped into the man's line of sight. In all his years, Dash had never seen the marquess look so... vulnerable. No longer strong and robust, Eynsford still wore that damned wig, but his face was gaunt and his skin so pale that Dash could have seen straight through it if he'd looked close enough.

Dash doubted whether the man would even be able to hold his own weight, slight as he now was. For a brief moment he felt a twinge of regret for what might have been, though it passed just as quickly as it came.

"The bastard of Eynsford. The scourge of Eynsford. The monster of Eynsford. What's the difference? Get out."

The man's mind still worked, however. He was

the same old rotten blighter, despite his decrepit state. "Charming as ever, I see," Dash replied conversationally.

The old man snorted. "Did you come to ensure your inheritance, boy? Don't worry. I haven't disowned you, not for lack of trying. Damned entailments. But you'll still have to wait until I take my last breath."

He turned his head away, as though he refused to acknowledge Dash's presence. "At least I'll never have to see such a travesty with my own eyes. A monster like you inheriting all I've built. My family seat. My wealth. It's intolerable."

Cait stepped up to Dash's side and tugged his sleeve. "Introduce me," she whispered.

It was amazing that she could be so calm about all this. Dash shrugged. "Father, though I loathe the very idea of putting her into your hate-filled path, I want to introduce you to my wife, Caitrin Brimsworth."

"The monster takes a bride?" the old man gasped. Then he coughed so hard it racked the bed. Dash feared he would expire before their very eyes. But the marquess eventually calmed and leaned back against the pillows, exhausted.

"Are you some kind of anomaly, too, Lady Brimsworth? Why else would you take someone such as my *son*," he laughed at the word, "as your husband? It's because he'll be terribly rich when I finally pass, isn't it?" He tapped his temple with his index finger. "It appears you found a smart one to tolerate you, Dashiel."

"Actually, my lord, I'm a witch," Cait said as she approached the old man. Dash sent her a warning glance that she promptly ignored.

The marquess grunted. "And she has a sense of humor to go with her death wish, I see."

Let the man think she was joking. He didn't particularly care.

"It's a pleasure ta meet ye, sir," she finally said, though her face told the truth. It wasn't a pleasure at all. Her dainty nose was scrunched up, probably from the smell. And no smile graced her beautiful face.

"A Scottish lass?" The marquess blinked his silver eyes.

"Aye." Cait inclined her head, and then she surprised him when she said, "A Scottish lass who isna afraid ta tell ye that ye smell terrible." She turned and motioned for the maid to open the window.

"He doesn't want it open, milady," the maid said.

"If he wants it closed, he'll have ta get up and close it himself," Cait replied.

The girl hesitated until Dash nodded his head for her to follow the order. Then the young maid rushed to do their bidding. The smell had to bother her, too. There was no odor as unkind as that of an unwashed, bedridden body.

Once the window was open, Cait inhaled a breath of fresher air. "That's better already. Call for a bath. The marquess is in need of one." The maid hesitated again. Cait said quickly and decisively, "Now!"

The girl quickly took heed, scurrying from the room as fast as her feet would carry her. "We'll need clean linens," she mumbled to herself. "And clean night clothes." She glanced quickly around the room.

"Cait," Dash started. It wouldn't matter what she

did. Her efforts wouldn't be appreciated. Nor would they be heeded. "I'm not sure this is a good idea."

Cait completely surprised him when she sat down on the side of his father's bed and took the old man's gnarled hand in her own.

"Ye smell terrible. And I and his lordship," she said, gesturing toward Dash, "would like ta spend some time with ye. Will ye consent ta a bath for me, and bein' cleaned up a bit?" Then she did the unthinkable and batted her pretty blue eyes at the man. She could charm just about anyone by blinking her lashes. And she took full advantage of that fact.

His father nodded absently. "I'll do it for you. Not for him, mind you. But I'll do it for you, because you're a pretty little thing, and it's been a long time since I've been a host in my own home."

"Then ye've something ta look forward ta?"

"It would seem so."

Dash's heart swelled to the point it was ready to burst. Cait had broken the ice for him, somehow softening the old buzzard up. She was making it all right, succeeding where he would have failed. She was doing the impossible. She was being Cait, the love of his life.

Thirty-Three

"WHAT A CHARMING FELLOW," CAIT SAID AS SHE FLOPPED down on the bed in their guest chambers. "I can see why ye dinna want ta make the journey."

"Warned you about that." Dash sat beside her and kissed the top of her head. "But you are amazing, Cait. I never would have believed it, if I hadn't seen it with my own eyes."

"Believed what?" She tipped her face up to see him.

"You turned the grouchy old lion into a lap-cat."

She couldn't help the snort that escaped her. No one who'd ever laid eyes on the Marquess of Eynsford would call him a lap-cat. The man was a ball of pent-up anger.

"Hardly. I just have a bit of practice managing difficult men."

"Indeed?" Dash asked, his brow high with amusement.

Cait smiled at him. "Hmm. My husband, for example, is a very difficult man."

Faster than lightning, Cait was on her back with Dash hovering over her. "Do you mean to manage *me*, angel?" It came out a low throaty growl, but a roguish grin tilted his lips.

Desire raced through Cait and settled low in her belly. All it took was a look from him to make her insides melt. She giggled and tugged on his ear. "Every day of my life."

"Witch," he accused, lowering his mouth to hers.

Before she could kiss him back, a scratch came at the door and Dash bolted off the bed to keep whichever servant was on the other side from catching them. "Come," he called.

Cait pushed up on her arms as the door opened and the aged butler peered inside from the threshold. "Lord Eynsford is asking for Lady Brimsworth."

Even though there was no blood between Eynsford and her husband, and only shared animosity, Cait could feel Dash's disappointment. Even after all this time, it seemed he craved his father's approval or perhaps merely his acceptance. She stood and smoothed the wrinkles from her dress.

"Thank ye, Price. I'm fairly tired from our journey. Perhaps Lord Brimsworth can keep him company for a time."

Dash shook his head. "Go on, Caitie. It's you he wants to see."

"Ye're his son," she countered, though they both knew that wasn't true.

He stepped toward her and lowered his voice. "You saw the vision. You said it meant something. I came to terms with the man's rejection many years ago."

She didn't believe that, however. His voice almost cracked, and that seemed a very telling sign to Cait. Still, she wouldn't push him to do something that made him uncomfortable. She squeezed his hand. "Very well, my lord."

Dash smiled at her, urging her to go. So Cait stepped around him to where Price still waited in the hallway. She followed the ancient butler to the other wing of the house where he scratched at the door before he opened it for her.

"Lord Eynsford, her ladyship is here."

The room smelled a little better this time around, and the marquess, lying in his bed, looked as though he had a bit more color to his cheeks. Cait stepped inside and crossed the room, dropping a curtsey once she reached her father-in-law. "My lord, ye are lookin' well."

A cynical sneer tugged at his lips. "You are a liar, Lady Brimsworth, but a pretty one, I'll grant you that." He pointed to a wooden chair at his bedside. "Sit."

Cait wasn't even part Lycan, but she felt as though she was being ordered about like a dog. She sat anyway. "Ye wanted ta see me?"

A sigh escaped his lips. "A word of advice, my lady. Take your things and run as fast and as far from my *son* as you are able."

Cait sucked in a breath. She supposed she shouldn't be surprised at the man, but she was anyway. "Lord Eynsford."

The marquess was unmoved by her chastising tone. "You seem like a charming lady, and I'd rather not see you hurt by the likes of him. I'm not long for this world, and there's very little I can do. But I'll see to it that Brimsworth settles you with a nice allowance. And—"

"I'm no' leavin' my husband," she said more harshly than she meant to.

Fear flashed in his eyes, and his pale skin became even more so. "The full moon is only days away, my lady. You can trust me... you do not want to be around him then. You'll not want to see the monster that lives inside him."

"I know what he is," Cait said softly. "What he's capable of. And he's not a monster."

Eynsford closed his eyes. "I wonder if Philippa knew what his true sire was."

"I beg yer pardon?"

The marquess' face twisted in pain. "You may think you know what he is, and I am surprised he told you—but you cannot possibly know what he can and will do to you, Lady Brimsworth. I don't think my wife knew, and she was never the same."

A sickening uneasiness settled on Cait. Eynsford knew who Dash's father was—his *real* father. She could hear it in his voice. She sat forward in her chair and clutched his cold, trembling hand. "Who are we speaking of, my lord?"

"Brimsworth," he spat the name at her, his eyes now narrowed with contempt. "Haven't you been paying attention?"

Cait nodded. "Of course, sir. I wasn't certain if we were still speaking of Dashiel or of his natural sire."

Eynsford snatched his hand away from her and winced. "I've not spoken that blackguard's name in nearly three decades. Why would I speak of *him*?"

He did know. Cait breathed a sigh of relief. How could she get the marquess to divulge the information? "I dinna kent ye were aware of who he was."

"Of course I knew," he grumbled, which then turned to a series of coughs that racked his body.

Cait rushed to a side table and poured him a glass of water from a porcelain pitcher. She returned and brought the goblet to his lips.

When he was done, the marquess brushed her hand away and then sank back against his pillows, closing his grey eyes once more. "I brought the scoundrel into my home."

Cait listened quietly for fear that any interruption would end his story. She resumed her seat and took his hand once more.

"Foolish of me," Eynsford continued, running his tongue over his parched lips. "I was flattered by his praise of my speeches in the Lords. I was vain even then, it seems."

He was quiet for a time, and Cait imagined that he was recounting past events, like reading the pages in a book. "I had no way of knowing the man was a monster, that he'd take my wife out to the woods and reveal the animal he truly was to her."

Eynsford winced and his words slowed as though the memories were painful.

"Philippa, so young and pretty. She'd been trying to give me an heir for so long, but I was old even then. I think she fell in love with the man. I was upset when I learned of their liaisons, and I knew the child wasn't mine when she told me she was expecting. But she promised not to see him anymore. I let it rest with that promise. I needed an heir, you see."

His eyes rose to meet Cait's, as though silently begging her to understand. "She came back with scars on her neck. And I firmly believe it was that night with Radbourne that killed my Philippa because she was unable to survive the birth of that *thing* everyone calls my son."

Dash. Eynsford blamed him for the death of the marchioness. She could hear the pain still in his voice. Though it wasn't fair, she could understand it. No man enjoyed being cuckolded.

Caitrin reviewed the marquess' words. Radbourne. She had a name, as well as the beginnings of a very sad story. The marquess thought Dash's mother had been left scarred and weak from her encounter with Radbourne under the light of the full moon. Cait swallowed past the fear the story brought to her.

She assumed she bore the same scars, the bite marks left when Dash had claimed her, yet she was not affected by them, aside from a brief moment of pain. And Elspeth hadn't seemed any worse for the wear after her marriage to Benjamin. She had bounds of energy, in fact, even for an expectant mother.

Eynsford turned his head and pierced her with his silvery eyes. "You say you know what Dashiel is, but I am worried for you. Pray leave before the full moon, my lady. It's not too late for you. I wouldn't have you or any other woman subjected to my Philippa's fate, being forced to carry a monster within her own body."

Cait rose from her seat and pressed a kiss to the marquess' brow. He didn't quite seem the tyrant she expected. And he'd suffered his own heartache, it seemed. Then she smiled down at him.

"Thank ye for yer concern, my lord. Please try

no' ta worry for me. Dashiel is all that is warm and considerate. He would never hurt me."

❦

Dash wasn't so certain about that. He would never intentionally hurt her, but he wasn't in control of himself during a moonful. He doubted he ever would be.

Eavesdropping wasn't something he could control either, and especially not when his Cait's soft lilt was anywhere in the vicinity. Radbourne. He'd never even heard the name. No idea who the man was. His father. Knowing the name was a bit like bringing the man to life, making him real for the first time ever.

Dash ran his hands along the dark stone walls of the windowless wine cellar. The musty smell of the room brought back many memories, none of them good, of the nights he spent chained up in this room. The marquess had insisted it was for his safety, but truly it was for the safety of everyone else at Eynsford Park.

The lessons were so imbedded in Dash's mind that even after he'd left Eynsford's home, he'd still had himself bound and cuffed before each full moon to keep those around him safe. Though he had no intention of mating with Caitrin during a moonful, the disturbing story from the marquess' ancient lips only solidified that decision in Dash's mind. He would never forgive himself if he hurt Caitrin. He'd sooner take his own life.

A creak at the far end of the cellar announced the arrival of a servant, and Dash stepped further into the darkness of the room. Then his nostrils were assailed by the scent of honeysuckle, and he closed his eyes.

How had Caitie tracked him to this godforsaken place?

"Dash," she called softly as she pushed the door open.

"Go back upstairs, Cait," Dash called, refusing even to look at her. He wanted her gone. He didn't want her to see the evidence of the beast that lived within him. "I'll be up in a moment."

"I wanted ta talk with ye," she said, her pert little eyebrows drawing together as she gazed about the room. "What are ye doin' down here?"

"You shouldn't be here," he said, knowing his tone was a bit too harsh.

"And, why no'?" she asked. Damn the woman.

"Because it's dirty," he lied.

She snorted. "Ye think I've never seen dirt before?"

Dash sighed and moved toward her, ready to steer her from the room. And use bodily force, if necessary. If she saw the shackles in the shadows of the room, he'd be forced to face her questions. Thankfully, she let herself be steered away.

"I just finished talkin' with yer father," she said, a sneaky smile stealing across her face.

"Yes, I know."

"How do ye ken?" She stopped and faced him, her hands on her hips.

Dash pointed to his ears with a sigh and an eye roll and said, "Nice to meet you, Cait. I'm a Lycan. We have extrasensory hearing."

She giggled. Just when he was fully prepared to be an ass, she giggled. Damn her for being so perfect.

"Ye can really hear from that far away?" She softened and leaned into him. She fit so perfectly there that he couldn't keep himself from wrapping his arm around her.

"I can hear the stable hands talking about the horse race that's coming up." He tilted his head and listened again. "I can hear the maids in the kitchen prattling on about how the monster has returned home and now they'll all be ordered from the grounds before the moonful. And I could hear you discussing my parentage with my father. Yes. I hear it all."

"And?" she prompted, a small smile tugging at the corners of her mouth.

"And what?" he asked. It was more of a grunt and he was aware of it, but he couldn't seem to keep himself from being a bit surly.

"And the marquess told me who yer father is." Her blue eyes twinkled with merriment.

"Radbourne." Dash nodded.

"Do ye ken who he is?"

"I haven't a clue," Dash replied, and then he bent to kiss her forehead. He needed to get away from her before he said or did something to upset her. "I need to go and talk with my father's steward. And take a look at some of his books. Will you be all right by yourself for a bit?"

Cait tensed. She could apparently see right through him.

"I'm perfectly fine by myself. But ye shouldna be runnin' from me." She brushed a lock of hair from his forehead. He closed his hand around hers and brought it to his lips.

"As the moon gets fuller, it becomes harder to stay in control. I'm sorry."

"If I'd wanted a man who was in control all the time, I'd have married someone else. It's no' as though I dinna have offers." He turned to walk away, but she grabbed him.

"I kent what ye were before I married ye. And I wanted ye anyway. And I always will. Now, run off ta sulk if ye need ta. But ye canna blame it on the moon or the fact that ye doona want ta hurt me. Because I'll never believe ye could do so."

"I wish I was as sure," he sighed. "I'll see you at dinner." He turned to walk down the corridor, feeling as though her gaze was hot enough to bore holes in his back.

"Dinner will be in the marquess' room!" she called to him.

"Witch," he muttered, shaking his head, unable to contain his grin.

"Big lout," she said beneath her breath.

"I heard that!" he called.

"I meant for ye ta hear it!"

Dash couldn't help but chuckle. Only his Caitie could take him from the depths of hell to a place where he couldn't keep from smiling. Damn the woman.

Thirty-Four

CAIT SAT ON THE SIDE OF THE MARQUESS' BED AND helped him don his robe as the footmen bustled about, setting a small table with fine linens, china, and silver.

"I wonder what's keepin' Dashiel," she muttered to herself as she rose and crossed to the window again. "I told him we'd be dinin' with ye here."

The old man grunted in response. Dash might not be his natural son, but they did share some traits.

"Are ye sure ye doona feel up ta sittin' at the table?" Cait asked as a maid fluffed the pillows behind the marquess and helped him to sit up.

"I don't think I have quite the legs for that, my lady. But I am very happy to have the company, even if Dashiel can't be here. It has been a long time since I've shared a meal with a fine lady."

"Even if that fine lady just happens to be mine?" Dash boomed as he strode through the bedroom door.

Cait was so happy to see him that she couldn't even scold him for his tardiness. He bent and kissed her softly. "I'm sorry to be so late. It's terribly inconsiderate of me not to be on time for a dinner engagement," he said as he bowed quickly toward his father.

"Quite formal, are we?" Cait muttered.

Dash turned and winked at her. "Some of us like to stand on formality."

Of course, he would know much more about what his father expected than she did.

The marquess finally said from his bed, "Not even the fact that she's yours could make me dislike her, Dashiel. How did you find such a wife?"

Cait saw Dash bristle. She slid her hand into his and squeezed softly. "Down, boy," she whispered.

Dash immediately relaxed and said to his father, "I bumped into her quite by accident, actually. I was visiting some friends, and they'd all gone out for an evening of entertainment." He threw a huge grin at Cait.

"And she happened to stumble into my path on her way to find a book in the study. It just happened to be where I was sequestered, and I knew immediately that I had to claim her as my own."

Cait had to fight to keep from giggling at his twist on the story.

"Lucky incident there, Dashiel. You should consider yourself very fortunate. You could have done much worse."

"On that, we agree," Dash said as he held out Cait's chair at the table. After she sat, he took a spot beside her and motioned for the footmen to begin serving the meal.

"How long do you intend on remaining at Eynsford?" the marquess asked as a servant ladled turtle soup into his bowl.

Cait glanced at Dash, who shrugged. "Until my countess has had her fill of you."

"Then what?" the old man asked as he brought a spoonful of soup to his mouth.

Dash shook his head. "I've never known you to be so interested in my plans, sir."

"I'm certain there are a great many things you don't know," his father snapped.

Cait suppressed a gasp. Her sensibilities wouldn't make this meal any more pleasant. "We'll return home," she told him soothingly. "Dashiel has hired a broker in Edinburgh, and we are lookin' for a residence near my father and friends."

The marquess' steely eyes focused on her as though she were a foreign species. "Scotland? Surely you jest."

Cait smiled as sweetly as she was able. "As I *am* Scottish, I canna imagine why ye would think I was jestin', my lord."

Eynsford waved his gnarled hand around in a circle as though to encompass the entire room. "Brimsworth has a duty, my dear. I do not believe it has escaped your notice that I am dying. If I had a choice to leave my holdings to someone more… well, more suitable, I would do so.

"But fate was not kind to me in that regard, and your husband *is* my heir. I have worked my entire life building my empire, and Brimsworth cannot see to it being run properly from *Edinburgh*." He sneered the last as though the mere thought of Scotland left a bad taste in his mouth.

"You've never needed me before now, sir," Dash said amicably, which was a tone Cait rarely heard from him. Very strange, since she had expected growling. "Besides, it is important for Cait to be near her father."

Near her coven was what he meant, and Cait's heart warmed at his words. She hadn't made any demands on Dash, yet he knew what was important to her. He knew what she needed, and he was willing to give it to her.

The marquess frowned down into his soup as though he didn't have an appetite any longer. Then he raised his gaze to his son. "It won't be long, Dashiel, before you are a peer of the realm. We have rarely seen eye to eye, but I did not expect you to turn your back on your duty."

Dash sighed. "You make it sound as though Edinburgh is on the other side of the world. I assure you it is not, Father."

But was it close enough? Cait sent her husband a sidelong glance. Was she being selfish by wanting to stay in Scotland? The circle of her coven had never been broken, though she knew the time was coming that Elspeth would spend a good amount of her time in England. Perhaps it was time for a change. She wished she could see what was supposed to happen.

"The session will begin soon," the marquess began. "Do you not intend to even take my seat in the Lords?"

"You are still among the living," Dash replied quietly.

The old man shook his head. "I will not be by the time the session begins."

A blanket of silence fell upon the evening, and Cait looked from one man to the other. She'd never imagined that she'd find herself married to an English lord. The thought had never entered her mind until it happened.

So many of her countrymen had fled Scotland during the clearances, pushed off their small farms and looking for opportunities in Canada and America. Having Dash's voice in the House of Lords might be a happy circumstance for her fellow Scots. "I am certain that my husband has every intention of fulfillin' his obligations, my lord."

Dash growled beside her. Truly, it wasn't her place to speak for him.

She turned her most charming smile on her husband, hoping to appease him. "The Westfields will be in London for the season... well no' this comin' one with her condition, but that is the plan for future years."

"What does that have to do with anything?" The marquess scowled. "And who are the Westfields? Do you mean Blackmoor's family?"

Cait nodded at her father-in-law. "My dearest friend is married ta His Grace's youngest brother. They are residin' in Edinburgh most of the year but plan ta spend the season in London each spring."

"Hmmph." Eynsford's frown darkened. "The current duke has done nothing to recommend himself. He's never taken up his seat. Too busy skirt chasing and gambling to be of any use to the country." His silver eyes held Dash's gaze. "Is that the sort of peer you aim to be?"

It was certainly the sort of man Dash had been before he married Cait, if his little journal was any indication, though she held her tongue. He said his days of debauchery were over, and she believed him.

Dash glowered at the marquess. "I intend to be the sort of man who takes care of his family first, fulfills his obligations to them, and *then* sees to all others."

The marquess grunted but seemed to be placated by Dash's announcement of his intentions. "Try to do a better job of it than I did," he finally said.

"That leaves me quite a bit of room for error, doesn't it, Father?" Dash replied dryly before meeting the old man's gaze.

The marquess snorted loudly just before he threw his spoon into his bowl with a loud clatter. "I couldn't let a monster ruin everything I'd worked for. It was a judgment call. One I'd probably make again."

Dash stood up slowly. "I'm *not* a monster."

Cait motioned for all the servants to leave the room in haste. As soon as they all bustled out the door, she stood up beside Dash and slid her hand into his. He squeezed it gently as he looked down at her and smiled softly.

Dash continued his speech. "I am a Lycan, Father."

"What kind of nonsense is this?" The marquess faltered, tripping over his words in surprise.

"It's not nonsense. It's the truth. I was led to believe all my life that I was an anomaly. But I recently met more men like myself. We're Lycans. Werewolves, if you will."

"Rubbish," the marquess grumbled.

"It's not *rubbish*," Dash bellowed as he smacked his open hand onto the table. "It's the truth. Only you're too blind to see it. And too stubborn to think

I could be anything but that bastard child who killed your wife."

"Do not speak of her!" the marquess bit out, his face reddening.

Cait rushed to his side with a glass of water as the man sputtered and coughed. He held up a hand for her to step back.

"Why can't I speak of her?" Dash asked the room at large, directing his question toward no one in particular.

"You," the marquess said as he pointed a finger at Dash, "cannot speak of her because *you* are the one who killed her, by God! You and your true sire, monster that he was."

The breath Dash drew in was almost painful to Cait. She covered her heart with her hand when Dash released it. Then she reached for him, but he was so quick that he was outside her grasp almost immediately.

"I didn't kill her." Dash made that small statement, his voice quiet but succinct. "And neither did Radbourne."

❧

Dash watched all the color drain from his father's face at the mention of his sire. "He did," the marquess insisted. "He took her into the woods under the light of a full moon. And he—"

Dash held up a hand and growled, effectively stopping his father's recounting of the events. He didn't need to be told what Radbourne had done.

Dash motioned for Cait to come closer. "We Lycans, most of us, can take our true mates into the woods with us, or anywhere else. When we claim them as our own, it's beautiful. Not draining or demeaning like you suggest." He looked into Cait's soft blue eyes, and his heart expanded. She was so lovely, so trusting, so damned perfect. He rubbed a hand along her cheek. "Caitrin wears my mark, the mark that means she's my true Lycan mate. She was meant for me."

"Blasphemous," his father grunted out.

"It's true," Cait said quietly from her place beside him. Dash couldn't stop himself from drawing her within his arms and pressing a kiss to her forehead. She'd always stand up for him. She'd always be on his side. She was the only one who ever had.

Cait's voice was a bit louder when next she spoke. "He's no' a monster, my lord. He never has been. He's a Lycan, as he says. I know others of his kind." She moved to sit down on the side of his father's bed. Such kindness was in her. Almost enough to temper Dash's fire, but not quite.

"But the moon comes," the marquess said harshly, his words grating, even to Dash. "You've obviously never seen him when there's a full moon."

"Have ye seen him yerself?" Cait blurted out.

God, he loved that woman. He wanted to wrap her in his arms and never let her go, never let any harm come to her, not even from himself.

"I was the first to shackle him when I saw what damage he could do." His father's chin jutted upward with a stubborn tilt.

"Ye say that as though ye're proud of it, my lord."

"Proud to have chained the monster? Yes, I was." The ruddy color was back in the man's cheeks. He obviously was ready to fight. "I couldn't let him hurt anyone."

"And he admits it so freely," Dash said quietly as he

sunk heavily into a chair. "You can stop, Cait. He'll never understand. He'll die a bitter and lonely old man who has no one to love him."

"I have never needed anyone to love me. I am a resourceful man. Look at my position in the House of Lords. Look at my estates. Look at all this." He motioned around the room. "I have not failed at anything."

"Yes, you did." Dash stood up on legs that were a bit shaky and crossed the room. He tugged a curtain on the wall until it slid back to reveal a portrait of his mother. She was nearly breathtaking in her gentle beauty with golden curls that billowed around her shoulders, a peaceful smile that graced a full set of lips, and eyes so green the artist must have embellished them.

When Dash was younger, he would sneak into the room when the marquess was gone and study the portrait of the woman with the smiling face who looked so happy. And dream. He'd dream of a life he could never have. Because monsters didn't find happiness.

Dash pointed to the painting. "You failed at this."

"I failed at *nothing*," the man growled, his breaths becoming more and more labored. "Close the curtain. I do not want to see it."

"Does her smile make you sad, Father? This must have been painted before she met you. She actually looks content. Ecstatic, even."

"That was finished a few days before your birth. When she was huge with her belly full of *you*." He sneered the last word, spittle flying from his mouth.

Cait's soft lilt reached his ears. "She did love ye, Dash. Ye can see it in the paintin'. I think she was happy ye were ta be born."

"Quiet!" the marquess yelled. "Out! Both of you, out!" Then a fresh wave of coughs gripped him.

As Cait leaned forward to offer the man some water, Dash saw the marquess move out of the corner of his eye. But he felt so out of kilter, realizing his mother was happy to be with child, with him, that he couldn't prevent what happened next. His father raised his arm and swung it with all of his might, the back of his hand making a cracking sound as he struck Cait across the face. She landed on the floor with a dull thud.

"I said, 'Out!'" the old man snarled.

Dash could see nothing but the redness of fury behind his eyelids. He crossed the room in three quick strides, yanked Cait to her feet, and then thrust her immediately behind him.

Somewhere in the back of his mind, he felt her tugging frantically on his arm, trying with all the strength she had to keep him from moving toward his father. But her slight form was no match for him.

He wrapped his hands around the marquess' throat and actually felt a rush of glee at the thought of killing the old man. Eynsford's face turned red, then purple. Then he sunk back against the pillows, the fight moving out of him.

Where tugging and pleading hadn't worked, Cait's gentle voice did. She said very plainly in his ear, "Please, Dash, I love ye. Doona do this." Then she repeated it, pulling him from his haze. Dash looked down at the old man dying beneath his hands and loosened his hold.

The marquess gasped in a few lungsful of air. "See.

I told you. He'll always be a monster," his father croaked out. Then he pointed a weak finger at Dash. "Always! You can't run far enough or fast enough to leave behind the monster that's within you."

"If you ever touch my wife again, I will kill you," Dash growled. Then he quickly quit the room, escaping as fast and furiously as he could, despite Cait's pleas that he wait. Despite her pleas that he stop. Despite the fact that he was still livid with rage.

Thirty-Five

LYING IN BED, CAIT CLOSED HER EYES AND WILLED DASH to return to her. She didn't have the first clue where to search for him. Eynsford Park was sprawling, and she didn't know her way around at all, especially not in the dark. She wouldn't find Dash until he wanted to be found, though Cait was certain that wherever he was, he knew she was waiting for him. He had to have heard her calling his name for the last hour.

There was nothing to do but to wait. And perhaps do a bit of research. At least it would keep her mind off where her husband had escaped to.

Cait rolled to her side and opened Eynford's copy of Debrett's. She flipped through the pages, searching for the right entry. She went through the listings of dukes. Radbourne apparently wasn't a marquess or an earl, either. Then she smiled when she finally found the page she sought.

"Radbourne of Baslow, Derbyshire, Viscount," she whispered to herself as her fingers trailed across the words. The first in the line was a Timothy Hadley in 1573. Cait glanced at the bottom of the page, only reaching a Clarence Hadley in 1596. She flipped two pages, then two more, until she felt as though she was getting closer to the listing she needed.

There it was. The current Viscount Radbourne was Archer Hadley, born 1793. But that would make him younger than Dash. She moved up a paragraph, and then a sick feeling took her over. If the current Viscount Radbourne was younger than Dash, then his natural father was gone. Dash had never gotten the chance to meet the man. He'd never know what his father was like, never be able to judge for himself.

With a trembling finger she touched the name Edward Hadley, born 1765, died 1797. Good heavens! He'd been gone twenty years.

"Edward Hadley married Violet Archer in 1792, the eldest daughter of John Archer, the sixth Baron Wardley. He had issue by his lady three sons, Archer Hadley, the current viscount, born 1793, Weston Hadley, born 1795 and his twin, Grayson Hadley, born 1795," she muttered softly.

Cait stared at the words on the page. Edward Hadley was gone, but Dash had *three* brothers. Three brothers he'd never met, never knew existed. She wasn't sure how he'd react to the news, and she sighed. How long was he going to keep himself from her?

❧

Dash prowled the grounds of Eynsford Park, cursing Eynsford for being such a miserable prig, himself for letting the old man still get to him, and Cait for making him come to this awful place to begin with. He wanted to bolt, to run as far as he was able, as far as it took for his father's words to stop echoing in his ears. *He'll always be a monster.* He didn't want it to be true, but he knew in his heart that it was. Other Lycans managed to control the beast that lived inside them, to tamp it down when necessary. He would never have that sort of power over himself. He was too wild.

If Caitie hadn't begged him to stop, he'd have squeezed the air from his father's body. He didn't doubt it for one moment. He still had the urge to do so, to storm back inside the manor house and hasten the old buzzard's demise.

Dash increased his gait, stalking toward Eynford's rectory. The old sandstone building caught his eye under the light of the moon, and he stopped in his tracks. He wondered if Mr. Nelson was still there under his father's employ. During some of his darkest hours as a child, he'd taken comfort in the old rector's teachings. Peace, forgiveness, responsibility.

Dash leaned against the stone fence and stared at the old wooden door that led to the rector's residence. No heartbeat came from within. No breathing. Not that he was surprised. Mr. Nelson had been ancient when Dash was a child. Still, the memories of the old man's kind face and soft words washed over him and brought him a bit of peace.

Cait accepted him. He knew that in his heart. He could see it in her eyes whenever she looked at him. Dash smiled as her image filtered into his mind. He could almost smell her flaxen hair with its honey-suckle scent. She deserved far better than he. She deserved a man who wasn't wild and dangerous. If he was honorable in any way, he wouldn't have forced himself into her life. But he'd been a selfish ass.

Perhaps it wasn't too late, though. Perhaps he could still protect her from himself. He could send her back to Edinburgh where her coven sisters awaited her return.

God, he was a fool. How did he let the marquess get him so angry? Dash took a deep, calming breath and then another as he watched the moonbeams dance around the rectory. When his soul seemed more at peace, he hiked back toward the manor house, hoping Cait would accept his apology.

He ignored the reproachful look Price shot him as he strode through the front door. The butler could go straight to the devil. Dash didn't give one whit what the man thought about him. Of all the people currently inhabiting Eynsford Park, only Cait mattered to him.

Dash found her sleeping on their bed in a gossamer nightrail, lying atop the counterpane, her glorious hair draped over one shoulder. She looked like an angel, so ethereal and heavenly. She must have waited hours for him to return.

He doused the lamp, then quickly shed his jacket and waistcoat before tossing his shirt to a damask chair near the bed. When he sat down beside her to tug off his boots, Cait rolled toward him, a smile upon her tempting lips. Dash brushed a curl from her face so he could see her better. "I love you, Caitie. I'm sorry I'm such an unruly beast."

She sighed in her sleep, and he couldn't help but smile at the way the sound soothed him. He tugged his boots off, then finished with the rest of his clothes. Gently, he eased the counterpane from beneath her and pulled it up back over her before sliding into bed beside her.

Dash lay down but sat back up at once when something hard poked him in the head. He retrieved a book from beneath his pillow and frowned.

What the devil was she doing with a book in the bed? The answer was obvious, however. She must have been passing the time waiting for her wayward husband to make an appearance, and a fresh wave of guilt washed over him.

Dash glanced at the title. *Debrett's Peerage of England, Scotland, and Ireland?* It didn't exactly make for light reading. It was worse than 'Genesis' with all those begats. He tossed the book to the chair where his shirt was, but it fell to the ground with a thud. He frowned at the sound and fell back against his pillow. Could nothing go his way?

"Dash?" Cait said sleepily.

"I didn't mean to wake you. Go back to sleep, Caitie," he said, as she snuggled against him, her sweet scent teasing his nose.

"Are ye all right?" she asked.

He was as good as he was going to be, stuck in Kent. "I'm fine."

Before the words were out of his mouth, she smacked his chest. "Then ye are in trouble."

"Yes, lass, I am in trouble," he agreed, scrubbing a hand across the spot she'd assaulted. "But there's no need to hit me."

Cait sat up and stared deep into his eyes. "I called ye and called ye, ye lummox," she complained. "Ye should have come back."

"I wasn't in any condition to be around you, Cait. Trust me on that."

"Listen ta me, Dashiel Thorpe." One slim finger jabbed at his chest. "I am yer wife, and ye doona get ta shut me out and stay away all hours of the night. I dinna ken what ta think, and I was worried about ye."

Dash sighed, not relishing a fight. He was too tired for that. "There's nothing to worry about, Caitie. I'm a Lycan. What do you think is going to happen to me?"

"Just because ye're a Lycan doesna mean that ye're invincible, Dash," she said softly.

He tugged her back to him and brushed his lips across hers. "Don't chastise me, lass. It's been a long day."

"I ken it has." Cait's arms slid around his neck, and she held him tight. "But ye're part of me now, Dash. Ye canna just run off."

"Caitie," he whispered before kissing her again. "It's not safe for you to be around me when I'm out of control."

Her sweet breath blew across his lips, and Dash groaned as he ached to find solace inside her, to erase all the anguish and pain of the day within Cait.

"Are ye in control now?" she asked, as her fingers trailed down his chest.

Dash rolled her beneath him. "Teasing the wolf?" he asked against her soft skin, grazing her shoulder with his teeth. "That's a very good way to get yourself bitten."

Cait giggled. "Now who is teasin' whom?"

❧

Dash loved waking up with Cait in his arms. Her bare breasts pressed against him, her pretty hair spread out across his chest.

She shifted beside him and then rose up on her arms to look at him. "Good morning." Her soft blue eyes twinkled.

He'd never seen a more beautiful sight, and Dash sucked in a breath. He'd deal with the future later, when she didn't look so desperately in need of a kiss.

"Good morning, angel," he whispered, leaning forward to brush his lips against hers. She tasted heavenly, like sweet summer berries.

After a moment, Cait gasped and reared back from him.

"What?" he asked, feeling as though his favorite plaything had just been snatched from his grasp.

Cait threw her leg over the edge of the bed. "I forgot. I told Price that I would help the marquess with his breakfast."

Dash couldn't help the growl that escaped him as he reached for her but missed. "The man has been feeding himself for seven decades. I think he can manage on his own."

Standing before him without a stitch, Cait folded her arms across her delightful breasts. "He hasna been eatin' well. Price said the little bit of soup he had last night was the most he's eaten in quite some time."

"If he chooses to starve himself, I don't see why we have the right to stand in his way." Dash stared up at the ceiling to avoid the scathing look he knew she sent his way.

"That is a horrible thing ta say, Dashiel Thorpe."

Perhaps, but he was unmoved by her protest and focused on a tiny crack in the molding. "He's a horrible man."

She huffed and then stalked toward the dressing room. In an instant, Cait yelped as her foot made contact with something heavy and she fell back on her bottom. "Ouch!"

Dash bounded off the bed to help her.

Cait ignored his outstretched hand as she clutched the Debrett's tome to her chest. "Dash, there's somethin', I have ta tell ye."

He scowled at the book in her arms. "I have something to tell you too, Caitie. That thing jabbed me in the back of the head last night. You shouldn't go around hiding books under pillows."

A beatific smile lit her face, and then she erupted into a fit of giggles.

He'd obviously missed something. "Just what is so funny, lass?"

"That's where I'd hidden it, yer wicked little journal. Under my pillow."

She'd obviously lost her mind this morning. Dash raked a hand through his hair. "Impossible. I burned the thing. Is your head all right? Did you bump it on the way down?"

Cait laughed even harder. "No, ye silly wolf, that night in the inn when ye were searchin' for it. I had it hidden under my pillow. Ye were rummagin' through my trunk, up ta yer elbows in chemises and frilly drawers." She fell backward, nearly breathless from all her laughter. "I wish ye could've seen yer face when Jeannie walked in on ye."

Dash leveled her with his most scathing glare. "I thought you were asleep."

She rose to her feet, still clutching the heavy tome against her chest. "Well, ye were wrong. I'm sure it willna be the last time." Cait leaned forward and kissed his brow. "I found Radbourne last night." She handed the book to him.

Dash's mouth fell open. That's what she'd been up to. He wasn't certain whether to kiss her or toss her over his knee for plodding forward without him. "I'm not sure I'm ready to meet him, Caitie."

Her light eyes started to water, and her lips drew up tight. "I'm sorry, Dashiel, but it's too late."

Radbourne was dead. He could see it in her tortured expression. "How long?" he choked out. A moment ago, he wasn't sure he was prepared to meet his sire, and now he knew he would never get that chance. He felt it from his heart to the pit of his stomach.

"How long?" she echoed, shaking her head in confusion.

"How long has he been gone?"

"Oh," she said softly. "Twenty years. I am sorry."

Dash shook his head. It shouldn't matter. He hadn't even known the man's name until yesterday. It shouldn't matter that he was gone, but somehow it did, which made no sense at all.

"His name was Edward Hadley—"

Dash raised his hand, silently halting her. He didn't want to know any more. His gut was clenching, and he didn't want her to see him weakened.

Cait's eyes softened, and she leaned closer to him. "There's more, Dash."

"I don't want to hear it, Caitie."

She pursed her lips stubbornly. "Ye have brothers," she blurted out.

"Brothers?" he echoed as the room began to spin.

Cait nodded. "Ye have three brothers."

Thirty-Six

Upon further reflection, Caitrin thought it might have been a bad idea to tell Dash about his brothers. He'd thrown on his trousers and shirt and fled from the room without another word. No amount of pleading or calling his name had brought him back to his senses. It was the second time in as many days that he'd stalked off, leaving her alone.

"*Mo chreach*," she grumbled to herself. "Temperamental wolf." It was so frustrating that she couldn't see his future. It would have brought a bit of relief if she could at least know he was safe.

Cait sighed as she quickly dressed herself without the help of a maid and then arranged her hair in a simple chignon. She and Dash were going to have a serious talk about his ill-mannered departures and propensity to brood.

Just as she started for the door, she heard a faint scratch. She opened it to find the butler in the hallway, grimacing. "Price, what is it?"

The old man shook his head. "It's his lordship, Lady Brimsworth. He's fading away before my eyes, and—"

"I'll get him ta eat somethin', Price." Cait smiled, hoping to comfort the man. "I'm sure he'll be fine," she lied. Though "fine" was probably a relative term. What she did know, what she could clearly see, was that the Marquess of Eynsford would not make it another day. What she didn't know was whether or not he would find peace with his son before he passed away, and vice versa.

Steeling herself for a difficult day, Cait followed Price to the marquess' suite of rooms. "I've never seen his lordship take to someone like he has you, my lady. I am glad you've come to visit."

Cait squeezed Price's hand. "Ye are ta be commended for yer loyalty."

The butler preened a bit at her words, which warmed Cait's heart. She knocked once on the marquess' door before letting herself in. "Good morning, Lord Eynsford," she called brightly.

The drapes were drawn closed and very little light filtered into the room. The marquess' labored breathing could be heard from the door, and Cait quickly crossed the room to his bedside. She wished Elspeth was here, as she could ease the man's passing.

Cait settled into a chintz chair beside him and straightened his wig. "I understand porridge is on the menu for breakfast, my lord."

He glowered at her. "I'm not eating *that*. Not even for you."

Cait laughed softly. "It's no' my favorite either," she confessed. "A dear friend of mine is always makin' the horrid stuff. I doona ken how she stomachs it."

"I'm dying, Lady Brimsworth."

"I ken." Cait studied his ancient face. Even the bit of color he had the day before was gone, but his mind was still sharp, his tongue just as biting.

"And I'm not going to eat anything I don't want."

She could see his point. Cait placed her hand on his. "I willna force the porridge on ye then, my lord. Is there somethin' ye do want?"

The marquess shook his head. "Just stay here. Talk to me. It's been forever since anyone just talked to me."

Cait nodded. "Of course, my lord. What shall we talk about?"

"Scotland," he suggested before coughs racked his body, shaking the bed beneath him.

Scotland? He was literally on his deathbed, yet he wanted to talk about inanities? "How about Dashiel?" she suggested instead, offering him a sip of water.

Eynsford shuddered and refused the drink by clamping his lips shut.

Cait resumed her seat. "Ye said yerself that ye were dyin', my lord. Wouldna ye like ta be rid of the animosity between ye and Dash before it's too late?"

He shook his head. "What's done is done, my dear. It doesn't have to be so for you, however. The moon is full tonight, but it's not too late for you to come to your senses and hide yourself away from the monster."

Cait tried to be patient with the man. He was old. He was dying. He didn't understand. "He's no' a monster," she said softly. "The line of Lycans is a benevolent one." Or so Benjamin Westfield had told her often enough. "They have helped to shape history as ye ken it, and Dash is as noble as his ancestors."

He frowned at her, folding his thin arms across his

chest, but Cait could tell he was listening. She took a deep breath and continued.

❧

Watching the sun begin to set from his father's old desk, uneasiness washed over Dash and he refocused on the ledger before him. He'd been dreading the coming of this moon more than any before, though he'd never been particularly fond of any of the moonlight-drenched nights. Until a month ago, he had always spent them shackled and chained, alone, fighting the pain that came with being out of control.

He hadn't confided his plans yet to Cait, as she'd been holed up with his father, whispering for most of the morning. He hadn't wanted to interrupt. He hadn't wanted to see either of them. And now as Eynsford Park was swathed in the glow of a sun-filled day, he decided it might be best to take the coward's way out, to sneak off like a thief and face the moonful alone, rather than have her bewitch him into staying there and accepting the risk that he could hurt her.

He simply couldn't. It wasn't conscionable. He would not, under any circumstances, be with Cait during the moonful. The only way she'd be safe was if he was shackled and chained in the same room where his father had first left him to face the beast within him on that moon-soaked night so long ago. Dash would spend it wrapped up in the irons he hated, but she would be safe, which was the most important thing.

He'd briefly contemplated leaving Eynsford Park before the moonful, but without adequate ways to secure himself, he'd just smell her honeysuckle scent across the river. Hell, he'd probably smell it if he was all the way back in London. Then he'd be traipsing through the woods to get back to her. And he'd probably make it. So, shackled in the room below stairs would work well, or at least it was the best he could do for now.

He considered sending someone to clean the room, to make it a bit more habitable. But he'd spent years with the cobwebs and dust. He could spend one more night.

He remembered the way she had awakened in his arms that morning, her sweet breath tickling the hair on his chest and her hands upon his skin. Lust immediately began to cloud his brain. And then he heard her soft footfalls down the corridor. Bloody hell. Of course, she would seek him out when he was feeling melancholy. She would find him the very moment he grew hard with want for her.

The study door cracked, and she poked her head inside. "Dash," she called softly. He fought to ignore her for a moment. He just needed long enough to clear his head. "Dash," she tried again, this time more urgently.

"What is it, Cait?" he barked, immediately sorry for his tone. But he didn't even raise his gaze to hers. He couldn't. Because he didn't want to see her love for him shining there. Finally, he couldn't keep from glancing up at her ever so briefly.

"Ye sure are in a fine temper, Dashiel," she said sternly as she placed her hands upon her hips and glared at him. God, those hips that he just wanted to hold onto so he could ride her through the night.

He slammed his desk drawer, trying to draw himself from his desire. "I'm busy, Caitrin."

"Aye, I can see that. And so am I, ye big lout."

He finally threw his quill down on the desk and slouched back. "What have you been doing?"

"Oh, now he has an interest?" she asked sarcastically.

"Cait," he groaned as he pinched the bridge of his nose between his thumb and forefinger in frustration.

"Yer father's cough grew worse durin' the night, and he's havin' a difficult time of it."

"Sorry to hear that," Dash mumbled, lowering his head back to his ledger to regard the numbers he'd lined up in neat rows. They swam before his eyes. Almost as though they wanted to swarm together and spell out her name.

"Damn it," he said as he slammed the book closed. "Why are you here, Cait?"

"Do I need a reason ta visit my husband?" Her blue eyes sparkled with irritation.

"No, but I imagine that you have one. So out with it."

Cait crossed the room toward him, her stockings whispering softly as she moved slowly in his direction. It made him think of the last time he'd removed her stockings and the new way he'd made love to her.

"Ye need to go and visit yer father, Dash. I'm afraid his time here will no' be much longer."

"Are you hoping I'll wrap my hands about his throat and ease his passing? If so, let's hasten to his room, Cait."

Dash saw the subtle warning that was anger in the reddening of her face. She turned quickly and picked up a vase on a table and threw it with all her might, straight at his head.

He ducked and the vase flew right by his ear, so close he could feel the wind it created. "Cait," he growled as he took in the broken shards that lay scattered on the rug.

"Ye've run from me twice, Dash. Ye havena sought me out all day, and I've been patiently waitin'. But the time has come ta an end, and ye need ta go and see yer father." She stomped her tiny foot. "Ye will regret it if ye doona go. He's askin' for ye."

Dash's ears perked up. "Why would he do such a foolish thing? He abhors the very ground I walk upon."

"He needs ye." She shrugged. "That's all I ken."

Dash scrubbed a hand down his face and took a deep breath.

"Do ye need me ta go with ye?"

His words escaped on a heavy sigh. "No. I can do it alone. I just cannot guarantee he'll be any better because of my visit. If he survives it."

"I'll go with ye," she resolved.

"If you think that's best," Dash grumbled as he strode quickly past her, holding his breath as he neared her for fear of unleashing the beast within him simply by inhaling her beautiful scent. "Stubborn witch," he mumbled.

"Irritable lout," she murmured at the same time.

"I heard that."

"I meant for ye ta."

Dash tried, unsuccessfully, to bite back his smile.

❧

Cait followed him, fully aware of the battle that waged within him. The beast in him wanted to rule, while the man in him wanted to wrest control back. And the little boy in him still wanted his father's approval.

That was the saddest part, knowing how much Dash craved Eynsford's love. Knowing how much he needed to belong, if only for a moment. Just as one misplaced word could leave everlasting scars, one well-thought word could heal old wounds.

Dash knocked lightly on the door before he stepped into his father's set of rooms and walked slowly toward the bed. The marquess lay so still, she immediately saw the fear in Dash's eyes that he'd been too late. She saw the regret, and it tore at her heart.

"My lord," she called to the sleeping form.

Then she smiled when he grumbled softly at her, "Go away." She heard the weakness of his tone and saw how he fought to open his eyes.

"Dashiel is here," she said.

The marquess opened his eyes, searching the room until he found Dash standing at his side. "Did you come to finish the job?"

"I came because Caitrin said you'd asked for me." Dash glowered at her.

"Why in the bloody hell would I do that?"

She shrugged her shoulders when the marquess confirmed her lie. But what else was she to do? They were both too stubborn for their own good, even now at this late hour.

Dash looked as though he could commit murder. Only it was directed at her this time. Cait fought to keep from shuddering. "If he'd been thinkin' clearly, he would have asked for ye," she said, hoping that both father and son would simply take advantage of the time that was left to them.

"It appears as though my wife has taken it upon herself to torture us both," Dash growled. "And since neither of us has a desire for me to be here, I'll take my leave."

The marquess said quietly, "Since you're here, you may as well stay."

Dash sat down so quickly on the edge of his father's bed that Cait tugged her earlobe, wondering if she'd missed the command to sit. But there he sat, looking as eager as a pup waiting for a treat. It nearly broke her heart.

"How are you?" Dash asked.

"Dying," the old man choked out, coughs raking through his body.

"I'm sorry," Dash said quietly.

Cait immediately wondered what he meant. Was he sorry his father was dying? Sorry for the way he suffered? Sorry for past actions? Sorry for being a bastard? She waited, nearly as eager as Dash appeared to be.

Tears pooled in her eyes when the old man reached out and covered Dash's hand with his own. "It's I who should be sorry, son." She could swear Dash trembled a bit. But he sat quietly and let the marquess continue. "It appears as though I love your wife."

Dash chuckled, his voice only shaking a bit. "I'm not too worried about you stealing her away from me."

The marquess motioned to Cait and asked, "Will you open the curtain there?" He pointed toward the one that concealed his late wife's portrait. Cait happily scrambled to reveal the picture of the beautiful, smiling woman.

"That's it, now," Eynsford murmured, settling peacefully against his pillows, a weak smile upon his lips.

Dash didn't make a sound.

"She loved you," the marquess finally admitted. "She was very happy to be with child. She talked of nothing more than her desire to hold you in her arms."

"Why didn't you ever tell me?" Dash asked quietly. Cait covered her sniffle with a small cough.

"I was angry. You took her from me, even before your birth. She loved you more than she ever cared for me. And then she was gone. Because of your origins, it was easy to assume you killed her. And it alleviated my guilt. I wasn't able to help her at the end. No one could."

"She loved me?" Dash echoed, and this time, Cait had to turn away to keep from spilling her tears on the both of them. Else she would have spouted like a big watering pot.

"She did," Eynsford whispered. "And, though I never understood the beast within you, your lady explained it all to me today. And so I feel I need to set things right while I still have time."

"It's not important," Dash began.

The marquess held up one finger, and Dash immediately quieted, like a good little pup. "I have been a fool, Dashiel. And I am sorry. I am proud to leave you all my worldly possessions. And I leave you my respect as well, son. Now go away so I can rest."

"But," Dash said, as though he needed to say a thing or two of his own.

With his eyes already closed, Eynsford squeezed Dash's hand, and Cait watched with awe as Dash turned his over to hold the marquess' tightly.

When his father slept, Dash moved to a chair across the room and sat. "I think I'll just stay a bit," he muttered, his words choked with emotion.

Cait walked quietly from the room, closing the door softly behind her. Father and son needed a bit of time alone. And she would give that to them.

Thirty-Seven

CAIT PACED BACK AND FORTH ACROSS THE ENTRYWAY of Eynsford Park, grinding her teeth so loudly that Price shot worried glances in her direction.

"Ye're certain he dinna leave a note? Or tell anyone where he'd be goin', Price?"

"I'm positive, my lady," the stoic butler said, avoiding her gaze.

"Are all the horses in the stables?"

He finally looked at her. "They are. I just sent Owens to verify it. His lordship did not leave on horseback."

It had been hours since Dash had vanished. According to Price, he'd lingered with his father until the man finally slept fitfully. Then he left the room quickly and had not been seen since.

The sun sank low on the horizon as Cait stared out the window of the parlor, wishing Dashiel was standing with her so they could share the fall of the sun in the sky and the rise of the moon. So they could be husband and wife. Lycan and mate. But she was alone. Shadows danced across the grounds as the sun sank and the moon rose to take its place, but Dash was still nowhere to be found.

"Are ye certain he dinna go out with an old friend, Price? Perhaps ye missed the comings and goings, since ye were checkin' on the marquess throughout the day."

The man puffed his chest out, his face falling as though she'd dealt him a harsh blow. "I do not leave my post unattended, my lady. And I have already asked the footmen for every bit of news they could share. No one has seen him."

"I'm sorry, Price. I'm simply worried."

Something flashed in the man's eyes. A bit of regret perhaps? If so, what would he have to be sorry for? Unless… unless he *did* know where Dashiel was.

Cait approached him slowly, trying to keep a congenial smile upon her face. "Ye have a bit of dust on yer sleeve, here, Price," she said casually as she reached to brush the sleeve of his jacket. Just as she'd thought would happen, the man was so flustered at the thought of soiling his clothes that he stopped and intently began to search for the offending dirt.

"I don't see it, my lady." He raised a questioning gaze to her.

"Have ye taken ta cleanin' chimneys, Price?" she laughed as she brushed the dust from his shoulder. "My butler back home has never gotten so dirty."

"I had some special chores to do today, milady. Beg your pardon." He stood a bit taller and raised his nose in the air, not appreciating her appraisal at all. Could the butler's vanity be his downfall? Perhaps.

"What were yer special chores, Price?" she asked

casually as she went back to the window to look again at the deepening shadows.

"I… I…"

She turned to face him, giving him her most haughty glare. "Yes, Price?" she snapped.

"I wanted to clean one of the rooms that we haven't used in a while, my lady."

"And what room would this be, Price?" She narrowed her eyebrows at him.

"Simply an old chamber, Lady Brimsworth," he mumbled as he turned from her.

"By any chance, did his lordship ask ye ta clean this chamber?"

"Which lord, my lady?" Price asked.

That was quite enough. Cait placed her hands upon her hips and stomped her foot. "If ye ken where my husband could be, Price, I would suggest ye tell me. Or I will be a very unhappy lady. And ye would no' like ta see me when I'm unhappy."

"I imagine not, my lady," Price grumbled.

"Well?" If the man didn't get on with it, she would have to get out her herbs and make a very special tea, just for him. One that might torture him for days. Oh, yes. That would be very nice.

"I'm not supposed to say, my lady." He pressed his lips together in a thin line.

"On whose orders?"

"The marquess?" Price said. But it came out more like a question.

"So ye mean ta tell me that the marquess is upstairs fighting for breath, and he cared about some old dusty chamber enough ta tell ye ta go and clean it?"

The man nodded quickly. "That's correct."

"Where is this chamber? I'd like ta see it for myself."

"I can't tell you." He pursed his lips again.

"Fine," Cait spit out. "I'll just go and ask the staff until *someone* tells me what I want ta ken."

"That would be why his lordship sent me alone, my lady. He didn't want anyone to know."

"Surely someone saw you comin' and goin'," she said, taunting him on purpose.

She could tell he thought hard. "Oh, I hope not," he finally sighed, squeezing his eyes together tightly.

Cait lowered her voice. "I *will* find out. So, ye might want ta make it easier for us both, or I'll go ahead and sack ye now."

"You wouldn't dare!" Price cried.

"Are ye sure about that?" Cait asked as she picked an imaginary piece of lint from her sleeve.

"The marquess isn't even in the grave yet!"

Caitrin felt a little niggle of regret for her outburst, but it only lasted a moment. "But he will be soon, Price. So, ye might want ta remember who will hold the terms of yer employment in her very own hands."

Price hung his head back with defeat and groaned. "The marquess had me clean *the room*." He said the last two words with enough inflection that Cait took a step back.

"The room?"

"Yes. The room. The marquess had me clean Lord Brimsworth's room. It hasn't been used for several years. So, I cleaned it. Fresh linens. A good washing. I must admit it's almost inhabitable. I even had a new bed brought from above stairs to replace that old cot.

His lordship has spent the nights of the full moon in it when it looked much worse."

"Then why did he have ye clean it now?"

"He said he wanted his son to be comfortable on this night that is so painful for him."

"He did?" Cait covered her chest with her hand. "How thoughtful."

Just then, a footman approached Price and said quietly, "All the maids have been sent from the property, just as you asked. And with little time to spare, I might add. The chains are already rattling down there."

Price cuffed the boy on the side of the head. "Watch your tongue around the countess." He nodded toward Cait.

"Beg your pardon, milady."

Cait tried to put together the pieces of the puzzle in her mind. A dirty chamber that was now clean. It was on a lower level because Owens had said *down there*. Chains. Cait blew with frustration.

"I just hope the chains hold the monster," Owens mumbled as he walked away. "I've never known him to get so agitated so early in the night."

Cait's gasp drew Price's glare.

"You can't go down there, my lady," the butler said, rushing toward her.

"My husband is in the *cellar*? That dark and dirty place I saw the first day I was here?"

"It's not so dirty anymore," Price mumbled, shuffling his feet.

"*Mo chreach*, that's where he is!" she cried as she ran in that direction.

"Where are you going, my lady?"

"Ta my husband!" she called back, unable to stop the smile that crossed her face at the thought of finding him and spending the night with him under the light of the moon.

❧

Dash was already fighting the chains. He'd fought his shift into wolf form as soon as the moon rose above the horizon, but some things could not be stopped, and the emergence of the beast was one of them, he knew from experience.

Now, the beast within him wanted to escape the shackles and escape the cellar, then go find his wife and have his wolfish way with her. But it wasn't going to happen. He wouldn't allow it.

Dash wore nothing more than the golden fur that adorned his body and a titanium collar that imprisoned him and kept him from going to find his heart's desire. He shivered at the very thought, a drop of drool dropping from his mouth to land on the stone floor.

The hair on the back of Dash's neck stood up when he heard Cait's soft lilt calling his name. He danced on four feet, tugging at the collar that bound him to the point of pain. She called for him again.

Unable to resist, he raised his snout into the air and called back to her, his howl deep and rich.

Oh, God! What had he done? He'd called for her. Perhaps she hadn't heard him. But then he heard her soft footfalls. Dash whimpered, dancing again in agitation. Cait! He needed her. He wanted her. But he could not have her.

"Dash?" she said from the other side of the heavy oak door.

Cait! He cried out in the only way he knew how. But then he remembered. He remembered what he was. He was a Lycan. He was dangerous. He couldn't have her. Perhaps if he sat quietly, she would leave.

The bars on the door were made to keep Dash in, not to keep others out, so there was no way to bar her from the room. He crept into the shadows, walking as far as his tether would allow. Perhaps she wouldn't see him, if she did step inside his cell.

A heavy thunk sounded as Cait removed the bar from the door. Then she slid the lock free. The door creaked open. Dash sat in the shadows and tried to keep from rushing to her. Then the honeysuckle scent of her reached his hyper-sensitive nose and he had to lick his lips to keep from drooling again.

"Dash?" she asked again as she stepped farther into the room.

He could see in total darkness because of his Lycan senses. But his little witch could not, he gratefully remembered. She turned and left. Dash's heart clenched within his chest.

He wanted her more than the air he breathed. He wanted her more than his next drink of water. He wanted her more than he wanted his very existence. He cursed in his head and tugged at the shackles that bound him to the stone room.

A moment later, a flash of light caught his eye as it filtered through the crack in the doorway she'd left open. Dash tilted his head to the side so he could clearly hear her. She hummed a spirited little tune.

Cait pushed the door open fully and stepped back inside, holding a lamp high so that it could illuminate the room. Dash came to his feet and crouched low, growling. She had to leave. She just had to.

Cait jumped and placed a hand to her chest. "*Havers!* Ye frightened me."

Good. She *should* be frightened of a feral wolf. If not, the woman was simply daft. And that was one thing he'd never assumed about her. She may be annoying as the devil, but she was completely sane.

Cait bent at the waist and placed her lamp on the floor, then took a step toward him. He growled low in his throat.

"Will ye stop makin' that noise?" she snapped. "I simply want ta take a look at ye. I willna do anythin' ye doona want me ta do."

Dash growled again. He didn't want to keep her from doing *anything*. That was the problem.

Cait put her hands on her hips and scowled at him. Dash was nearly overcome with the desire to hold his paw out for a shake. He shook his head to clear it. Damn the woman.

"Why are ye trussed up so, Dashiel?" she asked as she walked to where his tether was anchored to the stone wall.

Because I could hurt you.

Cait ran her fingers along the metal links until she was within his reach. She was so close he could smell her hair. He could almost taste the valley between her breasts. And then he began to think about the little crease where her thighs met her hips.

"Ye look like ye want ta gobble me up," she said

absently as she rose and began to search the shelves in the room for something. What could she be looking for? Then he heard the clank of metal against metal. He groaned when she found the key. "And now ye sound like ye had some lunch that didn't set well in yer stomach."

Not lunch, angel, but I could gobble you up and you wouldn't even see me coming. You wouldn't be able to move fast enough to get away from me.

She held out the key in her dainty little fingers. "I hold the key ta yer freedom." Then she tentatively touched the top of his head and unlocked the titanium collar at his neck. The moment he was free, Dash was surprised to feel the pain of changing from beast to man. He'd never changed at will before. But, there he was, his nose shortening, his ears flattening, his shaggy hair receding.

When he stood before her as a man once more, he closed his eyes and breathed deeply of her. He stepped closer but was afraid to touch her. Instead, he decided to tell her what was in his heart.

"I believe you've held the key to my freedom since that first night, Caitie."

Thirty-Eight

THOUGH SHE FOUND SOME SECURITY IN THE AMBER depths of his eyes, Cait still shivered when he reached out a hand to touch her and then drew it back. She rocked toward him like there was an invisible pull, but he quickly stepped back from her.

She tried to keep the quiver from her voice as he turned away, but she was fully aware the rest of her life depended on this one moment. "Dash," she began, but he cut her off.

"I imagine you're thoroughly disgusted by the very sight of me," Dash said quietly. He stood with his back to her, his glorious body naked, his muscles gleaming in the candle light. She wanted nothing more than to touch him. But sensed that would not be the right thing to do. Not for him. Not for her. Not tonight.

"I'm no' disgusted." Cait snorted.

"Frightened?" he asked, his tone a little deeper.

"Only that ye will continue ta shut me out."

"You've seen what I am. Now you understand why I shackle myself when there's a full moon. No one wants to deal with a beast. And I'll not expect you to, either. You are much better off without me."

Cait fought the blinding rage that crawled up her spine. "Ye think me spineless enough ta let ye walk out of my life, Dashiel Thorpe?" She stepped close enough she could feel his breath against her cheek. But he didn't touch her. She could tell he wanted to. But he held himself in check.

"Not spineless, Cait." He tapped his temple with his forefinger. "Smart."

"Ye're full of compliments today, I see," Cait grumbled. "But, I see one problem."

"I can't help what I am. Believe me, if I could stop being a wolf I would."

"Oh, shush. That's no' the problem. I have ta keep ye around. For, without me, who will keep the big beast on his best behavior? Ye need someone ta manage the shackles, I imagine. Ta get ye in them and out of them." Or to boil them in enchanted oil until they melted. She could make a door knocker out of them. They'd not be used to imprison her husband ever again.

"Price can do that," Dash mumbled, his face falling as she'd hoped it would. He didn't want to be shackled. He wanted to be wild and free. With her. But old wounds run deeply, she realized. She wasn't a healer, but she could help with this.

"I doona think I can allow ye ta put Price in danger that way," she said, faking a sigh. "It's me or no one."

"I've never wanted to devour Price, angel," he offered. "You, on the other hand…"

Cait spun around the room and noticed the bed in the far corner. "Was that here, before?"

"I've never seen it before, no," Dash replied, his brow furrowed. "I believe Price did some work down here this morning."

"Aye, at yer father's orders."

Dash's head snapped up. "Pardon?"

"Yer father. He had him clean this place up and make it less of a prison." At Dash's confused glance, she further explained, "He wanted ye ta be comfortable." Cait stretched her arms over her head and yawned dramatically. "And I, for one, am very glad he did. I'm exhausted."

"You can't stay here, Caitrin. You have to go."

Cait let a smile cross her lips as she tugged at the laces of her dress, loosening it until it gaped open in the front. Dash spun away, flexing his hands at his sides. The muscles of his bare bottom clenched.

Cait shrugged out of her gown, pulled her chemise over her head, and tugged all the pins from her hair. As she let each one hit the stone floor, Dash flinched again and again. If not for the spontaneous movement, she'd have sworn the man was made of stone for all the response she got.

When she was naked, she walked slowly toward the bed, allowing her shoulder to brush his arm as she did so. Dash trembled a bit and turned to face the other direction.

"Come here, Dash," she said quietly, knowing full well he'd hear her.

"I can't, Cait." The words came out with a tortured groan.

"Why no'?"

"I don't want to hurt you, Caitie. Please don't do this."

She could see the battle he fought within himself. And loved him all the more for the care he took with her.

"Bring the shackles. I'll tether ye over here. At least ye'll be able ta get some sleep."

"I sincerely doubt that."

"Ouch!" Cait suddenly cried.

He was beside her within seconds. "What is it? Are you hurt?"

She smiled a mischievous smile at him. "No' anymore," she said as she stood on tiptoe and wrapped her hands around his neck. She pressed her naked body against his and rubbed like a cat.

Dash's hands came up to her waist to set her away from him, she was sure. "You naughty little witch," he growled. But with his knees against the back of the bed, she shoved with all her might until he toppled backward onto the counterpane. She landed on top of him, her body pressed down the length of his. Immediately, she felt the hardness of him against her belly, and moved her hips against him. Dash looked away and gritted his teeth, as though she submitted him to torture after torture.

"I have somethin' ta tell ye, Dashiel," she said, her tone conspiratorial as she sat up, her thighs open over his abdomen as she looked down at him.

"Make it quick, Caitie," he growled. "I can't take much more of this."

She leaned close to his ear and purred, "From this day forward, the only shackles ye will wear are mine." And the only part of her beast that would ever be shackled was his heart. The rest of him, she'd take exactly as he was.

❧

Dash closed his eyes to the sight of her breasts, so close to his face as she leaned over him that he could easily touch his lips to a taut little peak if he but lifted his head.

Cait sat up, still straddling him, her flaxen hair hanging about her shoulders. She put a finger to her lips and pretended to look perplexed. "Oh my, did I forget ta tell ye? I love my wolf, exactly as he is." She rested her weight on the flat of her hands, which pressed against his chest. "Do ye really think ye can fight the love I have for ye? That ye can run far enough or fast enough ta make me stop lovin' ye?"

"Cait," Dash ground out. "I could hurt you. Don't you see?"

She leaned so that her mouth nearly touched his and breathed across his lips, "I'd like ta see ye try." Her blue eyes flashed with challenge. "I'm a powerful witch, or have ye forgotten?"

"No, but that doesn't mean—"

"It means everythin'," she insisted.

"What do you plan to do now?" Trepidation laced his words.

"I plan ta make love ta ye," she said, danger flashing in her blue eyes. "Do ye submit?"

"Do I have a choice?" Dash grumbled.

"Stop lookin' so distraught, Dashiel," she said, slapping at his chest. "Ye're ruinin' the moment, ye big lout."

"Apologies," he mumbled.

"I ken ye want me," she said quietly as she moved her hips over him, letting his shaft slide along the slippery wetness of her skin.

"More than air," he admitted, looking into her eyes for the first time all night. All he saw shining back was love for him. A joy filled his heart like none he'd ever felt. He let his gaze roam down her naked body. She was his. Loved him exactly as he was.

She squealed as he suddenly rolled her beneath him.

"What are ye doin'?" she gasped.

"Anything I want," he growled as he nipped at her lips. He laughed when a curse crossed her lips.

"You said you wanted me," he gently commanded. "Now take me as I am."

Cait lifted her head and touched her lips to his, tender and reverently at first. But before he could have even expected it, her tongue slid inside his mouth to war with his.

"I love your lips, lass. But I want to taste more than that," he said, raising his eyebrows as his gaze traveled down her body.

With no self-consciousness at all, she arched her back, bringing her nipple closer to his mouth. He slowly sucked it inside, teasing her with his raspy tongue and slow licks, until she nearly purred beneath him. Then he switched to the other breast.

He filled her in one swift stroke. She cried out, which only stoked his passion. He'd never seen a more beautiful sight, with her mouth hanging open, her eyes closed. "I think you like being at my mercy, angel," he breathed, staying completely still within her.

"Please, Dash," she whispered.

Cait rocked beneath him, her legs rising to wrap around his waist.

He brushed the hair from her forehead, and he

could finally see the need shining in her eyes. "If ye doona start ta move soon, I'll endeavor ta make yer life unbearable when the moon begins ta wane."

"You little witch," Dash mumbled. His angel was a devil in disguise, the little minx.

"Take me, Dash?" she asked as she lifted her head and rained kisses against his chest, still rocking her hips.

He was amazed that he had enough strength not to devour her. Not to hurt her. He wanted just a moment to enjoy the feeling. To enjoy a cycle of the moon. To enjoy *her* and all that she stood for.

Finally, he began to move, impaling the full length of him into the wet sheath of her body. Her eyes closed as she milked him, small gasps leaving her mouth with every plunge, her breasts still pressed to his chest, the hard peaks teasing him endlessly.

"Look at me, Caitie," he whispered by her ear.

Cait did as he directed, her hands rising to bracket his face. He watched with rapt sensation as she took him, each thrust harder than the last, her lips parted with desire. He moved faster and faster. Dash felt like he could explode just from the sight of her slender body moving beneath him and the way her blue eyes held his.

"Do you want to come, Caitie?" he growled by her ear.

She nodded tightly.

"Let me take care of you." She was too far gone even to recognize the no-nonsense tone he used. He moved his hand down between them, so he could rub the sensitive bundle of nerves that was her center.

Cait gasped, her movements growing unsteady as she

neared climax. Her mouth hung wide open now, her body tense, like an arched bow, ready to be released.

"That's it, Cait," he soothed as he bent his head and took her nipple into his mouth, drawing strongly on the perfect little peak. When she topped the crest, a tear rolled down her cheek. He wiped it away with his thumb. "Oh, Cait," he soothed.

"Doona give yerself too much credit, Dashiel. I always cry when Lycans make love ta me on the night of the full moon."

He chuckled lightly.

Her wet flesh quivered around him, and it was all Dash could do not to follow her into release. But he wasn't ready to end their encounter, not anytime soon.

When the clenching of her inner walls finally stopped, she looked at him with so much love in her eyes that it nearly hurt, a sheepish smile on her face. Dash pulled out of her and set her on her knees. She protested softly with a grunt of displeasure.

"I'm not done yet, Cait," he said as he took her hand and showed her how hard he still was.

"Oh," she gasped. "I'm sorry."

"Don't be." He silenced her with a nip to her shoulder. "I'll let you fix it."

Dash slid in behind her and pressed his hardness against her bottom.

"Dash, I doona—" she began.

"I know. I do. You trusted that I wouldn't hurt you. Now trust that I'll please you, as well. No matter how I want it. Or how I give it to you. I want to take you as a beast takes his mate."

A smile crossed her face. "What are ye waitin' for?"

With one arm around her middle, Dash bent her at the waist, pressing her shoulders toward the bed. Then he sunk inside her in one fluid motion that made her cry out, again. For a moment, that same doubt entered his mind, that he'd been too rough with her.

Damn his Lycan-hating upbringing. His whole life had been about restraint. He'd missed out on… this.

Finally, he could be free. He could be whole. He could embrace the beast inside him and never look back.

She rocked back against him, moving on him. He wrapped his hands around her hips and set a rhythm as old as time. He took her harder than ever before and gave her more pleasure than she'd known was possible. And only when she erupted around him time and again and begged and pleaded for him to end the sweet torment he delivered to her body and soul did he follow.

Cait sank to the bed, her breath heaving in and out in huge gasps as he collapsed on top of her. He brushed the hair from her shoulder and gently kissed the tender flesh that bore his mark.

"My little witch," he murmured against her skin.

"My beautiful beast," she breathed back. Then he rolled to his side and pulled her into his arms.

Thirty-Nine

"LADY EYNSFORD." PRICE CLEARED HIS THROAT, STANDING in the doorway of Caitrin's informal sitting room.

Hearing the name in regard to her was still something she was adjusting to, even though it had been nearly three weeks since Dash had assumed his father's title. In time, the name would feel more like her own, she was certain.

From her small writing desk, she looked up at the ancient butler. "Aye?"

He nodded in deference of her position. "Your guest has arrived, my lady," he said, taking care not to say the man's name as she'd directed.

Cait shot out of her seat. "Is he in the green parlor, Price?"

She wasn't certain at all how Dash would take her meddling in his affairs. Actually, she had a fairly good idea. He wouldn't be happy about it, especially as he forbade her weeks ago from contacting Lord Radbourne. But it was for the best, whether Dash realized it or not.

Even though he had come to terms with the late

marquess' feelings toward him and put many of his old demons to rest, Cait could still see the lost look in her husband's eyes from time to time. And that came from not knowing where he truly belonged. She'd seen that expression countless times on Elspeth's face in the past, back before she was reunited with her father, Major Forster.

Dash would forgive her; at least she hoped so.

Cait made her way toward the green parlor but stopped in her tracks when Dash emerged from his study, blocking her path. He sniffed at the air and then turned his intimidating amber gaze on her. "There's a Lycan *here* at Eynsford Park?"

Blasted sensitive nose. She would much rather have met the viscount before Dash got wind of his arrival. Made preparations, warned the man what to expect. Cait feigned a look of innocence. "Yes, there is," she cooed, reaching for him and sliding her hand up his muscled chest. "And he is incredibly handsome. How fortunate for me that I'm married ta him."

Dash's gaze darkened. "I know my own scent, Caitie, and that is not it. What are you up to?"

"Did ye become more suspicious when ye became a marquess, Dash?" She stood on tiptoe to press a kiss to his jaw, hoping to beguile him before he caught on to her plan.

"Yes, with good reason." He wrapped his arms around her waist. "I have not forgotten your potent sleeping draught, lass. I'm never quite certain what you're capable of."

Cait giggled, though she knew he hadn't exactly meant it as a compliment. "A wife is allowed some secrets, is she no'?"

❦

Not when one of them was another Lycan in their midst. The unfamiliar scent became stronger, and Dash frowned at his lovely wife who was trying her best to distract him. "You're up to something." He sniffed the air again. It definitely was not one he recognized. Not a Westfield. Not a Forster. He shook his head trying to place it, to no avail. "It'll go better for you if you confess your nefarious scheme now."

"I canna tell ye a thing. It's a surprise." Her light blue eyes twinkled mischievously, which made his trousers embarrassingly tight. God, he'd never have his fill of her. At the moment, he wanted nothing more than to whisk her up the steps to his room and force her to tell him. If he could get her undressed, he'd have the truth out of her in less than a second.

"I don't like surprises. Last chance, Caitie," he growled softly. "Tell me or else."

She playfully smacked his chest. "Go back ta yer lair, my lord. I'll call for ye when I'm ready."

If she thought for one moment that he was going to leave her to deal with some strange Lycan this close to a full moon, she was out of her pretty head. But before he could sufficiently frighten the truth out of her, a stranger appeared at the end of the corridor.

"Are you looking for me?" the mysterious Lycan asked. He was tall, younger than Dash by a few years and with rather ordinary brown hair that was a bit longer than was fashionable; but his eyes, a deep amber, seemed to look right through Dash. *Radbourne.* His half brother. He didn't have a doubt in his mind.

Dash's lungs wouldn't release the breath they held, and he felt a jolt in his chest and clenching that made it impossible to talk. Caitrin, apparently, couldn't leave well enough alone, even though he'd expressly asked her not to meddle.

His wife stepped from his embrace and walked toward the other man, her hand outstretched in greeting. "Lord Radbourne, I am sorry ta keep ye waitin'. I was just on my way ta meet ye."

"Am I to assume you're Lady Eynsford, then?" the man asked, raising Cait's fingers to his lips.

Dash had never felt such a flash of jealousy is his entire life. His hands were actually shaking with the intense desire to physically toss his brother from his home when his lips lingered a bit too long on Caitrin's skin.

Cait glanced over her shoulder at Dash, a warning in her eyes. "Indeed." She turned back to the man. "Thank ye for payin' us a visit."

"Well, I must say," the man shot an inquisitive look at Dash, "your letter was most intriguing."

Letter? What the devil had she said in this letter? A low growl escaped Dash's throat. He wasn't ready for this interview. He might not ever be ready. Blast Caitrin for forcing it on him.

"How ill-mannered of me ta keep ye waitin' in the hallway. Please, my lord, let us retire ta the parlor."

Dash swallowed. Though he wasn't prepared for this conversation, he'd be damned if he would let Cait conduct it without him. He quickly made his way to her side, possessively dropping his hand to her shoulder. "After you, my dear."

Cait looked up at him, smiling sweetly, before preceding the men into the green parlor. Radbourne's eyes dropped to watch her tempting backside until Dash's growl made his gaze rise once again. Brother or not, if the man glanced in Cait's direction one more time, he'd tear his damned head off.

Dash looked his brother over. Aside from their hair color, they did look similar. The same aristocratic nose, same strong chin. Their eyes were nearly identical. Dash gestured him inside the parlor. "Please, Radbourne."

Once inside, Dash claimed the spot beside Caitrin on a dark, damask settee. His eyes flashed to hers. "When this is over, I'm going to toss you over my knee," he whispered, though the quirk on Radbourne's lips confirmed he'd overheard the threat.

His half brother settled into a high-backed chair across from them, and he smiled charmingly at Cait. "It is a pleasure to meet you, Lady Eynsford. Your correspondence captured my interest right away."

She didn't even have the good sense to look ashamed for ignoring Dash's wishes. Instead, she sat forward in her seat and graced Radbourne with a very pretty smile. "Thank ye, sir. And this brutish man beside me is, of course, the Marquess of Eynsford. I do hope ye'll consider remainin' here as our guest as we negotiate the details."

Negotiate what details? Dash was certain his face was on fire. What exactly was she doing? "Cait," he grumbled softly.

"I assume ye did bring the sketches with ye, my lord," she continued, completely ignoring Dash.

"Cait," he said louder. "I would like to know exactly what is going on."

Finally, she tilted her head to see him. "It was supposed ta be a surprise, but ye canna bear for me ta keep any secrets from ye." She gestured to Radbourne with a sweep of her hand. "The viscount is sellin' a patch of land in Lancashire. I'd planned ta acquire it for yer birthday, Dash."

More like she'd planned to bring him face-to-face with his brother, and his birthday wasn't for another month. "How sweet of you to think of me, lass."

Radbourne chuckled to himself. "I wasn't sure what I'd find here, but this certainly wasn't it."

Dash frowned at the man. "What does that mean?"

His brother shrugged and then sank back in his chair. "When I received word from Lady Eynsford about the property in question and mentioned it to my mother, I thought she would faint dead away. She told me who you are, Eynsford."

"Who I am?" Dash echoed.

Radbourne folded his hands in his lap. "What I don't know is what you want. That's why I've come."

Dash's mouth went dry. What was he to say to that? He didn't want anything from Radbourne. Now that he truly examined the man, he noted that the viscount's clothes were a few years out of fashion and his boots were scuffed terribly. "May I ask why you're selling this property?" he asked, though somehow he knew in the pit of his stomach.

"The same reason any noble family sells off unentailed land, Eynsford—for the money. Now are we going to continue playing games, sir? Or will you tell me what you want with me?"

Cait rose from her seat. "I'll just leave ye."

"Oh, no, you don't," Dash said, tugging her skirt until she sat back down. "You got me into this mess." Then he turned his glare back to Radbourne. "Until a month ago, I'd never heard your name. I want nothing from you."

"Then why the pretense of bringing me here?"

Cait sighed beside him. "Because it was the perfect excuse ta bring ye here. My husband would never have sought ye out on his own."

Radbourne scratched his chin. "So, I'm here. Now what?"

Cait squeezed Dash's hand and, though he was thoroughly annoyed with her, the pressure reminded him of her love. "Tell us everythin' about him, your father. Doona spare any details."

But Dash spoke at the same time. "How bad is your financial situation?"

"Dashiel!" Cait scolded, her brow furrowing at him.

Radbourne just lifted one eyebrow, looking as though he found amusement in their questions.

"Your father died when you were young?" Dash continued.

"*Our* father died when I was young, yes," Radbourne corrected him.

Cait opened her mouth to speak, but Dash reached over and squeezed her knee, wordlessly warning her to stay quiet.

"Your wife is delightful," Radbourne said quietly, his amber eyes skimming over her.

"Perhaps you'll find one of your own some day," Dash warned the man subtly. Then he reached for the sketches Radbourne had brought. "My wife is meddlesome. But I love her, despite that fact." He opened the parchment to take a look at the drawings. "This is a large parcel of land."

Radbourne just nodded.

"Let's adjourn to my study, shall we, so we can discuss your situation? I believe I can help without you having to sell your holdings."

The men rose, and Caitrin stood up to follow. "We'll see you later, angel," Dash said as he kissed her forehead.

Cait protested, "But—"

"I promise I'll tell you everything." He couldn't help but chuckle at her crestfallen expression.

When they reached the end of the corridor, he heard her say softly, "Beast."

"I heard that," he called back.

"I meant for ye ta hear it!" she returned loudly. Then she whispered, "And I love ye."

"I heard that, too," he called again, happy when her laughter reached his ears.

Epilogue

"YER BROTHERS ARE DELIGHTFUL." CAITRIN SMILED OVER her shoulder at Dash as he unbuttoned the back of her dress.

He scowled in response. "They're a pack of hellions."

"They're a pack of *Lycans*," she corrected, slipping out of her dinner gown. "And it is very obvious they've been lookin' for a pack leader."

Dash groaned. "I didn't sign on for that role." He tugged at his cravat and then threw it across the room. His jacket followed a moment later.

Cait felt his eyes land on her, searing her through her chemise, and she couldn't help but grin. He was adorable in his shirt sleeves. She loved seeing him so relaxed. Finding his brothers had done that for him, no matter how he protested otherwise. "It is also very obvious how much ye adore *them*."

A smile tugged at his lips. "I do," he admitted.

Indeed the trip to Hadley Manor had been healing for Dash. He seemed to have found a purpose he'd been missing before. He was no longer a lone wolf, a wild Lycan. He was part of the Hadley horde in more ways than one. In addition to his three half brothers accepting him without question into their ranks, even Lady Radbourne adored him.

Cait retrieved a gossamer nightrail from the wardrobe, only to have it snatched away from her grasp. She spun around to see Dash toss it across the room. "I'm only going to rip it off you in a few minutes, Caitie. It's best not to even put it on."

"Ye are very sure of yerself, Dashiel."

"With reason. You can't keep your hands off me."

She rolled her eyes to keep from encouraging her husband. Then Cait walked around him toward the bed and picked up his discarded jacket from the floor. It was heavier than it should have been. "Have ye taken ta hidin' rocks in yer pocket like a young lad?"

His expression dropped, and he reached for the jacket. "Let me have it, Caitie."

Well, he was certainly hiding something. She slipped under his arm and scooted to the far end of the room. "What are ye keepin' from me, Dash?" She reached into his pocket and her fingers found a little leather book. Cait slid it from the jacket and her mouth fell open. *His journal of debauchery?* She frowned at him. "Ye told me ye burned it."

"I did," he rasped. "It's not the same book. Let me have it."

Cait glared at him. "Dashiel Thorpe, do ye think I'm daft. This is the same book!"

His face turned bright red. "Open it, then."

"I've already read it cover to cover."

His blush deepened, which she didn't even know

was possible. Dash snatched the journal from her and opened it, then began to read.

"I am not sure what I ever did to deserve Caitrin. She is my angel, my salvation…"

Cait's mouth fell open. He'd written about her?

"…I'll spend the rest of my life trying to be worthy of her love…"

Cait threw her arms around him and kissed his chest and his jaw and his lips, hoping to show him that he didn't need to prove his worth.

"…And when she takes me into her body, it's magical." Dash grinned at her. "Particularly when she's on top."

Cait smacked his chest and snatched the book from his hand, proceeding to read a few more lines to herself before she slammed it shut.

"You're blushing all the way to the roots of your hair, angel," Dash teased.

Cait hid her embarrassment by tucking her face into his chest. Then Dash tossed the book to the bed and enveloped her in his arms. "It's not the same book, Cait. I did burn the other one. There's only one woman I want to remember."

IT
HAPPENED
ONE BITE

Black Dragon Inn, south of Edinburgh
March 1797

Alpina Lindsay breathed a sigh of relief. It hadn't been easy locating a vampyre none of them had ever met, but finally, after nights of searching for the man, there he was! He certainly matched the description of the man Fiona Macleod had seen in her vision. Leaning against the stone façade of the old inn, Lord Kettering drew deeply on his cheroot as he gazed up at the crescent moon, seemingly without a care in the world.

Alpina narrowed her eyes at the gentleman who was, indeed, handsome, dashing, and more powerful than anything or anyone she had ever faced. The bairn in her womb kicked and Alpina protectively smoothed a hand over her belly while Fiona Macleod's warning echoed once again in her mind.

"Are ye certain ye want ta do this?" Bonnie Ferguson whispered in her left ear.

Alpina caught Rosewyth Campbell's eye and nodded, as there really was no choice in the matter.

The man before them had to be dealt with. Otherwise, her daughter's life and future would be in danger. That couldn't be allowed.

From her right, Moira Sinclair's dainty hand slid inside Alpina's, reminding her she wasn't alone. Together they could thwart the evil Fiona had seen in her vision. Together they would ensure her daughter's future.

A twig snapped beneath one of the witches' feet, and Kettering stood at attention. "Hello?" His crisp English accent sliced through the night air.

It was now or never, and Alpina couldn't take the risk that Kettering would escape. She stepped from the mist that had until now shrouded the coven from his view, pulling Moira alongside her. "Good evenin', my lord." Somehow she managed to keep the fear from her voice.

A charming smile settled on the man's face, and his white teeth sparkled in the moonlight. "It is now." He tossed what was left of his cheroot to the ground and stepped toward the pair. A seducer if ever there was one. "What a delightful treat. Not one beautiful lass, but two."

"Actually, there are five of us," Fiona's waspish voice came from somewhere within the mist.

"Five?" Kettering echoed.

And in the blink of an eye, Moira's misty shield evaporated and Kettering found himself in the middle of their circle. The five witches clasped hands together, trapping him inside the ring.

The Englishman looked from one to the other, confusion lighting his too-handsome face. "Why?" he asked.

"Because of what ye are," Alpina answered. "We cannot allow ye ta harm anyone."

He shook his head. "I've never harmed anyone," he professed.

Fiona Macleod snorted at that. "I've seen what ye are and what ye will be with my own eyes, my lord. Pray doona deny it."

"And what are *you*?" he asked.

"Justice," Fiona sneered. "For all yer victims—past, present, and future."

"*Cadail, uilebheist. Caidil gu bràth!*" Alpina's voice rang loud and clear.

"*Cadail gu bràth, cadail gu bràth,*" the others chanted.

Power surged through Alpina's hands where she held onto Moira and Bonnie within the circle. She'd never felt such intense energy. Sparks erupted from their clasped hands, arcing across the circle and creating a perfect, five-pointed star. Thunder cracked above them, and Kettering let out a pained cry. He crumpled to the ground and everything was silent.

The five witches slowly released their hold on one another, stepping closer to the man at their feet. If Alpina hadn't known better, she would have thought he was dead.

"His maker will search for him," Fiona predicted. "The knight will go through Edinburgh, Glasgow, and Aberdeen."

"But no' the Highlands?" Alpina asked, the answer mattering more than her next breath.

Fiona smiled. "Nay. No one will find him at Briarcraig, but we must hurry."

Alpina nodded. Then she knelt beside Kettering,

wishing they could have done more than place him in a dormant sleep; but it would have to do.

"As he is imprisoned, so shall remain his soul," Fiona said as she lifted his hand to stare at the ring that adorned it. She tugged it from his finger and tossed it to Alpina, who caught it in mid-air. The ring glowed, warm and vibrant in the palm of her hand.

"But vampyres have no soul," Alpina said with a shake of her head. "No life."

"As a descendent of Blodswell, *he* could." Fiona pointed her finger at the lifeless man at their feet.

Everyone knew the story of Blodswell. The tale was passed from witch to witch, from cradle to grave. It was a story of true heroism. It was the reason why the rings had been gifted to the knight, as a harbinger of hope, a promise for the future. But the prophecy could only be fulfilled if the wearer of the ring remained pure. For only love could heal the blighted soul.

"The ring contains what he holds most dear," Fiona continued. "It's the essence of him. And his link ta his maker. Take it and go. If ye doona leave with it, he'll seek its power and wake soon."

For the first time today, Alpina doubted this deed. But Fiona had foreseen it. If they didn't take immediate action, the vampyre would wreak havoc upon their lives and upon her daughter in particular.

Alpina stood back and watched as her four coven sisters made quick work of depositing the vampyre's body in the awaiting Macleod coach. They exchanged quick hugs before the four women crowded inside as well.

It didn't feel right to leave her sisters exposed to

such danger. "If he wakes, ye might have need of me," Alpina called out, as the coach lurched forward.

Fiona answered from inside the conveyance, "Ye hold his heart in your hand. Without it, he is but a shell of a man."

A shell of a man. Somehow Alpina doubted that. However, the further the coach moved down the meandering lane, the more the ring lost its shimmer and warmth. With a shrug of her shoulders, Alpina threaded the ring onto a cord she wore around her neck. No one could ever take the relic from her, and her daughter's future would be preserved.

AVAILABLE MARCH 2011

About the Author

Lydia Dare is a pseudonym for the writing team of Tammy Falkner and Jodie Pearson. Both are active members of the Heart of Carolina Romance Writers and have sat on the organization's Board of Directors. Their writing process involves passing a manuscript back and forth, each one writing 1500 words after editing the other's previous installment—Jodie specializes in writing the history and Tammy in writing the paranormal. They live near Raleigh, North Carolina.